STEEL HEART IRON CLAWS

THE GODKISSED BRIDE
BOOK THREE

EVIE MARCEAU

Cover Designer: Trif Design trifbookdesign.com

Content Note:

The Godkissed Bride series is a fantasy romance with sexually explicit scenes, violence, trauma, and adult language.

Are you new to the Godkissed Bride series? *Steel Heart Iron Claws* is Book 3, and for it all to make sense, I recommend starting with Book 1, *White Horse Black Nights*!

THE ANCIENT IMMORTAL COURT

Vale the Warrior, *King of Fae*
Iyre the Maiden, *Goddess of Virtue*
Artain the Archer, *God of the Hunt*
Solene the Wilderwoman, *Goddess of Nature*
Popelin the Trickster, *God of Pleasure*
Meric the Punisher, *God of Order*
Samaur the Sunbringer, *God of Day*
Thracia the Stargazer, *Goddess of Night*
Alyssantha the Lover, *Goddess of Sex*
Woudix the Ender, *God of Death*

PRONUNCIATION GUIDE

HOUSE DARROW
Sabine Darrow: sah-BEEN DAIR-oh
Lord Charlin Darrow: CHAR-lin DAIR-oh
Lady Suri Darrow: SOO-ree DAIR-oh

HOUSE VALVERE
Lord Rian Valvere: REE-an val-VAIR-ay
Lord Berolt Valvere: BEH-rohlt val-VAIR-ay
Lady Runa Valvere: ROO-nuh val-VAIR-ay

THE IMMORTAL FAE COURT
Vale: vayl
Iyre: EYE-ur
Artain: ar-TAYNE
Solene: soh-LEN
Popelin: POH-peh-lin
Meric: MAIR-ick
Thracia: THRA-see-uh
Alyssantha: ah-liss-AN-tha

v

Woudix: WOO-diks

Samaur: sah-MAR

OTHER NAMES

Basten: BASS-ten

Folke: FOHLK-uh

King Rachillon: RAH-shee-yon

Captain Tatarin: Ta-TAR-en

PLACES & VOCABULARY

Astagnon: AH-stag-non

Volkany: VOHL-kah-nee

Monoceros: mon-oh-SAIR-ous

Tamarac: tam-UH-rak

CHAPTER 1
BASTEN

Blackness roars inside my skull. Pain stabs behind my left eye like a hatchet to the brain, and I grip the sides of my head before the gods-damn bone splits apart. But there's more than just pain, isn't there? There's something worse.

Darkness.

Nothing.

A fucking *void*.

Remember her! a voice screams in the back of my mind.

But the memory of whatever—whoever—my mind is trying to cling to slips out of my grasp. I chase after it, stumbling through the midday woods, swiping my hands through empty air as though I can catch the fleeing memory like lightning bugs. But, of course, my hands come up empty.

Before I can drag in my next breath, the void roars again.

Wait...what was I even trying to remember?

A curse rumbles out of my chest and echoes among the

1

trees, sending a flock of crows into flight. Their frenzied wings make me flinch.

My damn armor is too tight. Something is wrong. I'm forgetting something important. *I can't fucking breathe…*

In unsteady footsteps, I rip at the buckles of my breastplate as I lurch toward the sound of voices ahead through the trees. With my godkissed senses, I should be able to pick up on every word from hundreds of paces away, but now, everything is a blur. The voices blend with the sound of the clouds roiling overhead, of crows screeching, of my own raging pulse.

I stumble to the edge of a clearing filled with elegantly dressed lords and ladies who make their way toward a row of waiting carriages. Their backs are to me, so I have a moment to observe and try to figure out what is happening.

Why is my head so damn foggy?

The clearing's tents are black—a foreboding color. A red-robed priest carries an elm staff and a gilded copy of the Book of the Immortals. A patch of freshly turned dirt sprinkled with rose petals reeks of earthy clay.

It's a gods-damned funeral.

Lord Berolt's funeral.

Thank fuck—it's coming back to me now.

The blessing over his ashes. The notably dry eyes of attendees who loathed the man. Then, after the ceremony, Lady Eleonora pulling me into the tent with Rian to confess a long-held secret that upended both our lives in a second.

"Wolf?" Lady Suri notices me first. She's the young widow of Lord Charlin Darrow, a loathsome minor lord from Bremcote who did her a favor by choking on his own blood. She cranes her neck to search behind me as though surprised I'm alone. "What…what are you doing back here?"

Her pretty brows pinch in concern.

I open my mouth, but there are no words. Why *am* I back here?

The last thing I remember, I was leaving Lord Berolt's funeral in a rush, determined to plunge deep into the woods, away from the crowd, with no intention of ever returning. For all I cared, everyone in this gathering could fuck off to Old Coros and leave me in peace.

But I wasn't alone. *There was a woman in the woods with me...*

Lady Suri's question draws the attention of the other attendees, who turn and stare at me in utter shock.

What the hell? Is there a wildcat clinging to my back?

Wildcat.

Something about the word triggers that void where a memory of someone is missing, and my chest feels tighter than ever, so tight that my lungs scream with the force of a thousand gales. No matter how much I pull at my breastplate's buckle, it won't loosen.

I can't fucking breathe!

Panic cuts into me like a knife. I drop to my knees, loose hair falling over my eyes, bracing one arm against the dirt to keep from falling.

Remember! You bastard, remember!

But there's only blankness.

Blankness.

Blankness.

Rian shoves his way through the funeral crowd and draws up to a sharp stop in front of me, staring down with incredulity on his face—but I don't have time to think about Rian. The emptiness in my head swallows all my reason until I'm clawing at the dirt, a roar tearing from my throat.

"Wolf, what the fuck happened?" Rian clasps my shoulder to calm me. "Where is—"

The instant I feel his touch, I toss his hand away with enough force to knock him back onto his ass. That triggers his guards, who draw their swords in one fell motion.

Without hesitation, they swarm me.

And that's when I *really* fucking panic.

My mind goes blank. My body takes over. Acting on instinct like a cornered cur, I shoot to my feet, throwing a punch at the nearest guard's chin, which sends him hurtling backward. I dodge the second guard's sword, only to square a strike in his side.

Screams ring out from the crowd. The voices sound strange, too far away. The whole clearing reeks of impossible smells. Winterberries. Fallen snow. An ocean breeze.

My godkissed senses are going fucking haywire.

My heart thunders in my chest, blood roaring in my ears as I pivot on my heel, evading a sword aimed at my midsection. The blade grazes my shirt, and I lunge forward, driving my shoulder into the guard's chest, feeling the impact ripple through my bones. He stumbles back, and I slap my hand over his on the sword hilt, twist the sword from his grip, and swing it around in a wide arc.

My senses explode with information, each breath sharp with the scent of pine resin and iron. The guards' movements slow to a crawl in my mind's eye, every twitch and flinch telling me what they're about to do.

I duck the nearest guard's swing, his blade hissing through the air where my head was a heartbeat ago.

The taste of copper coats my tongue as my teeth gnash together, biting into my tongue.

I ram my elbow into a third guard's throat. His windpipe collapses with a sickening crunch. He drops to the ground, gurgling, his sword clattering beside him. The world blurs at the edges, but my focus narrows to a razor's edge.

"He's having a panic attack," Rian says.

He snatches the elm staff from the old priest's hand and rams it straight into my solar plexus, knocking the wind out of me.

I double over as pain shoots through my nerves. It's enough of a pause to give the guards a chance to wrestle my arms behind my back and force me to my knees.

Chest heaving, I watch through my sweat-soaked hair as Rian tosses the elm staff aside and squares up to face me. He slowly sinks to one knee so we're eye-to-eye and grips my jaw to force me to look at him.

"In the name of the fucking gods, Wolf, what's wrong?"

Fighting for words, I murmur haltingly, "I was...with a woman...in the woods."

"Sabine," Rian says plainly, as if it's the most obvious thing in the world.

My heart clamps like a fist in my chest.

Sabine?

Despite my body's reaction, the name means nothing to me.

I slowly shake my head, struggling to push through the haze clouding my memory. "She had fire-red hair down to her waist. A white gown with a red key embroidered on the chest." I spit a line of blood into the dirt. "Fey lines on her arms. Fucking pointed ears, too. It was the Maiden. *Immortal Iyre.*"

A deafening silence falls over the crowd. No whispers

5

follow. Not a word of gossip, not even from that snake, Lady Runa Valvere.

What I've said has robbed the words from dozens of mouths. Even the wind seems to die down until not a single leaf quakes.

Rian finally breaks the silence by grabbing my shoulder. "Immortal Iyre approached you in the woods? You vow to this?"

"*Tamarac*." It's our boyhood word for complete honesty with one another. I spit out another line of blood. "I'll swear by whatever god you name that it was her. She appeared in human form but then dropped her glamour. She confessed with her own glowing lips who she was."

The crowd lets out gasps, and someone wails.

"Release him." Rian signals to the guards, who let me go. Then his eyes dart to Maximan, the gruff guard who's been in the Golden Sentinels even longer than Rian's been alive. "Maximan. Take some men to search the woods."

"Don't bother searching for Iyre," I say. "She's gone. She cut a portal in the air and stepped through it as easily as crossing a threshold."

Lord Gideon Valvere murmurs to Rian's grandmother, Lady Eleonora. "It will be chaos in the streets when this news reaches Duren. We must make haste before the riots begin."

Already, the crowd erupts into chaos, faces pale with terror as people shove past one another, scrambling for their carriages. Wheels creak and horses snort, hooves striking the ground as drivers whip the reins, desperate to flee to Duren and warn their families before it's too late.

My eyes latch onto one of the only figures remaining behind: Lady Suri. Her russet arms are folded tightly over her small chest. Her usual sunshine smile has vanished, and now her face is as stark as the night sky.

She drops to her knees next to Rian and grips my arm tightly.

"But where is Sabine, Wolf?"

Again, that name. *Sabine*. Who are they all so worried about? I told them that Immortal Iyre walks the earth, heralding the Third Return of the Fae, and they seem more concerned with a stranger.

I shake my head. "Did you hear what I said, my lady? The fae are waking. Immortal Iyre has risen from a thousand-year slumber, and we have no idea which of the other ten have also risen. Truth be told, we're lucky it's only Iyre. If it had been Woudix, or Meric, or Vale himself—"

Suri lays into me with an open palm slap to my right cheek.

Her walnut brown cheeks are flushed, her eyes sparking furiously. "I heard you plain as day, Wolf Bowborn! Did you not hear *me*? Where is Sabine?"

"Lady Suri, calm yourself." Rian grips her hand to keep her from slapping me again, but she shoves him away.

"She's my friend!" Suri cries. "And she was your fiancée until an hour ago, Rian!"

"Fiancée?" I spit out the word like sour grapes. It's so preposterous that I almost laugh. "Rian has no fiancée."

As soon as I say the words, however, a pain in the back of my head throbs.

Suri explodes at me, "Right, because you took her for your own! You promised to keep her safe! You said you'd put your own life above hers! So where is she?"

I couldn't be more stunned if Immortal Artain himself had shot me with a gold-tipped arrow. *My own* fiancée? By the gods, I don't have a fiancée. I've barely even slept with the same woman twice. My eyes dart between Suri and Rian, waiting for one of them to break and admit this is some twisted farce, when it's the last time anyone should be joking.

They remain speechless.

I say, "I have no idea what you're talking about, Lady Suri."

Suri launches herself at me, shaking me hard enough to throttle a rabbit. "You *bastard*! You said you'd love her until the end of days!"

Her voice is so laden with pain that it breaks through my irritation. My lips part, uncertain. She must be confused. Gone mad with fear at the fae's awakening, maybe. But her conviction clearly isn't in question, and it softens something in me to see a woman so violently committed to a falsehood.

"I'm sorry," I choke out. "I wish there was something I could tell you. But I know no woman named Sabine—"

At the same time, shooting pain stabs through my heart until I have to double over and brace my hand against my knees.

Rian hauls Suri off me, taking the blows that were meant for me as she flails against him. "Let me go! You're no better, Rian! You were an ass to her!"

Rian's heard enough insults in his life that he doesn't even flinch. "Lady Suri, stop. Lady—calm yourself, woman!" He plants her firmly on the grass. "Think about what Wolf is saying."

Suri still struggles, more insults poised on the tip of her tongue, but then a dawning realization crosses her face.

She gasps. "Iyre has a memory affinity."

"Exactly," Rian hisses. He gently touches his jaw where

one of her blows landed as he mutters, "Did *I* really merit that punch?"

She doesn't think twice. "Yes."

Once their tempers cool, and their breathing returns to normal, they slowly turn to me with eyes full of pity.

Pity? Pity for *what*?

All of this makes as much sense as laying a trap for a shadow. If this mystery woman was Rian's fiancée, there is no world in which I would ever take her for my own. If I'm sure of anything, it's that I would never betray the man who's like a brother to me.

Maximan comes striding back into the clearing with his usual dour look. Quietly, he murmurs, "We tracked Lady Sabine and Immortal Iyre's footsteps about three hundred paces to the south. The tracks vanish into nothing."

As he always does when he's thinking, Rian takes out his Golath dime, running it over his knuckles.

Suri huffs resolutely as she motions to a servant to bring her dappled mare around. "If Sabine's tracks are gone, then she's gone. You two are welcome to stay here and chase a ghost. I'm going back to Sorsha Hall. To the library, to see what the scholars have to say about fae portals."

She gracefully swings up on her mare and takes off in a cloud of dried leaves.

Rian offers a hand to help me up. I'm unsteady on my feet, reeling like a stallion kicked me in the ribs. The funeral encampment is a ghost town now. Everyone has fled back to Duren except for a few servants and Golden Sentinels still searching the woods.

"You look like death incarnate," Rian says low to me.

I feel like we're boys again, when he dragged me out of the gutter countless times and nursed me back to health. In

9

all my life, he's the only one who's ever given a damn about me. Even now, knowing that I'm the true heir to the Astagnonian throne and his greatest threat, he steadies me with a concerned hand.

I drag a hand through my hair. "Rian, I get that there are gaps in my memory, but I wouldn't have betrayed you."

His lips firm into a flat line as if remembering a distasteful meal. "Ah, but you did."

I stare at him like he's grown a second nose.

"This isn't a game of Basel, Wolf." He grabs me hard by the shoulder. "It's love and war. You fucked my bride on a holy altar in front of me. You gave up a throne that should have been yours by blood for her. And now you've lost her— you really don't remember?"

His look is keen, curious, even a touch fearful, as though my feelings on the matter truly carry weight.

Quietly, I say, "I can't miss a woman I don't remember."

"You truly remember nothing? You feel nothing?" He leans closer, and I feel like I'm on damn trial here.

I shake my head and try to resist the overpowering urge to glance over my shoulder at the shadowed woods. Something calls to me from those shadows. The adrenaline coursing through my veins urges me to *hunt*. To find the object that I've lost.

To find *her*.

But who am I kidding? I don't even know what this mystery woman looks like. If she is tall or small. The color of her hair. The contours of her face. Already, I can't recall the name they said only moments ago.

Rian's shoulders ease as he releases a held breath.

"You need rest," he says. "Come back to Sorsha Hall with me, and we'll get to the bottom of this."

"Right." I smooth a shaking hand over my face, raking back my sweat-soaked hair again. And though my heart urges me not to, I signal the servant to bring my horse. "I'll follow you anywhere, Rian." I pause before adding, "As always."

CHAPTER 2
SABINE

"**B**asten!"

It's the last thing I yell before Iyre pulls me through the portal cut in the forest air, her strength as much as three grown men's. My heart thrashes like a cornered beast, ready to strike with its last ounce of life. As I struggle against her, the invisible portal door fades away.

My final glimpse at Basten in the sun-kissed glen, breathless and confused, vanishes. I hurtle myself at his fading image, fingernails clawing at the air.

"No!"

But it's too late. The glen is gone. *Basten* is gone.

Now, I'm staring at a different forest. This one is filled with sky-high evergreens that cloak the world in shadows. Strangely colored light comes from the forest's dark recesses. In a way, it's beautiful. But it's a dangerous, intimidating kind of beauty. There's something eerie about this place. It's too dark. Too cold. The chilling mist brushes like ghostly fingers around my ankles.

I touch Basten's twine ring on my fourth finger, working it anxiously.

This cold place is my ancestral home?

Iyre releases me without warning, and I tumble forward toward where the portal was, but my hands swipe through empty air now.

I crash to my hands and knees, ripping my wine-red gown with the golden chain straps. A rock slices through the fabric into my left knee. Blood spills out, but I only stare at it in a daze.

I should feel the pain, but I'm numb.

The real pain is in my side, a phantom ache that feels like Iyre tore out one of my organs when she cut me off from Basten.

Basten is my other half. Since the day we met, I've been connected to him on a cosmic level. He hurts, I hurt. He suffers, I do, too. How can I function without being whole? Scholars say an invisible pull binds the Earth and moon, and that if that bind were ever severed, the moon would freefall into the black void of night.

That's exactly how I feel. *Freefall.*

I thrust my fingers into the soil to root myself in the here and now, letting the loamy, cool earth bring me back from the edge of panic.

"He didn't know who I was," I spit between clenched teeth. "You stole his memories of me—give them back!"

"They're gone," Iyre says flatly, slipping a small, round yellow bottle into her gown's pocket.

With a cry, I fling a fistful of soil at her face. In a second, I'm on my feet in my tattered gown, lunging with claws bared, ready to shred her pale fae skin down to the bone. "You lie! I've read the Tale of Iyre's Memory Bottles a thousand times. I know you keep your stolen memories bottled up—are those his? In that yellow bottle?"

I lunge for her pocket, but Iyre moves a step to the right with preternatural speed, causing me to crash down to the ground again.

A branch scratches my arm.

I cry as I push to my feet again to attack from behind. Iyre's face remains passive as I rush at her. The only emotion she shows is a slight flicker of annoyance as she again steps to the side, evading me, and this time catches me by the upper arm.

She tugs me close.

"Do you wish me to take your memories, too?" she threatens, pointed incisors flashing, as she digs her fingers against my temple. "I can make you forget all about that man in the same way. I can make you forget *everything*."

My temple tingles under her fingertips. My breath huffs out of my lungs in tight bursts.

I go perfectly still. A caught rabbit. I've already lost Basten—I can't lose my memories of him, too.

"That's a good little human." With one hand coiled in my hair, she shoves me to my knees in front of her. She hikes up her skirt to show the tip of her white leather boots. "Now, make a sacrifice to your goddess to prove your obedience." She wiggles the tip of her boot. "A kiss will do."

My body bristles under her hold as a wave of revulsion leaves me shaking from fingertips to toes.

This is too familiar. I've done this before.

A memory rushes back to me out of the deepest recess of my mind:

. . .

I am ten years old. Standing outside the imposing wooden gate to the Convent of Immortal Iyre. My white dress is freshly pressed. My long hair in an immortal crown that took my maid all morning to braid.

My little heart beats fast. More hopeful than anything— because this could be a fresh start.

The gates creak open.

"Keep your eyes lowered," Charlin Darrow barks. "And your mouth shut."

"Yes, Father."

He delivers a slap to the back of my head as the gates fully open to reveal an elderly woman with a long coil of gray hair that falls down the back of her red robe.

I dare a slight glance up at her through my lashes.

She saw my father hit me, didn't she? Is she going to say anything? She's a devotee to the Goddess of Virtue, after all, and beating one's children can't possibly be condoned.

But she only frowns.

"Matron White." My father shoves me forward. "Here's the girl. You'll get your payment the first of every month."

Matron White pokes at my little arms. "You said she could help in the fields. She's all skin and bones."

"And?"

Matron White cranes her neck to look at the carriage behind us. "And throw in that horse of yours, too, or else we don't have a deal. I need something that can pull a plow."

My father grumbles, but after the Matron sweetens the deal with a barrel of cider from the convent's orchard, he's all smiles again. After a promise to send Myst back with one of the servants, he leaves without saying goodbye, more concerned with ordering the footman to load his cider in the trunk.

The gates close.

My heart hammers as I dare to gaze up at my new guardian with hopeful eyes.

She grabs me by my immortal crown. Pain digs into my scalp as she leads me, wincing and stumbling beside her, to the statue of Immortal Iyre in the center of the cloistered courtyard.

She shoves me to my knees in front of the statue. The vines growing up the statue ruffle, strangely, as there's little breeze.

"Kiss Iyre's toes, girl. Swear fealty to her. And maybe she'll bless you with an ounce of usefulness because, right now, you're nothing but a burden."

I curl my hands into tight fists, nails cutting into my palms so that the bite of pain pulls me away from the memory.

Adrenaline floods me as Iyre twists her fingers harder in my hair, forcing my head closer to her real-life toes.

My stomach seizes as panic inches closer...

But then, something rustles in the tattered velvet fabric around my knees, and I hear a small squeak.

Mouse-talker? a gentle voice whispers in my head. *I'm here. I'm with you. You aren't alone.*

The forest mouse!

My limbs go weak with relief, and I briefly close my eyes. The mouse might be small, but her soft, warm little presence gives me courage.

I inhale, then look up at Iyre. "No."

"No?" A flicker of amusement crosses Iyre's face. "You think you have a choice?"

Her hand twists harder in my braid. Wetting my dry lips, I scan the forest. All around, towering trees box me in. I can't even see the sun overhead to know which direction is south, back toward Astagnon.

Let me run, the mouse says. *There are beasts in these woods. They will chase me and give you a chance to escape.*

I don't dare glance down at the mouse to give away her presence.

I won't let you risk yourself, little friend, I answer. *Back into my dress. Hide. It is my duty to protect you, not the other way around.*

The mouse squeaks in concern but does as I say.

Still, her suggestion gives me an idea.

Extending my godkiss, I whisper in the back of my mind, *Creatures of these woods, make yourself known.*

It takes a few moments before the animals, curious and brave, begin to respond.

A snake hisses, *Meeee.*

A barred owl overhead lets out a hoot.

A community of voles under the ground says in unison, *Lady needs help?*

A grasshopper on a nearby leaf chirps, *Who are you?*

Other voices come, too. Voices with a strange reverberation. They are the voices of unseen fae beasts, deep in the woods, watching.

A stranger who can speak to us.

The king's blood in her veins.

A lost girlie.

Iyre loses her patience and shoves my head down toward her boot. "Do it, Lady Sabine. Show your obedience to your gods."

My vole friends, dig! I cry out in my head. *Dig hard! Now!*

At first, the soil underfoot vibrates so minimally that it would be almost undetectable unless you knew what to feel for. I fight against Iyre's hold, clawing at her grip on my hair.

17

The ground beneath her feet gives way. The dirt cracks and crumbles into loamy crevasses. She stumbles back a step, which causes a cave-in that has her pinwheeling her arms as she crashes to the ground.

Cupping a protective hand over the mouse in my skirt, I hoist up my mud-stained hem, scramble to my feet, and run into the woods as fast as my feet can carry me.

Thank you, little helpers! I call back to the colony of voles.

I plunge into the darkest part of the forest, swallowed by a cool mist that hovers knee-high, hiding all paths from view.

Behind me, Iyre starts laughing. "Where do you think you'll run to, little princess?"

CHAPTER 3
BASTEN

I wake to too much silence.

Jolting upright, sweat pouring down my bare chest, I can barely catch my breath. Dreams scatter into the shadows like rats under a light, disappearing before I can catch a single one. *Her.* I was dreaming of her, I know it. My mystery woman. Whose name I can't even remember. Her face was there for a second, but now, it's gone.

"Fuck," I spit vehemently, throwing off the coverings.

I'm in Rian's opulent bed, though I barely remember stumbling in and passing out after returning from the funeral encampment. My mind and body feel utterly ravaged, at war with one another, and I have no idea if I've slept one night or three. A tousled blanket on the leather settee tells me that Rian gave me the bed and took the floor for himself, though there's no sign of him now.

I dunk my head straight into the wash basin's frigid water, shocking me out of my stupor. I shake the drips from my hair like a dog and, mopping a towel over my bare chest, shove open the window pane.

The third-floor window of Sorsha Hall overlooks the Golden Heights neighborhood, a collection of upper-class houses bordering the Eastern Market. It's normally a bustling square filled with vendors and promenading ladies with small, yappy dogs.

Today? It's as quiet as a graveyard.

There are no carriages rumbling down the streets. No one out walking. No servants sweeping the front steps. Half the elegant manor homes look boarded up and abandoned. A single curly-haired dog barks at something in an alleyway.

The only significant activity is from a family in the corner house, who hastily carry out trunks and boxes and load them on a wagon parked in the street.

"*Hurry, Eloisa,*" a mother says to her teenage daughter. "*Bring the candlesticks. Your father wants us out of Duren by midday.*"

"*Is Immortal Iyre truly awake, Mama? The servants said she stole Wolf Bowborn's memories.*"

"*Hush now. That's only gossip.*" The mother hurries her daughter to the wagon. "*But we all knew the Lone Wolf and the Winged Lady story would end in tragedy.*"

I jolt at the sound of my own name.

My stomach tightens, threading unease throughout my body.

"Lone Wolf and the Winged Lady?" I repeat aloud in a murmur, confused.

There's something familiar about the story's name, but I can't summon it to mind. I remember standing in Duren's arena, hearing the crowd chant for me: *Lone Wolf! Lone Wolf!*

But who's the Winged Lady?

"You don't remember the story, do you?" a voice says from behind me.

I snap into a defensive stance, unnerved that my senses didn't pick up on someone approaching.

I'm still hazy. Not myself.

Lady Runa Valvere leans in the door frame, toying with a ribbon on her satin gown's plunging neckline. Rian's deceitful cousin. Or, rather, *my* cousin. It's hard to wrap my head around the fact that I'm actually a Valvere by birth.

Honestly? I think I was better off as a street rat.

I unball my fists, but my muscles remain tightly coiled, wary of danger from this soft-skinned viper.

"The Lone Wolf and the Winged Lady," she repeats, sauntering over to Rian's desk. "It's a story that the people of Duren made up about you and Lady Sabine. They called her that because she had the godkissed ability to speak to animals. I suppose, when Iyre took your memories of her, everything related to her vanished, too. Do you remember escorting her here from Bremcote?"

My right eye twitches. "I remember making the journey from Bremcote. Alone except for a damn stubborn mare."

Runa smiles as she drags her index finger over the desk, then rubs away imaginary dust between her fingers. "The story of the Lone Wolf and the Winged Lady is based on a story from the Book of the Immortals. The Tale of the Fated Lovers. Do you know it?"

"I haven't voluntarily read a page of the Book of the Immortals in my life."

Runa plucks a quill from the golden holder, twirling the feather lazily. "In a time before time, a handmaid from Golath and a baker boy from Spezia dreamed about one another every night, though they had never met. Aria would fall asleep at midnight after a long day polishing her mistress's jewels, when she was charmed by nightly visions of a handsome boy. He was dusted with sand, surrounded by an open fire, with eyes like molten gold. Aron, who rose at midnight to begin the day's baking, was equally tormented by dreams of a beautiful girl surrounded by jewels, with hair like spun gold and emerald eyes.

"Aria thought her mystery man was a desert warrior. Aron thought his mystery woman was a high-born lady. Immortal Alessantha toyed with the two strangers, besieging them with dreams of the other until they thought they would go mad from longing. Only then—in a typical bout of fae capriciousness—Alessantha drew their paths together at the Dramaine festival. Aria's mistress had brought her to help with her dress's train. Aron was there to deliver the ceremonial bread loaves."

I shift from foot to foot, tapping my toe with impatience, but Runa remains indifferent as she runs the quill's feathered tip against her chin.

"The fated lovers met at the Dramaine," she continues. "Aron wasn't a desert warrior covered in sand—he was merely a baker boy dusted with flour. Aria wasn't a high-born lady bedecked with her own jewels—only a handmaiden tasked with polishing them. Still, the lovers recognized each other instantly. Time held its breath, and for once, the gods smiled upon mere mortals. For the rest of their lives, they lived happily."

Runa drags the feather down the ample curve of her bosom, tickling the tops of her breasts in coy indifference as she leans back against the hard edge of Rian's desk.

"Bullshit." I grab an apple from the basket on Rian's desk. "The gods don't give happy endings."

I take a large bite that drips juice onto my bare chest.

Runa arches an eyebrow as her attention sinks to that

drop like she wants to lick it off. "Perhaps. In any case, the people of Duren thought you and Sabine were the same: Alessantha's Fated Lovers reborn."

My hand freezes, the apple still clutched in my fist.

"Say her name again." Though my voice is deep, we both hear the edge of begging. "That...woman's. The Winged Lady's."

Runa gives a lupine smile as she makes the gesture of locking her lips and throwing away the key.

Anger simmers deep in my chest, driving me to grab this viper by her long neck and throw her out—but she's royalty.

And me?

Hell, I have more royal blood in my veins than her. But on paper? I'm a nobody.

"Poor little Wolfie." Runa pouts in mock sympathy as she traces the quill feather down my sweat-soaked temple. "Iyre really did a number on you, didn't she? And here I thought Lady Sabine was the one who ruined you."

Sabine.

My eyes fall briefly closed. Somehow, it's the first time I've heard it, yet as familiar as the grooves in my palm.

I jerk back from Runa's feather-light touch. My eyes warn her off as I say, "What do you want, Lady Runa?"

"You can drop the honorifics with me, cousin. You're not Rian's lowly servant anymore." She leans in as she whispers conspiratorially, "You're the rightful king."

Eyes snapping to the hallway to make sure we're alone, I fight the urge to clamp a hand over her mouth to silence her.

Instead, I hiss, "Never speak that aloud again if you value your tongue."

She taps the feather on the tip of my nose as she tuts.

"Such a hot temper. Don't worry yourself—only those of us in the family know your secret."

"I wasn't loyal to Rian because of his title."

She snorts. "You weren't loyal at all—not when it came to Lady Sabine."

I lift my chin, narrowing my eyes as I calculate how many years in the dungeon I'd get for throwing a royal lady out the window.

At my silence, she slinks over to the window, gazing down at the ghost town below in mild interest. "Sabine Darrow seduced you. She used you. She drove a spike between you and Rian. And now she's disappeared with the fae back to her father's enemy lands."

I scoff, "You think she went willingly with Iyre?"

"She's a Volkish princess. A natural-born traitor. For all we know, King Rachillon sent her to Astagnon to drive a wedge between you and Rian because you two have the strongest claim to his rival throne." She leans out the window and cups her hand theatrically around her ear. "Can't your gifted ears hear what the townspeople are saying? They're turning on her. They finally understand that she's always been our enemy."

Though I remember nothing about this mystery woman, a fierce instinct to protect her rises in me, and I grab Runa's wrist off the windowsill.

"You didn't know—" I pause. "Didn't know—"

Fuck!

Already, my mystery woman's name is gone from my memory.

Sensing my inner turmoil, Runa spins the feather lazily in her hand, her eyes lowered to my bare chest. She licks her lips as her gaze slides to the mussed bed sheets.

"Are you sure you don't want me to stay?" she asks.

I recoil, releasing her wrist like she's a burning branch. By the gods, I'm her *cousin*.

Disgusted, I shove her away. Grabbing one of Rian's black shirts, I slide it on and start to button it roughly, though it's tight around my arms. "Get out."

She drops the quill, letting it flutter to the rug, and grabs my shirt collar instead, stopping me from buttoning the upper half.

In a low whisper, she says breathily, "It's my task to pack the Valvere jewels for the trip to Old Coros. Diamond pendants. Ruby earrings. Fae ear caps inset with turquoise. Do you know what else I found? A locket Rian commissioned when he was first betrothed to Lady Sabine. It has her likeness painted inside."

I jolt like I've been bitten by a deathrattle snake. Narrowing my eyes into slits as fine as the quill's point, I say, "What are you offering?"

"The locket, of course. It might be a poor substitute for a full memory of your so-called Fated Lover, but it's the best you're going to get. In exchange..." She perches her plump bottom on the desk's edge, foisting her half-exposed breasts up, knowing that from my height, I can see damn near everything. "...I've always wanted to wear a queen's crown."

I might be a Valvere by blood, but I haven't been schooled in political machinations as they have—so it takes me a second before realization smacks me across the face.

Her flirtation, her cunning smiles, her emphasis that I'm the true heir.

Fuck me.

This woman is a predator.

I stalk toward the desk, resting my blanched knuckles on

25

either side of her perfumed little ass, bringing my lips to within an inch of hers.

"You would steal the throne from Rian?" My voice purrs with a barely contained threat.

"*You* are the rightful king—you would be doing the stealing. I would simply be wearing your ring."

I almost want to laugh at the gall of this pretty snake. She comes to her cousin's bedroom, touches his belongings, and so sweetly conspires to stab him in the back with the man who has always been at his side.

This is the family I was born into?

In a move so fast she can barely gasp, I grip her neck in the vice of my hand and squeeze until I can feel her trachea close off. As her painted lips contort for air, I lean in close enough that my loose hair drags across her cheek.

"Listen closely, *cousin*. I will never betray Rian Valvere. I'd be a damn fool not to lick the filth off his boots in gratitude for all he's done for me. I gave him the throne—and I would again tomorrow and every damn day after. I'd rather be buried to my balls in fire ants and doused with honey than marry you. And unless you want me to tell Rian about your scheming, you'll stay the hell away from me."

I release her with a shove that sends her collapsing backward on the desk, rasping for air as she massages her throat.

"Get out," I snap.

She stops at the door. "You'll rethink this, Wolf Bowborn. A lot can change in a matter of days—look how much already has."

CHAPTER 4
SABINE

I don't dare look back.

Chest heaving, I race through the maze of towering trees, throwing glances upward in hopes of seeing the sun through the thick mist. My boots crush a crop of glowing orange mushrooms that release a stench like rotting corpses. As I duck under a low pine branch, a vine falls on my shoulder, slithering with a mind of its own.

I clap my hand over my mouth to muffle my shriek as I fight to free myself from the vine and plunge deeper into the woods. I run blindly, as hard as I can, until my thighs burn. When I can't run another step, I drop to my stomach behind a copse of waist-high ferns that I hope will conceal me.

I'm no fool—I've seen how fast Iyre can move. She's practically godkissed with speed. Trying to outpace her in a foreign land would be a mistake.

All I can do is hide.

My breath strains against my ribs. My shoulder-length hair is a mess, filled with tangled thorns. My arms are covered in scratches and welts. The ground beneath me is unnaturally cold, so cold the mist around me leaves the ferns frost-tipped.

Closing my eyes, I listen, wishing I had Basten's senses.

Leaves rustle in the steady wind. An insect trills overhead. At any second, I fear footsteps approaching.

The *last* thing I expect is for a curious voice to chirp, **Whatcha doing, girlie?**

I flinch, swallowing a yelp, and go tense in case I need to fight. But when I look to my left, a friendly face with a lolling tongue greets me.

My lips part, but I only sputter for words.

The creature is the size and shape of a fox, with a fox's thin lupine face and sly black eyes, except that this one's feet don't touch the ground. Its glossy silver-blue fur floats like it's swimming, its silver-clawed paws treading the air.

You're a cloudfox, I say in surprise.

It paws the air to float up higher, nose sniffing, tilting its head this way and that to examine me. Its head jerks sharply to the right, silver ears swiveling toward a sound I can't hear.

Girlie is being hunted, it says. **Follow me!**

Before I can utter another thought, the creature bounds off through the trees. Its paws barely skim the ground as it does its floaty-swimmy movements, gracefully arcing around vines and ducking under branches.

Wait! I cry, frozen in a moment of indecision. Hiding still seems like the best course of action.

But the cloudfox is nearly out of view...

I curse and shove to my feet. In the next breath, I'm racing after it.

There's no hiding my sound now. My boots are loud on the fallen leaves. Branches snap as I rush to keep the cloudfox in sight ahead of me. Its silver-blue color is so striking amid the shadows that it's easy to spot as it effortlessly bounds deeper into the woods.

Wait! I cry out. *Please, take me south! To the border wall!*

Girlie, follow me! it answers in a sing-song voice.

A frustrated huff slips out of my mouth, but I duck under a branch and go after the cloudfox. My feet ache, my thighs burn, and a stitch in my side has me clutching at my ribcage.

Not far now! it chirps with a lupine laugh.

I muster my strength and push myself harder over the steep, rocky terrain. It's a scramble for me, but the cloudfox merely floats on the updraft.

If I can get to the border wall, I know I can find a way across it. Basten and Rian discovered a tunnel, and if there's one, there's probably more.

As I scramble up an outcropping, a brief ray of sun breaks through the mist to warm my face.

I pause to catch my breath, and my thoughts turn to Basten. My hand drifts to the twine ring on my left fourth finger.

Where is Basten now? Is he safe? Does he remember anything about me? For so long, he's been the one looking out for me. He's been there for me when I didn't even know I needed someone. Sheltering me. Watching over me.

The truth is, the only home I've ever had is with Basten. And now? Has he forgotten me completely? If I have to turn the world upside down to right that crime, I will.

Almost there! The cloudfox floats backward on its skipping paws to encourage me. *Just ahead! Hurry, hurry!*

My fingernails are broken and bloody by the time I heave myself over the outcropping, drag myself onto my knees, and then stagger to my feet. The cloudfox circles me, yipping at my heels in encouragement.

I don't know how much longer I can go on.

My muscles are growing slack.

My vision begins to blur.

The trees sway around me in a way where I can't tell if it's in my head or if they're actually moving in a sentient way. The cloudfox's faintly reflective fur is my beacon, the only thing I cling to.

Just keep going...

The next step takes me out of the trees.

I'm in a clearing. The smell of roasted meats and campfire smoke hit my nostrils. Indistinct voices and a nearby blacksmith's hammer pound against my ears. Ahead, a moss-covered, thirty-foot-high stone wall runs as far as I can see in each direction.

The border wall.

Reeling and weak, I take in canvas tents painted indigo with a starburst emblem, and my heart surges again—this time in fear. I've strode into an army encampment that flanks the border wall.

A *Volkish* encampment.

The cloudfox winds between my feet, grinning up at me with a cruel smile that reveals its sharp silver canines.

Silly girlie!

Anger tears through me like an avalanche, pushing past my exhaustion until I'm lunging toward the floating creature. "You deceitful thing! You tricked me!"

Surprised soldiers rise to their feet from around a nearby campfire, taking me in warily. A few of them carry axes strapped to their backs. Others have rows of small knives belted to their leather breastplates. From somewhere beyond the tents, a roar that belongs to no animal I've ever encountered shakes the ground.

Whatever it is, it's *big*.

I sink into a crouch to steady myself. My adrenaline surges out of control. Every voice in my head tells me to *run*.

But my body can't keep going. I'm worn out as a dish rag.

I take a single step backward, and the circle of tents seems to spiral as I sway on my heels.

The soldiers around the campfire make no move to attack me, but two women in indigo cloaks emerge from a tent and silently move behind me, cutting off any retreat into the woods.

I stumble, on the verge of panic.

"Little princess," a voice sneers as Iyre steps out from behind one of the tents, her glowing fey lines reminding me of the sentient vines, the cloudfox, and all the other deceitful magic in this cursed kingdom. "How kind of you to run exactly where I was going to bring you anyway."

From behind her, the cloudfox gives a lupine snicker.

I narrow my eyes as rage burns through me.

I had thought there was no strength left in my bones. That I was one breath away from crumpling like a leaf. That my beautiful future with Basten might be closed off forever when Iyre sealed the fae portal.

But I underestimated my hatred for the gods.

"You." I jab a finger at the cloudfox. "You and I aren't finished." Then, I square up to Iyre, my real enemy, and lift my chin. "You think you rule this land? You think you rule *me*?"

"Well, *yes*." She stands before me with her hands primly

folded in a farce of modesty, the exact pose from the statue of Immortal Iyre back at the convent.

In a flash, I'm back within those high stone walls.

My hands are blistered and bleeding from scrubbing the Sisters' floors for hours on end. Finally, I reach the end of the hallway where an alcove holds that damnable statue. The vines have been growing like crazy since I arrived—no matter how many times I pull them off, they grow back within days.

"Immortal Iyre showers the righteous with good fortune," Mother White's grating voice drones from behind me as her boots stop an inch from my scouring brush. She adjusts a candle set in the statue's clasped hands. "Because we worship her, she gives us the bounty of strong cider, a roof over our heads, and lamb stew enough to feed the entire convent."

She turns, hiccupping from all that 'strong cider,' and leaves fresh, muddy tracks where I just finished cleaning.

I clench my jaw. I harvested apples and brewed their cider. I climbed onto an unsteady ladder to rethatch the roof. I slaved over a fire all day, stewing lambs who had only hours before pleaded with me for their lives. And I never even got more than a few bites to soothe my groaning belly.

Now, that beaten-down, ten-year-old girl inside me cries out for help. I'm not a child anymore.

I'm a force of nature.

I dig my nails into my palms for the grounding bite of pain.

The sly cloudfox has slunk over to the campfire, still

grinning its self-satisfied smile as it paws around a turkey bone dropped in the dirt.

Like a lantern, my rational mind switches off.

I'm only dimly aware now of what's happening, as though I'm watching myself like an owl from overhead branches. I feel outside my own body. This has only happened once before, in Duren's arena, when Rian let a tiger loose upon an innocent boy. He'd wanted to test my powers. To push me to the limit of my capabilities beyond where I was willing to go.

At the time, I hated him for it.

Now, I whisper a word of gratitude that he showed me what I'm capable of.

Watching from above, I see myself rise to my full height, no longer bowed by exhaustion. The scratches on my arms ooze blood that dribbles to the ground. My eyes are cloudy, glazed over with a strange silver sheen.

The soldiers shift their stances, murmuring uncertainly to one another, preparing to block me should I try to run.

My head snaps like a child's doll toward the cloudfox. Lips moving silently, I feel like I am both in my body and outside of it.

Light up this camp like a fireball, I command it.

The cloudfox snarls and paws the dirt, fighting against my compulsion.

I focus more intently, thrusting my will into its mind until it *must* obey me. It contorts its body, leaping through the air in strange, jerky flails, but I drill my thoughts in further until I can feel its rapid heartbeat stuttering behind its small ribs. So delicate. So small. If I wanted to, I could crush that heart with a single thought like stamping out a butterfly.

Light it up! I demand.

The cloudfox twitches one final time before its soul retreats into some dark place to make room for mine.

Now, it's *my* mind within the little fox's body, baring its silver teeth, moving its feathered paws. Dimly, I'm aware of the soldiers' cries of confusion, but they might as well be gnats in my ears. My hands twitch as I puppet the cloudfox, forcing it to jump in unnatural, jerky leaps toward the tents.

Already, I can feel a strange energy crackling within it. A bright power I somehow knew was there even though I've never seen a cloudfox before.

In the Book of the Immortals, cloudfoxes are described as playful, mischievous creatures. Unlike starleons, who spread plague on their wings, or goldenclaws, bears the size of carriages, they present no real threat.

But somehow, this deep, second self within my body knew that wasn't true. That cloudfoxes have always been more powerful than those ancient scribes knew.

DO IT! I command.

The cloudfox's final resistance vanishes as it falls entirely into my thrall. As its body quakes, a bolt of lightning shoots out from its feathery, floating fur to strike the roaring campfire. The logs explode with a shower of sparks, throwing out splinters and billowing smoke.

The soldiers fall back, confused, but they're trained for the unexpected. The encampment fills with the sounds of iron blades being drawn.

I remain perfectly still, only vaguely aware of their presence on the edges of my periphery.

I haven't stopped staring at Iyre once, not even to blink.

At my command, another lightning bolt shoots out from

the cloudfox, striking an elm branch overhead. The branch snaps off, crashing to the ground to smash two tents.

Someone cries out in pain.

The nearest soldier, a beast of a man with a thick braided beard, draws a foot-long serrated knife from his holster. Before he can stab me, I force the cloudfox to hurl another lightning bolt at him. The man flies back five paces to crash in a roasting spit that impales his thick bicep.

All around, soldiers rush into fighting mode.

But Iyre?

Iyre remains calm. Amused, even. Her eyes flash with dark delight. "Is that the best you can do, princess?"

My rage boils over until I'm ready to break the world in two. It hurts the cloudfox to channel lightning bolts—I can feel its heart faltering, its small body gripped in pain. For a second, I doubt myself, but then another soldier comes at me with a mace studded in metal spikes.

With a cry, I force an explosion of lightning out of the little fox. Bolts radiate across the encampment, sending soldiers flying, tents catching fire and going up in flames. Shouts and screams pierce my ears.

The cloudfox's body twitches on the ground. *The ground.* It doesn't even have the strength to bound through the air anymore. Curled into a ball, it quietly yips in pain.

But this darker self within my mind? The one that can control beasts?

She knows no pity. Pain does not sway her. She wants revenge for a lifetime of wrongs at the hands of this deceitful fae goddess, and she will burn the world down with lightning until she is back with Basten.

I scream an inhuman cry, ready to tear the cloudfox

apart to destroy the entire encampment and Immortal Iyre with it, when my voice is strangled.

My jaw is hinged open, frozen.

I can't move my eyes from side to side.

Even my heart doesn't beat in my chest.

Suddenly, the darker self within me is gone like morning mist.

Now, it's just me, Sabine, a bloodied and spent girl. From my periphery, I can tell that it isn't only me. Every single soldier in the clearing is frozen in time like a statue. Not even the flames flicker in the campfire.

Is...is Iyre doing this?

But then, from the corner of my eye, I spot one of the indigo-cloaked women moving among the bodies, her lips working silently as she holds her hands in front of her, lowering one finger at a time as though counting down.

She's petite, though her broad-shouldered armor and cloak give her the look of someone much larger. Her skin is the soft brown color typical of northern Kravada, her silky black hair twisted into a loose braid. Above her cloak's brooch, I can make out a godkissed birthmark.

"Lady Iyre," she says to the goddess in Astagnonian, with a heavy accent. "I cannot stop time for more than ten seconds."

Already, half her fingers are lowered—which means I have five more seconds of being immobile.

Iyre is the only other person impervious to the godkissed soldier's frozen time. She approaches me languidly, smoothing back a strand of hair off my face.

Four more seconds, I count.

"Ten seconds is sufficient, Captain Tatarin," Iyre replies calmly.

Three seconds.

Iyre picks up a heavy iron chain from a pile near the campfire that a blacksmith was mending. She hefts it in her hands, then approaches me with that ice-cold smile.

Two seconds.

"If you're going to act like an animal, princess, then we'll treat you like one."

She wrenches my hands to my front, and I'm powerless to stop her. She binds them tightly together so that I can't move my fingers to puppet the cloudfox.

One.

When time finally restarts, I'm a girl in chains.

CHAPTER 5
BASTEN

E yes like the ocean shallows.

One perfect freckle on her right cheek.

Those *breasts*.

I'm moaning aloud like a thirteen-year-old boy when I wake, all tangled in Rian's sheets, a sheen of sweat coating my skin. She's there. Right at the edge of my mind. In the dream that's slipping away...

"You filthy fucker." A pillow smashes into my face. "That's the last time I give you *my* bed."

Groggy, I blink awake to find Rian folding his blanket from where he slept next to the fireplace.

I run a hand through my damp hair. "What—what are you on about?"

"If anyone's going to stain my sheets with nighttime spunk, it'll be me. With the town's latest whore. Now clean yourself up and finish packing. The carriages will be ready to leave at dawn. Unless you've changed your mind about coming to Old Coros? Decided to stay here and make love to my mattress?"

I throw the pillow back at him. "Fuck you. I'll be packed."

It doesn't take me long to gather my things. I nod to the guards as I leave the castle and head for the city gates.

As I make my way to the game warden's cottage I call home, I'm struck by how deserted Duren is. Most of the shop windows are boarded up in fear of looters. The markets are empty. The only increase in traffic comes from more drunks and opium hounds than usual, staggering down alleyways or passed out in doorways. I guess everyone deals with the news of the Third Return in their own way.

In another life, I'd probably be with those bums. Drooling into the filth. If Rian hadn't seen potential in me all those years ago.

When I finally shove open the door of the game warden's cottage, I take a moment to look at my home—my life—with a stranger's eyes.

The unmade bed.

The carelessly stocked cupboards.

The single chair by the fireplace.

Rian gave you a chance to make something of yourself, and this is the best you did? Bravo, Wolf. Bravo.

It doesn't take long to pack my knapsack with my few belongings. My bow and quiver go into the pile of things to take. My hunting knives in their leather roll-up bag. An extra pair of boots and two pairs of woolen socks. When I get to Old Coros, my backwoods forest garb will make me look like a caveman compared to the capital's prissy highbrows, but so be it.

I tug out a few extra pairs of trousers and shirts, but when I root around in the back of my dresser drawer, an unexpected scent smacks me in the face.

Before I can stop myself, I grab a ratty old shirt and press it against my face. I breathe in deep, like an opium addict getting his next hit.

Violets.

Instantly, I'm slammed with desire so strong that my heart tries to fight its way out of my chest. My pulse flares, sizzling like oil tossed onto a fire. All that's nothing compared to the damn surge of blood to my cock, which instantly hardens.

It's her scent. It has to be. She must have borrowed this shirt.

The faceless woman I only know as the Winged Lady, because a single minute after hearing her name, it keeps getting sucked back into that yawning abyss in my head.

But this? The scent of violets? The muscle memory of a woman's skin smooth as petals? *This* I haven't forgotten. It lives somewhere beyond the part of my mind that Iyre ripped out.

My legs go slack, and I sink down to my bed like a sack of beans, causing the joists to groan under my weight.

A matching groan rumbles out of my chest as I bury my face in the shirt again, rooting like a damn pig for every last trace of her scent, breathing her in as fast as my lungs can fill.

My arms start shaking uncontrollably. A rush of panic rises in me, the feral urge to swing at anything that dares approach me, blinded by a need to remember, to REMEMBER...

I growl into the shirt, fingers twisting in the fabric, ready to tear the world apart for a single memory of this woman.

"Wolf? May I enter? Um—is this a bad time?"

A woman's soft voice at my door makes me jump, and I

stuff the shirt into my knapsack, though it's a challenge to convince my fingers to let it go.

"Lady Suri." My voice is gruff as I quickly curse myself for leaving the front door open. "Is there something I can help you with?"

She steps into the game warden's cottage apprehensively as though I might have set snares in the floorboards. As her wide brown eyes scan my humble pantry, the underwear hung to dry by the fire, the piss-bucket under my bed, I take a closer look at the Lady of Bremcote.

Truth be told, I've never paid much heed to Suri. When I first met her, she was an afterthought. The pretty young Kravadan girl unfortunately married to Charlin Darrow.

When Charlin came to Duren to blackmail Rian and brought Suri with him, I found her a curiosity. She managed to maintain a sunny disposition even while married to a drunken lout. Hell, she even cried at his death. Somehow, she'd been able to see the sliver of good in him when no one else could.

Fuck if I know how.

Suri stops her inspection of my meager belongings when she spots my half-packed knapsack. Eyebrows lifted in surprise, she says, "You're going to Old Coros with the Valveres?"

I flip closed the knapsack flap, protective of the shirt with *her* scent on it.

"Of course. I owe Rian everything, least of all my service."

Suri's lips press tightly, her face at war with itself, before she blurts out, "If rumors are to be believed, you owe him nothing. Not when *you* should be on the throne—"

I cut her so sharp a look that it silences her. For a long

moment, we stare at one another as the wind makes the ceiling joists creak. The first fat raindrops of a coming shower plink on the window glass.

"I overheard Sorsha Hall's servants packing your own bags this morning, my lady," I say evenly. "I could just as easily demand to know why *you're* going to Old Coros."

"I'm going for a book."

Her answer comes so swiftly that I feel like a crow smacked me in the face. Scrambling, I scoff, "What, there aren't enough bedtime stories in Sorsha Hall's library?"

"I'm not after a bedtime story." Her cheeks flush as she smooths back the dark curls framing her face. She drops her voice. "I'm looking for a book Sabine was searching for."

I step back in surprise.

Lady Suri closes the cottage door behind her and says quickly, "Before Lord Berolt's passing, Sabine came to me for help. I wasn't watched as closely as she was, so she thought I had a better chance of searching unnoticed." She hugs her arms against the cold of my cottage. "She was after a one-of-a-kind set of volumes written after the First Return. She found the first volume in Sorsha Hall—apparently, it explained how the fae gods were awakened. But the second volume was missing."

Suri glances toward the window as if the storm outside unnerves her. "Supposedly, that one reveals how humans two thousand years ago put the fae *back* to sleep."

My eyebrow arches. Back to sleep? In the thousand years since the fae last walked the earth, people have spread all kinds of hair-brained lore. But not even the most far-fetched tales I've heard implied that humans could exert any power over the gods.

I grab a pair of socks to stuff in my knapsack.

Suri twiddles her thumbs anxiously. "Have you changed your mind about searching for Sabine?"

My hand freezes at the sound of the name. My knuckles go white without me even realizing it, as my heart pounds so damn hard it rivals the driving rain. I hesitate, thinking back on what little I remember of last night's dream. Of my mystery woman. No—of Rian's former fiancée.

I turn sharply back to my belongings on the bed. I shove the socks into the front pocket of my knapsack. "Sorry, Lady Suri, but you nailed it when you called me a bastard. I don't *know* her. And from what I hear, she's a traitor to the realm."

"For all that is holy! Wolf, you can't actually believe that!" She throws her hands in the air. "Do you truly remember nothing?"

A muscle ticks in my jaw.

Sabine, I remind myself before the name slips away again. *Sabine. Sabine.*

"Nope."

Suri's brow wrinkles as her sympathetic nature bleeds through, and she says more softly, "She loved you. And you loved her. They wrote ballads about the two of you. A week ago, if she'd been taken, you would have scoured the earth from here to hell to bring her back. You're a master tracker!"

"I don't *know* her!"

The force of my shout startles even me. Suri's eyes somehow go even rounder, the velvet brown irises reflecting back my face like two silver mirrors. I scrub a hand on the back of my neck, pacing in front of the bed as my blood surges.

Sabine, I repeat in my head. *Remember her name, you bastard.*

Once my temper cools, I grip the bedrail, hair curtaining my face like a confessional.

Quietly, I mutter, "You don't understand, Lady Suri. When Iyre took my memory of Sabine, she took *everything*. I don't remember what she looks like. Hell, I couldn't even remember her name until you said it just now. I know nothing about her habits, her movements, her associates. I have nothing to go off. I can't track a shadow."

Suri's lips press together as she watches me, and I can't fathom what must be going through her head.

After a moment, she bites gently on her bottom lip. "There's the story of Immortal Iyre's Memory Bottles. If Iyre put your memories in one of her bottles, then you could get them back—"

"None of those old stories are true," I mutter dismissively.

"You don't know that."

I keep my jaw tight as I continue to pack my bag.

A stretch of silence follows, and then she reaches into the inner pocket of her cloak. "I worried that Rian might pour poison in your ear about her, so I brought you something. To remind you of her. This belonged to Charlin."

She takes out an envelope. It's yellowed around the edges.

She continues, "Iyre stole your memories, but not even a goddess can strip away every last thing." She pauses. "She lives in more than memories."

I glance sidelong at the envelope, swallowing.

I'll give Suri credit. I've had my walls up since the beginning of our conversation, but she seems determined to break them down. Poor girl—she doesn't realize that she's poking a beast with iron-thick skin.

I grab the letter. "Whatever this is? Yeah, I don't care. I don't think about whoever this woman is. I don't dream about her. I don't miss my lost memories. So good luck finding your little book in Old Coros. I'll be right where I belong. At Rian's side."

I make a big show of crumpling the letter and tossing it into the cold hearth.

I tie my knapsack with jerky movements, then sling it over my shoulder. I'm twice Suri's size, and in a few steps, I've herded her to the door.

Her eyes spit fire at me, furious that I would so easily turn my back on the woman I supposedly loved. And damn, if I'm not a little jealous of a friend like Suri. When everyone else has turned away from my mystery woman, Suri has stayed true.

I lean in the doorframe, letting my height intimidate her, as I bark, "Now scamper off before the rain ruins your gown."

Suri's cheeks bleed red with disappointment. She tips her chin up, looking me in the eyes like she can see right through my forced bravado, and murmurs, "I knew Rian didn't deserve her. I thought, maybe, you did. But you and the High Lord? You only deserve one another."

She slams the door behind her.

I let out a long exhale, running a hand over my face. I listen for her departing footsteps outside.

As soon as she's gone?

"Fuck it." I scramble to the hearth and unfold the crumpled letter, reading greedily.

Dear Papa,

My thirteenth birthday was last week, and I think you would be astonished by how much I've grown. I can now reach the highest shelves in the chapel. Matron White says I shall soon tower over Sisters Rose and Scarlet, which will be useful when it comes time for spring cleaning. You will be pleased to hear I am diligent in my studies and have not missed a prey session all year, even when I was ill with the wintertide fever.

I am happy to report that Myst is in good health, though the confinement of the convent does not soot her free spirit. I've spent my time on useful pursuits, such as tending to the goats, brewing cider for the Sisters, and honoring Immortal Iyre by polishing her temple's floors. I am not always perfect in my obedience, according to Matron White, but I promise you that I shall not stop striving to correct my failings until I make you proud of me.

I was sorry that you were unable to visit on my birthday yet again, though of course, I understand you are needed at the Bremcote estate. I miss you and the servants deerly and would like to come see you. It would hearten me greatly to pay my respects to Mama's grave. I know you have said no in years past, but this year, would you grant me permission to return for a visit?

Your daughter,
Sabine

The letter shows the hallmarks of an uncertain young girl trying her hardest to paint a happy veneer over misery. The handwriting is careful to the point of shaky perfection, as though she rewrote the letter a dozen times to get it right. The girl behind these words is so transparently desperate for even table scraps of her father's attention. The few misspellings—prey for pray, soot for suit, deerly for dearly —cause my brick-hard heart to soften.

She was so young when writing this. So damn alone.

A child.

And her bastard of a father probably didn't even respond.

A surge of anger at Charlin Darrow—at everyone who failed her—screams at me to crumple the letter, but I force myself to resist the urge. Because what Suri said was true— this is a piece of my mystery woman.

She lives in more than memories.

I sink onto my bed beside the knapsack, smoothing out the letter to re-read it. With every pass, I feel like I know this girl a little bit more. The way her "t's" are crossed with an upward tilt betray a hopeful spirit even in the midst of her imprisonment. Her naive devotion to a man who couldn't give a damn about her shows her unfaltering kindness.

I'll tell you what I *don't* see—the slightest glimmer that this girl has a traitorous bone in her body.

It fills me with a cascade of questions that tumble over me until I'm drowning. Now that Sabine is grown, is her spirit still as unbroken as the girl who wrote this letter? Does she feel rage toward the Sisters who neglected and abused her? Does her drive to find the good in the world persist?

I trace my finger along the name at the bottom of the letter.

LOVE, SABINE.

As long as I have this letter, I'll have her name. But letters can burn. Be destroyed or lost. And if someone found this letter on me? I might as well fuck Rian's fiancée in front of him all over again.

As the rain drives against the tin ceiling, I spare a brief moment to take a breath. My fingers knit, wanting to hold onto the name like a gods-damn jewel.

That brief breath is all I can spare.

I fall on my knees by the bed, tearing through my knap-sack until I get my hunting knife. The blade gleams in the rain-washed light from the window.

Jaw clenched, I roll up my lefthand sleeve to my elbow, then set the knifepoint against my flesh.

The blade is twelve inches, a brutal tool, but I'm prac-ticed enough with it that I could skin a pygmy mouse without nicking a single organ.

Biting down on the inside of my cheek against the pain, I begin to carve the letter *S*.

CHAPTER 6

SABINE

My thighs ache worse than after sex.

For three days, I've been forced at the sharp end of a spear to ride on one of the massive fae goldenclaws that the Volkish army uses as war beasts. My velvet dress from Lord Berolt's funeral hangs in tatters around my bruised and scratched limbs. The soldiers robbed me of my boots, knowing I couldn't run far barefoot through the forest. My wrists suffer the most, bound in heavy iron chains like I'm chattel.

No, wait.

I take that back.

Worst of all? *It's the smell.*

Riding a goldenclaw who's gone longer without bathing than I have is infinitely unrecommended.

"I need to pee," I call down sweetly to Captain Tatarin, the mage soldier with the godkiss of freezing time. The poor captain has been tasked with babysitting me, which means she, too, must suffer the goldenclaw's reek. "Shall I piss on this bear's fine saddle?"

Captain Tatarin flicks me an impatient glower. "We stop for a midday rest in an hour, Highness. You can empty your bladder then."

I lift my eyebrows. "So you *do* want me to piss in the saddle."

"Go ahead," she answers, matching my mock cheerful tone. "You'll sit in your own filth for three more days until we reach Norhelm."

My eyes narrow into slits that she called my bluff.

That's been more or less the extent of conversation with my captors since my abduction. Most of the Volkish soldiers don't speak Astagnonian, and Iyre prefers to ride in a small, enclosed carriage carried on a goldenclaw's back at the head of the party.

The terrain has gradually grown steeper and rockier the further north we traverse, yet the six goldenclaws carrying the carriages and supplies lumber effortlessly over the uneven ground, their giant paws leaving behind tracks dusted in gold.

My goldenclaw—unimaginatively named Two because she is second in the line of six—and I settle into a tentative routine. If I scratch the mite bites behind her scarred left ear, she graciously avoids the low branches that would otherwise slap me in the face.

As we plunge deeper into the forest, I can't help but put aside my anger to marvel at the delicate wildflowers glowing in impossible shades of sapphire and indigo, their petals shimmering like moonlight on a still lake. Eerie fungi cling to tree trunks, casting an emerald glow. Beetles with luminescent spots dotting their wings leave light trails in their wake. Occasionally, a sentient vine will snake across the fallen leaves to curl around my ankle before a soldier severs it with his sword.

I never knew such a place existed. A land of cold magic, of living shadows.

I'm a princess of a place I've never been.

In the evening, the soldiers drag my aching body down from the goldenclaw and plant me, chained and bound, at the base of a tree while they set up camp. Amid the bustle of erecting tents and roasting spits over campfires, I'm all but ignored.

The hem of my dress ruffles as the mouse peeks out the tip of her snout, her twitching whiskers tickling my bare feet.

She runs through her daily report: *I **smelled standing water** after breakfast, followed by **wildflower nectar** before lunch, then **pine resin** for the remainder of the day.*

Great job, I commend her. **Now stay hidden. I'll save you some supper crumbs.**

Between the two of us, we've been charting Iyre's course from the border wall to Norhelm, the capital city of Volkany, so that if we get a chance to escape, we can find our way back. Few people know this, but humble as they are, mice are excellent scent trackers. Between the two of us, I have a good mental map of our trek.

Standing water? *That means a swamp.*

Wildflower nectar? *A field laid bare by a massive fallen oak.*

Pine resin? *The forest we've traveled through all afternoon.*

As I hug my legs close and rest my cheek on my knee, I let out a long exhale.

Who am I kidding? I'm fantasizing about an escape for the mouse's benefit, not mine. We have no real chance of escape. We already tried. I definitely don't want a repeat of what happened before—my stomach churns with guilt when I think of putting the little cloudfox through so much pain.

Plus, I'm not a skilled woodsman like Basten.

I can't help but think of him as I tip my head up to look at the moon overhead, visible through a break in the tree canopy.

Are you looking at the same moon now, Basten?

I swallow back the lump in my throat before Iyre, Captain Tatarin, or any of the other soldiers see a hint of vulnerability that they can exploit.

A few minutes later, Captain Tatarin drops down beside me with two bowls of stew. She fishes out a key from a piece of twine around her neck and unlocks my shackles.

"You know," I say as I massage my wrists. "There are other job opportunities besides kidnapper."

She dips her spoon in her stew. "Kidnapper, eh? That's an interesting perspective."

"What would *you* call it?" I stab my own spoon in my bowl.

She thoughtfully chews on a tough hunk of venison. "Highness, no one has kidnapped you. This has been a rescue operation from the start. Your father has gone to great lengths, even sending a woken goddess, to bring you home."

I burst out laughing so hard that soup sprays out my nose. Dabbing at my chin, I croak, "A rescue? In chains?"

"The chains are your fault," she counters. "You tried to kill my soldiers."

I huff another bitter laugh, quieter this time.

Patiently, she blows on her stew to cool it. After another few bites, she points the end of her wooden spoon at my chest, where my tattered dress's neckline shows my birth-mark. "I've never met someone who can speak to animals."

I bristle, remaining silent, only opening my mouth for stew. But once my hunger fades, my mood slightly improves.

I've been watching Captain Tatarin closely for days now. She doesn't cheat when she plays dice with the other soldiers. She thoroughly brushes down the goldenclaws after each ride. Puts ointment on any cuts on their tender noses. Even kisses their foreheads when she thinks no one is watching.

Plus, I'll be honest—it's getting boring to only talk to a mouse.

I sigh. "My godkiss doesn't help me much now, does it? I've asked that goldenclaw you have me riding to run away a dozen times, but she only wants to play riddles."

Captain Tatarin nearly chokes on her stew. "Did you say *riddles?*"

I groan. "All day. Every day. That's all goldenclaws think about, other than their bellies."

She cocks her head, curious and a little awe-struck. "Tell me one."

I shift to pull my legs cross-legged beneath me as I scoop the last of my stew. "What do you see if you follow a horse?"

My goldenclaw, Two, stumped me with that one yesterday.

The captain wrinkles her nose. "Its stable?"

"Its backside.'"

She laughs so hard that a few surprised heads turn from the nearby soldiers to look at us curiously. "One more."

I lean back on my arms. "What is gold but never shines?"

"Hmm. I don't know."

"Honey."

"How like a bear," she chuckles. She sets her empty bowl in the grass at her side and sits cross-legged, too, then pulls around her braid to start to unwind it. "You may call me Tati, by the way. All my friends do."

I snort. Because we *aren't* friends.

I wipe the remnants of my stew with my bread, savoring the flaky crust. Finally, feeling a little mellowed, I clear my throat. "Do you really believe you're rescuing me?"

Her eyebrows rise as though it's obvious. "Of course, Highness. Your father is the king. In Norhelm, you'll be granted all the luxuries that a princess of your station deserves. You'll have gowns threaded with silver and gold. A bed draped in the finest furs. You'll dine on the rarest delicacies."

I look away. "Can't say I care about that—except maybe the food."

A knowing smile creeps over Captain Tatarin's face. "You'll have safety, too. The protection of gods and kings alike. Not to mention freedom. In Volkany, women are not locked away or sold as unwilling brides to the highest bidder. We can choose our lovers. We can hunt or serve in the army." She taps her captain's rank brooch. "And you'll be with your family, that's the most important thing. Your father."

The most important thing? I toe the dirt as I think back to Charlin Darrow, who I once considered a father.

A soft snow falls on the Mistlemas tree by the convent's gate. I've been sitting here for hours, by the road, my little muscles stiff. A bundle at my side filled with the meager Mistlemas presents I've been able to craft in my evenings: A bookmark made out of bark for my father. A candle made from leftover beeswax for the servants. Kitchen scraps for our barn's animals.

The snow grows heavier.

I wait all day, but my father doesn't come to pick me up.

"He isn't coming." Matron White jerks her head for me to come back inside. "Probably hit the bottle too hard. In any case, myself and the Sisters can't delay our trip to Old Coros for the holiday. You weren't supposed to still be here."

"I—I'm sorry, Matron White." A tear rolls down my cheek, landing in the snow.

She mutters under her breath, "Can't leave you to traipse around the place on your own, eh? Have you poking around through all our things? Pilfering the kitchen?"

As my teardrops fall, I realize the sky has stilled. I look up, marveling. "The snow—look! It stopped! That means Father will be here at any moment!"

She scowls up at the calm sky, darting a suspicious glance at me as though I had something to do with it. Briefly, she confers with the Sisters, who have their wagon loaded and are throwing impatient looks at the rising moon.

"Too late. Snow or not, we have to leave. Come with me." Matron White returns to grab my ear, dragging me to the cellar beneath the apple barn, where the trap door is open. "Down."

I climb down the ladder, and the Sisters drag it up after me. Matron White throws down a blanket. "You have a water barrel in there and apples. We'll be back in a fortnight."

She slams the trap door. I'm alone—again.

"Highness? Come with me."

I snap back to the present to find Iyre standing behind

me with an empty chalice in hand. Both the cup's rim and her lips are stained in a dark red liquid that looks too thick to be wine.

My stomach tightens with a bad feeling.

She passes the empty cup to one of the field cooks.

I realize my hands are so tightly balled that my fingernails have carved into my palms. As my anger simmers, I turn back to the campfire. "I'll pass."

"It wasn't a request. We can talk in my carriage." Iyre clicks her long red nails together, and I sigh heavily before pushing to my feet—she always holds the threat of stealing my memories of Basten away from me if I don't behave.

I toss Tati the rest of my bread as I follow Iyre to her carriage, which rests on the ground now while Six, the gold-enclaw who carries it, snores softly beside it. I ruffle his metallic fur as Iyre opens the carriage door.

She snaps, "Paz. Out."

A handsome soldier with dark brown skin slinks out, buttoning his open shirt hastily. "Yes, Lady Iyre." He presses a kiss to Iyre's waiting hand before grabbing up his baldric belt and sword and heading off toward the infantry tents.

I crane my neck at Iyre. "Patron goddess of chastity, huh?"

"I don't fuck Paz, if that's what you're wondering. He's useful in other ways." She smiles wolfishly. "Now get in."

I have to hoist myself up to enter. Giant coiled springs on the underside of the carriage keep it from being thrown *too* violently from side to side when it's mounted on Six, and make it rock slightly now.

Inside, the carriage smells of rich, spiced pipe herb. It's a small space—I have to stoop when standing—with two narrow benches cushioned in velvet facing one another.

Iyre climbs in behind me and flops onto one of the benches. Though a lantern swings from the ceiling, her glowing fey lines provide all the lighting the small space needs.

She shifts her knee an inch—all the accommodation she'll make for me.

"Sit," she says. "Let us share a drink."

I settle awkwardly on the narrow bench opposite her, such close quarters that our knees brush. My fingernails curl so tightly on the seat cushion that they nearly rip the fabric.

My insides churn as I glower. "A drink? Do you mean that same wine that was in your chalice? It was wine, right?"

She tips her head back and laughs devilishly. "I have something better suited for you than what I was drinking."

She opens a compartment that reveals several glass bottles of different sizes and colors. My eyes latch onto a small, round, yellow bottle—the same one she had in her hand in the forest.

She finds a standard wine bottle and two stemmed glasses.

To my relief, she pours what looks like regular wine as she asks, "Did you know you have a tic when you're remembering something painful? You press your fingernails into your palms. Show me your hands."

Reluctantly, I hold my hands palm up to reveal half-moon calluses caused by my nails.

"See?" She clicks her tongue. "I've seen you do it a few times now. You're trying to force unpleasant memories away. Substitute one kind of pain with another."

"So?" I ask quietly, keeping my eyes on the bottle compartment.

She passes me a wine glass. "Though you're determined

to believe I'm the enemy, I assure you, I'm not. I asked you to my carriage so we could get to know one another. I can help you."

I take the glass but don't drink. "The same way you *helped* Basten?"

She peers at me curiously. "The man in the forest? Don't worry about him and his memories, Lady Sabine. You have a much greater fate ahead of you than being with that peasant."

My eye twitches. I shift on the bench, unable to get comfortable. My skin feels itchy in places I can't scratch.

I dart a glance at the round yellow bottle in the compartment. "You don't have any idea who he is."

She tuts and leans back in the seat, sipping her own wine. "I know that man hasn't prayed to the gods a day in his life."

"So, you cursed him?"

"A curse? Little princess, what I did was a blessing. For you both. It's better that he forgets you and moves on. That man's destiny is bound to Astagnon. As yours is to Volkany." She continues quietly, "Basten Bowborn isn't right for you."

I lean forward, clutching my glass hard. "So you *do* know who he is. Can't your fae wisdom see that he carries the blood of a king?"

"The blood of one, perhaps," Iyre says with a yawn, swirling her wine. "But not the will of one. There are better matches for you. Men with ambition in their veins and armies at their call."

I sip my wine slowly, keeping my eyes on the bottle compartment. According to the Tale of Iyre's Memory Bottles, Iyre keeps her stolen memories bottled up in a secret, high room of Drahallen Hall's Aurora Tower, the door locked with magic. Inaccessible.

Unless someone could fly.

As though reading my mind, Iyre runs her fingers lightly over the bottle assortment. Her voice takes on a strange tone as she says, "You'll simply adore Drahallen Hall. My chamber is in the Aurora Tower to the southwest. Security is exceptional. Protected with wards. Only those with fae blood can enter my tower's doors and windows."

The message couldn't be clearer: None of my winged friends are getting into her tower.

"I thank you for the wine," I say tightly. "But I'm not interested in your help. I'll take my leave."

She shrugs. "Suit yourself."

A knot tightens in my stomach as I grip the door handle, peering through the wooden window lattice. Tati is pasturing Three and Four for the night, petting their thick metallic fur as she secures their iron collars to chains attached to the ground.

Suddenly, a streak of silver floats out from behind a leafy branch. When it spots me looking, it ducks back down.

The cloudfox.

We've traveled at least ten miles from the border wall. Is it following us?

Uneasy, I open the door and slip out into the fresh night air. There's no sign of the cloudfox now, but the uneasy feeling in my gut tightens.

It feels like the strange magic of this kingdom has only begun to toy with me.

CHAPTER 7
BASTEN

The rain is relentless as I ride Dare, my roan gelding, to Sorsha Hall's courtyard.

It's a gods-damn circus.

A line of six carriages and fourteen wagons fills the space as footmen in rain-slick oil cloaks bind tarpaulins over the furniture, trunks, and other household goods the Valveres will need in Old Coros.

The journey to Old Coros takes six days in good weather, and already, my stomach grumbles to have to spend it in the midst of such fanfare.

Servants—drenched to the bone—hold wooden panels over the Valvere family members' heads to protect them from the downpour as they take their places in the carriages. Lady Eleonora takes the first one with Serenith, Sorsha Hall's Castlekeep, as her travel companion. Lord Gideon and Lady Runa take the second. The rest are filled with distant cousins and high lords who somehow managed to glom onto Rian's favor enough to earn a place in his reign.

Lady Suri takes the final place in the last carriage, snagging my eye with a disapproving look.

She hoped not to see me here—that I'd be scouring the woods for Sabine.

I seem to disappoint everyone these days.

I swallow a lump in my throat as I absently rub the wrist guard strapped to my left forearm. The leather panel does a good job of hiding the bandages. Not that anyone would bat an eye at a bandage, anyway—I spent years as a soldier and a huntsman.

Still, I prefer it to be secret. A wrapped present only for my eyes. A *name*. A name that, now that it's carved into my skin, is also locked into my memory.

A clatter of metal like a tin drum makes everyone turn. The last wagon, the largest and strongest, which is usually reserved for transporting army cannons, holds an enclosed iron cage that's ten feet long and nearly as high. There isn't a single window or bar, only a door secured with a staggering number of locks.

Another metal crash rattles my teeth as the whole box shakes.

Captain Fernsby shouts the command, "Add an extra set of chains!"

Dare dances beneath me, nervous; his nostrils scent the air. Almost nothing spooks him, which is why he's my choice of mount from the Valvere stable. A huntsman needs a ride with confident footing.

But the thing inside that iron cage has Dare writhing like a snake scenting a fox. And it doesn't take a genius to guess what it is.

"What are you fucking thinking, Rian?" I murmur under my breath.

To my surprise, an answer comes.

"When going to war," Rian's deep voice says from behind me, "It's wise to take one's most powerful weapon, wouldn't you agree?"

Rain forms rivulets down his black wool riding cloak as he sits astride his horse, Colossus.

I shift in my saddle, hiding my surprise that he's out in the rain instead of with the other Valveres in gilded carriages.

Recovering fast, I point out, "Unless that weapon is a fucking monster."

The monoceros in the box, Tòrr, is twice the size of even the largest Valvere stallion and meaner than one of Rian's caged tigers. Its three-foot-long horn made of pure solarium can harness sunlight to incinerate an entire city to the ground.

Rian knows this. He's seen the monoceros trample half a dozen sentinels to death. Hell, he's seen it stab his own father through the chest.

Truth be told, though, I understand why Rian would bring the monoceros to Old Coros despite the risk. Leaving the equivalent of a powder keg bomb in Sorsha Hall's basement, without any supervision, would spell Duren's destruction the first time someone forgets to feed Tòrr his favorite honey grain.

Besides, possessing a monoceros won Rian the Astagnonian throne over Grand Cleric Beneveto's campaign. There wasn't a chance in hell Rian was going to leave his prized weapon behind.

Rian's mouth curves in a wry half-smile. "Good thing you're coming along to protect me from my own idiotic tendencies."

"Well, someone has to."

"Truth be told," Rian says in a low, dangerous voice that pulls my attention from the shaking box, "I'm less worried about being stabbed in the back by the monoceros than by you."

I sit straighter in the saddle, cold rain dripping from the tips of my loose hair. I ask carefully, "What do you mean?"

Keeping his eyes on the line of carriages, he takes out his Golath dime and runs it over his knuckles. "My family held a meeting at dawn. The verdict was that I should poison your coffee at the first waylay stop on our journey and leave your body to rot in the woods. They think you're a threat to all of us, given your birthright. The terms of our deal have changed, after all. I gave you Sabine in exchange for the crown, and now Sabine is gone. What's to say you won't renege on our deal?"

He catches his coin tightly in his palm, glancing at me. He speaks about plotting my murder as casually as discussing the route we'll take to Old Coros.

I shift again in my saddle, trying to keep my face as much a mask as his own. "Is it wise to share a murder plot with the victim, my lord?"

A smirk flits across his face as he finally looks me plainly in the eye. "Tamarac?"

I pause. "Tamarac." *Complete honesty.*

I'm not going to kill you, Wolf. You'll be pleased to know I told my family that I'd sooner poison their coffee than yours. Yes, there's no denying it: You fucked my bride in front of me, you bold, golden-cocked bastard. But do you think I'd let a woman come between us? After everything we've been through? After you gave me the crown that should be yours?"

His tone is jovial like we're boys again, wrestling in Sorsha Hall's rose garden. But I know that Sabine is no mere distraction like the pretty chamber maids we used to flirt with at Midtane parties. She meant something to him, too— I can see it in his eyes, in the slight tremor as he smooths a hand over his damp brow.

Rian spurs Colossus closer to Dare as he tosses and catches his Golath dime. In a cheerful voice that doesn't quite reach his eyes, he says, "In fact, instead of death by coffee, I've decided to make you First Sword upon my coronation."

He flicks his coin in my direction, and I reach out to catch it on instinct.

Opening my palm to look at his prized coin, I croak, "First Sword?"

It's the title given to the king's personal advisor, his right-hand man. The shock of it leaves me reeling, more wary than ever, but I force a cheeky smile. "Bit of an upgrade, my lord. From, well, my death."

He winks. "A bit."

I stare at the coin again before closing one finger over it at a time.

Captain Fernbsy calls to him that the convoy is ready to depart, and with one curt nod, Rian spurs Colossus to the front of the line.

I finally let out the deep breath I've been holding, letting it bow my posture against the pounding rain as I slip his coin in my pocket.

First Sword? By the fucking gods. The title would be a great honor to any soldier, but I'd sooner drink the poisoned coffee. Leadership isn't in my blood. The solitude of the woods calls me, not army barracks.

"Congratulations, Lord Basten." A Golden Sentinel nods to me as I pass, and I fight the urge to roll my eyes at the honorific.

"Lord Basten," another soldier says with a bow.

Bristling against the praise that everyone showers on me with more force than the punishing rain, I kick Dare into a canter and ride apart from the travel convoy, a few horse distances from the nearest carriage.

Finally—a moment to think.

Folke, naturally, takes this prime opportunity to sidle his horse up beside me. His gray-touched hair is pulled back messily. His shirt could use an iron. He looks as rough as the day I met him, half-drunk in the army barracks back when we were both trainees.

"They let *you* into the convoy?" I say.

He grins. "I'm Rian's best spy."

I glance over my shoulder to spot Ferra in the traveling party. Perched primly on a Palamino mare with a silk umbrella open over her curls, she couldn't be more of a contrast to Folke. As the Valvere's godkissed beauty sculptor, she maintains the epitome of city fashion.

It baffles me daily that the two of them ended up together.

"You're Rian's best spy only because *I* beat the answers out of your victims." I hold my left hand up in a fist that I feign swinging at him.

He smirks and dodges, then frowns. "What happened to your forearm?"

"Nothing." I shut down as I snatch back up the reins and study the road ahead. But the silence roars at my ears, so I quip, "Anyway, it's *Lord Basten* now to you."

"Ha! Yes, First Sword. Congratulations on the promotion. Some might say Rian bought your loyalty with that shiny new title."

"He doesn't need to buy me," I snap, annoyed. Only Folke could get away with such a jab. "I don't play those political games."

"Well, where we're headed, you'll have to learn to play. Hekkelveld Castle isn't like Duren. You can't go around throwing punches in the hallways. There, it's *all* about the game. You'll need to bluff. Know when to fold. Most importantly, know who holds the winning cards."

I slide him a close look. "You sound like you're already in the game."

He shrugs. "A wise player knows what he's walking into, including the other players. There are a lot of men with power in Old Coros. Women, too. I might have been sending a few messenger crows back and forth over the last few weeks, it's true. While there appears to be one top player for now—" he looks pointedly at Rian "—it doesn't mean he will always be on top. There could be other players, say, a *wildcard* who was born with the winning hand but traded it for fuck-all."

My jaw clenches. He's venturing close to treason here. Quietly, I mutter, "I told you that I'm loyal to Rian."

"Who said anything about Rian? We're talking hypotheticals, my friend." He steers his horse closer and leans in. "The Astagnonian throne is no game of chance. And the stakes are the *fucking* lives of an entire kingdom. Do you really think the Lord of Liars is the best man for the job when there are..." He pauses as his stare drills into me. "... *wildcards?*"

I spur Dare forward into a canter, eager to be away from Folke and his insinuations.

Does it surprise me he's scheming? Hell no. But I'd rather his schemes not involve *me*. Because if he thinks I'd make a good king, he hasn't spent the last ten years at the bottom of a tankard with me.

As Duren's city gates appear ahead, an enormous black streak covering the side of the grain warehouse steals my attention. I pull Dare aside and draw him to a stop beneath a blacksmith shop's awning, then dismount.

The warehouse's south wall is covered in what looks like a mural of a woman with golden hair in seemingly endless waves, but now it's covered with black paint. Someone has smeared her painted face with charcoal. Over her mouth is written "TRAITOR."

All that's visible of the original mural are a few butterflies painted at the top corner, a curl of hair at the bottom, and the elegant curve of the woman's neck leading into a pointed chin.

A sharp pain punches me in the gut, making me clamp a hand to my stomach as I double over from the overwhelming force.

I remember this mural—at least, I remember the fact that there was a mural here. But for the life of me, I can't remember the face beneath that black paint.

It was her, I think. *It was a portrait of Sabine.*

The earth seems to shift under my feet. The air grows unseasonably cool for late summer, and goosebumps erupt along my skin. I clamp my hand over the bandages that hide the name carved into my skin.

Breathing hard, I can't tear my eyes off the few remaining portions of the mural, lapping them up like crumbs. Even from that glimpse of her chin and a lock of her hair, I can tell that she's the most stunning woman I've ever seen. No wonder Rian was so taken with her. Even with her face blacked out, it's easy to imagine why the public wrote sonnets about her. They've tried to cover her up, but she's still radiant beneath the black paint.

She lives in more than memories.

A man shouts a second before his carriage side-swipes me, and I jerk back in time before a pure white mare runs me over.

The mare stops short an inch in front of me. Though her driver curses and whips her, she remains standing.

I can only stare.

It's Myst.

The mare feels as much like an old friend as Folke: the kind who are as much trouble as they are someone to rely on.

It's strange. I remember Myst perfectly, including our ride from Bremcote, her snorts and head-tosses, yet my memories of that time are blurry around the edges.

Blurry because Sabine *should* be in them.

"Myst." I give a huff that's somewhere between a laugh and a scoff. "You old troublemaker."

I reach to stroke her forelock, but she tosses her head up and gives a hard stomp to my foot.

"Ow!" I double over, clutching my toes. "What the hell was that for?"

Myst pins me with her black eyes. I don't have the gift to talk to animals, but this horse and me? We've always under-stood one another. And right now, she's telling me that I'm a complete and utter *fool.*

"Yeah, well, Lady Suri beat you to that conclusion," I murmur.

The carriage driver lifts the whip. "My apologies, Lord Basten. Don't know what's gotten into this one."

I step aside, motioning for Myst to go. She side-eyes me one more time before trotting on.

Breathing hard, I realize I'm standing in the street like a stray dog.

As I mount Dare and rejoin the travel party passing through the city gates, I press my wrist guard hard enough to reopen the wounds. Blood weeps down my knuckles, mixing with rain, dripping into the mud.

CHAPTER 8
SABINE

On the fifth day, we emerge from the steepest mountains. A few farmsteads dot the hilly landscape, hacking out patches of garden space and pastures amid the forest terrain.

As the valley widens, villages crop up. At first, they're only a few clusters of homes. As midday approaches, they turn into larger settlements, some of which have trading posts or an inn. But even in these bastions of civilization, the forest always feels barely contained, as though if the villagers don't keep a close eye on the woods' perimeter, they'll wake to vines snaking through their windows.

It can't be an easy life here, yet perplexingly, every horse we pass is fat, and every wagon is overflowing with bright orange pumpkins. The people do not appear destitute. Children laugh as they play Blindman's Bluff in the fields. Shopkeepers nod to our long line of soldiers. Happy, dusty dogs chase alongside the goldenclaws.

"You look vexed, Highness," Tati observes, walking alongside Two.

"In Astagnon," I start haltingly, "we know little about Volkany, but what we glean does not suggest it is a prosperous kingdom. I was told stories of beggars. Thieves. Starving families eating tree bark."

Tati chuckles. "Volkany may be a wild kingdom, but it has always been blessed. In every Return, it has been the first to worship the newly woken gods. So, it has earned fae favor. Those who sacrifice to the gods are richly rewarded."

I shift on my goldenclaw saddle, toe-tapping anxiously, and look over my shoulder at the soldiers following us in formation. Like the Volkish villages, the Volkish army is different from what I'd expected. To be sure, there's plenty of passed brandy, dice games, and eye-watering course language. However, the presence of female soldiers seems to balance out the regiment's energy, bringing a kernel of civility.

From what I can tell, most female soldiers belong to the mage faction, commanded by Tati and composed entirely of godkissed soldiers, but I've spotted women in the infantry and archery factions, too.

What would you think of this place, Basten?

As soon as I think of Basten, my smile fades. Where is he now? My heart sinks like a stone dropped in a lake. All our months together might mean nothing to him. If I'd been captured two weeks ago, he'd stop at nothing to rescue me. But now, I can't have faith in that. All of Duren thinks I'm a traitor—I can only imagine the poison he's hearing about me.

As I struggle to swallow the lump forming in my throat, I become aware of two eyes watching me.

I twist sharply to find the cloudfox ducking behind a glowing emerald fern. My heartbeat rattles off-kilter.

You again? I snap. **What do you want?**

Despite my angry tone, guilt twists my stomach in knots until my breakfast threatens to come back up. I can't shake the awful feeling of being inside its head, forcing it to expel electric charges, agonizing along with it under the punishing crush of pain.

Yes, the cloudfox wronged me—but the fact that I caused it pain feels like a betrayal of everything I hold dear. Maybe it's *me* I'm really angry with.

Its silver-tipped ears disappear behind a fern, only to appear again a few minutes later, this time on the far side of a fallen log.

Why are you following me? I ask warily.

The cloudfox's blue eyes glow the same cool hue as a moonlit glacier before it turns and bounds off into the shadows.

On the seventh day, we clear the last mountain pass and get our first view of Norhelm. A deep valley plunges below us in a dramatic V shape, carved by a raging river that tumbles down cliffs to form a series of waterfalls.

Our line of soldiers—stretching back further than I can see—stops to take a final break while a mage scout runs ahead to announce our arrival.

I find a quiet nook at the top of a cliff, where I grip a sapling for safety and gaze down at my father's capital city.

From here, the capital city looks like a black beetle on the horizon, its spired rooftops forming a glistening shell of menacing spikes. The tallest spires belong to Drahallen Hall, my father's home and the place of my conception.

Mother, I whisper. *Why did you run away?*

Of course, ghosts don't answer.

I found out at my father's death that my mother had been a concubine to King Rachillon. Her unearthed journals revealed that she stole Myst from the royal stables and fled to Astagnon when she discovered she was pregnant. But her journals didn't explain *why*.

Iyre sidles up to me, puffing on a long pipe as she gazes down at the view.

"It's a striking city, is it not? Two thousand years ago, devotees constructed Drahallen Hall in the King of Fae's honor after the First Return. The five towers are named for ancient fae monoceros steeds—Aurora, Hailstrom, Sunflare, Stormwatch, and Cloudveil. When we fae awoke for the Second Return, the castle served as the seat of the immortal fae court. As it shall be for this Return."

"Fascinating," I say flatly, tightening my grip on the sapling. "All I know of Drahallen Hall is that something so terrible happened within those walls that the idea of birthing a daughter there caused my mother to flee for her life. And mine."

Iyre blinks calmly. "And now you've returned."

"And now I've returned," I echo with an edge.

"Lady Iyre!" the mage scout shouts, scaling the loose scree at the top of the cliff path. His cheeks burn red from exertion. "His Majesty's Blades approach from the north."

The serenity on Iyre's face falls away. She strides away to her carriage, harnessed atop Six, as she murmurs something under her breath in a language I don't know.

Among the crowd, I spot Tati testing Three's harness in preparation for the descent down the mountain.

"Who are the king's Blades?" I ask.

Tati's hand pauses on the harness as a shadow briefly crosses her face. "The Blades are His Majesty's bodyguards. They serve as your father's advisors. Tasked with carrying out his most vital orders." She grimaces as she strains to tighten the girth strap, and when she finally buckles it, she parts her lips, a wariness in her eyes. "About the Blade Boys—"

Before she can warn me, a breathtaking chestnut gelding crests the mountain path, followed by a dappled stallion, then a blue roan mare, and every soldier within eyeshot stops to stare. The horses are beautiful—but their three riders?

Their riders can only be described as absolute *fantasies* stepped straight out of a painting.

This...is unexpected, I think.

The lead rider is a god of a man, with the typical tanned skin and white-blond hair of the Volkish people, along with a jawline that could slice bread. He wears iron-studded leather armor that cuts into a deep V over chiseled bare abs that would rival river stones.

The second man is a head taller than the first and no less handsome, with skin the color of warm shadows and thick, dreadlocked hair pulled back to show off simmering, hooded eyes.

The third man is all contrasts: raven hair and pale skin. His dark eyes gleam with a strange cloudiness that throws me off, making me unsure where his attention rests. A sleek female hound follows at his mare's side.

I realize I'm gaping and quickly shut my mouth.

The three men are gorgeous, yet a voice in my head warns me away. I toy with the twine ring on my finger. They lack Basten's gritty, dark, imperfect beauty, like a diamond hiding in coal.

There's such a thing as *too* pretty.

The female soldiers, however, don't seem to share my sentiments as they transform into swooning fools instead of the deadly archers and sword-wielders I've traveled with for days. Even Tati, who has a solid head on her shoulders, surreptitiously cups her hand over her mouth to check for bad breath.

I roll my eyes, and she quickly pretends she was only scratching her nose.

She nods in their direction. "Ghost, Whisper, and Night. Those are the Blade Boys' code names. Ghost"—she motions to the white-blonde one—"Whisper"—she points to the one with dreadlocks—"and Night." She indicates the dark-haired one with the hound.

A chill coils in my belly. There's something about those names that echoes how Basten spent years at Rian's side, doing his dark bidding without the dignity of his real name.

"Wolf," I murmur to myself.

Tati frowns. "Pardon, Highness?"

I shake my head as I stutter, "N—nothing."

The Blade Boys, as Tati calls them, dismount and call for water and wine, which are promptly delivered. They banter with one another, swapping mischievous smiles, commanding the soldiers with effortless confidence.

Ugh, they remind me of Rian.

Iyre strides up to the trio with a sneer. "Boys. What do you think *you're* doing here?"

The tall one called Whisper barely spares her a glance, even though she's a goddess and he's a mere mortal. "King

Rachillon commanded us to escort his daughter the final stretch to Norhelm."

Iyre narrows her eyes. "I am perfectly capable of—"

"Is this her?" The blonde one—Ghost—with shoulders as broad as an archer's bow stalks toward me with a gleam in his green eyes. He's walking arrogance. I don't think that smirk has left his face for a second.

I fold my arms tightly across my chest, chin tipped up casually as though I'm unbothered.

Ghost slowly circles me with an appraising eye. "Mmm," he purrs pensively, letting his eyes travel down my body. "*She's* certainly worth the hunt."

I bristle and hug my arms tighter.

Whisper smooths a hand over his dreaded locks as he grins wolfishly. "Brighter than the sun itself."

Night—the one with raven hair and clouded eyes— stalks forward with his sleek hound pressed unwaveringly against his left side. "I'll take your word for it."

He's blind. The realization slams into me with a touch of confusion. One of King Rachillon's most trusted bodyguards lacks sight?

"May I, Highness?" Night slowly removes one of his black leather gloves, one finger at a time, and flexes his pale hand in the air between us.

It takes me a moment to realize what he means.

"*Oh*. Um...I suppose so."

His hound leads him forward until he's half a step away. Hesitantly, I take his wrist and guide his fingers to touch my face. His skin is so cold that I shiver on instinct. His fingers are rough and calloused yet as finely wrought as a sculptor's.

He skims his fingers over the contours of my face,

reading my features with a touch that's somehow both respectful and scandalously intimate.

He lowers his head in a bow. "Lady Sabine. Beautiful as ever."

"As ever?" I blurt out.

"We've been told of your beauty," Night clarifies. "By the raiders who witnessed your battle in Duren's arena."

My muscles tense, unwilling to unwind, as Ghost circles me again while running his thumb over his bottom lip. "What I would do for one night alone with this one."

"Easy now," Whisper teases. "You're drooling, Ghost. If you want fresh meat, visit the cooks at Drahallen Hall, not the king's daughter's bed chamber."

I choke at these men's gall.

My cheeks flare red as I spit out, "Bold of you to think I won't slit your throat if you even dare a step toward my bed." I hold up my hand with Basten's twine ring on my fourth finger. "In any case, I'm already called for."

I expect them to beg my pardon, but instead, all three chuckle. Ghost leans close to the raven-haired Night to explain the twine on my finger.

"I'm serious!" I announce. "Laugh if you want, but whether the ring is of twine or gold, I'm engaged to Basten Bowborn of Duren!"

"Highness, forgive us," Ghost says, sobering quickly, though a hint of mockery still dances in his eyes. "We do not laugh at *you*."

"Indeed," Whisper adds. "We laugh at Immortal Alessantha, who was so cruel as to make you believe this love of yours was real."

I go so still that I can barely feel my heart pounding in

my chest. They talk of cruelty? I'm not sure I have ever heard anything so cruel as their mockery of my love.

I turn away sharply and stomp off to the campfire. This close to the flames, the air is thick, smoky. But at least the Blades lose interest in me in favor of the other, more willing women who sidle up to them.

Girlie. A soft, almost pleading voice comes from behind a flowering shrub. I spin, muscles tensing, and let out a tight breath when I see the cloudfox peeking between the iridescent blue blossoms.

I press my lips together tightly. My first instinct is to tell the cloudfox once more to get out of my sight and leave me alone. I hurt it before—it should know better.

But instead, I ask warily, *Why have you been following me? Aren't you afraid I'll hurt you again?*

The cloudfox's silvery eyes flash, showing the whites, her paws anxiously prancing a few inches above the grass.

Yes, yes, to the hurt. Her voice trembles, but she holds her ground. *But now we are even, yes? Girlie looked into my mind...I looked into girlie's, too.*

I wrinkle my brow, still braced for danger. *What do you mean?*

I saw... Her voice softens to a hush. *I saw girlie has the power to grant a name. I saw what girlie really is. I am... pulled...to girlie.*

I glance over my shoulder, instinctively checking that we're alone. *You want a name? That's what this is about?*

She nods eagerly, her blue tongue lolling.

I twist my twine ring, unsure if I can trust her. The request shouldn't completely catch me off guard. Regular animals—mice, cats, birds—don't care about names. They can't grasp the concept of a name's meaning. They simply identify one another by rudimentary features like feather color or tail shape.

But fae creatures, I'm learning, *crave* a name.

For them, names hold immense power. They cannot give themselves a name; it must be uncovered like a long-buried treasure, revealed only with patience and insight. It took me weeks, but when I finally discovered Tòrr's name, I was able to achieve the impossible—to mount and command him.

I will find your name, I promise the cloudfox, *but in return, you must do something for me.*

I glance at Iyre's carriage. She keeps it locked and guarded by Paz, her companion, so there is no way to sneak in to access the bottles now. I'll have to wait until she moves them to her tower room.

The cloudfox's bushy tail wags, throwing off small puffs of cloud that dissipate into the air. *Name your task!*

I pause. *First, how can I trust you?*

Her rump wiggles as she prances. *We will strike a fae bargain!*

I'm unsure what exactly she means. *And if you lie again?*

Does girlie not know anything? Fae bargains are binding! She sits straight and recites a singsong rhyme. *'A pinch of earth to close the deal; what's given now, the ground will seal.'*

She scratches her silver claws in the dirt and looks at me expectantly.

I scoop a small pinch of the loosened soil and rub it between my fingertips. *Like this?*

Yes, yes. We mix our earth. The deal is sealed.

She drags her paw through our two piles of soil until they're one.

This is new information to me. The Book of the Immortals mentions fae bargains only in passing. As far as I know, fae can lie, cheat, and steal with impunity. The fact that anything at all can bind them is...powerful.

Slowly, I brush the dirt off my fingers.

When we reach Drahallen Hall, I say, **Come find me. I will give you instructions.**

The cloudfox bobs her chin excitedly. She crouches to bound off into the woods but then pauses and turns back.

Girlie should be more careful around the woman in white, she warns.

I let the last of the soil fall between my fingers as my blood runs cold. **Why?**

Your cup held wine, she says. **But the fae's cup did not.**

The cloudfox doesn't wait for my response. With a flick of her tail, she springs off into the woods, disappearing in a blur of silver-blue. I watch her vanish, my heart pounding harder than it should. Her final words echo in my mind, making my stomach twist.

I glance back at Iyre's carriage. *Your cup held wine. But the fae's cup did not.*

My throat tightens, a bitter taste rising.

Blood. I knew it. Iyre had been drinking blood.

But why? Is that what she does with Paz? What does she gain from it? I've read every story in the Iyre chapter of the Book of the Immortals, which say nothing about drinking blood.

I press a hand against the tattered ribbons on my bodice, forcing myself to breathe, but the knot in my stomach only tightens.

When I turn back around, Iyre is right behind me.

I jump, sucking in air. "Iyre!"

Her eyes glow faintly. "We're almost to Norhelm, princess. And I need to remind those boys who's really in charge here."

My shoulders ease as I realize she didn't see my exchange with the cloudfox. I glance over her shoulder at the Blades gathered around the campfire, their laughter cutting through the smoke. "How exactly are you going to do that?"

"Easy." As she reaches toward my temple, I realize a second too late what she has in mind. "Like this."

My muscles tense, but there's nowhere for me to run. Iyre's silken fingertips graze my hairline to the left of my brow, and before I can even suck in my next breath, everything goes dark.

I fall, fall, fall into a void as black as night.

CHAPTER 9
BASTEN

New city, same damn pageantry.

After six days of travel, we enter Old Coros with all the pomp that a rising king should expect. Golden banners—in honor of the Valvere color—drape from the main gate to dust us with glitter as we enter. Scrolls displaying the Valvere coin emblem hang from every municipal building. The streets are lined with the capital's residents, so eager to glimpse their new regent that they throw elbows and climb onto rooftops.

I can't help but let out a snort. Rian, the golden boy, being fawned over as the future king.

He must fucking *love* it.

I'd like to say that the public's enthusiasm stems from deep devotion to Rian, but that would be a lie. The Valveres ruled Duren, sure, but that's a trashy backwoods town to most of these aristocrats—they only care that he's fresh blood.

Young, handsome, and full of promise for juicy scandal.

I'm sure he'll deliver all that and more.

I shift in my saddle, pulling at my collar to release the noonday heat. I'm grateful to ride midway through the travel party. Not at the head, where Rian rides Colossus like a conqueror surveying his domain.

It isn't lost on me that, had fate been different, *I* would be heading this procession. It would be me the crowds fawned over. Me wearing the golden circlet of the rising king.

Well, thank the fucking gods it's not.

Still, as I adjust my seat on Dare, there's a tiny prick of remorse, like a splinter under the skin. A part of me wonders what it would be like to have accepted my rightful title, to have the power to change things. Was it right for me to shirk that mantle onto another's shoulders? Am I missing my calling from the gods? But then I remember the responsibility, the constant scrutiny, the damn starched collars, and I snort.

Besides, screw the gods.

Every kingdom needs a rogue, and I wear *that* title like a second skin.

It isn't my first time in the capital city, but as I ride through Old Coros, I find myself studying everything with new intensity. It's famed throughout the seven kingdoms as the pinnacle of human achievement. The streets are laid out in a precise grid. Canals with stone embankments transport riverboats from one portion of town to another. Even Hekkelveld Castle's five towers are named for human virtues —Honor, Wisdom, Faith, Mercy, and Charity.

Sure, the presence of the gods is felt here. Mostly in pubs named "The Fae Charmer" or "Popelin's Lark," and in the Red Churches devoted to the ten godly orders.

Still, the lion's share of the statues gracing crossroads

are of human heroes, not gods. During King Joruun's peaceful days, with the fae deep in their subterranean sleep, it didn't matter.

But everything's changed now that Iyre is awake.

I find myself pressing my fingers against the pain blooming in my left temple before I let my hand fall.

I hope like hell Rian knows what he's doing.

Ferra, riding a few horses behind me, clicks her tongue as she murmurs to Folke, "I miss Duren's Sin Streets already."

"Old Coros has a legal vices district, too, my jewel," Folke replies, his voice light with amusement.

"It's hardly the same." Ferra's sigh carries a note of longing. "In Duren, you could be who you really are. Even in the filth, there was a sense of freedom. But in Old Coros, you always have to pretend."

"Being yourself is a luxury few can afford anywhere," Folke counters.

The theme of their conversation pricks my ears. I've always considered myself an open book, never hiding behind masks like Rian or other politicians. But here, listening to their words, a troubling thought creeps in. Maybe I am pretending. A true king forced to act the part of a soldier, playing a role like everyone else.

The realization settles uncomfortably in my chest.

"Besides," Folke chides good-naturedly. "No one plays pretend quite as well as you."

Ferra's reply is quick, defensive. "What's that supposed to mean?"

Folke strokes the back of his hand down her cheek. "It was only a reference to your godkiss. You can change your face as easily as a new set of clothes. Thriving in Old Coros should be child's play to you."

Ferra's voice snaps with annoyance. "Shifting appearances isn't as carefree as you think. It's a curse to always have to change. To never show your true face. You think it's a gift, but it's a prison."

Folke chuckles. "And how many prisons have you been in, my jewel?"

Ferra yanks on her horse's reins. "One, if you count being with *you*." She spurs her horse forward, passing me, and riding ahead to flank Suri's carriage.

A trumpet blares, making me jump.

Ahead, the limestone towers of Hekkelveld Castle rise above the buildings.

Soft exclamations sound throughout the travel party. It doesn't matter how often a person sees Hekkelveld Castle—each time, it's as though for the first.

Old Coros may be an homage to humankind's achievements, but in those castle walls, the presence of the gods can't be denied.

Like all ancient fae castles, it's laid out in a five-pointed star pattern. Sorsha Hall is the same. Likewise, Drahallen Hall in Volkany is well known to have been Immortal Vale's primary residence and the seat of the fae court.

Correspondingly, Hekkelveld Castle was originally built to honor Immortal Meric, God of Justice and Punishment, during the First Return.

However, in the two thousand years since then, the original fae style has been covered up by human additions. The carvings of Meric's knot symbol are worn away, visible only in the castle's ancient foundation. The sections where the fae stonework meets newer human additions are largely obscured by greenery. Meric's original maze, used to punish criminals, is now a carefully manicured garden.

A welcome party awaits us on the front steps. The banners here are notably not Valvere gold in color. They're gray, emblazed with silver ravens, and the message is clear: It doesn't matter where Rian came from—now, he is a servant of Old Coros.

I can't help but smirk to see the downturned corners of Rian's mouth, as though he just ate undercooked cod. Gods help the King's Council if they think they can tame Rian Valvere into wearing gray.

A white-haired man in slate-colored robes announces, "Your Grace, Rising King Rian, future regent of the great kingdom of Astagnon, it is with profound honor that the King's Council welcomes you today!"

I stifle a yawn, noting the nine other equally white-haired men, their faces a blur of indistinguishable wrinkles. It seems that the members of the King's Council aren't so far away from joining Old Joruun in the grave.

The spokesperson continues, "Though untested and new to the burdens of leadership, we recognize the unique tools at your disposal to forge a path through tumultuous times ahead. With your rare assets, you stand poised to lead Astagnon through its challenges. May your reign be marked by unwavering success. Long live Rising King Rian!"

Rian's face remains as immovable as the castle's limestone bricks. As innocuous as the welcome sounded, it was what the advisor *didn't* say that stings.

Not one word about the Valvere family name. No praise for Rian's integrity. Not a mention of wisdom, valor, or compassion.

"*All they care about,*" I overhear a soldier whisper to the man next to him, "*is that he has a monoceros.*"

Damn, if I don't smile to think of how Rian is going to show all these white-haired asses how a Valvere gets things done.

A valet bows deeply as he holds Colossus for Rian to dismount. The crowd at the castle's steps—lords and ladies, dukes and counts—is noticeably better dressed, not to mention better *smelling* than the ones we left in Duren. Here, it's all rose oil and sandalwood, not the cow manure scent of the masses.

Whatever. They still piss in a pot.

Rian bows to the King's Councilors, though not as deeply as is customary. I can hear his molars grinding in his jaw as he forces a proud smile. Until the crown rests on his head, he isn't their king yet—he has to ingratiate himself.

"My deepest thanks," he says steadily, casually resting one hand on his sword and closing each finger slowly around the hilt, which melts the smirks off their faces. "It is with great honor that I accept the role bestowed upon me by gods and men alike. I vow upon Immortal Popelin's sacred chalice to serve the kingdom with honor."

I roll my eyes before thinking better of it. Immortal Popelin might be his family's patron god, but Popelin would sooner watch a kingdom burn just for the entertainment factor.

The travel party begin the arduous task of unpacking. While the bulk of Rian's staff disperses to be assigned their new castle roles, the Golden Sentinels parade off to the royal barracks. The Valvere family and other courtiers are ushered into Hekkelveld Castle's cavernous entryway.

Rian pauses at the grand brass double doors, which are

cast with the twin city mottos of BRAVERY and FORTITUDE. Looking around, he hunts me out from the crowd and beckons.

"Wolf. Come."

"Great," I murmur under my breath. As First Sword, I can't slink off to the barracks in peace.

Inside, the castle is blessedly cool after the midday heat. A round mosaic of a raven surrounded by olive branches is set into the floor. The foundation rocks are thousands of years old, so ancient that my heightened vision can pick out the fossils of tiny fae sea creatures trapped within the pressed siltstone.

Absently, I clasp the wrist guard over my left forearm, rubbing my thumb over the bandage's soft edge.

A voice calls, "The Lord of Liars makes an oath, and we are to believe him?"

A ruggedly handsome man in royal armor and a silver chainmail sash descends the steps toward Rian. That sash marks him as Lord of the Iron Banner—the envoy bridging communication between the royal family and the kingdom's army.

My hand goes instantly to my sword. Before the Lord of the Iron Banner comes to a halt, I sweep to Rian's side and draw my weapon.

"You dare to insult the Rising King?" My voice cuts with the same promise as my sword. Glaring through my loose hair, I ready myself for a fight. I might have only been named First Sword a few days ago, but I've spent a lifetime defending Rian.

A metal ring echoes in the air as the royal guards flanking the entryway draw their swords.

Like a thunderclap, electricity sizzles in the air.

My ears pick up the agitated murmurs from the crowd of servants and King's Councilmen, speculation about who the man is who dares to draw a weapon in Hekkelveld Castle's Raven Hall.

"*...they call him the Lone Wolf.*"

"*The one Immortal Iyre robbed of memory.*"

"*He's spent a lifetime at the Rising King's side...*"

The Lord of the Iron Banner merely blinks, perfect calm. "No greater dare, I should think," he says, "than drawing a sword in Raven Hall. This is sacred ground. Deemed by the late King Joruun to forever be a threshold of peace."

"Well," I point out, "Joruun is dead."

Rian laughs, masking it with a cough, and rests his hand on my shoulder in a calming gesture. "Relax, Wolf. If one person in the world is allowed to insult the Rising King, it's Kendan Valvere."

Kendan Valvere?

I haven't seen Rian's eldest brother in fifteen years, not since he and Lord Berolt had such a violent disagreement that Kendan stormed out of Duren and never returned. Rian has met with Kendan over the years, when traveling or in Old Coros, but I wouldn't have recognized him.

At first glance, he has none of the Valvere elegance. The Valveres are all polish and precision. Even Rian, known for his restraint with adornment, is partial to a swipe of smoky blue kohl on his lashlines. Gods know his hair and beard are tamed within an inch of their lives.

Kendan, in contrast, has all the lean angles of a falcon, both deadly and striking but also plain in its feather coloration. His hair is as raven black as Rian's, though at ten years Rian's senior, a touch of gray dusts his temples and the stubble hugging his chin. Though his armor is carefully polished, it doesn't hide a constellation of knicks and dents. Apparently, the Lord of the Iron Banner title doesn't mean his hands don't occasionally get dirty.

Slowly, I sheath my sword, and the royal guards follow suit.

Kendan's mouth lifts in a calculated smile, and *there*. I see it now—a hint of the famous Valvere ability to perfectly contain one's emotions.

"Welcome." He grips Rian by the shoulders in a hearty embrace, but his eyes shift to me over Rian's shoulder, alight with a cryptic gleam. "*Brother.*"

I jolt enough to rattle my armor.

Kendan might as well have splashed a bucket of water on my face. It's a struggle to stay impassive, to wear a mask like the two of them do so effortlessly.

By the fucking gods, does he know?

As soon as the words are uttered, Kendan switches back to the perfect role of teasing older brother. He gives Rian a heavy pat on the shoulder, all genuine smiles now.

But my heart races, and my mind buzzes with unease.

"Rian—and I'll call you that until the crown is on your head, eh? You have no idea how proud I am to have my little brother about to warm his ass on Hekkelveld's throne."

Rian chuckles deeply as he rubs his hands together. "Well, a fine ass it is. Best in the family."

"Let the ladies of court be the judge of that." Kendan leans in devilishly to murmur for only Rian's hearing, "You're going to have your hands full of women clamoring to be queen now that your previous engagement is null."

A lump forms in my throat as I flex my left hand, drawing my attention to the bandage beneath my wrist guard. I ache to peel back the bandage, to see the letters etched into my flesh.

But I can't. Not here, not now.

"Cousin Kendan!" Lady Runa makes a point of fluttering her peacock feather fan as she inserts herself into the conversation. "What a dashing man you've grown into. Is that *gray* in your beard?"

"Silver," Lady Eleonora interjects, leaning on her diamond-tipped cane. "Valveres don't gray, we *silver*."

"Grandmother." Kendan steps forward to place a kiss on her wrinkled cheek.

Lord Gideon Valvere and the rest of the cousins preen for his attention, but Kendan only has eyes for the young woman trying to sneak off toward the stairs—Lady Suri.

"And who is *this*?" Kendan asks.

Suri jumps, spinning around with a forced grin as she smooths out her gown. In the sunflower dress with golden trim, she shines brighter even than Eleonora's diamond.

Kendan looks gobsmacked. Once he recovers, he continues, "Brother, if I'd known you had such beautiful maidens in Sorsha Hall's court, I would have returned home more often." He bows to Suri, offering his hand. "My lady, I do not believe we've had the pleasure of meeting. I am Lord Kendan Valvere, Lord of the Iron Banner, and I will be devastated if you tell me we're distant cousins."

A laugh bubbles out of Suri's throat before she can tame it back into a polite handshake.

"This is Lady Suri Darrow." Rian makes the introduction with a breezy flick of his hand. "The recent widow of Lord Charlin Darrow of Bremcote and the stepmother of my former fiancée."

Kendan's eyes twinkle with mischief as he turns back to

Rian. "Ah, yes, your former fiancée. Didn't she end up being the kingdom's greatest traitor? I always knew you had a knack for picking women with a flair for drama, Rian."

The words strike a nerve in me, an instinctive surge of protectiveness flaring up like wildfire. My fingers twitch at my side, aching to defend this woman I don't even know. I clench my jaw, forcing the impulse down.

Rian's laugh is forced. "Yes, well, everyone needs a scandal in their life, don't they? Keeps things interesting."

Kendan's smirk widens. "True, but not everyone *marries* theirs." Kendan turns back to Suri. "Widow? Did I hear that correctly? I'm so sorry for your loss."

His broad smile negates his words.

Suri's eyes sparkle with amusement. "With those kind words, my lord, you have already proven yourself more of a gentleman than your brother."

"And why is that?" Kendan asks. "Did my little brother speak ill of your late husband?"

"Actually, he murdered him," she answers sweetly.

A scowl plunges Rian's face into shadow.

Kendan chokes on his next breath, doubling over to mask his surprise as he turns briefly to face the wall, pinching his nose to stop from laughing. "Dear lady, we are lucky to have a prize such as yourself in this fair city."

Rian taps his foot, unamused with their flirtation.

"Lady Suri is here at *my* invitation," Rian emphasizes, eyes sparking with jealousy over their instant comradery at his expense. "She will be a great credit to *my* leadership of Astagnon. In fact—" His eyebrows arch sharply, "—I've decided to grant her the position of Castlekeep."

A murmur breaks out from the senior staff lining the

wall, who have been silently waiting to be presented to the future king.

An elegant older woman with a cherrywood cane pinches her lips, fingers twisting on the cane. The current Castlekeep, I assume, given her obvious displeasure.

Suri's cheeks darken. "What?" she sputters, eyes round as the moon. "I'd sooner clean a pig barn than take a rag to your castle—"

"You deny a direct order from your Rising King?" Rian challenges, tipping his chin so he can look down from his full height.

She juts her chin defiantly, but she's still a head shorter. My ears detect a rustle as she pushes herself to tiptoe, a fact hidden from everyone else by her skirt. "You invited me here as a member of your court, not a servant."

"Lady Mildred is Countess of Edgewood," Rian says as he motions toward the current Castlekeep, grinning as he enjoys the irritation pinching Suri's pretty lips. "Kendan is Duke of Gwendolyn in addition to Lord of the Iron Banner. Even Wolf has a title now! And yet they all *serve* Hekkelveld Castle." He adjusts the set of his circlet crown atop his skull. "Some would say I, as king, am, in fact, the realm's greatest servant."

"Perhaps the realm's greatest *ass*," she mutters.

"Pardon?" Rian says, touching his ear.

She presses her lips together.

I stifle my snort behind my fist.

"Besides." Rian softens his tone. "The Castlekeep doesn't scrub or scour—the position merely oversees the castle's junior staff. I assure you, you won't be dirtying your pretty hands."

Suri balls her small fists, but with so many witnesses, she can hardly expect to deny her king a direct order.

Kendan strokes his long chin, observing her like a falcon, waiting to see if she proves herself predator or prey.

Before I realize what I'm doing, I step in. "As Castlekeep, Lady Suri will have keys to every room throughout the castle, isn't that correct? The storerooms, the attics, the *library*?"

Suri's initial look of confusion shifts into understanding as she gazes up at the second-floor hallway, where the top of the library door is barely visible. If she wants that book Sabine was looking for, here's her golden opportunity.

Both Rian and Kendan cock their heads in identical curiosity. Maybe they aren't brothers by birth, but they both have the Valvere curiosity.

"Well? Is that true about the keys?" Suri blinks her bird-like eyes at Rian, waiting for an answer.

"Why?" Rian asks slyly. "So you can sneak into my chambers and slit my throat, as I did to your odious husband?"

"Murder would not be the *first* thing on my mind, Majesty," she says sweetly.

"Oh?" he leers.

Her cheeks pinken as she blurts out, "Neither is your bed!"

Rian's grin only stretches wider.

"Keyguard is one major responsibility of Castlekeep," Kendan offers as he strides over to the current Castlekeep, and, after a brief exchange of words, returns with a jangling keyring balanced on one finger.

Rian swipes it from him with a glower, then offers it to Suri.

No sooner have her fingers closed around the clattering iron keys than a sudden crash of metal from outside makes everyone jump. It comes again, clanging louder than that damn Valor Bell.

A fine layer of dust rains down from the wooden ceiling joists as the ancient foundation groans.

Suri shrieks, and Kendan sweeps forward to offer her a steadying arm. She gazes up at him with round-eyed appreciation. Lady Eleonora nearly loses her balance, too, but no one rushes to *her* aid.

A sense of foreboding snakes over my skin as I turn toward the great brass doors.

The crash comes again, followed by an unearthly shriek like a thousand banshees.

"What," a pale-faced Kendan enunciates, "is *that?*"

Just visible through the open double doors inscribed with BRAVERY and FORTITUDE, the monoceros's prison rattles the chains lashing it to the wagon as Tòrr slams his metal hooves against the walls, hard enough to dent iron.

"That," Rian says proudly, his velvet-brown eyes simmering with dark delight, "is *my* prize."

CHAPTER 10
SABINE

Warm tendrils of sunlight caress my cheek, and I blink awake with a start.

It takes a moment for my eyes to adjust. Everything is blurry until I shade my face from the direct, mid-morning rays cutting through an arched window.

Holy gods. I'm in the strangest bed chamber I've ever seen.

The heavy wooden furnishings feel swathed in shadows, even with morning light at the window and candles flickering in sconces. There's a mineral smell in the air reminiscent of ancient stone. Gnarled vines push through chinks in the mortar to climb in intricate patterns up the walls, their vibrant, maroon blooms taking the place of any artwork or tapestries.

The four-poster bed seems to have been carved from one giant tree trunk. Fur pelts drape over crisp satin sheets. The bed's canopy is sewn to mimic papery dried leaves.

All together, it gives the feeling that nature has overtaken the room and yet, at the same time, exists in a perfect balance.

As I sit upright, my clothes rustle loudly.

Alarmed, I look down to find I'm no longer wearing the dirty, tattered velvet dress from Lord Berolt's funeral. Someone has dressed me in a fresh gown of heavy obsidian silk with a plunging neckline, dark crystal beads, bat-winged sleeves, and a serpentine lace corset.

Even worse? They've also bathed me.

The dirt is scrubbed from my nails. My feet are buffed to soft perfection. My hair is freshly washed, dried, and twisted into what feels like an intricate fae crown braid.

Panic grips me as I run my hands down my body, trying to recall who did this. Who touched me. Where there should be a memory of someone getting me dressed, there is only a void.

My lungs seize up, unable to pull in a deep enough breath, and I fight with the coverings to scramble out of the massive bed.

This terrible void...is this what Basten felt when Iyre took his memories?

With a pang of longing, I frantically twirl the twine ring on my finger.

Thinking of him causes the room to spin, and I rush to the window, shoving open the hinged wooden lattice. The air is fresh, with a trace of an unfamiliar floral incense. An eventide chant floats through the air, calling to me strangely, like a siren's song. It isn't exactly soothing...more like an intoxication. I find myself leaning out over the sill, closing my eyes, breathing in deeply.

When I open my eyes, Norhelm unrolls beneath me.

There's an eerie sense of barely-tamed wilderness to the

capital city. Mountain cliffs flank both sides of the valley, dotted with gnarled, wind-blown trees. Enormous elms shade the buildings, and a natural system of streams weaves among the streets like a tapestry. They feed into a raging river that surrounds Drahallen Hall on three sides. The castle itself juts out over the rocky river valley on a promontory.

If I were to fall? I'd crash down sixty feet to jagged rocks.

Still, despite the dramatic setting, the small city has a bustling charm. I don't quite know what I expected from Norhelm. Perhaps haunting, shadow-laced spires. A city the rest of the world has forgotten. From the looks of it, Norhelm *is* all those things—but also much more.

Like the villages we passed on our journey, there is no obvious sign of squalor in the streets. Carriages rumble down cobble-lined lanes, and residents greet one another with waves. I spot a market beside the river, packed with customers jostling to peruse an unbelievable bounty of fresh fish, as though the fishermen simply whistled and salmon jumped into their nets.

I do a double-take when I spot a man riding a saddled moose. Near the market, a woman sells cloudfox pups from a basket on her arm, leashes securing the wriggling little pups from floating away. A small girl strolls down the street, sipping nectar from a flower bud in place of a teacup.

This is no bleak city full of indentured workers beholden to my father's reign. In fact, at first glance, Norhelm looks... charming.

Ta-DA! A small voice calls up from the woven rug.

Spinning around, I find my forest mouse darting out from under the bed. She turns in a circle with a flourish of her tail.

Little friend! There you are! Relieved tears puddle at the corners of my eyes as I fall to my knees to cup her in my hands. *I was afraid we were separated when Iyre knocked me unconscious!*

I told you I would always find you. She preens her tail proudly.

A laugh bubbles from my throat as more relieved tears roll down my cheeks. *Have you explored the castle?*

The kitchens are on the ground floor. There's a pantry for everything. Root vegetables. Salted meat. Even a confectionary.

I smile because, of course, a mouse first thinks of food. *What else?*

The castle has five towers with five walled gardens between them. There are crawlspaces between the floors, so I can travel easily and unnoticed. Oh—and the cloudfox? From the forest? It was at your window this morning, but I couldn't—

A sharp knock at my door cuts her off.

We both jump.

Hide! I tell the mouse even as she is already bounding across the rug to duck under the wardrobe.

I hurry to the door, pausing to marshal my emotions before opening it.

When I see who it is, I take a staggering step back. "You!"

Grand Cleric Beneveto waits in the hall. He doesn't wear his cleric's cassock, instead donning riding trousers and a loose black shirt open at the collar. It's his hair that I know him by—the telltale white streak over one eye, giving him a look that's more roguish than holy.

He gives a slight bow. "Highness, allow me to welcome

you to Norhelm. Your father thought you might be more at ease if greeted by a familiar face."

My fingers curl into my palms to quell the desire to deliver a sharp slap to his face. "I believe my father might be confusing familiarity with fondness." My fists tremble at my side when his only response is a smug smile. "I suppose your being here means Rian was right about you. He always suspected you were disloyal to Astagnon."

Beneveto wraps his hand around his neck like a noose, grinning. "Guilty."

Oh, this insufferable man.

On second thought, I give in to the urge and lay the flat of my palm across his fresh-shaven cheek.

"Traitor," I spit.

The smack reverberates down the hallway. A sting pulses in my fingers, and I shake out my hand, answering his smug grin with one of my own.

A scowl deepens his wrinkles as he gently taps his cheekbone. "Is it traitorous to defy evil? Or merely prudent?"

I wipe my hand down the length of my gown's bejeweled bodice to banish his skin's feel on my fingers. "Do you refer to Astagnon? Evil is a harsh word for the kingdom you supposedly shepherd."

As he leans forward in the doorway, his white streak of hair falls in his gray eyes. "A kingdom that did *you* no favors, either." He straightens, tossing back his mane of hair, then combing a hand through it until he's restored a semblance of formality. "I am still shepherd of the souls in Astagnon. That is why I am here, Highness. Working with your father to give those poor lost souls a better life."

My gown's tight bodice squeezes my ribs. "Even at the cost of war?"

Instead of answering, Beneveto scratches his eyebrow. "You should speak with your father if you're going to bring up war. Come, Highness. I'll take you to him."

I fold my arms like a shield, presenting a hard outer shell, hoping it hides how my heart is hammering inside.

After twenty-two years, I'm going to meet my real father?

Swallowing, I nod for him to lead the way.

As we move through Drahallen Hall, I can't help but be begrudgingly curious. The stone walls are chiseled with the ten fae symbols. Servants pass in fine, glittering uniforms with asymmetrical hemlines. Tapestries hang in the stairwell with portrayals of the stories from the Book of the Immortals:

One shows the Night Hunt, with Artain chasing Solene disguised as a doe.

Another shows Aria and Aron, the fated mates who Alessantha brought together.

A third shows Meric's cursed prisoners wandering the Labyrinth of Justice.

"Volkany is blessed under your father's rule." Beneveto's irritation at me seems to have mellowed by the time we reach the third floor. He motions to a young servant boy carrying firewood to the upper bedrooms. "King Rachillon is ushering in a grand new era. That boy, for example, will live to witness the Third Return of the Fae."

I mumble a vague answer, not wanting to voice what I truly think: that the poor boy will be nothing but a plaything to the fae.

Like all of us.

A pretty young noblewoman, dressed in a midnight blue gown and wearing silver ear peaks, nods politely to the

Grand Cleric as we pass. A godkissed birthmark winks on her russet brown skin above her breastbone. She extends a hand toward an unlit candle, and a flame springs to life at her fingertips.

"Good day, Grand Cleric," she says with a heavy Kravadan accent.

I glance back over my shoulder to watch her continue down the row of candles, lighting each one for the evening with her godkiss.

"She is Kravadan?" I ask.

"You will find that many residents and servants in Drahallen Hall come from across the seven kingdoms. It stems from your father's efforts to locate the sleeping fae. He requires ample godkissed people to search for their eternal resting places."

My stomach cinches. "You mean they've been kidnapped and forced to serve him. Like the godkissed people who went missing from Astagnon."

Beneveto doesn't blink at the accusation. "Many were brought here forcibly, yes, but you'll find that few wish to return to their homelands. Moreover, most are pleased to have been given the opportunity for a better life. That noble lady we passed lighting candles? Lady Caelena? She was a slave girl to a desert warlord. King Rachillon's fleet of godkissed searchers freed her, brought her here, and your father rewarded her contribution to Volkany with a title."

I press my lips together, not wanting to give voice to the doubts in my head. Tati assured me that I was wrong about Volkany being a cursed kingdom. Every instinct in my body bristles against accepting that, but can I deny the evidence I've seen with my own eyes? The prosperous villages? A thriving city? A castle filled with people who celebrate the fae as gods, not monsters? Then again, could there be greater proof of their evil than Iyre?

Beneveto stops at a gilded doorway guarded by a soldier in iron armor. "Here is where I shall take my leave for the time being. Your father awaits within."

He nods curtly before he leaves me.

My stomach shrinks as I face the soldier, who towers over me a full head taller. Silently, he opens the door.

My feet don't seem to want to move. My hands smooth over my bodice, working out nonexistent wrinkles. My father is beyond this door. Not Charlin Darrow, the drunken lord who locked me away in a convent.

My real father.

I force myself to take a step inside. The room is windowless and dark, making it nearly impossible to judge the size. At first glance, it could be a closet or a cathedral.

My eyes adjust to the darkness, picking up the glow of low lights from the walls. There's something strange about the lights. They don't flicker like candles.

I cautiously approach one, my shoes padding softly on the stone floor. Surprisingly, the glow comes from phosphorescent plants set in wall sconces.

When my eyes fully adjust, I find myself in a room of waist-height marble pedestals, each one illuminated by glowing plants. An enormous glass water tank is set into the far wall. Fanciful glowing fish swim within, their dorsal spots radiating impossible colors.

I seem to be alone, so I step cautiously to the first pedestal, which holds the long iron needle that Iyre used to cut a portal from Astagnon to Volkany. I glance over my shoulder before snatching it up and poking at the air like she did—but all that happens is I accidentally jab my finger.

I sigh.

No surprise—you have to be fae to use fae tools.

The next pedestal displays a leather-bound book locked in an iron chain, and the others contain a rusted horseshoe, a fisherman's net, and a lasso woven from human hair, among others.

At the water tank, I tap gently to attract the attention of an eel-like fish with glowing fins, and gradually, I become aware of a pair of human eyes looking back at me from the other side.

Shrieking, I jump backward.

A figure slowly approaches from the far side of the tank, his features cast in the eel's electric glow. My heart seems to stop as surely as if Tati had raised her ten fingers.

A man enters the room like a slow, heavy mist. The air grows tense, charged with an almost palpable sense of power. His beard is graying, yet his hair is still a honey blond, pulled back into a thick knot at the base of his skull. The ten points of his crown, rising like the points of a star, are etched with the symbols of the fae court. A steel brooch pinned to his doublet is cast in the size and likeness of an anatomical heart.

It's *him.*

When he steps into the brighter light, it's like all the air is sucked from my lungs. I never saw myself in Charlin Darrow's bulbous features.

But in King Rachillon's?

He has my straight, restrained nose. My same sea-blue eyes. From what I can tell, the same long hair, too.

"Daughter." His voice is raspy and deep like he's spent a lifetime around campfires. "I've waited a long time to put eyes on you."

My body refuses to move, lips frozen, trapped between fear and awe. The king places his hands on the sides of my face as though trying to find himself in my features, too.

Shaking, I let out a held breath.

He slowly tilts my head down and brushes a kiss on my forehead. When he releases me, he touches his anatomical heart brooch and whispers, "By the gods. You look so much like her."

Though my throat feels too dry for words, I force these across my sandpaper tongue: "My father—my adopted father—often said that I carried my mother's features. I was too young when she died to remember what she looked like in detail."

Rachillon strokes his long beard. "Isabeau was a beauty. But she was more than that. She had a defiance that I see in you. Which is why I know that, as much as you pretend not to be, you're seething with anger that I took you from Astagnon."

You took me from more than Astagnon, I think. *You took me from Basten.*

I seal my lips to school my temper.

Measuring my response, I say slowly, "I'm not willing to embrace a kingdom—even my parents' kingdom—that kidnapped hundreds of godkissed people and slaughtered innocent citizens." I tilt my chin upward toward the glowing ferns, their cool light washing over my skin. "I was there. At Duren's arena. I saw what your raiders did at your command. The starleons, too."

On the rare occasions that I stood up to Charlin Darrow, he corrected me with a slap that ached for days. King Rachillon, however, takes my challenge with a flare of pride in his eyes.

"I don't relish the death of innocents." He paces toward a pedestal that displays a pair of worn leather gloves. "Yet such is war. The gods blessed me with my own godkiss; I cannot deny it, as you cannot silence the animal voices in your head. I must do as the gods bid. They *want* me to wake them. To do so, I required godkissed people for their ability to find the fae resting sites."

"And?" I place the marble pedestal between us, leaning forward over the seemingly mundane gloves. "You think the gods will thank you? Reward you? The gods will just as soon put you in a grave and dance upon it."

I tense for the slap I feel sure to come—but instead, Rachillon throws back his head and laughs. When he finally wipes the mirth from his eyes, he says simply, "You are right that the gods can be capricious."

Capricious.

As if they're baby goats butting their half-inch horns against one another.

He picks up one of the leather gloves with as much reverence as if it were a crown jewel. "Do you know what these are? They are Immortal Artain's hunting gloves. Whoever wears them shall have perfect aim. Come. Look at this."

Rachillon steers me to the next pedestal.

"This knife—" he hovers his hand over a vicious curved blade with a serpent carved into the handle, "—is called the Serpent Knife. It was used in The Sacrifice of the Golden Child. Do you know the story?"

I shake my head softly. "In the convent, we only read the stories from Immortal Iyre's chapter."

He runs his finger over the serpent design. "In a time

before time, Immortal Vale promised favor to a farmer if he sacrificed the prize kid out of his goat herd to the fae. The farmer, greedy and half-mad, used the knife to kill his youngest son instead and placed a chalice filled with the boy's blood on an altar. Vale drank from the chalice, thinking it was wine. According to legend, that was the first time a human life was sacrificed to the fae. Vale didn't mean to drink human blood, but he did, and it gave him far greater powers. It's what turned them all from long-lived fae into *gods*."

He speaks as casually of a boy's murder as describing the supper menu. Ice runs through my veins as I think about the blood on Iyre's lips.

Our blood fuels their powers.

He leads me to the next pedestal, which holds a delicate vase that swirls with mystical dark blue bubbles frozen in the glass.

"I've collected these fae artifacts at great expense over the course of nearly forty years," he explains. "A diver died bringing this one back from a shipwreck. It is Immortal Thracia's midnight vase. Her most prized possession, according to lore, as it was a wedding gift from Immortal Samaur during the First Return. He called upon the sun to heat sand from beneath a glacier, giving it its unusual color. It can keep any bloom alive for eternity, even without sunlight."

His hand on my back steers me toward the next pedestal, but I step away from his grasp, a hand pressed to my dress's tight bodice.

"If your rule is so just and your kingdom so great, then why did my mother flee?"

His blue eyes shine in the low, iridescent light that keeps

shifting as the eels circle in their glass enclosure. Finally, he looks into the middle ground and sighs.

"Isabeau was an actress—did you know that?"

I can't hide how much this unexpected fact shakes my world. The truth is, as much as I loved my mother, I knew almost nothing about her. For ten years, she kept her past a mystery. At night, when I would ask her to tell me about when she was a little girl, she would make up fantastic tales and tickle me until I giggled myself to sleep.

Rachillon smiles at my reaction, knowing he's hooked my interest.

"Isabeau's godkiss allowed her to glamour herself and any objects in her possession. As you can imagine, it was the perfect gift for an actress. She could change her face to match any role. But her talent extended beyond appearance. She was a wonder on stage. Her words, her eyes—she could convey entire worlds in one expression."

In the softness in his rasping voice, I can almost believe that he loved her.

"I first saw her in a production of The Night Hunt," he continues. "She was playing Immortal Solene. I courted her for months until she agreed to give up the stage and commit to servicing me. A concubine, yes—I couldn't marry a commoner. Still, we were together day and night, always as equals. But then—" His throat bobs with a hard swallow. "—she fell pregnant. I was overjoyed. Though we were not married, I wanted nothing more than a child produced by our union. A godkissed seer predicted you would be a female and also godkissed...three days later, Isabeau was gone."

My limbs are left shaken by this information. All my life, I would have paid a king's ransom to have known my mother's history, and now it's given to me freely.

And yet, greedily, I'm salivating for even more.

"Why?" I press. "If you were so in love, why did she run away?"

Rachillon turns to the fish tank, running his fingers over the surface to trace the fish's movements. "Isabeau feared the coming war. She could sense its approach, whether in one year or thirty. She wanted to hide you from it." He tilts his head so I can see his profile glowing in the eel's shifting light. "I didn't think you should be hidden. I knew, in my soul, you would be key to the war's outcome. And so, she fled. She didn't want you to live the life of a revolutionary. She wanted you to simply be... happy."

Happy. The word skewers me through the ribs.

It feels like a fairy tale. A fantasy. Maybe if my mother hadn't died, I would have had a chance for happiness in Bremcote. Learning to sew and dance from her, marrying a boyishly sweet minor lord, having children of my own. But she *did* die. And everything that happened after?

Not exactly *happy.*

I take my time soaking in this knowledge, tucking it away deep inside me, locked in a place more treasured than this fae artifact room.

My mother loved me. She wanted to protect me.

After a lifetime of guessing, this information is water to a girl dying of thirst.

Rachillon lets the silence stretch, and for that, I am grateful. If there's ever a time not to be rushed, it's now.

Finally, I bring myself to look him in the eyes. "One more question. How did you know exactly where I would be, unguarded in the woods after Lord Berolt's funeral, for Immortal Iyre to capture me?"

He laughs to himself, but there is no mirth in it—only sadness. Pity. For *me*. "I was told the exact time and place."

"What?" I blurt out. "By whom?"

He turns back to the swimming eels, the light shimmering over features so like my own. "Don't you know?"

The fae artifact room spins on its axis, and I grip the marble pedestal before I lose my balance.

A wave of nausea rolls up my throat as I close my eyes, praying to every god who has ever walked the earth that it's not the name I think it is.

Hands trembling, I hear the warning hum of every spider within Drahallen Hall.

"*SSSSsssss, tck-tck-tck, sssSsssss, TCK-TCK-tck...*"

They sense my pain. They're trying to ease it. Hoping to soothe the unbearable wail in my soul.

But only one thing will make me feel better about learning the identity of the person who betrayed me to the Volkish enemy.

...their gods-damn *death*.

Rachillon rasps quietly, "The man who sold you out was Rian Valvere."

CHAPTER 11
BASTEN

The first few days in Old Coros pass in a blur of unpacking, coronation planning, and getting lost in a damn castle that rivals the size of Duren's arena.

My bedroom alone is larger than Rian's sprawling chambers back in Sorsha Hall. Who needs a bed that could sleep four and two fireplaces? On top of that, my chamber is stocked with peonies that make me sneeze. I immediately give them to the first maid I see with instructions to take them home to her mother.

Whoever the former First Sword was, I hope he appreciated the luxuries bestowed upon him. Because I sure as hell don't.

Give me a campfire and moss for a bed.

Yeah, it's no surprise, but I'm dismayed to learn that I loathe the formality in Old Coros just as much as I expected to. These bastards really expect the king's First Sword to comb my hair *daily*.

Still, as painful as the days are, the nights are torture.

As soon as half-sleep seeps in, Sabine steps back into my dreams. Between the Valor Bell's last chime for the night and the first for dawn, it's a gods-damn orgy of every possible way our bodies can connect. Mouth on mouth, my lips on her perfect breasts, our hips writhing together. In my dreams, she smiles, laughs, and talks for hours about, I don't know, chipmunks—and I've never hung on someone's words so damn much. Whatever she cares about, I care about, too. Her passion is contagious.

Then, that damn Valor Bell jolts me awake, and before I can even race to a quill or pen to write down the dream's details, it's already gone.

"Lord Basten." A crisp knock sounds on my door. "Rising King Rian has asked for you."

"Tell him to sit on his spurs!" I groan.

I wrestle with the silken tunic that feels too stiff beneath my armor, pin on the silver sword brooch that marks me as First Sword, and try not to get lost on my way to Rian's chambers.

The First Sword pin jabs me in the chest as a maid directs me to a balcony leading down to Rian's private garden, where I find him frowning at a rosebush.

"Joruun loved roses, or so I'm told," he says as I approach. He plucks a velvety red blossom to run between his fingers. "Frankly, I find the smell cloying. Eventually, I'll have them all mown down and plant oleander in their place. A more pleasing scent. As a bonus, they're poisonous."

I rub my nose, which has been itching from the overpowering scent of roses ever since I set foot in Rian's apartment. "Always been partial to violets, myself."

Rian freezes, then slowly looks over his shoulder at me.

"What?" I ask, wiping my jaw for any traces of coffee on my stubble.

"Violets. Little violet. It's what you used to call..." A cloud passes over his face. "Never mind."

My hand drifts to my left forearm, squeezing the wrist guard.

He gestures for me to walk with him down a path lined with circular water gardens. According to legend, these pools were once natural springs where Immortal Meric would host debauched orgies of fae and human decadence —but now, they merely hold lily pads.

"I want you at the coronation tonight," he says.

I start, nearly tripping on a flagstone. "It's tradition for the coronation to be a private affair between the king and the crown bearer priest."

"Fuck tradition." He smooths his fingers over his chin, but the habit doesn't seem to ease his tension. "I want you and your sword there. I don't know these damn people yet. And I don't let anyone near my neck without you nearby."

I tilt my head. "Of course, Majesty."

We meander among the labyrinthine walls that Immortal Meric once used to torment criminals. According to the Book of the Immortals, if the jails were full or he felt particularly cruel that day, he would toss a condemned sinner into the labyrinth to face the deadly fae beasts within. Fingernail marks—much too worn away for the regular eye to detect—still scar the stones.

"Majesty." Maximan strides down the length of the garden walk, pebbles crunching beneath his heavy boots. Beneath his helmet, his face is even more dour than usual.

He takes a knee before handing a rolled parchment to Rian. "A missive arrived from our northern army general. Word has spread to the border towns that Iyre is risen and in league with Volkany. Villagers burned straw effigies of her in protest, and in return, Volkany sent a flock of starleons to rain down plaguedust. They're saying the casualties are already in the dozens." He removes his helmet and wipes his sweat-plastered brow. "In retaliation, Astagnonian villagers are attempting to tear down the border wall to attack the Volkish people."

Rian snatches the missive hard enough to crumple it in his fist. "That wall has stood for five hundred years. Ropes and pulleys aren't going to budge a brick."

The damn First Sword pin jabs again into my pectoral. I shift, trying to dislodge it discreetly, and Maximan slides me a disapproving frown.

Rian crumples the letter. "Tell the general to send two battalions to the border villages. One each of archers and infantry. Keep the calvary on hold. If this is the start of war, then our soldiers should be fighting it, not farmers and woodsmen."

His order hits me like a strike to the solar plexus, knocking the wind right out of me. I swallow hard, my throat as dry as sandpaper, and force myself to breathe. *War?* Already? The word echoes in my mind, a relentless beat that portends dark times ahead.

Maximan gives a crisp nod. "Yes, Majesty."

His footsteps crunch over gravel long after he's out of sight.

Rian pulls in a deep breath, gazing at a point somewhere amid the darkening clouds. The weight of the sky seems to press down on him, the first few raindrops splashing on his cheek.

"Damn it all, maybe it should have been you, Wolf. This

kingdom deserves a good man on the throne. And I'm not a good man." He wipes away the rain.

This rare flash of vulnerability sends a shiver down my spine.

Guilt is not the first—hell, not even the twentieth—sentiment that Rian Valvere is known for.

"You think I'm any better?" I bark. "You must not remember the debauchery we got up to in the Sin Streets."

He laughs flatly, turning back to the roses.

I know better than to ask questions of a man who plotted his own father's murder. I'm not sure there's a soul alive who holds more to himself than the future king standing before me—and I can't help but wonder what has him feeling so guilty.

The coronation ceremony is blessedly brief. A smear of holy oil on Rian's forehead, a prayer from the priest, and Rian's recitation of the sacred vow.

Boom.

Crown? On head. Throat? Intact.

The celebratory banquet, well, that's another story. If the coronation itself was small and sacred, the banquet is anything but that.

Hekkelveld Castle's Grand Hall is filled with tables laden with roasted peacocks, succulent venison with herb oil, and pies bursting with fresh berries. Nobles bedecked in silks and velvets mingle, and some already take to the dance floor. It's a more restrained form of opulence than Sorsha Hall's balls, where a fistfight was a common sight. The fashion here isn't fae-inspired, with no pewter earpiece or asymmetrical hemline.

My stomach growls. The assault of so many smells on my senses makes me wonder when I last ate. Yet, as I saunter over to the head table to take my place at Rian's right hand, my stomach revolts.

A roast peacock sits on my plate, drowned in orange glaze with a fat hunk of walnut bread, a practically over-flowing glass of wine reflecting the candlelight.

All I can think is: *Today, an army marches on the border. Villagers are dead from plaguedust. And we're fucking eating peacock.*

Rian smiles as he holds court at the head of the table, looking resplendent in the steel crown cast to look like raven feathers.

Not six hours ago, he gave the order for war.

Now he's laughing?

The last thing I could do was smile after issuing a death sentence. But as I tear into my bread, there's a gnawing guilt that won't let go. Some senseless part of me almost *wants* that damned throne, if only so that Astagnon gets the moody, scowling king that it deserves.

Decorum? No, I'd fail at that.

But pure bloody strategy? I'd fucking dive in.

Lady Suri sits to my left, taking such small, birdlike bites that midnight will toll before she finishes. Kendan sits across from her, refilling her water glass after every sip she takes. He makes sweeping hand gestures as he describes his latest diplomatic mission to Kravada.

The rest of the table is filled with distant Valvere cousins, the white-haired councilors I can't tell apart, and nobles whose names I'll have to eventually learn.

"I'm glad *someone's* having a good time," Suri whispers to me when Kendan gets up to speak with a general. She subtly points her butter knife at the dance floor.

Folke and Ferra are among the couples, though unlike the graceful Corosian couples, their movements do not convey polite restraint.

Folke has one hand clasped firmly on the globe of Ferra's ass beneath her feather-adorned gown, holding her so flush to his hips that I think we might be toasting a baby in nine months. Ferra's long tresses are colored gold in honor of the coronation, and they boldly spill down her back in loose waves. Their giddy faces are red-cheeked, eyes glassy, feet stumbling as they catch one another.

"Looks like they partook of the wine early," I observe. "And often."

Suri muffles a laugh. "I'm just glad they made up. It's like springtime with those two, isn't it? A storm overnight, sunny skies by the afternoon. The next day, the same thing all over again." She sighs, twirling her fork in a delicate waltz through the air. "It's heartening to see a true love match."

"Speaking of a match," Lady Eleonora interjects from the other side of the table. "Now that you are crowned, Rian, it is time you find a queen."

Rian sips wine with a wry, indulgent half-grin for his grandmother. "So eager for a great-grandchild?"

"Producing an heir is the duty of every king." Lady Eleonora dabs at her wine-stained lips, and I have the uncanny feeling her wine intake began even before Ferra and Folke's.

Hell, probably at dawn.

"To ensure the kingdom's succession," she continues.

"Why, look at all the chaos caused when Joruun died without an heir. The Grand Cleric was within a god's whisper of wearing that crown."

"Mmm," Rian observes, swirling his wine glass. "Speaking of, I can't help but notice that our dear Grand Cleric Beneveto is not in attendance tonight."

Suri sets down her water and pipes up, "The previous Castlekeep informed me that the Grand Cleric is unwell. Matron White, of the Convent of Immortal Iyre, is here on his behalf to represent the Red Church."

My attention shifts to a dour woman sitting two tables away with a small gathering of Sisters, all dressed in stiff red cassocks. The Matron glares down her hooked nose like a hawk, her eyes as cold and stiff as a prayer stick.

The moment I lay eyes on her, my muscles tense like a bowstring drawn tight. An instinctive wave of revulsion surges through me, making my skin prickle, though I can't place why.

"*That* old witch?" Rian slams down his glass and leans over his plate, his dark eyes spitting venom. "She must have the balls of Immortal Vale himself to show her face to me after what she did to Lady Sabine."

I jolt at the name. My jaw clenches hard enough that I bite my tongue, the metallic taste of blood overwhelming my senses. I rub a hand over my face to hide the panic rising in my throat.

That old woman hurt Sabine? That's what Rian is saying?

Even though I couldn't tell you the color of Sabine Darrow's eyes, I still woke this morning moaning her name.

She means something to me—something I can't put my finger on.

Something that's sliding into obsession.

Lady Eleonora snaps, "Do not speak that girl's name. You're a king now, Rian. Your former fiancée is a traitor. It doesn't matter if Matron White tied her up for the vultures to pick clean. She's none of your concern."

For a few tense moments, they all pick at their peacock and feign interest in the harpist's solo. I use the time to tune in my ears to the gossip circling around the Grand Hall.

At the end of the table, the army generals are discussing the movement of the troops they dispatched that afternoon. At the next table, a count and his wife are speculating about the real reason Grand Cleric Beneveto is absent.

"I heard he hasn't been seen in Old Coros for weeks," the countess whispers. *"They say he is still plotting against Rian."*

"Nonsense. The truth is nothing so complicated. The crown was almost his," the count says, *"and he couldn't bear to see his rival wearing it."*

"Lady Suri." Rian cuts sharply into his peacock as he says matter-of-factly, "As much as Astagnon has greater concerns, my grandmother does have a point. I will need a queen soon to produce an heir. As Castlekeep, it falls to you to find me a match. I want you to locate the kingdom's best women for me. Arrange a...parade, let's say."

Suri's eyes simmer with indignation as she sputters, "A *parade* of women?"

Rian jabs the bite of peacock into his mouth and mutters around it, "For simplicity's sake. I'd like to see them all together to compare their qualities."

Suri's dark cheeks positively catch fire. Her chest rises and falls in her bodice as she says tightly, "You forget that I was there when you sent the order for Sabine to *parade* naked across half of Astagnon. I was the one who arranged her hair to cover her body. I saw her trembling in the court-yard, trying to be brave. You think I would voluntarily encourage any woman to spend a lifetime with a man like you?"

The table falls so silent that I can hear the soft woosh of the candles' flames.

Lady Runa leans in, practically salivating at this scandalous comment. Kendan shifts in his chair, eyebrows knitting together as he carefully sets down his silverware to keep his hands free—for what, I can only imagine.

The air feels so tense I could prick it with a needle.

Rian leans casually on his elbow, stroking his chin as he looks studiously down his long lashes at her. "Are you aware you're speaking to a king, Lady Suri?"

Her hands tighten on the edge of the table. Biting her tongue, she says carefully, "I will not arrange a *parade* of women for you, Majesty."

Lady Runa pops a grape into her mouth as her attention volleys between them.

Rian sits back in his heavy oak chair, his steel crown aglow from candlelight, as he appraises Suri with newfound interest. I don't need my godkiss to see the mischief dancing behind his eyes.

He loves this—loves her hatred.

He stands and walks slowly to Suri's chair, then grips the chair back and leans in to purr in her ear, "Very well. If you do not find me an acceptable bride, then I suppose I will have to marry *you*."

Suri doubles over, coughing into her cloth napkin. It takes her a moment of composure before she can eek out, "Majesty, surely you jest!"

Rian shrugs one shoulder as he returns to his place to

take a long drink of wine. "I am quite serious, in fact. You're young. Healthy. Of a noble line. I believe that checks all the boxes. Not to mention, it would save me an immense amount of time." His eyes jump to her with a dark, cruel kind of triumph. "Of course, should you not wish to wear my ring, I'll expect you to present the top candidates next week."

After tipping his glass to her, he strides off to speak with the generals.

Suri is left trembling with rage to the point where I can hear her fingernails clicking. She murmurs, "He truly is psychotic."

Resting my hands on either side of my plate, I murmur, "You've done the worst thing you could, Lady Suri. You caught Rian's attention."

"I *insulted* him!" she hisses.

"That's the problem." I tuck a loose strand of my hair behind my ear. "Rian has only ever known hatred. His father did terrible things—things you couldn't imagine. His brothers abandoned him. His grandmother—well, you know Lady Eleonora's wrath. And so, the fact that you, also despise him? He *likes* it, if only because it's familiar. Love and hate—they're all mixed together in the Valvere family. The more you hate him, the more he'll enjoy torturing you back."

She presses a delicate hand on her neckline to clear a tremor from her throat. To her credit, she faces this news bravely—with a thoughtful head tilt—instead of blanching.

"What does that mean for his feelings toward Sabine?" she asks.

I jolt again, hearing the name. Hot candle wax on my

balls couldn't make me writhe with as much pleasure and pain.

"W—what do you mean?"

"Did he ever love her?" Suri asks softly, eyes hunting out Rian in the crowd as he whispers low into a general's ear. "Or was it a confusion—love and hate?"

I pause, hanging on the verge of answering, yet my thoughts go blank. The truth is, I have no idea how Rian felt about Sabine. Like all memories that surround her, it's a void.

Across the hall, Rian signals to me.

"Excuse me, Lady Suri." I push my chair back.

Rian motions me to a quiet corner of the Grand Hall, where he says in a low voice, "Someone needs to shadow Kendan."

I try to hide my surprise. "Your brother?"

"There are stirrings that he's been meeting with the wrong kind of people."

A chill creeps up my spine, because I'm usually very good at sniffing out traitors. And I haven't gotten so much as a whiff of suspicion from Rian's older brother.

Arrogance? Oh, yes. But not deceit.

I give a curt nod. "I'll do it."

Rian rests a hand on my shoulder, shaking his head. "No, Wolf, you're above that now. You're First Sword. Send Folke instead."

Folke?

I spot the man in question swaying drunkenly on the dance floor, his face buried in Ferra's ample chest, much to the affront of the elegant Corosian ladies watching.

I've been friends with Folke long enough to know that he can sober up quickly. One word from Rian, and he'd be stalking the shadows as the best spy in the city within the hour.

But seeing him lovingly tuck a strand of Ferra's hair back does something to my damn hardened heart.

For a second, I almost remember what it was like to love someone—

Before those thoughts drift too far, I cross my arms over my chest, staring at the dark city beyond the banquet hall's glass windows, shifting as the First Sword pin once more jabs me in the chest.

"I'll do it," I repeat, and then add, "I miss getting my hands dirty."

CHAPTER 12
SABINE

"That gods-damned *bastard!*"

I storm out of Drahallen Hall with all the force of a hurricane, angry tears leaking out of the corner of my eyes, the world spinning in a dizzying blur that keeps me from knowing up from down.

Overhead, the stars are pinpricks against the night sky, glittering like the jewels that drip from every surface of Rian Valvere's home. Long grass tangles around my shoes, streaking them with gossamer-silk spiderwebs and midnight dew. The air holds a smoky, herbal scent. I catch myself on the back of a wrought-iron garden bench, doubling over to try to fill my screaming lungs with air.

The man who sold you out was Rian Valvere.

My corset pinches my lungs to the point where I can't breathe. Its obsidian jewels may be beautiful, but they're beyond restrictive. I tug at the crimson ribbons holding the corseted top together until they finally loosen.

The tops of my breasts spring free. Clinging to the bench for support, I pull in breath after shaky breath.

"Highness? Are you all right?"

I toss my head up, all too aware of my mussed hair and tear-streaked face, to find Captain Tatarin exiting a gate, concern written in her dark brown eyes. She reaches a steadying hand toward me, but I straighten quickly, tugging my dress to smooth out the wrinkles.

"Oh. Tati. It's you."

Her eyes go wide. "Highness, you're crying! What happened? Shall I call for the healer?"

"No!" I press a hand against the loosened corset. "Please, don't. I only need... I only need... Oh, damn it all! I need a noose around Rian Valvere's *throat!*"

Tati hesitates, glancing back toward the castle. But instead of calling for the guards, she unwinds the maroon scarf around her neck and presses it into my hands.

I nod a shaky thanks as I use the scarf to dry my eyes.

Tati tuts in sympathy. "Rian Valvere, eh? I...think I can guess why you want to throttle that particular man."

I nearly drop her scarf in surprise. "You do?"

She clears her throat. "I hope you do not hold this against me, Highness, but I was the one who met with Rian Valvere at the border several weeks ago to make the deal."

Under normal circumstances, such information would have me bolting upright and demanding answers. But with my heart already contorted in knots, I only narrow my eyes.

"Tell me everything."

Tati keeps her voice low. "We had positioned Grand Cleric Beneveto to take over after King Joruun's passing so that we would have an ally on Astagnon's throne. Beneveto had been working with us for well over a year as a clandestine agent. Whatever your father asked of him, he would have his Red Priests and Red Sisters do. But then, Rian

Valvere sent a messenger crow with a compelling offer. If King Rachillon would help put him on the throne instead of Beneveto, he would give up your location. Your father ordered Beneveto to rescind his claim."

My fingers curl hard around the garden bench. "I thought—I thought that in his own way, Rian loved me." I gaze up at the soft, twinkling lights in Drahallen Hall's windows. "I think, maybe, I've been wrong this entire time about who my enemy is."

Tati rests a soft hand on my shoulder.

I close my eyes. "Now it makes sense why Rian gave me up to Basten with so little objection. He had already traded me for the throne once. It meant nothing to him to do it again. He's the Lord of Liars. I—I should have known better."

I pinch my nose to keep the tears at bay. Still, a tear rolls down my cheek and splashes onto the top of my chest. I wipe it away, realizing my breasts are practically spilling out. "Gods. My dress. I look like a mess, don't I?"

"It is no great concern, Highness. Here in Volkany, we don't care about formalities. See?"

She motions to her own loose-fitting men's trousers and oversized shirt. It's the first time I've seen her out of her armor.

I sniffle. "Female soldiers are allowed to wear men's clothing?"

"When we are off duty, we may wear what we like. As well as drink and curse and smoke Wicked Weed."

"Wicked Weed?" My ears perk up. I've only ever heard the elicit substance whispered about in the Sin Streets of Astagnon.

"Haven't you tried it, Highness?"

I chuckle darkly. "No, I grew up in a convent."

Tati's eyes light up mischievously as she grabs the end of her scarf, using it as a lead to tug me toward a walled garden. "We have a saying here: 'Inhale the weed, exhale your troubles.' Come—try a toke. It will help you forget all about Rian Valvere."

I hesitate.

Exhale my troubles? Yes, *please*.

The herbal, smoky scent lacing the air grows stronger as I follow her into the walled garden. The rise and fall of soft voices catches my ear, broken with peals of laughter. A greenish haze of smoke hangs around an enormous hemlock tree whose branches sweep the ground. A cozy, intimate glow of lanterns comes from within the hemlock boughs.

She sweeps aside a low branch like a tent curtain. The way the branches hang low forms a natural canopy, screening the smokers inside, forming a private space.

Curious, I crane my neck, trying to glimpse between the pin-like needles—only to make out someone with fire-red hair combed back from pointed ears.

"*Iyre*? No. No way. I'm not sharing a pipe with a fae."

I quickly ball up Tati's scarf and shove it at her as I turn back toward the castle, ready to spend the night chatting with my mouse—but Tati grabs my arm.

She says with big eyes, "The fae are awakening, Highness. There's no going back to life as it was before. There's only moving forward in the new world they are about to create—and if you want to thrive in that world, you must know their ways. Good *and* bad. Starting with Iyre."

I'm about to tell her *she* can go cozy up with that fae bitch, but then pause.

If Iyre is here...then she isn't in her tower room.

I tilt my chin upward, where the Aurora Tower's peak is visible over the rest of Drahallen Hall's rooftops. The lanterns are off in the highest room. From the corner of my eye, I scan the dark, walled garden, looking for a flicker of silver-blue.

Cloudfox, I ask in my head. *Are you here?*

For a few moments, there's no answer. The mouse told me that she was at my window earlier, but she might have left. Returned to the forest. But then, the bushes rustle, and a voice chirps:

Here, girlie! Her small silver face peeks out of the leaves.

A thrill rises in my chest as I tell Tati, "*One* toke."

She grins.

As I duck into the tree's tent-like canopy, I whisper to the cloudfox, **Go to the Aurora Tower. The highest room. Search inside for a small, round, yellow bottle. I'll keep an eye on Iyre.**

The cloudfox nods enthusiastically.

The space beneath the hemlock boughs is surprisingly large, easily accommodating the dozen or so humans lounging within, all holding court around Iyre. They drape themselves over wooden furniture or recline on quilts. Over-flowing fruit trays rest on low tables, along with ample bottles of wine. Round glass orbs filled with candles hang from the highest interior branches like miniature moons.

All conversation stops at my entry. Faces turn my way. I recognize Paz, but most of the others are strangers.

The Blades are here, too—Ghost, Whisper, and Night—accompanied by Night's hound at his side. It's strange. I didn't notice before, but I can't seem to hear the hound's voice in my head.

Hello, friend, I try, but the dog ignores me, keeping her chin on Night's knee.

I feel the creeping feeling of being watched and find Iyre studying me from behind her long lashes, her glowing fey lines casting harsh shadows on her angular face. Slowly, she blows a perfect smoke ring into the air.

"Highness," she says, flashing her pointed incisors. "Bold of you to join us."

Chuckles ripple among the crowd.

Ghost stands up, preening as he combs his long, fair hair over one shoulder and offers me a dazzling smile. "Take my seat, Highness."

He flexes his exposed biceps as he motions to the bench.

I feel suddenly locked to the edge of the gathering. Gods, is it a mistake to be here? What if the cloudfox tricks me again? Am I a fool for trusting our fae bargain? My cheeks are still streaked with dried tears, and the last thing I want is to show them any weaknesses.

Oh, and my breasts are popping out of my loosened corset.

Great.

Warily, I sink into the seat Ghost offered, subtly trying to tighten the corset ribbons.

"That's the spirit!" Tati laughs as she collapses onto one of the blankets. She takes the pipe from Iyre, draws in a toke through the foot-long stem, and then releases a puff of green smoke up toward the sky.

Sighing contentedly, she offers me the pipe.

All eyes watch me in unabashed interest as I take the pipe, holding it with as little skill as I would a blacksmith's tongs.

"Like this," a deep voice says. The raven-haired Night takes my wrist, trailing his other hand up my shoulder to find my chin, and then guides the pipe to my lips. With his cloudy eyes pinned somewhere in the distance, he murmurs in my ear, "Breathe in through your lungs, not your mouth. Here."

His hand slides down my side to rest above my ribcage, over the slackened corset ribbons, his rough thumb grazing the top of my breasts. My heartbeat picks up. I shift on the bench, uneasy. There's nothing overtly seductive about his touch. Still, I'm not used to strange men touching me.

"Thanks," I croak.

On the count of three, I suck through the pipe. A spark shoots down my throat, and I double over, coughing out clouds of green smoke.

"That—that *burns!*"

Iyre cackles as she reaches over to take the pipe and then draws a long, practiced toke. "You'll learn, little human."

My lungs feel like they're on fire, but after a few minutes of throat-clearing, I'm able to finally breathe steadily.

The Wicked Weed shoots straight to my head. Soon, my muscles soften like warmed honey, my worries falling away. I drape myself against the bench between Ghost and Night, staring up at the orb-shaped lanterns.

Tati nudges my foot with hers and passes me a slice of beautyberry cake. My stomach growls to alert me that I'm ravenous. I pounce on the cake, devouring it in two bites and then moaning as I lick my fingers.

"Easy, Highness," Ghost teases in my ear as he stretches his muscular arm on the bench's back behind me. "Save some of that appetite, and I'll give you something better to lick off your lips later. One night—that's all I need. One night, and you'll never look at another man again."

Grimacing, I shove away his arm. "I've had better offers —from men who don't trip over their own egos."

He wiggles his eyebrows. "Doesn't seem to bother half the women in Norhelm."

I can't do much other than stare at this pretty, pompous buffoon. With his theatrically bulging muscles and perfectly coiffed hair, he's the definition of a foppish dolt. Harmless? Absolutely not—he must be one of my father's top body-guards for a reason. And yet he might be the most unserious man I've ever met—and I was engaged to *Rian Valvere*.

"If that is true," I counter as I scoot away from his knee, "Then you'll have no trouble finding company tonight other than me. Or better yet, leave the poor ladies alone and plea-sure yourself."

He tips his head back for a deeply amused laugh.

I suddenly feel too warm, crammed on the narrow bench between Ghost and Night—two men whose beauty would rival Basten's if it wasn't so skin-deep—and move to Tati's quilt.

With a soft smile, she passes me the pipe again.

This toke, I only cough a little.

By the time I've passed the pipe on to the next person, I can barely remember why I was angry. My head swims. My muscles turn to jelly. I try to peer through the branches toward the Aurora Tower, but the night is too dark. I lose my balance, falling to my back on the quilt to gaze up at the hemlock.

"We've lost her," I hear Ghost tease Tati. "Wherever our little princess is going tonight, it will be quite a journey."

As the herb fades me in and out of reality, time begins to move in strange ways—

—*Suddenly, I'm on all fours on the quilt, with Night's dog's breath in my face as the hound licks my ear, and I'm laughing and scratching the dog's chin—*

—*Whisper and a pretty-as-a-peach girl are dancing beneath the orb lanterns hanging from branches. Another woman joins them, who looks uncannily like the first. Twins? The trio's steps are careless, their pupils blown from Wicked Weed—*

—*The twins are now seated in Whisper's lap, their bodices shoved down around their waists to expose heavy breasts as Whisper sticks his tongue down the closest one's throat—*

—*Tati, giggling, uses her godkiss to pause the other dancing couples in time as she counts down from ten on her fingers, and then their swaying movements restart—*

—*Not to be outdone, I jump to my feet and lift my hands to the hemlock boughs, calling to the night owls.* **Come, friends!** *I command in my head—*

—*The branches quake, and dozens of owls swoop through to peck at our leftover grapes and slices of cake, as the revelers gasp and clap—*

—"She likes you," Night whispers in my ear. Somehow, I'm seated in his lap on the bench, with one of his powerful hands circling my waist from behind to keep me from drunkenly tumbling to the grass. His dog rests her head on his opposite knee, gazing up at me with her big, black eyes.

"Her name is Hawk," Night whispers.

"I can't speak to her," I say, hiccupping. "For some reason, she doesn't have a voice."

—"No, no, no, little princess. Get your own." Whisper is holding back his wine goblet, wagging a scolding finger at me for trying to steal it from him—

—I'm dancing with Ghost now as he expertly guides me beneath the boughs, maneuvering our way between the roosting owls. His voice is breathy in my ear. "We've been waiting for you. Now that you're here, everything can begin"—

—I'm standing with my arms around the hemlock trunk. I could swear that I can feel the tree breathing in and out, in and out, the bark expanding beneath my embrace. **Go,** *the tree tells me, which makes me giggle because plants can't speak.* **This place is not for you.**

. . .

My senses snap back into place as I crash out of my Wicked Weed haze into the here and now.

Barefoot.

Wasted.

In a grass-stained dress as dawn rises on the horizon.

I look around. I'm not the only one hit hard by the Wicked Weed. The twins are trying to climb the tree. Iyre and Paz are half-naked on one of the quilts, splayed out as she kisses his neck. Two of the Blades are arm wrestling.

Oh—the cloudfox!

My legs are unsteady. I finally stagger to my feet, and once I'm outside of the hemlock tree, fresh dawn air douses me like a bucket of water.

I pause, blinking up at Aurora Tower.

"Highness, wait." Tati is breathing hard, her braid falling loose as she runs to catch up with me. Her throat bobs in a swallow as her fingertips dig into my upper arm.

"I need to—to get to my room." *To check on the cloudfox.*

She presses on, regardless. "I didn't tell you something about my meeting with Rian Valvere." She pauses, brow wrinkling. "He was distracted. Deeply bothered. When I asked why, he said that a man who was like a brother to him had betrayed him."

The haze around my mind disappears, and I snap my attention to her. "What?"

"I mention this to show you what kind of man is about to sit on Astagnon's throne. Why your father is so adamant about replacing him with someone loyal to us. I'll never forget what Rian said or the ice in his eyes. '*I considered him a brother. Now, I won't stop until he's muzzled. Chained. Broken as a hunting dog that bit its master and will never see sunlight again.*' If he said that about someone so close to him, what would he do to common folk he owes nothing to?"

I grab onto the back of a bench, shaken. I don't need Tati's examples of Rian's wickedness. I know Rian's crimes frontward and backward.

I have to warn Basten—before it's too late.

CHAPTER 13
BASTEN

For three days, I track Kendan through the streets of Old Coros, from Hekkelveld Castle to the Temple of Immortal Meric. From a three-story manor house in Lommer District to an opium den known for its eye-watering Wicked Weed.

As I move throughout the city, the fear in the streets is palpable. Doors are locked and barred, and windows are boarded up against looters. Every alleyway shrine to the ten gods overflows with offerings of victuals, coins, and even silverware as desperate citizens try to buy the rising fae's favor. Entire neighborhoods are vacant, left empty for the rats to move in by those seeking the safety of the countryside.

I can taste it like the energy before a battle: Tangy fear mixed with a sweet burst of excitement, about to bubble over into a boil.

As the Valor Bell tolls midnight, I shuffle back into my room, ready to fall into the sheets and sleep like the dead. I unfasten the First Sword brooch. I strip off my wrist guard and unwind the bandages, assessing whether I need to treat the cuts with vinegar to prevent infection, when distant footsteps give me pause.

They're one story down, moving east through the castle hallway toward the royal library. The person moves carefully, not making much sound on the creaky floors. This is no guard switching shifts. And all the maids are in bed.

I crack my bedroom door just enough to scent the air. Since the person is an entire floor away, their smell is faint even for me, but if I concentrate, I pick up on a trace of orange tea spiced with clove oil.

So, it's not a Valvere, either. They all drown themselves in sandalwood incense.

I grab my woolen cloak, shrouding myself as I make my way downstairs. As First Sword, I'm responsible for the king's well-being. He has a fleet of bodyguards, sure, but those stiff-spined asses are all about ceremony. They'd barely know which end of the sword to use against an assassin—only how to polish it.

I keep to the edges of the hallways, where the floor-boards don't creak as loudly. I hunker in the shadows, moving silently down the stairs and onto the second-floor hallway in time to see a figure in a silk cloak unlock the library door with a large brass key.

Now that I'm closer, I can pick up on a whiff of lavender hair oil mixed with the orange tea scent.

That and the key tell me exactly who I'm following.

My shoulders ease—this is no assassin. Rian isn't in danger. And my bed is calling for me.

Still, curiosity pushes me to slip into the library behind

the woman. Her heart is beating so loudly that she doesn't hear me until I press my palm against her mouth from behind to silence her.

"Lady Suri—do not scream," I murmur. "It is only me."

The whites of Suri's eyes flash as she twists to see me in her peripheral vision. Our eyes meet, and I give a slow nod. Her pulse beneath my grasp slows back to normal, and she matches my nod.

I remove my hand, taking a step back.

"What are you doing here, Wolf?" she demands in a harsh whisper.

"What are *you* doing here?" I counter.

The library's hush presses around us as we stare one another down, and then she finally raises her arms toward the shelves.

"What do you think? I'm looking for the book Sabine told me about."

I glance at the shelves. There must be fifty thousand volumes. "You'll be looking for years at this rate. Let me at least help you. I can read the titles on the highest shelves without a ladder."

She nods.

We each take a different section of the library. Suri starts at the low shelves flanking the fireplace, and I scan the uppermost ones. The library's calm, unnerving at first, becomes more comfortable by the time I finish the C's and move onto the D's.

She keeps turning toward me, on the verge of speaking, but then returns to the books.

Finally, she blurts out in a loud whisper, "Why is Rian such an utter *ass*?"

As I continue down the D's to the next shelf, I suppress

an eye roll. I have to remind myself that Suri doesn't know much about Rian's past. "Look at his family. Considering who raised him, you have to give him some grace, right? He's an ass, sure. But he *tries* not to be the typical Valvere viper."

"Tries and fails," she murmurs. I think she might let it drop as she moves to the next set of shelves, running her finger along the spines, but then she declares, "Lord Kendan seems perfectly agreeable."

"Lord Kendan probably perfumes his balls."

She gasps before her initial shock rolls over into a chuckle. "He does seem the type, doesn't he?"

We return to our books, but barely a minute passes before she whirls back around, sputtering, "I mean, what does Rian possibly gain from toying with people?"

The D's prove worthless, so I move onto the E's. "Entertainment, Lady Suri. And you seem to provide the most."

This silences her. She pulls a book out, moodily blows dust off it to read the spine.

I soften. "I'm not saying you should give Rian his damn parade of women. Only that there's someone for everyone out there, isn't that what the matchmakers say? *Some* heart-of-gold woman out there will want to find the good in him. A baroness who finds his antics as alluring as enraging. A countess who shares his love of himself. Don't begrudge him happiness because of a few lies."

She shoves the book forcefully back on the shelf. "If lies were gold, he'd be the richest man in the kingdom."

"He *is* the richest man in the kingdom."

She rests her hands on her hips. "My point exactly."

A floorboard creaks outside, and my head whips toward the sound.

"Wait," I hiss. "Quiet."

"What do you hear?" she whispers.

I hold up a hand for her to remain silent as I track the sound of footsteps through the castle's entryway, two floors down. These steps also try to be quiet, but the person has none of Suri's lightness. I hear the faint jangle of a chainmail sash.

It's Kendan.

"I have to go."

"Wait, Wolf, about Rian—"

But I'm already silently slipping out the library door, tiptoeing into the hall. Quietly, I jog down the central stairs and into the entryway. As I duck into the shadows, I see a small side door click closed.

Keeping a careful distance, I follow Kendan out of the castle, into the city streets. The wealthy neighborhood surrounding Hekkelveld Castle is tense but quiet, with royal soldiers stationed at every street corner to keep the peace from looters.

Once I cross into the city center, however, signs of unrest crop up like mushrooms. "MAY THE FAE NEVER AWAKEN" is painted across the side of a tavern. A straw effigy of Immortal Iyre with red hair made of dyed wool is propped against a street lamp with her straw wrists bound in chains. Angry protesters stand outside the Temple of Immortal Vale, chanting, "Fae built this city, but humans gave it life!" and "Death to Volkany and all fae supporters!"

Despite the unrest, my shoulders relax, and my stride falls into an easy gait. Here, among the riffraff, I blend in as well as a drunk in an alehouse. This isn't Duren, but the chaotic streets are the same. *They* are my childhood home.

I track Kendan's footsteps to a wealthy gentleman's

club, and spend an hour waiting outside, next to a nearby tannery, watching the club's doorway. The tannery's stench drives my senses mad, but it keeps everyone else from looking closely.

Finally, my patience is rewarded.

Kendan steps out of the club and, after a word to the doorman, crosses the street to enter the Temple of Immortal Meric.

I snuff out my pipe and cross the street, barely more visible than a shadow in my dark cloak and with my locks falling in my face.

Kendan moves with a brisk determination, and I keep a careful distance, slipping through the bustling night revelers like a wraith.

At this hour, the temple is empty. Wooden benches span the small nave, and a locked glass case contains a gilded copy of the Book of the Immortals. The scent of incense chokes the air, mixing with the damp chill of stone walls.

Kendan doesn't pause for prayers to the altar but heads straight for a side door.

I follow him down the temple's twisting corridors with all the silent focus that I give to stalking a deer. He stops at a locked iron gate, and my heart thuds hard with the thrill of the hunt.

This is it.

I flick open the flap on my hunting knife's sheath, ready to draw steel at a moment's notice. If he's meeting with the Grand Cleric—as Rian suspects—I'll need to be on my toes. That pompous holy man, Beneveto, swings a sword better than he recites prayers, and I'm betting he's more likely to stick a man with a blade than bless him with a sermon.

Kendan unlocks the gate and disappears into a dark

passageway that descends beneath the temple. I slip in behind him, my footsteps silent on the worn stone steps, anticipation coursing through me as I realize he's leading me to the city catacombs, a place where secrets are buried with the dead.

We emerge in a narrow underground chamber lined with ancient tombs. Kendan moves freely, but at my height, I have to duck to avoid the low stone joists. A spiral stairwell takes us back up to the surface, where, to my surprise, we emerge into the rear portion of a blacksmith shop.

The reek of iron and woodsmoke slap me in the face like a bucket of ice water. The blacksmith shop is vacant now, the chisels and hammers neatly hung on wall hooks, though the forge in the center of the warehouse creaks as its embers glow.

Kendan dabs a cloth to the sweat beading his forehead as he exits through a rear door.

Pausing, I get my bearings as I recall a map of these streets. There's an alley out that door that leads to a high-end brothel. Chances are, that's not his scene. He seems too self-righteous. However, at the end of the alley, there's a leech house for the poor sponsored by the Red Church, open at all hours, which would be the perfect place for a rendezvous.

As soon as I hear his footsteps recede, I silently open the rear door and step out into the alley—

And, *fuck*.

Someone immediately shoves a burlap sack over my head, while a second man presses a knife to my throat. The sack must be doused in lamp oil, because the smell is so overpowering I can't smell or taste anything else.

I freeze, hands raised in surrender, though my mind churns with ways to beat my two captors bloody.

The first one clamps a padded strap around my ears, muffling my hearing.

That's when I realize I'm *really* fucked.

These men know about my godkiss—which means I've just walked into a trap.

CHAPTER 14
SABINE

loudfox? I call out my window. ***Are you there?***

I wait, tapping my toes anxiously, but there's no answer.

Cloudfox! We made a deal! I need to know if you upheld your end. I've been thinking about your name. I'm getting close.

Again, no answer.

I turn away, cursing. The little troublemaker has been suspiciously absent since I sent her to steal the bottle of Basten's memories from Iyre's room. Either Iyre somehow captured her, which is doubtful since I was with Iyre all night in the hemlock grove. More likely, our fae bargain was just another trick.

Note to self—never trust a cloudfox.

"Dammit," I murmur aloud.

I look up at the daytime moon. *Basten, I'm coming.*

He might not remember me. He might even hate me. Believe that I'm a traitor. But Rian is scheming some kind of twisted, elaborate punishment for what happened at the

Midtane gathering. For all the times Basten rushed to my aide, now it's my turn to save him.

It takes a few days, but finally, I get my chance.

As midday light streams through the windows, loud voices in the hall snap my attention to the door. Footsteps rush down the hall, skipping more than sprinting, along with the excited cries of a handful of maids.

I throw open the door, curious. "What's happening?"

The guard posted there speaks to a maid whose face is as bright as a buttercup.

The maid cries, "Highness, we have blessed news! The king's searchers have located the resting place of Immortal Thracia! A godkissed mystic revealed during a trance that the Goddess of Night slumbers in the westernmost Cratian Island. Soon, your father shall awaken her, and we will have another goddess amongst us!"

I grip the edge of the door to hide how this news affects me.

Already, Immortal Iyre walks amongst us, and look at all the trouble that has caused. She stole Basten's memories. Destroyed happiness for both of us. Her awakening has sparked unease across two kingdoms.

And now there will be *two* woken fae?

What's worse, Immortal Thracia's affinity is healing. That might sound like a blessing, yet, in the last Return, she used that affinity to make her acolytes nearly invincible. If my father wakes Thracia with his godkiss, and she aids his army, then Volkany's soldiers will be undefeatable.

Astagnon will be decimated.

Another maid rushes up. Bouncing with excitement, she spares a perfunctory bow for me. Then, she grabs the first maid's hand. "King Rachillon has ordered a party tonight to celebrate the discovery of Thracia's resting place!"

"Ooh!" The first maid claps excitedly.

I glance out the window. From the point of the Stormwatch Tower where my bedroom is located, I can look down into both the kitchen garden, to the right, and the entry court, to the left. Messengers pour out of the castle to spread the news. The kitchen garden buzzes with servants gathering marigolds for garlands while a goatherd leads a beautiful white goat toward the castle.

My stomach sours, thinking of The Sacrifice of the Golden Child, and that poor goat's fate.

"We'll dress you so beautifully, Highness," the first maid says. "We can weave marigolds into your braid and fix your golden ear-tips to your ears—"

"Right," I hedge, thinking fast. For the past few days, I've always been closely watched. Expected to be in either my bedroom or dining at the head table with my father, Iyre, and the Blades.

This is the first time there's been a...distraction.

I clear my throat. "The thing is, I'm not feeling well. Volkish food is a lot heavier than I'm used to." I give a weak laugh as I press a hand to my belly. "That gravy last night got the better of me. The last thing I want is to be sick all over Immortal Thracia's altar. I'd better spend the evening alone in my room. Please extend my apologies to my father."

The second maid leans in with a knowing look and intimates, "That gravy always makes me sick, too."

I paste on a smile until the moment I can close the door. As my smile instantly falls, I drag the desk chair over to hook under the doorknob.

My father made a mistake by draping my chambers in riches. Maybe in another life, I'd be charmed by the crystal wall sconces that paint the walls with bursts of light, or the gilded jewelry box, or the priceless books lined up on the mantel.

But I'm a girl who grew up sleeping in straw. Jewels only matter now for how much I could sell them to bribe my way to Astagnon.

To Basten.

I stuff handfuls of the jewels and a few other belongings into a satin handkerchief, then drop to hands and knees in front of the wardrobe.

Little mouse, I whisper. *I need to get out of the castle unnoticed. Tonight. Once the party is in full swing. Didn't you say there is a crawlspace between the floors?*

Her nose pokes out, whiskers twitching. *We mice use it as a passageway. I think it is large enough for a small human to fit.*

Show me. I glance back at the door, beyond which comes the sound of more excited maids skipping downstairs.

The mouse leads me to the cold fireplace, where a metal grate is set into the floor with an ash box beneath for collecting ashes.

Lift the grate, the mouse commands. *The boards are rotted out beneath it. See?*

Sweating, I hook my fingers in the heavy grate and hoist it onto the rug. The sunken ash box is about two feet wide, two feet long, and nine inches deep. I plunge my hand into the downy ashes, coughing as they clot in the air, and feel for the back of the box.

Sure enough, the wooden board there is almost rotted

out. All it takes is a few hits with the metal ash scoop to break it the rest of the way.

And that's it. My path to freedom.

I stare into that darkness with a brick sitting in my stomach. In a way that defies logic, I don't want to leave. I want to give my father a chance. Rachillon has shown me nothing but generosity since I arrived at Drahallen Hall. Even bringing me here against my will could be considered a form of kindness: Returning me to the home—the life—and the family that should have been my birthright.

Is it madness to let Basten drive me away from the only true family I have? Basten doesn't even remember me.

But I remember him.

He is worth every ounce of my courage. If I have to become his sword and shield, without him even knowing who I am, then so be it—I'll fight to be the one who saves him.

I'm fourteen. Picking apples in the convent's orchard, singing "The Poor Lady Who Lived in a Pot." Sister Rose passes through, hunting for morels for supper, and stops to rest at an apple tree. Plucking one of the fruits, she bites it mockingly and says, "Poor Lady in a Pot? Why, that might as well have been written about yourself. Poor Lady Sabine has never had a home, have you? You'd probably be grateful for a tin pot to call your own."

I fall silent as I grab apples off the branch.

"No home," she continues. "No mother. A father who'll sell her to the highest bidder the moment she's of age. I do wonder what depressing ditty the school children will sing about you years from now."

Sister Rose chuckles as she throws the apple core against the back of my head.

My muscles tense.

I tell myself to hold my tongue. I still have welts on my back from the last beating.

But when the apple tree Sister Rose stands under suddenly drops a branch, crashing down right on her head and sending her to the infirmary for a week?

Then, I smile.

That night, I impatiently wait until the maids bring me supper in my room, then for the sounds of the party in the Hall of Vale below to reach a fever pitch, when I'm certain everyone is sloshed and thinking of anything but me.

I shrug out of my robe and fold it on the bedspread. My nightdress hangs loose around my knees, letting the chill kiss my bare ankles. My preference wouldn't be escaping in only a shift, but from what I can tell of the crawlspace, any beads or lace on a gown would snag immediately. Not to mention, whatever I wear will get covered in ashes.

I drop my bundle on the hearth—a bedsheet containing a dress to change into, a pair of shoes, and all the jewels from the gilded jewelry box.

As I lay flat on my stomach, the floorboards vibrate from the dancing below. A violinist strikes a high chord, making my stomach tighten.

Ready? The forest mouse pokes her nose up from the tin ash box, soft gray ashes covering her head until she sneezes.

Ready. I shove the bundle ahead of me into the crawl-space, then cast one final glance over my shoulder at my bedroom's gothic elegance, with its towering arched windows overlooking the high Vallen Mountains, the sumptuous dark furnishings, the intricately carved wooden bed frame, all bathed in the soft glow of candlelight.

In another life, I could imagine feeling safe here, wrapped in the cool embrace of this wondrously strange place. The cold, dark stones call to me with the same pull as the eventide chants to the gods. Something about this castle, with its ethereal, dark beauty, whispers in an unlikely way of *home*.

Coming? The mouse asks insistently. ***The feast below is well underway—you must go now when no one will notice you leave!***

I brace myself to crawl into the ash box, only to glance again at the door.

I'm sorry, Father. I'm not leaving because of you.

Hurry, mouse-talker! the mouse chides.

I lay on my belly and wriggle down into the ash box. It's deeper than I expected, and my hands sink into soft ashes that clot at my nose like goose down, making me fight the urge to sneeze. It takes some contorting to crawl down into the rotted-out section.

Once I've fully wriggled into the crawlspace, I lie flat and squint as I take my bearings. The space is barely a foot high. Once, it was probably stuffed with straw for insulation, but that's all long since disintegrated, and the space is empty now except for cobwebs. It's dark except for weak lines of light that filter in from gaps in the floorboards overhead.

In that faint light, I see the forest mouse dart ahead.

"This is...substantially...easier...for you," I groan as I scoot forward over rough-hewn boards that tear at my nightdress. Pushing the bundle ahead of me, I fight to crawl without collecting splinters in every inch of my palms.

The boards groan beneath me as, inch by inch, I arduously follow the mouse's path through the maze-like crawlspace.

My knowledge of Drahallen Hall's layout is fuzzy. Judging by the quiet overhead, mixed with the occasional scent of perfumed linens, I assume we're passing beneath more sleeping chambers. Below me are the muffled sounds of voices and clomps of shoes. The Hall of Vale is one floor down from my bedroom, but I can't be sure of its exact location. The party's music vibrates the floorboards, seemingly coming from all directions at once.

How much farther? I ask the mouse.

Not far now! she responds. *A loose stone ahead gives way to the roof above the Twilight Garden. You'll be able to climb down the gables.*

I pass over a shed snake skin in the crawlspace and suppress a shiver. My ears are pricked for the slightest sound of danger. For the music to stop. Boots stomping down the hallway over my head. The guards to shout that I've gone missing.

I have to wonder: Have I completely lost my mind? Once I reach the Twilight Garden, where will I go? All I can think is to run to the stables. Sneak an apple to one of the horses and beg it to help me.

The same plan that worked for my mother twenty-two years ago.

My heart clenches with a punishing wish to see Myst again. It's hard to believe my brave girl was once a carriage horse in this very castle's stable. She became so much more, first to my mother and then to me.

My best—my only—friend for years.

Until I met Basten.

My chest tightens with longing. Against all odds, we found each other at our lowest. Made our own fae tale come true. Only, the fae had nothing to do with it. It was our own doing—our messy, imperfect human love.

And I will not let Rian hurt him.

Somewhere across the seven kingdoms, there must be a godkissed healer who can mend fractured minds. Or a potion powerful enough to revive lost memories...

My nightdress snags on a nail, and I give it a sharp tug, but it holds fast.

Grimacing, I tug harder. The movement makes the boards creak beneath me. I can hear the party more clearly here, the sound of laughter filtering up from the floorboards.

What time is it? Midnight? The festivities will go on until dawn if I'm lucky. In my mind's eyes, I imagine dancing couples circling an altar dripping with riches that will only rot and waste away in a sleeping goddess's honor.

I pull harder on my nightdress, muttering a curse, but the fabric lodges deeper onto the nail.

"By the gods!" I kick my bare foot against the nearest joist, and as the fabric finally rips free, the joist creaks.

The boards beneath me buckle—

—and I don't have time to grab something to hold onto.

With one ear-splitting crack, the floorboards break.

The mouse was right that the crawlspace could fit a person's size.

But not weight.

Mouse-talker! The forest mouse sprints back toward me, tiny paw outstretched as though somehow she could stop the inevitable from happening.

It's too late.

I get one final glimpse at her black-bead eyes filled with fear before I feel the ground fall out from under me.

CHAPTER 15
BASTEN

"Fight back," a voice warns, "and it'll be a knife across your throat."

After dragging me across half of Old Coros, my attackers slam me into a chair and wrench my hands behind my back to secure with ropes. The oil-soaked, padded sack they've thrown over my head assaults my senses until my throat burns and my eyes water. I can't pick up on a single fucking smell beyond it. Can't see a damn thing. Can't hear much, either.

I shift in the chair as much as I can to try to pick up on clues—feeling with my boots for what type of floor is beneath me, rubbing my elbows on the armrests to detect the chair's style. Carved grooves would mean my abductors are wealthy, unsanded wood would mean bandits.

One of the attackers brushes against my left leg, and I use the opportunity to jam my knee straight up into his groin.

A muffled curse reaches my ears, and I smile darkly to myself before he smacks the back of my head.

With a sudden tug, the sack is pulled off my head.

"Fucking hell, Wolf!" the man behind me says. "I might want children one day!"

At first, the sting of light crashes over me. My senses are drowning, too many sights and sounds all at once. I'm in a house. Wait—scratch that. What *was* a house. The walls are covered in soot, and half the furniture is charred. The whole place reeks of smoke so gods-damn badly that I can barely pick up on the old scents of fresh-baked bread, rosewater, mint tea—what remains of a family that once lived here.

"Folke. *You bastard.*" I recognize his voice instantly and whip my head around, trying to see my so-called friend over my shoulder. "What the fuck is this?"

Folke moves to the front of the chair, cupping his balls with one hand as his face contorts with pain. He adjusts himself as he paces in front of the house's burned-out hearth. "You're a hard man to get alone. We had to jump you while you were away from the castle. Sorry about the sack. And the ropes. We knew you'd start swinging at the first shadow."

I lean forward as much as I can, my hair falling into my eyes as I try to process that my best friend doesn't seem to have kidnapped me for some hair-brained ransom attempt.

"You couldn't have sent a fucking *messenger?*"

"Not for this."

He adjusts his bruised balls once more as the second man comes around from the back of the chair. Before I lay eyes on him, my senses are already gathering information. The soft clink of a chainmail sash. A trace of cologne. Footsteps that move with grace.

"Kendan Valvere." I lean back in the chair, narrowing my eyes as he steps into my line of sight. Rian's eldest brother

155

has made an attempt at a disguise, dressed in a brown woolen cloak like Folke's, but his flawless skin, unmarred by malnutrition or pox, immediately clocks him as a nobleman. "You're behind this—this—what the hell *is* this, anyway?"

Kendan turns to Folke with a frown. "You're certain it's safe to free him?"

Folke pats the front of his pants. "He already did his damage."

Kendan reluctantly draws a knife and frees my bound arms. As the rope falls away, I massage my wrists, pausing over my left wrist guard. But they don't comment on the bandages.

"This," Folke announces to the burned-out husk of a house, "is a meeting that could get all three of us put in a nice deep grave."

A groan travels up the length of my throat. *Fantastic.* Exactly what I need right now, on top of a fae stealing my memories, dreams of a woman who haunts me each night, and a fancy new title that means I have to bathe regularly.

"Well?" I bark. "I'm waiting."

Folke looks to Kendan, who sweeps back his cloak so he can sit on a bench opposite me. His hazel-green eyes gleam. They're so like Rian's—and yet that is really the only similarity between them.

The cut of Kendan's jaw makes me feel as though I'm looking in a mirror, at a version of myself in a different life. A pampered life. A *well-fed* life. Kendan's hair is lighter than mine, his eyes hazel-green to my brown ones, but the resemblance between us as brothers is undeniable.

"Forgive the unorthodox greeting, Lord Basten." Kendan drags a hand over his square chin as though he, too, notes our resemblance. "I asked Folke to arrange this meeting on behalf of a small group of powerful individuals who bear deep concerns about the kingdom's future. Above all, given your news that Immortal Iyre is awake and the Third Return has begun."

"You're afraid of the fae?" I ask. "Good. You should be."

He smooths his hands together. "Not just the fae, but leadership in this kingdom that will have to go up against them. My brother is, shall we say, untested. That's the kindest word I can use in his favor; I assure you my associates use far viler words. If Rian is anything like our father, then he will only use his position as king to negotiate with the fae to further his own aims and bring ruin to the Astagnonian people."

Ah—so this is what's really going on. Kendan Valvere fancies himself a savior of the realm.

I want to snort in his face, but I begrudgingly have to consider the sizeable risks he's taking by questioning his brother's rule. He could be executed if caught.

I tip my face toward Folke. "And you agree with this?"

"I'm here, aren't I?" Folke holds out his hands.

"Rian suspects you're plotting against him." I watch carefully to see Kendan's reaction.

He shrugs, unbothered. "He's a Valvere. Everyone's plotting against him."

I rake my hair back. "Well, I can't argue against that. Lady Runa already suggested I murder Rian and marry her."

"Funny. She made me the same offer—except involving *your* death." Kendan leans closer, tenting his hands. "Lord Basten, I know the truth about your parentage. You are my full brother. You have Valvere blood in your veins. Which is a curse in itself—yet you were not raised in Lord Berolt's household. You were not taught to scheme and betray. For that reason, my associates and I have questioned whether you might be the superior ruler for this kingdom."

Oh, fuck.

"This isn't about putting *you* on the throne?" I bark.

"No." Kendan tips a long finger in my direction. "It's about putting you on it."

Treason? They're proposing gods-damn treason?

I whip my head around the burned-out house, looking for an old fire poker I can stab myself with. Because a quick death now would be vastly preferable to a lifetime in the dungeon.

Folke adds, "Of course, Rian won't give up the throne willingly. Even if we publicly reveal your true claim, there will be months of disputes. The only way forward is for Rian to suffer an...accident."

My blood goes cold.

Murder on top of treason would get a man flayed within an inch of his life, then drawn and quartered by plow horses, his ripped-apart body displayed on the four sides of the city walls.

I stare at Folke incredulously. "This is treason."

Kendan takes a deep breath. "Lord Basten—*brother*—the fact that you even care is why it is you who deserves the throne. Precisely because you do not want it. You do not see it as a path for your own enrichment. You do not enjoy political games. The political machine of greed and power hasn't ruined you."

I shoot him a stone-cold glare, but it's hiding a strange fire stoking to life in my chest. My throat bobs, but it does nothing to douse the feeling that maybe Kendan is onto something that I haven't wanted to admit.

By right, the throne should be mine—and by letting

another man sit upon it, am I shirking my responsibility? This kingdom is filled with so many boys like me, raised in the streets. Girls made to prostitute themselves or marry into misery. Am I turning my back on my former self, knowing I could have improved life for me?

Or am I unwavering in my loyalty?

I clear my throat and lean forward. "Listen closely."

Both men lean in.

I adjust my position in the chair, the wood groaning under my weight. Sweat drips from my brow, painting lines through the grime in my face.

In enunciated words, I say, "You were wrong before. Not everyone is plotting against Rian. *I'm* not. I don't give a fuck whose blood is in my veins. I made an oath. I swore to give up the throne to Rian, and my word matters." I shove to my feet, fists braced. "If you think I'm going to betray the man I owe everything to—"

"He sold her out." Kendan cuts me off sharply, eyes flashing.

A chill spreads through the room as I narrow my eyes. "What did you say?"

Silence slides between the three of us, the tension flowing as thick as water. Folke murmurs something under his breath as he digs around among a half-burned cabinet and pulls out an intact bottle of whiskey.

"At least let him have a drink first." Folke uncorks the bottle with his teeth and slides it to me across the table.

My body tense, I pick up the bottle and sniff. When I verify it isn't poison, I down half the bottle in one long glug before slamming it back down. "Now, let's try again. What *the hell* did you say?"

Kendan smooths a hand over his chainmail sash,

holding my gaze. "You made a deal with the Lord of Liars. Are you surprised he lied?"

"What do you *mean?*" I shove my empty chair over, tired of dancing around the point.

"One of my spies saw Rian meeting with a captain in King Rachillon's army." Kendan slowly slides the whiskey bottle to his side of the table. "Rian made a deal with Rachillon. And his bargaining chip was Lady Sabine Darrow's location."

I cock my head, not certain I can trust my ears. Maybe I breathed in so much lamp oil that my senses are confused. A bitter taste slides backward up my throat, and as my breathing grows quicker, I lean over and spit, "That's a fucking lie."

"Think about it." Kendan digs in his breast pocket as he drops his voice. "How else did King Rachillon know exactly where to send Immortal Iyre? Lord Basten, I have proof." He draws out a folded letter. "My spy recovered the letter that Rian sent by messenger crow to—"

I swipe the letter out of his hand, crumpling it before hurling it to the floor. "This is just another Valvere plot! Folke, you aren't seriously falling for this, are you?"

Folke swirls the whiskey bottle. "Read the letter, Wolf."

My feet are antsy. I can't stop pacing. My muscles twitch, begging for a fight. But there's a small, suspicious part of me. I drop down to pick up the letter.

It's dark, so my night vision switches on, the world going to shades of gray.

My hands begin to shake as I read. My *archer's* hands, which do not shake even if a wolf is bearing down upon me.

The handwriting is the same that I've seen for nearly

twenty years. It used to be the High Lord's signature. Now, it's the King's.

And it breaks me.

It breaks me into a million shards, all of which crash to the floor like the half-full whiskey bottle that I turn and hurl against the wall.

It breaks me until I'm nothing but ash—

—ash and *anger*.

CHAPTER 16
SABINE

I'm *falling.*

As I pinwheel my arms, my heart slams into my throat, lodging like a splinter. Cool air rushes past. I can't think. Can't breathe.

Then—impact.

My back hits hard, so hard I see stars. Broken boards crash into me. Pain shoots down every limb, and I gasp, clutching my ribs. My vision smears into swirling shades of gold and silver overhead, soft fabric beneath me, gleaming cutlery askew around me.

There's something wet on my cheek—blood?

I jerk, touching my face, looking at my fingers.

No, wait...it has...seeds?

Raspberry jam.

I blink hard, trying to piece together the chaos. I'm in the Hall of Vale. Lying in the middle of the banquet table. Wine soaks through my shift's hem, and a spilled tureen near my waist drips gravy onto an overturned boar flank. Above me, chandeliers sway, their dangling strings of black pearls catching the light, casting eerie shadows across the room.

Everything *aches*.

I force myself onto an elbow as I try to pull in air. Abruptly, the music stops, replaced by a tidal wave of disjointed chatter from hundreds of partygoers.

Squinting, I peer upward. The ceiling above me is shattered. Ashes and dust rain down like feathers, covering the table in a fine layer of filth.

Dimly, I realize: *I fell through the ceiling onto the head banquet table.*

Faces peer down from all directions. They're strange faces. Familiar but not, like peering at a warped painting.

Then comes the scrape of a heavy chair.

A brilliant blue glow blinds me. I wince, shielding my eyes with a trembling hand as the light moves closer, casting bright lines like rippling water over the wrecked feast. I know that particular kind of light—it only comes from fey lines.

I part my lips, trying to speak Iyre's name—

But it isn't Iyre towering over me.

Iyre sits near my feet.

The face staring down at me, looming from the pushed-back chair, is both King Rachillon's and not.

My *father's*...and not.

While the aquiline nose and heavy brow are the same, the grey in his beard gleams like quicksilver. There's a vibrancy to him now that shines as brightly as molten gold fresh from the forge. Through his slightly parted lips, I can make out sharp incisors.

No.

This can't be right. This can't be happening.

My heart skips painfully in my chest. I try to push myself up, but my body is numb. I'm still sprawled among the wreckage, surrounded by four strange faces around the head table, whose supper I ruined. Their eyes lock onto me, piercing and dangerous.

My father.

Iyre.

Ghost.

Whisper.

They're fae—they're *all* fae.

Ghost leans in to trace his finger through the raspberry jam smeared on my cheek. He licks it off, slow, deliberate, his lips curling into a grin as his pointed incisors flash. "Well, well, Lady Sabine. Dropping in unannounced, are we? Had we known you'd make such an entrance, we'd have kept our glamours on. But I suppose the secret's out now, isn't it?"

I. Can't. Breathe.

Panic sets in as all eyes within the Hall of Vale gaze down at me, splayed among the buffet fare, as though I'm the most delectable item on the menu.

I might not have landed on the altar, but I feel like an offering just the same.

CHAPTER 17
BASTEN

When people ask why I'm loyal to the Lord of Liars, I tell them about Beauty.

Beauty was Lord Berolt's prized hunting dog, a russet bloodhound of unbelievable swiftness with a nose that rivaled my own. If a fox was within ten miles, Beauty would corner it before the other dogs even caught its scent. Back then, when I was a gawky-eared lad of fifteen, I'd silently accompany the riding party as the Whip, tasked with rounding up the stray dogs and herding them back into the pack.

Once, a dog latched onto the wrong scent—a rabbit carcass—and led me far from the main hunting party. While I was tracking it, I picked up on voices ahead, as well as the sound of Beauty's pained whines.

Stopping my horse, I listened in on Lord Berolt speaking to the hunt master and Rian in the distance.

"*She's our strongest hound, Father,*" Rian argued, his teeth grinding so hard in his jaw that I could hear it from nearly half a mile away.

"*Which is precisely why you must do it*," Berolt ordered. "*The hunt is meant to make bumbling nobles feel as skilled at archery as Immortal Artain himself. Beauty is too good. She traps the fox before those dolts can even pull their fat asses into a saddle. She makes them look like fools.*"

Beauty's whines clawed against my ears—they must have tightly leashed her.

I waited to see what Rian would do. If he would heed his father's advice and slaughter the only competent dog of the pack to make some rich idiots feel better—or if he would spare Beauty.

"*Go, Beauty! Run!*" Rian yelled.

The forest filled with the sound of Beauty fleeing through the undergrowth with her leash trailing behind her.

"*You disobedient fool.*" The sound of a sharp smack echoed through the woods.

"*Fool?*" Rian seethed. "*Fools kill their best subjects to spite the stupidest.*"

After that incident, Rian was locked in his room for three weeks with only water, and when he was finally released, he'd lost thirty pounds—but not his cold, defiant smile.

That is the Rian I know, I would tell people.

Today, though?

Today, we aren't youths scrabbling over hunting dogs. Today, Rian sits on a throne that, by all rights, should be mine. The power he wields exceeds what Lord Berolt could have ever dreamed. If Rian wanted, he could better this kingdom. Keep the fae gods at bay. Hell, maybe even improve life for the common folk.

But Rian isn't still that boy who would defend the defenseless.

And I'm going to fucking *end* him.

After leaving Folke and Kendan, I head straight from the burned-out house to Hekkelveld Castle.

To Rian's floor.

When I kick open Rian's bedroom door, his decades of military training have him shooting up in bed, ready for a fight.

As soon as he sees it's me, he yawns and squints at the window. "Fucking gods, Wolf. It isn't even dawn."

He must not notice that his two bodyguards are slumped in the hall, bruises forming on their unconscious temples, swords lying as useless as broomsticks on the stone floor.

He scrubs a hand over his sleepy face. "Why the hell are you—"

I take a few powerful strides into his bedroom and cut him off with a hand around his throat. His thick eyelashes raise until I can see the whites of his eyes.

He tugs on my hand and garbles, trying to pry my fingers off.

"You. Sold. Her. Out." Each word is a swift strike, foreshadowing the dark urge to drive my blade into him until his sheets run red. Leaning in until our noses nearly brush, I seethe, "You told King Rachillon where to find Sabine Darrow."

His fingers freeze. For a second, the perfect still of his early-morning bedroom is broken only by both our heaving breaths, and then he lands a sharp kick right to my solar plexus.

It knocks the air out of me, and I stagger back, clutching my side. In a way, I wanted this. I welcomed it. Because I deserve it for even doubting the woman who haunts my dreams.

I thought *she* could be a traitor?

It's been him.

Rian, all along.

Straightening, I roll out my neck, muscles flexing in anticipation like a shark who's smelled blood in the water.

"Are you going to deny it?" I snap.

Rian swings out of bed, his bare torso rippling with the muscles hard-won from a lifetime of training as he massages his throat.

His eyes waver before hardening. "No."

"Then why?" I explode, barely able to restrain my fever-pitch temper. "Why cut a deal with a foreign bastard who wants to wake the gods?"

He grips one of the bedposts, pinching the bridge of his nose. "Beneveto was going to be named king. The Council had already determined it. I needed Rachillon to call off his lap dog."

"You sold her out for a fucking crown?" Before I can stop myself, I lunge at him. My fist flies toward his chin, but he manages to dodge it and slam his shoulder into my chest.

He's half-naked and groggy, but I'm still drunk on whisky and weak from being tied to a fucking chair—neither of us is anywhere near our sharpest.

With a growl, I loop my arm around his neck from behind and choke him. He snakes his ankle behind mine and sweeps my foot out from under me, sending us both crashing to the floor.

My knee connects with bare stone, but the crack of pain is so dulled by rage that I hardly feel anything.

I grab his calf and drag him across the rug until I can wrestle him in a bear hug from behind with his chest pinned to the floor.

"Don't pretend to know my motives!" he shouts, head contorted to try to spit at me.

With my full weight pinning him to the rug, he can't get free no matter how he struggles. "You never loved her!"

"What about you?" he counters, writhing under me like a snake. "You have no memory of her! Why the *fuck* do you care about a *stranger*?"

I slam his head to the ground. "Did you know Iyre would take my memory? Was that your idea?"

"Get the fuck off me!" He gets one hand free and grabs for an iron boot scrape, which he smashes against my temple before I can dodge the blow. Pain ricochets across my skull, and I stagger off him as I clutch the bleeding wound.

Rian scrambles across the floor to his desk, where he grabs the knife he keeps strapped underneath it.

He shoves himself to his feet.

His bare chest is slick with sweat, gleaming in the early dawn light.

Clutching the knife, he shouts, "It's where she belongs, Wolf! Hate me if you want, but if you think about it for one gods-damn second, you'll see that I'm right. Sabine stood out here like a swan among pigeons. *This isn't her home.* Her family is Volkish. Her people are Volkish. She has powers that run as deep as the earth's core, deeper even than she realizes, and you and I both know it. Do you think she'd be content for one day at my side, ruling the kingdom that's at war with her homeland? Or at *your* side, playing house with field mice while her people are slaughtered north of the wall?"

Maybe it's the blood loss, but I stagger back until I can catch myself against his bedpost.

I drag in a few strained breaths. Truth be told, I can barely process what he's saying. If it is right or wrong, sensible or folly.

I spit, "Don't pretend for a minute that you did this for her."

He tips his chin up, breathing as hard as me. "No. I did it for me. But I would never do anything that would hurt her —I swear that to you."

"You swear? As if your word means *shit*?" All I can see is a red wash of anger. "Rachillon is a madman!"

"And I am the Lord of Liars!" he explodes. "Do you think there has been a single monarch across the seven kingdoms, over three millennia, that has ruled like a fucking saint? Grand Cleric Beneveto is supposed to shepherd this kingdom's souls, and he sold them out. Hell, even old Joruun had his vices. Sabine stands a better chance of thriving there than she ever did here!"

I crack my knuckles, seething. "Tell yourself that one more time, and maybe you'll believe it."

Rian slams the knife hilt on the table. "You fucked her *in front of* me, Wolf!"

A moment of silence stretches to let his shout echo.

"That's what this is really about, isn't it?" I stalk forward. "She and I loved one another, when you wanted both of our love for yourself!"

He throws his hands sarcastically in the air. "Oh, what, have you magically recovered your memories? Did you find one of Iyre's fae bottles? You suddenly remember your love for her?"

I flinch. It's salt in a fresh wound.

In as steady a voice as I can manage, I say, "I may not

remember her face or the sound of her voice, but I know what happened. That she and I were in love. I dream about her, and even if the dreams are gone at first light, my heart remembers. So, I'm going to do whatever it takes to get her back. Her *and* my memories. If that means strangling Iyre, all the better. If it means strangling *you*, well, I'm not opposed to that, either."

Rian stares at me as though I've slapped the sarcasm out of him. His mask is gone now—his face is splotchy and flushed, his eyes wavering with a rare vulnerability.

His breath is ragged as it pushes out of his throat.

His brown eyes meet mine and don't look away—for what feels like years, we stare at one another as if seeing who we've become for the first time since meeting over twenty years ago.

He leans over and spits out a line of blood. "I wanted the crown. I wanted to hurt you. But do not *ever* say that I didn't love her."

I take my time stalking across the blood droplets on the floor, over the wrinkled rug, and past his twisted bed sheets until our chests are an inch apart.

I haven't forgotten about the knife clutched in his fist. Or that, at any second, more bodyguards will come charging down the hall to drag me to the gallows.

It's just that some things are more important than danger.

I rip the First Sword brooch off my shirt and drop it at his feet. The sound of it hitting the ground feels final, like a door slamming shut.

"Keep your throne," I growl. "I was a fool to follow you. To believe in you. I should have known right away. Should have seen it—the lies, the manipulations, all of it. I cared about you. And for what? You played me like you do everyone."

He adjusts his grip on the knife, biting back his words. "Wolf—"

"Basten, gods dammit! My name is Basten! I was stupid to think you ever gave a damn about anyone but yourself. But I see it now. You don't deserve loyalty. Gods, it's so clear. My dreams were trying to tell me the truth, but I wasn't listening. I am now. I'm getting my woman—she *is* mine, whether I remember or not—and the only reason I'm not ripping your heart out is because I'm saving that pleasure for her."

My shoulder knocks hard against his as I turn, shoving him back an inch onto his gilded desk, causing his priceless set of quills to clatter to the floor.

By the time the last one falls, I'm already storming out the doorway, stepping over the unconscious bodyguards.

As I make my way through Hekkelveld Castle's tortuous hallways, I'm barely aware of anything except for the sound of my own throttled heart. I take the Faith Tower hallway stairs up a floor to the Valvere family members' quarters.

The bodyguard stationed there glances at me, vexed, but he doesn't dare cross the First Sword.

"Lord Basten." He bows.

"Open her fucking door," I order.

The guard's throat bobs as he quickly turns the handle, looking away tactfully in case he should catch a glimpse of his mistress in early morning disarray.

At the sound of the door opening, Lady Runa shoots up in bed, her hand darting to the knife she keeps beneath her pillow.

She might be a coddled noblewoman who hasn't once

emptied her own chamber pot, but she's still a Valvere. And they all sleep with knives.

"Wolf." Her body softens when I step into the low light and nudge the door closed with my heel.

It's too dark for her to see the blood on my temple. All she sees is a beast of a man supposedly risking everything to enter her bedroom. Mistaking my intentions, she drags a hand along her low neckline, her breath growing shallow as her pupils dilate.

"Wolf, I knew you would come—"

She slinks out of the silk sheets and makes as if to touch my face, but I grab her wrist in the shackle of one hand and slap my other one over her mouth.

"Listen closely, you Valvere bitch. If you scream, I'll strangle you until you'll never make another sound. The locket. Point to where it is."

Her mouth is damp against my palm, her pulse rushing through her veins in a mix of fear and sick arousal. For fuck's sake. This is turning her *on*.

I wrench her arm harder behind her back. She moans breathily against my palm, and I roll my eyes. I wrench harder, and her moan finally turns to one of pain.

She uses her free hand to point to the wardrobe.

I drag her over and throw open the door. It's filled with the usual silk gowns and lacy underclothes. Her finger flails toward the top drawer. I pull it open so hard it falls out, spilling priceless jewels all over the floor.

I nudge through the pieces with my boot until I see a locket engraved with an S.

I snatch it up, wrenching it open.

And freeze.

It's not just a beautiful face staring back at me—though,

damn, she makes the fae goddesses look like heifers. It's the defiance in her eyes. Sea-blue eyes. Eyes that snag me like a fishing lure and reel me in, stranger or no.

My breath hitches, and an intense warmth spreads from my fingertips to my chest. It's maddening, this unearthly pull. I don't recognize a single curve of this face, yet I feel bound to her in a way that's beyond logic.

She lives in more than memories.

Yes. Yes, she does.

I close my fist around the locket, then release Runa with a shove toward her bed. She catches herself on the mattress, looking back over her shoulder with pupils completely blown. Slowly, she runs her tongue over her lips where my handprint still marks her face.

"Wolf Bowborn. If you fight like that, you must fuck like a god."

My jaw clamps so hard that my molars ache. As much as I want to shove this vile woman out the four-story window, I force myself to the door instead.

"The gods will be here to fuck us all over soon enough," I growl as I leave.

CHAPTER 18
SABINE

*M*y father is a fae.

Ghost and Whisper too.

The thoughts are so mind-shattering that it's all I can do to keep breathing. I'm splayed out on the Hall of Vale's banquet table, broken ceiling debris scattered around me, like some grotesque dessert waiting to be served.

All around, dozens of partygoers stare in bald-face shock. They're human. That's something—at least I'm not the only one. I spot Grand Cleric Beneveto in the crowd. Captain Tatarin, too. None of them seem surprised by the fae seated around the table.

I'm the only one.

I'm the only one who didn't know.

"*Tsk tsk.* What a mess you've made of the feast in Thracia's honor. If she were here, she'd be livid."

I flinch as Whisper's voice cuts through the air, his wicked smile curling as he plucks a fallen grape from its tray. As he pops it in his mouth, his chocolate-brown lips glow faintly at the edges, connected to fey lines running across his face's contours like crushed glowworms.

"You're—you're Immortal Samaur." The words slip out, my breath catching at his terrible, ethereal beauty.

The certainty crashes over me. Whisper is the God of Day. Our convent's copy of The Book of the Immortals showed Samaur as a white man with auburn hair, but that was an artist's guess. No one has actually laid eyes on him in a thousand years.

Regardless of his appearance, there's no denying his identity. The burnish on his dark skin is warm as sunbaked soil, and his blazing irises are the exact color and intensity of midday sun, so much so that I have to shade my face. Above all, there's his defense of Immortal Thracia. Goddess of Night. His other half.

"And here we were feeling sorry for you for feeling unwell." The man—no, *fae*—I knew as Ghost casually sips from a silver chalice. Long, white-blond hair falls around his perfect face, somehow even more beautiful now in its full fae glory. His eyes are the vibrant green of new-growth hemlock, flashing impishly beneath eyebrows that slope upward as sharp as a bow's point. The tops of his ears rise at a sharp angle, decorated with a small pewter arrow piercing through his ear's shell.

If his arrogant sneer didn't give away his identity, the arrow piercing would.

"You're Immortal Artain," I murmur, the words like ash in my mouth. *God of the Hunt.*

When he lowers the chalice, a drop of blood stains his lips. Fear cramps my stomach.

Blood—like Iyre drinks.

"Guilty," he says as he teasingly bites his pointed

incisors against his bottom lip. "Does this change your mind about spending a night together? One night with a fae, and you'll never be satisfied with a human lover again."

I shove up to a seated position, knee knocking a boar flank off the table. The smell of roasted meat and sticky-sweet raspberry jam makes my stomach seize, and I dig the heel of my hand against my nightdress.

Even corsetless, I can't seem to breathe. Panic sets in. My vision starts to blur.

Run.

Instinct takes over, and I follow the boar flank off the table, rolling unsteadily to a stand, my limbs still so clumsy from the fall that I have to brace myself against the table's edge.

I glance over my shoulder at the doors.

Open. Unguarded.

"Sabine." King Rachillon—no, not a king, at least not of humans—holds out his hand as though sensing I'm about to bolt for the door. His anatomical heart brooch catches the light, blinds me. "Breathe. Just breathe."

The air is tense as poison gas. So many bated breaths waiting to see what I'll do. I feel like one spark could ignite the entire ballroom into a fireball.

"I told you she wasn't ready for the truth," Iyre hums from her seat at the end of the table, barely glancing up from her meal. She plucks a glazed carrot from her plate and blows off the ashes, unconcerned by the wreckage I caused.

Captain Tatarin, dressed in linen trousers and a silken doublet, suddenly rushes up from the crowd to take my wrist's pulse. Her lips move, but it's like I hear her words through water.

"Highness? You're okay. Hold on—let me see if you're hurt."

I barely register her presence as she checks for injuries. Her hands feel miles away. My mind spins.

Whisper is Samaur.

Ghost is Artain.

And my father isn't just fae. He's *Immortal Vale*—King of Fae.

I can't deny it. The broad shoulders, the wild hair the color of honey, the quicksilver beard. It's all there, this time exactly like the illustrations from the Book of the Immortals. But seeing him like this—not wearing King Rachillon's delicate crown, but the heavy Battle Helm Crown from legend, forged of dark iron to resemble ancient Golathian war helmets—is too much. The weight of this truth presses down on me, crushing my lungs.

My vision begins to go dark around the edges.

"Breathe, Sabine," Vale urges again, his eyes locking onto mine. His tone is gentle, but there's an edge beneath it, something ancient and dark.

Breathe?

I'm not sure I can even blink.

My foot moves a fraction toward the door. Vale's expression darkens as his gaze flicks to Artain. The God of the Hunt snaps into motion like an arrow loosed from a bowstring.

Artain grabs a rope of strung pearls dangling from the chandelier, looping it into a lasso.

Finally, my body screams.

Run, now!

Bolting, I tear across the stone floor, bare feet slipping on the high polish. Members of the court shriek as I narrowly avoid barreling into them.

I hear the slow, confident thud of Artain's steps behind me but don't dare risk the time to look back.

"Clear the hall!" My father slams his fist against the banquet table, and the crowd immediately disperses to the room's edges.

I'm left alone. Exposed. Heart racing, I pump my arms as I sprint toward the exit.

The double doors are open. If I can make it to the stables, to a horse—

As I rush through the doors, I suddenly slam into a wall of rigid muscle dressed in a black leather doublet. Black gloves grip me by the shoulders to steady me, and in a daze, I tilt my head up to find myself face-to-face with Night.

The stoic third member of the Blades wears his dark hair loose today, hanging over his mist-colored, clouded eyes. His deathly pale face tips in my direction with a perplexed tilt.

"Lady Sabine?" His voice ripples like velvet. "What has happened?"

When I see that Night is human—rounded ears, skin unbroken by fey lines—a cry of relief breaks past my lips as I collapse into his hold, tears rolling down my cheeks.

Night places a protective hand on the small of my back as I bury my face against his broad chest. He pets my hair in slow, comforting strokes as his other hand gently loops around one of my wrists.

I'm no fool—I know that Night works for my father. He's a Blade, so he must know Ghost and Whisper's true identity. But feeling a human's protective touch makes me forget, if only for a moment, the crushing danger around me.

"Night." My breath condenses on the supple leather of his doublet. "Help me. *Please.*"

The rest of the Hall of Vale fades away. Here, in his arms, I feel sheltered from the storm. His warmth seeps into my bones, dissolving the chill that seems to have overtaken every inch of the room.

He tips my chin up with one gloved hand until I face him. He takes his time running his knuckle slowly over my cheek, his sculpted lips parting.

"Such a pretty soul," he murmurs. "One day, it will be mine."

There's something about his voice that forms a noose around my neck.

Oh. My heart beats off-kilter. *Oh, gods. No.*

I try to pull back from Night, but his grip on my wrist is a vice.

"You're—" I start, too awe-struck to finish. "You're—"

Night shoves me back into the Hall of Vale like a rag doll. My footsteps echo amid the rafters. The dance floor is empty now. Wide open. I stagger into the center, all alone. My bare feet leave damp prints as I turn in a slow circle.

"She's all yours, brother," Night says darkly to Vale.

That word. *Brother.*

Night rolls back his shoulders as fey lines break out along his skin. His ears and eyebrows lengthen. His skin pales to the pallor of death beneath locks as dark as crow feathers. This already devastatingly attractive man becomes more beautiful than anything I have ever laid eyes on.

A terrifying beauty—the beauty of the End.

"You're Immortal Woudix. The Ender. God of Death," I breathe between trembling lips.

His hound, Hawk, sidles up to him. Now, her glamour is dropped, too, and it's painfully clear why I can't communicate with her. Her flesh is patchy. Rotting. A portion of her cheek is missing to show her teeth.

She's dead.

My stomach clenches. A pain seizes my heart, squeezing out every drop of blood until I feel as spent as a candle stub. Any minute, my legs might give out. I feel my mind and body shutting down. Unable to process...this.

But *there.*

The tall, arched window at the front of the hall is open. Gasping, I take a step toward it.

Heavy footsteps approach me from behind as Artain murmurs, "Go ahead, Highness. Try to run. I like to play with my quarry before I catch it."

"*Artain!*" My father's booming voice reverberates like a bell strike. "Lady Sabine is a princess of this realm. Not some plaything for you to toy with!"

Artain's grin falters.

Panic seizes me. Dots form at the edges of my vision as if, at any moment, I'll faint.

I dart to my left, trying to find a gap in the crowd, but am blocked by Immortal Samaur. Heart racing, I double-back toward the right, but Immortal Woudix and his hound have moved to fill that place. I take a step forward, but Artain blocks me.

The only fae not hemming me in is Iyre, who continues to munch on roasted carrots disinterestedly.

Darkness roars louder around the edges of my vision.

Desperate, I sprint to the open window and pull myself onto the stone ledge. A draft of wind blusters up from the valley below.

I dare to look down.

It doesn't matter that the Hall of Vale is on the castle's

ground floor, because all of Drahallen Hall rests on a high promontory over the Ramvik River. The fall is thirty feet straight onto jagged river rocks.

Below, low-flying falcons glide in concentric circles between me and the river.

The partygoers immediately fall silent, holding their communal breath as I inch my foot backward toward the drop.

The smug grin on Artain's face vanishes.

My father's urgent rasp breaks the silence. "Sabine— don't. Think about what you are considering. You are human. You cannot return from a fall like that."

"Return?" My chest heaves as I look down at the falcons. A pair of eagles and a giant hawk have joined them, drawn to my need. "Return to *what*? A father who lied to me? A court full of deceitful gods?"

My father takes a slow, cautious step forward. "We were waiting to reveal the truth until you were ready to accept it."

All the fancy parties. All the riches. All the smiling servants. *All a ploy to win me to their side before they broke my world.*

But *I'm* the only one who decides my fate.

As gasps ring out through the crowd, I slide my foot back another inch, dropping my gaze to the river, counting the number of birds circling below, debating if I'll fall—or if I'm strong enough to fly.

CHAPTER 19
BASTEN

Dawn rises beyond the white limestone windowsills of Hekkelveld Castle as I stride down the hall after leaving the man I once called "master" broken and bleeding on his bedroom floor.

The locket with Sabine's portrait is clutched so tightly in my fist my knuckles are white. I shove it into my pocket, where it clinks against a coin.

I pause, taking out the Golath dime that Rian gave me when I became First Sword. For a moment, I run the pad of my thumb over it, thinking of happier times.

But then, someone shouts.

Within, oh, two seconds...the entire castle is in chaos.

Bodyguards thunder down hallways in a search for me, but it's almost laughably easy to avoid them. I hear their footsteps from halfway across the castle as they crash up stairs and race down hallways with swords drawn, ready to separate my head from my shoulders.

But they'll have to catch me first.

As a set of four guards descend from Wisdom Tower,

where they ransacked my room, I pull back into a spare guest bedroom. They tromp by me like clattering tin cans in their armor. Once they've passed, I slip out in the opposite direction to the senior servants' quarters on the fifth floor.

When I rap my knuckles against the last door on the left, I hear the sheets rustling inside as someone groggily flails his hand against the slumbering person beside him.

A male voice says, "*If you get it, my radiant jewel, I'll bury my face between your knees for a full hour tonight.*"

"*Oh, please,*" a woman's voice groans, "*I'd be bored after five minutes.*"

After a long-suffering sigh and the rustle of a dressing gown, the door is swept open, and a surprised face takes in the bloody mess that is *me*.

Ferra's face is scrubbed of makeup, and for once, her long hair is her natural ash-brown shade. I've grown so used to seeing her use her godkiss to give herself lilac locks or electric coral lips that I blink hard, startled by how young she really is.

I tip my head carefully, all too aware that massive blood loss from a head wound won't end well. "Lady Ferra."

Her initial surprise quickly gives way to feminine annoyance as she folds her silk-clad arms across her chest, her nails flashing like talons as she drums them against her upper arms.

"Wolf Bowborn? What are you doing here? All I need, the second man within a minute to prove he's utterly useless without a woman." She sighs as she looks over her shoulder at the lump on the other side of her bed.

Folke has the sharp instincts of a soldier, but after our night in the burned-out house, he apparently also gained the thirst of a drunk. The smells of booze and sex roll off him, but at least it's only Ferra's scent on his cock, and not some stranger's from the brothel.

"Folke, I believe this dolt is here for you." Ferra tosses a pillow onto the lump, and Folke grumbles from an impending hangover.

"Actually—" I snatch a satin scarf that's drooped over a nearby chair and use it to mop up the blood streaking down the right side of my face, "—I might need you, too, Ferra."

Outside, the Valor Bell begins clanging a relentless alarm. I wince. "It's, ah, urgent."

"Oh, you stupid man." She puffs out a blast of air. "What have you done?"

"Probably best if you don't know."

The alarm bell makes Folke shoot upright with both hands clamped against his ears. "Gods in hell, it feels like that bell is clattering inside my skull!"

Guards' boots sound one floor below, headed for the stairs, and I clench my jaw and push into Ferra's room, ripping the sheet off Folke's half-naked body. "Up. Now. I need to be out of this castle *yesterday*."

His hands fall away from his ears, and when he sees the look on my face that says I'm serious, he miraculously sobers up. Suddenly sharp, he swings his feet onto the floor. "Ferra, close the door."

She doesn't hesitate, and shoves a chairback under the knob for good measure.

"Get dressed, my jewel." Folke throws her a gown from her wardrobe, then finds his shirt hanging over the bedrail and tugs it over his head. Footsteps clatter up the nearby stairs loud enough for him to grimace.

"I guess there's no going out that way," he murmurs.

He throws open the single window, looks down, then

pulls a coil of rope out from under the bed. One end is already secured in a bowline knot to the nearest of the bed's heavy oak legs.

"You had an escape system at the ready in Ferra's room?" I ask.

He snorts as he shoves me toward the window. "I've spent enough time in the Sin Streets to know that these regal hallways are just as deadly—and no woman of mine is going to be a sitting duck."

Ferra scoffs as her fingers fly to put the dress over her shoulders. "I am no one's duck."

"Shut your quackery, my jewel," he argues as he spins her around to do up the buttons on her gown's back. "We can argue when we're twenty miles from here, alive and eating plum cakes. Now, quick. You first, Wolf. Then Ferra. I'll follow up behind."

I grip the rope and throw one leg out the window. I have to fold myself into a knot to fit through the narrow wooden frame, but I manage, and then scale down Wisdom Tower, bracing my feet against the limestone bricks.

Ferra descends next, complaining loudly as she fumbles down the rope until she's close enough that I can hoist her the rest of the way to the ground.

Folke crashes down the last six feet, still reeking of booze, but quickly recovers. He tosses his tangled hair off his face as he scans the oleander shrubs clustered around the headstones of the Reliquary Garden. "Where to now, you troublesome bastard?"

I jerk my chin toward Mercy Tower. "The stables."

The three of us make our way among the marble mausoleums of Astagnon's fallen kings. I listen keenly for the guards' movements and instruct Folke and Ferra when to pause and when to run. We reach a low stone wall that runs along the side of the stables and drop into a crouch.

"We need to draw the guards away from the stables," I say quietly.

"Drama? That's my specialty." Ferra's violet eyes practically glow as she taps one long fingernail against my chest. "I have an idea. Come with me, boys."

A row of tombstones stretches the length of the Reliquary Garden, lined up like dominoes waiting to fall. Without a word, Ferra presses her shoulder against the first stone. As it teeters, I begin to understand.

"Ferra, you aren't going to—" I start.

"Not on my own, I'm not. Help me!"

Folke and I join her and lean hard against the tombstone. The heavy granite stone totters slightly before finally crashing over onto the next one. Like a row of children's blocks, the headstones knock one another over all the way from the front gate to the castle wall.

Each tombstone crashes down with a ground-shaking thud that I feel down to my marrow.

Ferra claps excitedly. "That should do it!"

The stable guards shout at the sound and run to investigate.

Once the stable door is clear, the three of us make our way in a crouch along the stone wall, then duck inside. The cool, clean smell of straw replaces the stench of sweat and blood that clings to me.

I plunge my hand into my pocket to reassure myself of the locket with Sabine's portrait. My chest softens as my fingers glide over the smooth gold surface. All I want in this cursed world is to open it to see her perfect face again, but I have to wait.

It's torture.

It's a thrill.

Is this even actually happening? Are my dreams going to become real? The idea that I might hold Sabine Darrow in my arms fills me with such breathtaking awe that I have to clear my throat.

Ferra glances back at me, concern etched in her eyes. "Basten? Are you okay?"

"Yeah." My voice comes out rough, so I clear my throat and try again, my gaze scanning the horse names chalked on each stall door. "It's this one."

Folke and Ferra fall in step behind me as I unlatch Myst's stall door.

"Easy there, girl." Even though time is of the essence, my voice drops to a low murmur as I slowly run a hand along Myst's neck, fingers brushing over the spots rubbed raw by the carriage harness. Anger surges through me, hot and bitter, that a creature as powerful—and as stubborn—was ever reduced to pulling Rian's carriage.

"You remember me, right?" I murmur. "The poor bastard you tried to trample? We're getting out of this place to find Sabine."

She tosses her head, eyes wide as if to say, *You finally came to your senses!*

The Valor Bell continues to clang the alarm as my ears pick up the creaking wheels of army wagons rolling in with extra soldiers from Old Coros.

I quickly saddle Myst, working fast now that we're about to have company, but as I slide one foot in a stirrup to mount, she rears up. Prances her feet. Tosses her head.

I hold up my hands. "Whoa. Easy, girl. What is it?"

Satisfied she has my attention, she jerks her muzzle toward the far end of the stable.

A chill creeps over the back of my neck. There, in the shadows of what was once a tack room, rests the iron cage that houses Tòrr.

My stomach tightens.

"Crazy mare..." But I rub my hand over my chin, thinking. Half a dozen heavy locks are fixed to a chain spanning the cage door's handles. The iron material blocks my sense of smell, but I can hear steady breathing inside.

"Wolf?" Folke pitches a hay biscuit at my head. "Time to *go*."

Ignoring him, I take a slow step toward the cage.

"Wolf?" Ferra hisses. "What are you looking at? Wait. *No*. Have you lost your mind?" This time, she's the one who throws a hay biscuit.

I dodge it, wetting my lips as I straighten. Slowly, I quote Rian: "When going to war, it's wise to take one's most powerful weapon."

Ferra throws her hand toward one of the stable's high windows. "It's daylight! You open that cage, and Tòrr could snuff us out like ants under a magnifying glass!"

My heart kicks up with a warning. *She isn't wrong.*

"Myst will manage him." I smooth my hand over her leather saddle. "I've seen her calm his temper a hundred times. She wants Sabine back as much as I do, and she'll make sure Tòrr cooperates. Besides, how else will I get Sabine away from King Rachillon? Or my memories back from Iyre? I *need* a weapon."

"It's a big fucking gamble to think you can tame a monoceros, my friend," Folke croaks.

More footsteps cross through the Reliquary Garden. I'm

out of time. I have only a second of hesitation before I set my shoulder beneath the wooden beam to hoist it up. Groaning under its weight, I free it from the braces and toss it to the ground.

"I suddenly find myself a gambling man." I grab the first padlock, rattling it slightly. "Folke?"

"Wait. You want *me* to free the monster?"

"You can pick locks like you're godkissed."

Folke balks, rattling off curses, but I can see the spark in his eyes that draws him to the challenge. Finally, he waves me out of the way. "I need some space. And...this."

He plucks the knife from my hip holster with a pickpocket's grace. As I retreat to give him room, he sets the blade's point into the keyhole. Gnawing on the inside of his cheek, he angles the blade until the lock springs free.

"Ha! See that? We mere mortals can work miracles, too."

Ferra throws glances toward the end of the barn, keeping a lookout, while Folke picks the second lock.

"It's almost too easy," he scoffs.

He swiftly picks the third and the fourth locks. The fifth gives him some trouble, but he smacks the hilt of my knife against the side, and it springs free.

Only one left.

I focus all my senses on the ground, feeling for the vibrations of footsteps headed our way. From the growing rumble, it seems as though at least twenty soldiers are headed for the stable.

"Folke, hurry," I mutter.

"And...you're welcome!" Folke stands back triumphantly with the final lock in hand, bowing like an actor before an adoring audience.

"Congratulations," I say flatly. "Now move aside." I

immediately begin unraveling the chain from between the door handles, though Folke rests a hand on mine.

He asks quietly, "Are you truly sure about this, old friend?"

A muscle jumps in my jaw. Am I? Setting free an ancient fae creature with the power to level an entire city is not a move to take lightly. I've heard the servants recount the tale of Sabine triumphantly riding the beast in Duren's arena, though there's only a blank in my mind where that memory should be.

Rian and Kendan both believed that because she discovered its name, anyone could harness its power. But they're naive.

I'm not Sabine Darrow.

I can't speak to Tòrr.

Hell, I can't even speak to *Myst* to tell Tòrr to get his preening ass in gear. For all I know, the second I throw open his iron door, Tòrr will roast me like a sausage.

Sweat trickles down my face, but I tighten my fist on the door handle.

"Stand back."

It's all the warning I give before throwing open the monoceros cage. Folke raises his hand as though to shelter himself. At first, nothing emerges from the darkness inside, but then, my eyes switch to night vision, and I see a burst of steam. A cool fog rolls out of the monoceros cage, winding around my ankles.

Folke jumps back, touching his breastbone in prayer to the gods he doesn't believe in. "Shall I start digging our graves now, or later?"

Hoofbeats paw at the cage's iron floor.

Another burst of steam shoots out of the box.

A shriek like twisting metal pierces the shadows.

Myst, quiet until now, stamps her foot as if to say, *Stop being dramatic!*

One final, smaller burst of steam puffs out, and then Tòrr ducks his head to emerge from the iron cage.

I retreat a step, muscles tense and at the ready, before realizing Folke still holds my hunting knife. I snatch it out of his hand. But as Tòrr steps into the stable to raise his head to its full height, his solarium horn nearly brushing the ceiling, I dare to lower the blade.

Ten seconds in, and I haven't been smote. *Yet.*

That has to be a good sign, right?

Wrong.

Tòrr stomps up to me and plants an iron hoof directly on my boot.

"Ow! *Fuck!*" I slide my foot out and cradle it as I hop on my good leg. That's at least one broken toe.

Wincing, I turn to Myst and motion to Tòrr with the knife hilt. "You better convince this asshole that I'm on his side! This was your idea!"

Her ears swing forward. She looks between Tòrr and me, then nips him on the neck.

He snorts defensively.

I put some weight on my boot, relieved that he only shattered one bone instead of my entire foot. "Ferra." I bend my fingers to motion her forward. "I won't get a mile traveling with a monoceros. Can you alter his appearance to pass for a regular horse?"

"Oh, let me consult my guide to my power...I don't know! I've never worked on an animal before. Especially not a fae one."

I glance toward the stable door. "Will you try?"

STEEL HEART IRON CLAWS

She mutters under her breath as she plucks anxiously at the ruffles of her gown, tiptoeing close enough to cautiously run her fingers along Tòrr's neck. When he doesn't immediately sink his teeth into her shoulder, she takes a steadying breath.

"I'd better not lose any toes, Wolf. And even if this works, I have no idea if he'll maintain his fae powers in the glamour." She works cautiously, knitting her fingers through Tòrr's mane so that the metallic strands come away a dull, coarse black.

She delicately puffs air into each of his eyes, and when he blinks, his red-tinged irises fade to a walnut brown.

For the final task, she runs her palms over every plane of Tòrr's body as though wiping away dust, and when she stands back to admire her handiwork, he's shrunk at least a foot in height.

He's still the biggest damn horse I've ever seen—but at least he looks like a *horse*.

I give a low whistle. "I see why the Valveres pay you so much."

As she wipes her hands in satisfaction, she slides me a sidelong look. "I don't expect a thousand gold coins from you, Wolf Bowborn. Bringing Lady Sabine back will be payment enough."

The locket with Sabine's portrait burns a hole in my pocket. *I will*, I vow to any gods listening. *I'll bring her back or die trying.*

Folke squeezes my wrist guard as he gives me a knowing look. "Go get your woman. Your memories, too. We'll keep the guards off your back."

"Thanks, old man."

Folke smacks me fondly on the side of the head.

They each roll back one of the stable doors, letting in a burst of sunlight. A beam falls at my feet, illuminating the dust dancing in the air, and I have a second of doubt.

But then Myst nuzzles my shoulder, and I touch the outside of my pocket over the locket. I step on a mounting block and swing a leg over Myst.

"Okay, crazy mare. You tried to tell me what I needed to do, and I didn't listen. I'm listening now. I can get us to the border. I need *you* to manage that fae beast so he doesn't burn the entire kingdom in our wake."

Myst's head swings toward Tòrr as though giving him a stern look.

Tòrr stands tall in the center of the stable, swishing his black tail in impatience. He stomps one hoof. Even glamoured to look like a regular horse, he still has the arrogance of a fae.

"And you, Tòrr." I point a finger at his nose. "I'll make you a deal. No saddle. No bit. Not so much as a lead rope on your proud neck. But if you bolt into the woods and burn a couple of villages for fun, I'll hunt you to the end of the earth. Got that?"

I'm no idiot—I know I'm only talking to myself. Trying to convince myself that I have any control over either of these crazy horses is a fool's errand.

So when Tòrr pins his dark eyes on me and purposefully drags the tip of his front hoof through the straw dust on the floor, my jaw drops.

He moves his hoof forward, then down, then draws a circle.

O-U-T.

. . .

The letters are written in the dust, clear as day. I stare, gobsmacked, and he stamps a hoof to rattle me out of my stupor.

"Sure," I mutter, running a hand down my face. "Sure. So, you can write. Good to know."

He snorts a burst of steam in my face.

I signal Myst with my heel, and she pivots to face the exit. Tòrr falls into line with us, and I whisper a prayer that these two horses won't be the death of me before I can reach Sabine.

"Let's get our girl."

I kick Myst into a gallop. Her muscles fire beneath me, propelling us forward, with Tòrr striding along at our side. We burst out of the stables to the surprised shouts of soldiers, but by the time they nock their arrows, we've already thundered across the courtyard.

Once we clear the castle gate, I look back over my shoulder, a preternatural sense picking up something from the furthest corner of my vision.

Over the square mass of the wall, I can just make out the top of Honor Tower.

In the uppermost window, Rian braces himself against the sill, gazing down at me with an inscrutable expression.

To him, I must look tiny as an ant, but I can see the cold glint of his eyes even from this distance, sharp as the edge of a blade.

CHAPTER 20

SABINE

"**D**on't jump, Lady Sabine!"

Grand Cleric Beneveto shoves his way through the pale-faced courtiers, swatting away the resplendent fae gods with as little care as if they're buzzing gnats. His eyes shine in his skull like glass marbles, a sign he's hit the opium pipe too hard. Still, he remains remarkably sturdy on his feet.

"Sabine—Highness—don't jump," he repeats. "It would please these pointed-eared bastards far too much to know they'd gotten under your skin."

The crowd falls into a bated hush as they wait to see if Immortal Vale will crush Beneveto like coal for the insult, but my father remains stony-faced. Iyre cackles to herself as she licks sauce off her fingers, and the Blades—no, *Artain, Samaur, and Woudix*—paint smirks on their handsome faces.

My fingertips dig into the bricks on either side of the windowsill as my heart gives a seismic shift. Wind rushes up from below to whip my thin cotton shift around my knees. My toes curl around the ledge's rim as I glance over my shoulder at the river below.

A soft sputter escapes my lips as I lean an inch further out.

One step, and I'm free...

Beneveto steps forward cautiously, trying to catch my gaze like a lifeline.

"Let's talk, Highness. Human to human. I know more about the gods than you'd ever learn from fae tales. There's a reason I turned my back on Astagnon and am ready to put the Red Church's full weight behind their rule when the time comes." He pushes back his white streak of hair. "We went to so much trouble to bring you here. Don't make us hold your funeral tomorrow."

I curl my toes around the ledge.

The last person I should trust is a traitor with the reek of opium on his breath, but Beneveto's words make me pause. Beneveto is the second most powerful man in Astagnon, after Rian. He wouldn't gamble away that position if he weren't certain.

A squeak overhead catches my ear. I jerk my head up to see the forest mouse poking her head down from the hole in the ceiling.

Mouse-talker? she frets. ***Don't leave me! If you jump, I cannot follow this time!***

As the wind blusters at my back, I realize I can't risk jumping. The birds might catch me—or I might crash onto the rocks. Either way, I can't abandon the mouse. She's been with me since Mag Na Tir Forest, stowing away in Basten's knapsack, to his supreme irritation. And what about Myst? My brave girl is a kingdom away, a prisoner of Rian's stable, when she deserves to stretch her legs, free and wild. I can't just leave her there. And the goldenclaws? The cloudfox? Even though it tricked me, I promised it a name. I can't name it if I'm dashed against river rocks.

Let's not forget about Tòrr.

That prissy monoceros has the power to destroy kingdoms. Of all the powerful men whose hands he could fall into, did it have to be Rian Valvere's? Once upon a time, I trusted Rian, at least enough to believe he'd honor a bargain. I even thought he might love me in his twisted way. But he sold me out with the same careless indifference as a coin flip.

So, what horrors would he inflict upon a fae horse?

As I perch on the windowsill's precipice, dozens of eyes burn through me until sweat drips down my brow.

Stay?

Or jump?

With the wind whipping my nightdress, I slowly hold out a shaky hand to Beneveto.

Relief washes over his face as he steps forward to help me down, but then, Immortal Vale shoulders him out of the way to seal his own large hand around mine.

"Human to human?" Vale rasps. "No. Fae to human. If anyone owes her an explanation, it should be her father."

My stomach draws tight as a button as I stare at my hand in his.

I...don't know what to do.

"My father?" I finally murmur. "Is that what you are to me?"

"I am many things to you. But I am your father above all other titles." He steps back, sweeping out his hands, and like a gradual dusk, his true fae appearance melts away. His dark gold eyes fade to the dull shade of rust, and the silver in his beard settles into a salt-and-pepper gray. His shoulders, wide as an ox beneath his fur-line cloak, recede into a normal human male's width.

Nerves as soft as butterfly wings flutter over me, lifting goose bumps all along the length of my arms. The darkness still roars at the edge of my vision.

I feel faint...

A distant thought stirs in my head: If he is fae and my mother was human, what does that make me?

Before I can follow that line of thought, he continues, "Before you judge us—" he nods toward Artain, Woudix, Samaur, and Iyre, "—Let us talk. That's all I ask. A chance to explain. All of you, raise your glamour. Can't you see you're frightening her?"

He snaps his fingers, and one by one, the rest of the fae shift back into their human glamour as effortlessly as changing into a new set of clothes.

Now, they're simply flesh and blood.

Human, by all appearances.

Swallowing a lump in my throat, I spare one final glance at the birds circling the Ramvik River below.

On shaky legs, I step down from the window ledge, toward my father.

And, swaying, immediately tip forward into his arms as darkness finally claims me.

When I wake in my bedroom, groggy and disoriented, I blink at the sunlight streaming through the window. It catches on my desk's silver candlesticks, flashing bright lights against my retinas that are hauntingly similar to fey lines.

I groan and shade my eyes as everything rushes back.

Someone knocks on the door. Before I can croak for them to go away, a round-cheeked maid enters with a fresh pitcher of water. When she sees me sitting up in bed, her eyebrows shoot upward.

"Highness! You're awake. I'll alert King Rachillon—"

"*Wait.*" I practically claw my way out from under the fur coverings to slam the door before she can leave. Her eyes widen as I press my back against the door, trapping her. "Wait. Tell me what day it is."

"It's—it's Wednesday, Highness."

Wednesday. So, I've been out for a day. Not good, but it's better than knowing I've been lying there as soft and help-less as a baby doe for a week.

"Who dressed me?" I tug on the neckline of the fresh nightdress I'm wearing.

"I did, Highness." She sees how I'm desperately pressed against the door and sets the water pitcher on my wash-basin. She tuts gently, "There's nothing to fear, Lady Sabine."

"Half the fae court are traipsing around this castle's halls!"

She refolds the towel draped over the washbasin stand as though biding time for my outburst to pass, then says softly, "Everyone knows what happened at the feast in Immortal Thracia's honor—there's still a hole in the Hall of Vale's ceiling. And we all thank the gods that you didn't jump out of that window. Do not be frightened. The fae are a blessing, Highness. We've been praying for their return for one thousand years, and we are among the fortunate few who get to witness the Third Return."

As I listen, I can't help but sniff the air—something smells *wonderful*. And my stomach is growling.

I spy a plate of cranberry scones someone must have left earlier on my desk. I surreptitiously thieve a step toward it. "So, everyone in the castle knew their true identity? My father's? And the Blade Boys'?"

"Yes, Highness." She hesitates. "We were told to shelter you from information you might not be ready for. Letting you know only about Lady Iyre was meant to ease you into the full truth."

I don't like the pitying tone in her voice, like I'm a child who needs to be told the monsters under her bed aren't real. Still, she knits her hands in what looks like genuine concern for me. And, frankly, I trust what a maid has to say more than my father.

She has much less reason to lie.

She notes where I'm headed and picks up the scone plate to offer me one.

Slowly, I take the closest, trying to resist devouring it whole. "In Astagnon, people are as likely to curse the fae as worship them."

She chuckles. "Power can frighten the unenlightened. Not to say you aren't enlightened, Highness! Only that here in Volkany, we've never wavered in our devotion. Consider all the good Immortal Vale and the others have already bestowed upon us."

"Good? What good?" I nibble at the scone. Gods, it's *divine*.

"Why, just last week, Lord Artain cleared the forest of a wolf pack that's been picking off farmers' sheep. Lady Iyre visited elderly soldiers still traumatized by the Twenty-One Day Battle—she eased their minds by taking away the worst memories. And Lord Woudix helped a priest crushed under a cart to have a peaceful death."

I knit my mouth to the side as I chew, but can't manage to hold in my real thoughts. "You know they drink human blood, right? Artain probably *ate* the wolves. Iyre certainly bottled up those soldiers' memories to use later. And Woudix? Who knows if the priest would have even died without the Ender's "peaceful" assistance."

I expect a gasp, but the maid only looks at me with that same piteous gaze. Gently, she sets down the plate of scones before heading to the door. "I feel sorry for you, Highness. That you were taught to see the cruelty in the world before the kindness. I'll tell your father that you're awake."

She gives me a sad smile before leaving.

As soon as the door latches, I stomp over to the plate and stuff another scone in my mouth, but now, it tastes as dry and flavorless as sand.

I spit the mouthful out the window, staring southward over the mountains—the direction of Astagnon.

Who am I supposed to believe, a maid with stars in her eyes, or my own heart? Maybe if Matron White and the Sisters hadn't kept me locked away half my life, I would know what to make of the world. As it is, my experience with the wider world is limited to a handful of months spent in Sorsha Hall with Rian. And look at how well I read *that* situation.

In my heart, I know that the only person I've ever trusted to set my course straight is Basten. He's my North Star. My wayfinder.

And now, he's all alone in Rian's court of lies.

I'm not sure how long I stand at the window, but when the door swings open, I spin around with my heart in my throat.

King Rachillon—Vale—fills the doorway, glamoured, looking deceptively human in a simple dark gray cloak.

"Father." I grab a robe from the wardrobe, shrugging it on quickly over my nightdress. Clearing my throat, I cinch the belt tightly. "You don't need to hide yourself with this human glamour anymore."

I motion to his drab appearance.

He plucks at his round ear shell as he rasps, "I thought it would be easier for you."

"A wolf in sheep's clothing is still a wolf."

To my surprise, he chuckles as he crosses his thick arms over his leather doublet. "You have fire in you, Daughter. I like to see it. But before you go crashing through any more ceilings, I have something to show you."

I brace myself, taking a step backward, and trip over a copy of the Book of the Immortals on the floor. I've been reading the stories that I didn't have access to in the convent. Trying to learn everything I can about my new *family*.

"What exactly do you wish to show me?" I ask tightly. "The Serpent Knife? To my jugular? Did you bring me to Volkany to slit my throat on one of your altars like that poor farm boy in The Sacrifice of the Golden Child?"

He huffs a breath, amused. "Get dressed. And come to the Garden of Ten Gods."

When he leaves, I remain standing stock-still, unsure of what my options are at the moment. Finally, I decide they're extremely limited when one's father is King of Fae.

Once I'm dressed, guards escort me down the central

stairs and into the walled garden that sits between the star-like points of the Cloudveil Tower and the Aurora Tower.

Stone paths wind around topiaries shaped into fae beasts. A large privet tree is trimmed into a goldenclaw. A half dozen small holly shrubs are shaped like a family of playful cloudfoxes. When we emerge from the awe-inspiring topiaries, it's into an open, circular amphitheater with gleaming white marble steps.

Around the perimeter are ten statues twice a person's height—one for each of the gods. Offerings rest upon altars at the base of each statue: coins, wildflower bouquets, raisin loaves.

As much as I want to march in with cold-blooded confidence, I can't help but gaze in soft-jawed wonder at the statues' masterful craftsmanship.

Still, when I see the individuals seated haphazardly on the marble steps, my jaw closes up tight again.

Great.

Iyre, Artain, Samaur, and Woudix—with Hawk—sprawl on the various levels of the amphitheater steps while my father holds court in the center stage. They're wearing their human glamours, but with their ethereal beauty only rivaled by their stunning arrogance, I can't believe I didn't see the truth earlier.

"Do *they* all need to be here?" I fold my arms as I saunter down the first step.

"Nice to see you again, too, princess." Artain kicks out his feet, resting his head back on his clasped hands. He nods to Vale and says, "You know, if you had given me one night with her, as I'd asked, she'd never have tried to jump out a window—she'd never leave my bed."

"Try to put your libido out of your mind for a minute," Vale growls. "I told you, we're doing it differently this time."

My head jerks toward him.

This time?

Artain shrugs and leans back against the base of a statue. With a lurch in the pit of my stomach, I realize he's positioned directly below his own statue—a figure of Immortal Artain in nearly the same arrogant pose.

I roll my eyes.

Vale points a warning finger at the rest of the fae. "Lady Sabine is my daughter, not a prisoner. She's the future of this kingdom as much as the rest of you are. This isn't the first time we've had to pivot in our plans. Remember the First Return? The queen of Spezia's pirate fleet?" He looks pointedly at Samaur, who sheepishly adjusts his silk shirt collar. "Now, unless you wish me to hurtle each one of you over that wall into the Ramvik River, you'll fall in line."

I'm still curious about what he meant by "this time," though I suppose they *have* kidnapped a small army of godkissed people, which would lend itself to wanting to do things differently.

I'm distracted from those thoughts when I realize each fae, not just Artain, is seated below their own towering effigies.

Iyre admires her long red nails beneath a statue of the Goddess of Virtue. Samaur picks at his teeth with a knife next to the God of Day's statue. Woudix crouches beneath the God of Death's statue, stroking Hawk along the sharp ridge of her spine.

By all appearances, she's a living dog now. No exposed ribs. No rotted jaw. As glamoured as the rest of them.

My father turns to me. "Let us start by—"

I cut him off by holding up my wrists, which still bear red marks from when Tati escorted me to Norhelm in chains. "Forgive me for doubting that I'm not a prisoner, given that your soldiers shackled me to a goldenclaw."

Iyre smiles lazily as she plucks a fallen leaf from her statue's toes. "That *was* a good time."

I stomp toward her with balled fists. "You're fondly remembering my abduction? The worst day of my life? When you ripped me away from the one man I've ever loved?"

Woudix's head tilts upward. A muscle jumps in his jaw. "She loved a human man?"

"She *thinks* she did." Iyre flicks the leaf with her long nail.

"Oh, you fae bitch—" I hurtle toward her, but Vale snaps his fingers, and the stones under my feet begin to tremble. It's a tiny earthquake, limited to only a three-foot span. I tip forward, barely catching myself before falling. As I scramble for balance, the ground calms, and the stones return to their positions.

I straighten my gown. "Message received—you can crush your daughter with a finger snap."

"You need to listen to what we have to say." Vale's voice is hard-edged now. Impatient. "To understand our world— a world you're now a part of."

"Did my mother know?" I blurt out. "That you're fae?"

He runs a hand down his long beard before rasping, "She suspected. It was part of why she ran away."

I sink next to one of the unoccupied statue's bases, pinching the bridge of my nose. Measuredly, I say, "If that is so, then clearly, she did not believe this castle to be safe. Why should I trust you when my mother did not?"

"Isabeau didn't flee because she feared *me*." His boots plod on the marble stones at the base of the Immortal Vale statue. "What I told you before was the truth. She fled because she feared the war she suspected was coming. She wanted to hide you—shelter you—from that war. I wanted the opposite. To bring you into it like the powerful force of nature I knew you would become."

Something preening flutters under my skin, responding to his praise like a flower to sunlight. They're all so damn *beautiful*. And this place? The fanciful topiaries. The midnight balls. The gatherings beneath the hemlock tree. It would be so tempting to fall into their mythical world, where time loses all meaning.

I shift my stance, and a twig cracks under my shoe, returning me to the present.

I point to the other five statues and say gravely, "Thracia. Popelin. Alessantha. Meric. Solene. Half the court is still asleep. What do you intend to do about them?"

"We will find their resting places," Vale rasps confidently. "We always do, in each Return. Sometimes, it takes days. Sometimes, decades."

Samaur examines a glittering agate crystal on his statue's altar. "Thracia's location is already secured. It's just a matter of bringing her here and waking her."

"Waking her *how*?" I press.

Samaur nods toward Vale. "As King of Fae, your father has that power."

"But how does it happen? What does it take to wake a fae?"

"Why do you ask?" Vale says.

I pick up a small bronze antler from the base of Immortal Solene's statue, turning it over in my fingers. "I know how fae twist their words. I've read the stories. So, I want you to speak plainly. Truthfully. You owe me that." I press my thumb against the antler's sharp tip as my heart speeds. I'm not an idiot. I realize that a sharp bronze antler will not protect me from five fae gods. Still, I like the way it feels squeezed in my palm. Dangerous. *Like claws.* "Fae didn't become gods until Vale drank the blood of a farmer's sacrificed child. You could call that an awakening. Did you bring me to Volkany because waking a god requires a blood-line sacrifice?"

All five fae stare at me as though I've said the sea is made of the moon's tears.

Artain is the first to laugh, doubling over against his statue's knee to brace himself. "Now I understand why she was going to throw herself out the window! Vale, she thought you were going to gut her like a pig! Bleed her dry on Thracia's altar like in that old damn tale! What's it called—"

"The Golden Child!" Samaur slaps Artain on the shoulder as he, too, doubles over in laughter.

Iyre gives an ugly snort before covering her mouth with an embarrassed hand.

Woudix alone remains unfazed, his pale features still as a death mask.

I slam the bronze antler down on the altar. "You mock me? After I've seen you drink the blood of humans? Seen the Serpent Knife in the artifact room?" I snatch up a brace of skinned, field-dressed rabbits on the altar beneath Immortal Solene's statue. "Do not tell me you don't need sacrifice."

Artain and Samaur keep snickering until Woudix nudges Hawk. The dog drops its glamour. In a second, it's a half-rotted cadaver with teeth exposed from its torn jaw, growling low at the other two Blade Boys.

Their laughter vanishes.

Vale raises a hand toward the castle. "You've seen many of our acolytes. We take their blood, yes. Their breath. Their sex. Their prayers. They are all more than willing. They suffer no harm for this vow of sacrifice—in return, we shower them with mortal delights. Food. Wine. Pleasure. Whatever they desire. Our head acolytes are even rewarded with a special connection. A shared mind. Shared thoughts."

Jaw clenched, my mind lurches to find an argument. It's true that I haven't seen any dead bodies drained of blood. Paz and the twins Samaur was dancing with in the hemlock grove certainly seemed pleased to serve.

I shift my stance. "Is that why you've brought me here, then? To be an—an acolyte?"

I brace myself for more laughter. I almost crave it, because that would mean it was an absurd idea—but only distant birdsong answers me.

Artain gives a salacious grin. "Well, if you want to take me up on that one night together..."

I hurl the bronze antler at his head, but he manages to duck.

"Sabine," Vale says gently. "There is no trick. No deception. I brought you here because my daughter should be at my side. War is coming. There are five of us. Soon to be ten. We are strong, yes, but against how many millions of humans across the seven kingdoms who will resist us? We will need humans on our side. Like Beneveto. Captain Tatarin. And you."

As I wrestle with this, I tip my chin up to gaze at the marble statue eclipsing me. Immortal Solene is carved with vines winding up her legs, flowers growing from her hair. She looks like the very picture of peace. One with nature. Serenity itself. Hardly a monster.

"That's really all?"

"For fuck's sake, stop being so suspicious." Artain loops his arm around my shoulder with that dazzling grin. "We're missing out on valuable partying time."

I scowl at him, but it lacks its usual bite. Shrugging out from under his arm, I twist the twine ring around my finger, my stomach turning in knots, too. "If I am to stay here, then I need to send a message to Basten Bowborn."

My father tents his fingers. "A letter could be arranged, though it may take some time. My spies are deeply undercover in Old Coros. And all our messenger crows are currently completing other voyages." He rests a hand on my shoulder, his eyes soft. "Are you sure this man hasn't forgotten you entirely?"

I flinch, instinctively shooting a look toward Iyre. "It doesn't matter if he does; *I* haven't forgotten him. I have to warn him of danger."

"From what you've told me, this human male is more than capable of guarding his own back." Vale presses my hand between his, stilling my anxious twirling of the ring. "He hasn't reached out to you. We've received no crows. No letters. Perhaps he has moved on with his life. Perhaps you should, too."

I bristle, tugging my hand free. Heat bleeds into my cheeks as I tip my chin high. "I need to write that letter."

He nods, but his eyes tell me my hope is lost.

A familiar tension pulls in my side, but I can't tell if it's real or old instincts kicking in. I try to poke holes in my father's story, but nothing sticks. Yes, Iyre's a nightmare. I wouldn't trust Artain or Samaur after dark with a bottle in their hands, either. Woudix? Still a mystery I can't unravel.

But this place, these people—they're not exactly the monsters I thought. There's a pull here, a potential, like a half-remembered dream that calls me back each time I wake.

What if this is where I belong?

"If you're ready, Sabine," Vale says. "I'll reveal the truth —all of it. Who we are, the power we wield, what's been hidden from you."

Am I? Will I ever be ready?

I briefly touch the twine ring on my finger before hesitantly taking his hand. "Show me."

As the words leave my lips, a surge of something dangerous and thrilling courses through me. Family. Power. The possibility that this could be my world. A door swings open in my mind, and for the first time, I step forward into the unknown with something other than fear.

CHAPTER 21

BASTEN

We don't slow from a gallop until we're ten miles north of Old Coros. Tòrr runs with such effortlessness that not a drop of sweat mars his glistening black coat. But *I'm* huffing and puffing, and foamy sweat clings to the contours of Myst's shoulders, too. I can hear her breath straining with each stride.

Sure, she's a crazy old mare who couldn't stand me before she begrudgingly came to like me, but I have to give credit where it's due—she's relentless when it comes to keeping up with a monoceros.

Farmland stretches on either side of the road. A few barns dot the landscape, but there's no sign of any people.

I lead the horses off the road to a stream running along a pasture where they can drink their fill. I dismount straight into the stream, boots splashing in the shallow water, and crouch down to cup water around the back of my neck.

The coolness soothes my heated skin but does nothing to calm the storm inside me.

Damn you, Rian. Back at Hekkelveld Castle, rage wanted to burn through me like wildfire, but now, in the quiet of the pasture, it's choked out by blind faith—something I've never operated on before. The feeling is both terrifying and exhilarating, stepping off a cliff and trusting the wind to catch you.

Sabine? She's my wind.

She's my *everything*—my redemption, my revenge, my future. It may be the stupidest thing I've ever done to put my faith in a woman I can't remember, who the rest of the world branded a traitor. But for the first time in my life, I'm going to follow my heart.

Leaving the horses to drink, I park my ass on the grassy bank, then unstrap my wrist guard and run my fingers over the scars that spell out S-A-B-I-N-E.

Goosebumps ripple across the skin.

Next, I take the letter Suri gave me out of my knapsack. A smile tugs the corner of my mouth as I open it to reread thirteen-year-old Sabine's handwriting, which conveys a hopeful spirit that I can't help but believe she still has at twenty-two.

Then, I pull out my old shirt that Sabine must have borrowed. I can't resist burying my face in it, hungry for a scrap of that feather-light trace of her scent. A burst of violets fills my nose, as intoxicating as gin.

I mutter to myself, "Only an idiot would believe in fated mates, Wolf."

Which makes you an idiot, friend.

Shaking my head, I chuckle softly at my own bull-headedness as I set the shirt aside.

Lastly, I fish Rian's locket out and cradle it in my palm.

The golden "S" on the front winks in the dappled sunlight, tugging at some hidden corner of my heart. My mind screams at me to think logically about this senseless quest, but my heart? My heart is certain.

Her name on my arm.

The letter.

The shirt with her scent.

The locket.

That's all I need to lead me to this woman who I've dreamed about every night, tossing and turning, groaning with a visceral need to hold her.

The horses snort nearby, oblivious to my turmoil. I shift, trying to get comfortable on the streambank, but my body is too keyed up. Every muscle feels coiled tight, ready to spring. The knowledge that she's out there makes my pulse quicken.

I'm coming, Sabine.

I'm pulled out of my thoughts by a sharp stomp to the tip of my boot.

"*Ow!*" Clutching my boot, I shoot Tòrr an incredulous glare. "Stop doing that! You broke another damn toe!"

He stamps his hoof next to words he's written in a patch of damp soil beside the stream.

U-P L-A-Z-Y

"*Lazy?* Look, humans require this thing called rest. And two other extravagances called food and water. And if we're feeling really excessive? Coffee."

I wrench my cooking pot out of my knapsack to wave in his face.

Tòrr blasts steam as he stomps off toward Myst, tossing his mane and pacing until she admonishes his frivolity with a swift smack of her head against his.

"And I thought good, old-fashioned mortal horses were stubborn," I murmur as I stuff the pot back in my bag. "I don't know how Sabine put up with you."

I pull off my boot and grimace at the bruised second toe.

As I bandage it, I think more about Sabine. If we're truly fated to be together, I guess I'd better get good with animals real damn quick.

Horses. Monoceroses. Anything that crawls or flutters or fucking slithers. The gossip about her in Hekkelveld Castle was all *chipmunks-this* and *butterflies-that.*

It isn't that I dislike animals. Not at all. It's just that I've spent years avoiding them.

It started with Onno.

I loved that damn scruffy dog with every tiny bone in my ten-year-old body. He was the only joy I found in the abandoned stables where Jocki kept boys and dogs locked up when we weren't in the fight ring.

And when Jocki got jealous of my bond with Onno...

And forced us, boy and dog, into the ring as opponents...

Well.

Strangling your only friend at ten years old sets a remarkably solid foundation for a lifetime of psychological scars.

After Onno died, I ran away. Hating Jocki. Hating myself. Hating the gods-damned world. My godkiss made it easy to survive on the streets, though I was painfully alone.

Once, I wandered into a nicer part of town and saw a teenage girl leave a perfume shop with a beautifully wrapped package. The package was bathed in the smell of jasmine, but the odor of the bottle within made me stop in my tracks.

Thorn Apple is commonly known as an odorless poison, but that's only to the ungodkissed nose. Jocki kept a supply of it to use on his enemies, and to me, it always carried the faintest scent of grass. It can be easily confused with burdock root, a fixative for stabilizing volatile compounds like perfumes.

I snatched the package from the girl's arms and threw it into the North Innis River, causing a carriage to screech to a stop and dozens of onlookers to gawp.

"*That perfume was made wrong,*" I explained to the girl. "*It's poisonous. One spray would have killed you.*"

The girl swooned, falling all over me to thank me for saving her. "*Let me repay your kindness with a meal, you poor starving boy,*" she said. She insisted I follow her to a tavern.

As soon as we were down an alley, away from prying eyes, she spun on me with a knife to my throat. "*You idiot— you nearly ruined everything!*"

It turned out that the girl, Annabella, worked for the perfume maker, a portly woman named Madame Caleau, whose real business was poison. I'd nearly exposed their operation and probably would have lost my head for it, if Annabella hadn't paused long enough with her knife pressed to my throat to ask:

"*How did you know it was poison, boy?*"

Luckily for me, a godkissed boy able to sniff out any scent was worth something to a poison manufacturer.

Madame Caleau and Annabella gave me three square

meals and a cot in the perfumery's stock room, and more importantly, evenings filled with laughter as we would mix poisons and speculate about our clients' gambling debts. Annabella teased me mercilessly for my cracking preteen voice, at the same time that she would stay up until dawn sewing me new pants to fit my growing legs. Madame Caleau mothered me like a hen, always trying to tame my unruly hair, chiding me about putting more meat on my small bones, worrying herself when I didn't make it home from a delivery until dawn.

Their vocation was to take lives—but they *gave* me one.

My happy life with them came crashing down when a crime lord decided to take over the poison market for himself. While I was on a delivery, his men burned the perfumery with Madame Caleau and Annabella inside. They caught me when I returned, beat me within an inch of my life, and sold me back to Jocki.

And the Golden Sentinels? They looked the other way. Crime ran every aspect of Duren's economy from the Sin Streets to Sorsha Hall. And all of it was permitted, even promoted, by the Valvere family.

Who, of course, took a cut.

Suddenly, a snarl from a small copse of trees near the stream pulls me out of the past.

Immediately, the musty scent of fur hits my nose.

A huge gray wolf is crouched on the other streambank with his sights set on Myst while she munches grass, unaware.

Alarm shoots through me as I scramble for my bow. "Myst!"

Before I can reach my knapsack, Tòrr rears up from the middle of the stream. Water pours off his iron hooves as he paws the air, letting out another one of his unnatural shrieks. He lifts his massive head toward the sun, and a strange ringing sound starts.

Bands of shadow ripple across the ground as the air grows cold. The hair on my arms lifts like lightning is about to strike.

Then, a burst of light explodes across my eyes.

Crying out, I roll away, throwing an arm over my face. Intense heat licks at the back of my neck. When I ease my eyelids open, my vision slowly refocuses.

Where the wolf had been is now a pile of ash on burned grass.

I fall back on my elbows, eyes wide as I take in Tòrr.

He lowers to all fours in the stream, shakes himself, then trots over to rest his chin on Myst's neck.

"Okay." I smooth a shaky hand over my face. "Okay. Right. I guess you *can* still use your powers."

Myst nuzzles Tòrr as I go to inspect the wolf's remains. Other than some singed tufts of fur, there isn't so much as a claw left.

Curious, I point to the ruins of an old, abandoned shed on the far side of the stream. "Show me again what you can do. I want to see." Tòrr swings his head to peer at the shed. "Go ahead. As long as it isn't *me* you're crispifying."

Tòrr tips his head to the left, into a beam of sunlight pouring through the trees, and another fireball instantly incinerates the shed.

"Fuck! *Yes*." I bark an awe-inspired laugh. "Oh, murder horse, the things I would burn if I had your power."

Tòrr prances in the stream, excited by my tone. He swings his head around again until he spots a bustling sheep barn about three hundred paces away. His eyes widen gleefully, flashing the whites.

My grin falls. "Wait—"

A burst of light has me turning my face away. When I look up, the barn is nothing but a few smoking corner posts. Bleating sheep run panicked across the pasture.

A dog starts barking.

I wipe a hand over my face. "Uh, I think it's time for us to keep moving."

But Tòrr prances again, kicking up water in his excitement. A wicked gleam flashes in his eyes. He keeps tossing his head. Shrieking.

Fear runs backward up my throat.

Myst nips him on the neck, but he only snorts and nips back at her. His hooves dance over the sun-dappled river rocks. His ears swing forward as he hones in on a farmhouse about a quarter mile away.

That dog must belong to the family inside. Because already, I can hear a mother's concerned voice coming from the building. Two children's anxious questions. A father's heavy boot steps as he heads for the door.

"Tòrr, no!" I shout, crashing into the stream. He throws his head so violently that I can't grab him by the mane. "Tòrr, there are people in there! A family! Innocent people, you understand? Not kindling!"

I hold up my hands, trying to herd him back into the trees' shadows away from sunlight, but he blows an angry burst of steam at my face.

It scalds me, but I grimace and try again. "Hey! You're better than this. You're fae, aren't you? It's in your damn silver blood? You're supposed to be superior to humans. Illustrious. Exalted. Well, with your gift comes duty. So, take some fucking responsibility. You can't go around burning down the world because it hurt you."

Myst nips at him again, this time deep enough to draw blood.

He finally calms down, his lungs heaving as he fights for steady breath, the vengeful glee fading out of his eyes.

My shoulders sink, my own tension melting away.

Tòrr lifts his front foot and stomps right on my boot.

"Ow!" I double over, growling now, ready to punch this damn horse in the muzzle. "Hey! Listen, you fucker—"

Tòrr ignores me as he tromps to the streambed and writes out with his hoof in the mud:

K-I-N-G

He juts his head toward me.

I feel the sting of the accusation behind Tòrr's pointed ears, and scoff.

"Me? You're turning this on me? That's your answer?"

Tòrr stomps emphatically next to the word. His eyes bore into me. This damn horse is calling me out. *Hard.*

I grit my teeth. "I'm a hypocrite. I get it. My blood is supposed to mean I'm a king, right? With all those same responsibilities. But the difference between you and me? The world doesn't need someone like me in charge."

Even as the words leave my mouth, they feel hollow. The truth is, Tòrr and I are the same. Both of us have been betrayed, abandoned, and neglected by a world that never stops taking. We both want the world to burn.

My chest feels too tight as I pace in the stream.

"Maybe we're both animals," I mutter, the words gruff.

But the thought feels bitter on my tongue. From everything I've heard about Sabine Darrow, *she* wouldn't let this twisted world stand. She would tear the rot apart with a steel heart and iron claws.

She's stronger than me.

And, dammit, I need her strength right now. I need her to show me how to be the man I must become—the man who wouldn't let what happened to Madame Caleau and Annabella go unavenged.

I thrust my hand into my pocket and circle my thumb around the locket's edge, focusing on the face that won't let me sleep at night.

"Or maybe we both need to stop running." My voice is barely above a whisper now, but it feels like a confession. "And face our duty."

Tòrr huffs. I don't think he wanted this. Peace. Calm. He wanted me to join in his gleeful vengeance tour.

I kneel down and swipe my hand through the mud next to the word he wrote, writing:

M-Y-S-T

I jab my finger in her direction. "That mare, there? You love her. You don't want to lose her, but that's exactly what will happen if you don't tame your temper. I have a woman, too. One who I'm fighting for blindly with one hand tied behind my back. Because I have faith. You and I? We have a duty to this world, even if it's wronged us. Maybe *because* it's wronged us. Because we can make it right for those who come after us."

Tòrr watches me in silence, his posture slowly relaxing. He blows out a long breath, his ears twitching, and for the first time, the anger in his eyes seems to dim.

"We can be better." I stand up and rest my flat palm on his nose. "For them."

CHAPTER 22
SABINE

As the days pass, I slowly get used to my new reality. I reread the tales in the Book of the Immortals to sort fact from fiction. I explore the fae artifact room with fresh eyes. Through it all, I'm as cautious as curious. It would be easy to lose myself in the allure of the fae world, in the intoxicating sense that I'm a part of something ancient and mythic.

But for every story I read, I wonder what's been left unsaid.

For every artifact I touch, I feel the weight of promises broken.

Why doesn't girlie smile? a voice chirps from the window.

I jolt upright as the silvery-blue cloudfox bounds up onto my bedroom windowsill. Her purple-blue tongue lolls from her open jaw. Her eyes are bright, alert. Her fur floats gently like she's underwater.

It's you! I breathe out a long exhale. *I was afraid Iyre had caught you.*

She prances along the windowsill, heedless of the plummeting drop. *I have news that will make girlie smile.*

I dig my nails into the windowsill eagerly. *Did you get the bottle?*

Patience, patience. I snuck in the tower window. Found the yellow bottle but could not reach it. Locked cabinet.

I sigh, biting back my disappointment. *I'll have to find another way in. Still, you upheld your end of the bargain as best you could, so I will, too.*

The cloudfox bounds from one granite rainspout to the other, her long tongue lolling in excitement. *My name?*

Yes, little troublemaker. I've decided on it. I pause for dramatic effect. *It's Plume.*

Her tail wags frantically, tossing off bits of cloud that dissipate in the air.

Plume? she repeats. *What means this, Plume?*

It can mean a feather, as you are feather-light. I reach out and scratch her under her downy chin. *It can also mean a puff of cloud. Plus, the word's sound reminds me of how you're always bounding about.*

Proving my point, she lands on the windowsill only to immediately spring back to the waterspout.

Plume, she tests out. *Plume. I love it!*

A smile breaks across my lips as I watch her turn a cartwheel in the air from the rainspout to a decorative ledge.

A knock comes at the door. "Highness?" the maid asks. "Everyone is gathered in the Hall of Vale."

"Oh—one minute!" I shout.

I have to go, I tell Plume. *When I need you again, I'll call.*

I pause in front of the mirror, tugging at the fit of my

gown. I made a bold choice—the obsidian-studded one with batwing sleeves. For the first time, I fastened pewter ear caps to the tops of my ears—though they pinch. I touch my cheeks, worried I applied too much blush powder.

This is all…new.

I'm seventeen years old. Freshly bathed in a barrel of frigid water. Sister Rose attacks the tangles in my ankle-length hair with a vengeance. Matron White adjusts my dress's neckline, stuffing rags into my corset to shove up my breasts. No girl ever lured a wealthy husband with a flat chest, according to them.

The sky darkens outside, rain clouds rolling in to block the sun.

"This weather! It came out of nowhere," Sister Rose observes, closing the shutters. Then, she frowns at me. "She looks half dead."

"Indeed—that won't do." Matron White pinches my cheeks hard enough that tears fill my eyes as my blood vessels widen. "There. A touch of lady-like pink. It's amazing what a little blood can do."

I realize I'm fiddling with Basten's twine ring and, for a brief moment, consider taking it off. It's frayed. Dirty. It looks shabby against my other jeweled rings.

But then I squeeze it tightly. *You might have forgotten me, but I haven't forgotten you.*

My pulse pounds as I stride into the Hall of Vale, hoping I look more confident than I feel. All eyes turn to me, taking in my fae regalia, and I tug at the uncomfortable right ear cap.

Is it supposed to pinch this hard?

The musicians begin a lively tempo, and to my relief, attention shifts away from me as dancers move to the floor. It's a strangely beautiful melody that calls to mind the first stirrings of autumn chill. Laughter ripples across the room as partygoers play Basel on one of the dining tables, using fat green olives as gambling tokens.

"Highness!" Artain sweeps up and immediately shoves a heavy pewter mug in my hands. "Here. Ale. As much as you can drink, as fast as you can drink. That's the game."

"That's the game?" I slide him a doubtful look. "I was told tonight would be a fae competition for showcasing your powers...not your *drinking* prowess."

"What can I say? Drinking is one of my many powers." He places a hand on the small of my back to herd me toward the head table, where my father's chair is empty, but Samaur, Iyre, and Woudix fill theirs.

I come to an abrupt halt, gaping up at the still-broken ceiling.

Dust and debris still cover the table, but that hasn't stopped the revelry. Servants have simply placed new platters among the wreckage. Spilled raspberry jam still coats the back of Artain's chair. Samaur fishes a hunk of bread out of the mess and dips it in spilled herbed oil. Woudix's hound sniffs through the crumbs.

"You haven't fixed the ceiling?" I exclaim. "It's been days! You're going to leave this mess?"

"No, Highness. We aren't." Artain's eyes dance with mischief as he faces the crowd and announces loudly, "A toast to Lady Sabine, the fairest new member of our court!"

The courtiers cheer and lift their glasses. Since I'm

empty-handed, Artain waves the ale tankard in my face until I snatch it.

Hesitantly, I sniff the bitter ale and grimace. What was it that Tati said? *There's no going back to life as it was before.*

"Fine—but I want wine." I shove the ale back at him.

Artain laughs as he signals to a servant, who brings me a glass. "To Lady Sabine!"

"To Lady Sabine!" the crowd answers.

Cheeks warming, I take a small sip, but then Artain tips the glass's bottom until the sweet liquid fills my mouth. As wine spills down my chin, I cough and stagger backward, swiping a hand over my lips.

Artain pats me on the back with a grin. "Keep practicing, princess, and maybe I'll get that night with you after all."

"Not likely." Samaur raises his own flagon.

Woudix circles the base of his wine glass with one long finger, his cloudy eyes fixed to the middle distance. "One night with you, brother, and she'd beg me for death."

"Leave the poor girl alone, boys." Iyre lounges back in her chair, waving a silver chalice in the air. "Have you forgotten that she's taken? Look—she still wears that little string around her finger."

I bristle, placing a protective hand around the loop of twine. "It's an engagement ring. But of course, you know the full story about it, don't you? You've seen it in Basten's memories you stole."

Iyre merely chuckles as she sips deeply from her chalice.

I turn sharply away.

As my nerves jangle, I grab another wine glass from a passing servant and down it in one chug. These damn ear caps hurt like thumbscrews. On impulse, I tug them off and drop them in my empty wine glass, trading it for a full one.

Relieved, I massage the top of my aching ear.

"Are you looking forward to tonight's competition, Daughter?"

I jump to find Vale looming behind me. Like the others, he wears his human glamour, and without the dazzle of fey lines, I can clearly see myself in his features.

It steals my breath—it's something I've never had.

Clearing my throat, I motion my wine glass toward the ceiling wreckage. "Shouldn't we clean that up first?"

He winks. "You're absolutely right."

He claps his hands with a theatricality that makes my stomach feel giddy—apprehensive. He turns to address the head table. "Brothers. Sister. Come—Lady Sabine has rightly pointed out that this mess is unacceptable. Let us do something about it."

The music stops, and the crowd drifts forward amid whispered speculation, their curiosity palpable. As the other fae make their way to the front of the hall, my father lightly touches his anatomical heart brooch, begins his transformation from King Rachillon to Immortal Vale.

His wiry, graying beard smooths out until it gleams like molten silver. Fey lines break across his temples and down the sinews of his neck. His ears lengthen to fine points, curved at the end like goat's horns.

By the time the other fae come to stand beside him, they, too, shine in their full fae splendor.

"Lord Woudix." Vale sweeps a hand toward the wreckage. "The first turn is yours."

With Hawk pressed against his outer leg to lead the way, Woudix approaches the debris. He tilts his head as he lightly runs his hands over the table, feeling the dust and overturned silverware, his face as immobile as hardened clay.

He finds a full silver chalice, drinks deeply from it, and then tosses it to the floor.

A few drops of blood spill onto the stones.

My stomach tightens, dampening my mood. No one else, it seems, is bothered by the fact that he drank someone's—or something's—blood.

"Ah, now, we get to witness a true fae competition."

I jump at a voice to my side and twitch to find Grand Cleric Beneveto leaning close.

He tips his own wine glass in Woudix's direction as he quietly explains, "They'll each take a turn, trying to outdo one another. It's the best form of entertainment in one thousand years. Watch—Lord Woudix will use his fey."

"Fey?"

"It's what they gain from our sacrifices. What separates the *fae* from the *god*. It amplifies their powers, lets them achieve the impossible. Look."

As Woudix raises his hands over the table, bolts of energy spark from his palms like small crackles of lightning, the same bruise-black color as the fey lines that run down his temples.

Goosebumps crop up along my bare arms.

"The ceiling joist was rotten," Woudix announces to the crowd, holding his arms out over the table. "Weakened by pests."

A clicking noise fills the air, something strangely familiar, yet I can't place it. Suddenly, a woman shrieks as hundreds of tiny wood-bore beetles scurry out of the shattered ceiling boards, spreading down the table's legs onto the floor.

Their faint voices barely reach my ears—***hungry hungry hungry hungr***—when Woudix brings down his hands.

Bolts of energy pulse over them, and the beetles fall dead instantly, their carapaces clattering onto the floor like an overturned jar of buttons.

My mind reels, the echo of their voices fresh between my ears. *So much death.*

"That fey—it comes from us? Humans?" I try to keep my voice steady.

Beneveto signals toward a tall, raven-haired woman watching Woudix from the sidelines. "Arden is Woudix's main acolyte. She's dedicated her life to him. She fucks him, she worships him, she drains her blood for him to drink. In return, he kills the tumors that would put her in the grave."

Arden watches Woudix with the same blind devotion as the dead hound at his side. As soon as he lowers his hands, she rushes up to fall to her knees, kissing his boots. Mildly annoyed, he begrudgingly lets her fawn all over him.

Vale nods toward the God of Day. "Samaur. Your turn."

Samaur motions to the voluptuous twins in the audience. They saunter up, and the first one leans in as though for a kiss, but her lips and Samaur's don't meet. Instead, he breathes in her breath until she stumbles backward against a table, dizzy and giggling.

He repeats the act with the second one.

Then, he approaches the banquet table. Shaking his head dramatically, he *tsks* at the hundreds of dead beetles.

"You left an even worse mess, brother."

His golden eyes begin to burn as bright as the sun. The crowd murmurs excitedly. Fancifully dressed ladies bounce on their toes, squealing with impatience.

Samaur winks at me. "Watch this, princess."

The God of Day's affinity is fire, and when he lifts his hands, a bolt of flame-orange fey crackles over the table. The flashes of light illuminate the attendees' rapt faces. Faster than a blink, the fey burns the dead beetle husks—as well as the dust, debris, and spoiled food—while leaving tonight's banquet offerings untouched.

One of his twin acolytes cheers. The other raises her glass.

"To the God of Day!" the first one says.

"May he always burn hot as *fire!*" cries the second one.

"I'm not finished!" Samaur announces, then loops his arm around my neck and breathes in my ear, "Watch."

He shoots another burst of fey, which crackles over the broken glass shards from the fallen chandelier. The crystal pieces glow red, begin to liquify, and then form back into their original shape until they are as finely chiseled as when they first hung from the ceiling.

Samaur squeezes me hard enough to draw a squeak.

Servants hoist the repaired chandelier back into place. Bawdy cheering rings out, silenced only when my father lifts his hand. "Artain. It is your turn."

With his usual arrogance, the God of the Hunt loops his thumbs through his belt as he swaggers up to the table. Shirtless beneath his leather vest, his bare muscles shine with freshly applied oil.

A woman murmurs to her friend behind me, "I wouldn't mind if he hunted me down."

"Oh, darling," a man purrs, eyeing Artain's bulging muscles. "I know *exactly* what you mean." He fans his hand like a tiger's claw.

I hide a snicker behind a loose fist. Artain *is* exceedingly pretty—that's undeniable. A blonde-haired, chisel-jawed illustration stepped off the page with muscles on top of muscles on top of muscles, but I will never be able to take seriously a god who refuses to wear a shirt.

Artain takes his time collecting fallen nails from the wreckage, much to the crowd's confused murmurs. He holds one up to the light, frowning, and then licks a drop of raspberry jam off its point.

Next, he selects four arrows from his quiver and swaps out the pointed tips with the nails.

"Lady Sabine." He nocks one of the modified arrows. "Would you do me the honor of blindfolding me?"

I snort, rolling my eyes. He has to be joking.

However, the audience oohs and aahs in perfectly serious anticipation. "Oh—um." Feeling wobbly, I pluck at my dress sleeve, wondering what to use as a blindfold.

"With your *hands*." Despite Artain's smile, impatience rings in his voice.

I level a hard look at him. He thinks he's so clever? I can't let this preening dolt have any more reason to admire himself.

I down the rest of my ale, then slam the flagon on a table. "*Sure*."

For as broad as his shoulders are, Artain isn't especially tall. On my tiptoes, I can easily reach around from behind to cover his eyes. As he draws his bow, his loose hair brushes against my lips, and I grimace, trying not to make too much of a show as I spit it away.

"Lord Vale," Artain announces. "If you would please lift the fallen beam."

All eyes shift to my father, who leans back on his throne to evaluate the hole in the ceiling. My stomach tightens, unsure what to expect. Are my palms sweating? Gods, I hope not. I'd hate to give Artain the satisfaction of knowing I'm not as cold-blooded as them.

Vale brushes his hand over the broken ceiling joist. Blue bolts of fey crackle over it, slowly lifting the heavy beam into the air as surely as if hoisted by a rope.

Artain takes his time aiming, then lets loose the first arrow.

Even blindfolded, his aim strikes true. The nail-tipped arrow drills one corner of the suspended joist back into place. The spent arrow shaft rains down, and female courtesans scamper after it like a party favor.

Artain smirks at the cheers as he lets loose a second arrow. *Perfect aim.*

A third. *Perfect again.*

For the final arrow, he's preening with confidence, and I smile to myself. *Time to put him in his place.*

I push higher on my toes and lick his pointed ear.

His bowstring falters, sending the arrow shooting into the evening's honey-glazed roast turkey.

The crowd gags in surprise.

Artain whirls around to face me, knocking my hands away, an angry shade of red staining his cheeks. "You tricked me, princess."

I give a thin smile. "Now you know how it feels."

He stalks toward me, muscles coiled, hot energy rolling off him. His glowing eyes flash as he murmurs low, "If you want your tongue on me, just ask. One night together, and I'd—"

"Enough." My father's booming voice cuts him off. "Your turn has concluded, Artain. Go nurse your loss with a bottle. Iyre is next."

Iyre delivers a sharp poke with her long nail to Artain's exposed navel. "Step aside, brother. Enough with you males and your grandstanding. Your way of *fixing* still leaves a mess."

She sweeps her hand over the overturned dishware. As her eyes burn with a glow that holds both the blue and red of a flame, sparks of fey crackle from her palms.

The sparks, however, sputter. Plates clatter listlessly. A fork moves an inch.

Samaur laughs. "Is that all you've got, sister?"

Frustrated, Iyre scowls down at her palms.

Woudix murmurs, "You require a renewal of your power. You shouldn't have missed yesterday's offering ceremony in the Garden of Ten Gods. When was the last time you went through your offerings? Or took a sacrifice from an acolyte?"

She snaps her fingers sharply at Paz. "Paz. Get over here."

Paz, lounging to the side with Arden and Samaur's twin acolytes, wags a teasing finger. "I adore you, Lady Iyre, but I think you'll have to accept this loss."

The other humans chuckle, winking at one another, satisfied to see their gods imperfect for once.

Iyre purses her lips in barely contained humiliation.

"Paz is right, Iyre," Vale rasps. "Go find yourself a renewal source. Today, you've lost. The game is over."

Paz exclaims, "Wait, wait! Not all the competitors have shown us their talents yet!"

Iyre shoots him a cold look. "What are you talking about?"

"The fae played. Now, let a human." Mischievous mirth twinkles in his eyes. With one hand holding a sloshing bottle of wine, he points the other at me.

As all eyes turn to me, the blood drains out of my face.

I blurt out, "*Me?*"

It's such a silly idea that I could laugh.

I *do* laugh, then, and it rolls from a chuckle into a full-on fit as I double over in giggles. Oh. Great—I've had *way* too much wine. I feel my tipsy thoughts slide into unstable territory. It's preposterous, really. Not the competition. The fact that I'm here at all. That people are calling me "Highness" when months ago, I was shoveling goat manure. That my father is King of Fae. That half the gods are awake and prancing their pretty faces openly.

The fact that...I don't hate it.

As my laughter dies, I realize that everyone else watches me in perfect seriousness.

Quickly, I wipe the tears from my eyes. "Wait—you're serious?"

Paz grins. "You might not be fae, Highness, but you *are* godkissed. And it's time a human shows these gods that they're not the only ones with dominion over this world."

CHAPTER 23

BASTEN

I t takes the horses and me two days to reach the border wall, then one more to find the subterranean tunnel that breaks through the ward spells.

When we emerge into Volkany, I feel a shift in the air. It's colder here by at least ten degrees, plunged into perpetual twilight by towering pines. All I can think about is the last time I was here.

With Rian.

On that trip, I'd felt a whisper of distrust. A premonition that he would turn on me.

Why the hell didn't I listen to my instincts?

I dismount Myst to scan the forest, looking for tracks that might indicate an army encampment nearby that we should steer clear of.

A moth with iridescent wings flies by, leaving a trail of glowing dust in its wake. It's unnerving, sure. But no matter how many times I see the strange fauna of Volkany, I will always feel a little bit awed, too.

The horses, however, merely flick their tails at the magical moth.

Tòrr writes in the dirt:

N-O S-T-O-P

"Some of us are mortal," I tell him as I unbutton my trousers. "So, forgive my moment of awe while I take a piss."

For the rest of the day, we ride further into Volkany's interior. My senses are on edge here in a way they weren't on the Astagnonian side. The shadows are ice cold. The smells are stronger. The pines emit a sap that smells like sun-warmed bark and a moonlit stream, two things that shouldn't belong together but, here, do.

We make camp at the bottom of a cliff. I don't light a fire, not wanting to announce our presence, so I spend the night hungry and shivering with a saddle pad as a blanket.

But then, I dream of *her*.

And in my dreams, there's nothing but the warmth of her light. It pours into me, chasing away the cold that grips my bones. When her hand touches my chest, I feel a spark. Stirring coals. Some part of me remembers her, even if my mind won't.

I'm coming, Sabine.

I'm awakened by a thud.

Disoriented, I jolt upright. It takes my night vision a moment to focus. The forest is dark. It's still before dawn. Crickets play their midnight song from the trees.

Tòrr's front left foot is slammed to the dirt an inch from my boot.

I rake my hair back, blinking. "Tòrr?" I look from his iron hoof to his flaring nostrils and back down. "Hey—you didn't break one of my toes this time! That's progress!"

This modicum of improvement in our relationship fills me with a strange amount of joy—but it's short-lived.

Tòrr shoves his nose in my face to blast me with a snort, his eyes flashing white.

"Okay." My hand falls to the hunting knife at my side. "Okay. What has you bothered?"

Myst stands near the rocks, her tail flicking in agitation. My ears tune in to the forest.

Crickets. Shifting wind. An owl.

A mile away, someone sneezes.

"*Fuck.*" I dive for my knapsack, quickly readying my bow and arrow. "Myst. Tòrr. Time to go." As I quietly move around the camp, I train my ears on the distance, calculating.

"It's at least thirty soldiers," I whisper to them. "Coming from the west. They're moving quickly. They must have tracked us somehow."

Tòrr cocks his head questioningly.

"I don't know," I answer as I saddle Myst. "My guess is that they heard about your little performance at the sheep barn back in Astagnon. I bet the shepherd family went straight to the nearest army outpost, and spies got word about it over the border. Volkish soldiers have probably been following our tracks all day, though until now, they've stayed far enough back that I haven't heard them." I pause. "They're smart. They know night is the safest time to attack a monoceros."

I look up at the slivered moon, cursing.

Myst paws the ground anxiously. I swing up into her saddle and rest a hand on her neck. "I know, girl. Let's go."

We move at a quick walk into the river valley. I don't dare go any faster—the horses don't have my night vision for loose rocks and roots. My heart batters against my ribs as I throw glances over my shoulder at the dark woods.

The further we descend, the colder it gets. A thick mist swirls around the horses' legs, blanketing the ground so that I can't tell if we're headed for a road, rocks, or a cliff face. Within minutes, the mist has risen to mid-chest. Only the horses' heads are visible above it, giving the eerie sense that they're swimming through storm clouds.

Worst of all, the mist muffles my senses. It's strange—smoke can obscure my senses, but not mist.

Until now.

An uneasy prickle runs down my spine. I'm unfamiliar with Volkany, sure, but this mist? It doesn't feel natural for *any* forest.

I'm about to tell the horses to turn back when an arrow shoots out of the mist.

It strikes Tòrr's left haunch—but glances off. A spark flashes like when iron is struck.

"Stand together, facing opposite directions!" I hiss as I guide Myst to fall back next to Tòrr.

We face west. Tòrr takes the east.

The hair on the back of my neck raises. My heartbeat quickens. Though the woods are almost eerily silent, my ears pick up on tiny falling pebbles and the occasional squeak of leather gloves alerts me to our company.

An arrow shoots within an inch of my left ear.

"*Fuck!*" I curse.

Another arrow flies at my head from the north, but this one I see coming and duck.

Snapping into military mode, I aim my bow at the thick mist, waiting for a flicker of movement to give me a target.

As I wait, sweating, I pick up on the sounds of soldiers quietly drawing swords.

Infantry. Archers. But that doesn't explain the mist unless...

I groan as I mutter aloud, "They have a godkissed soldier with them."

Tòrr steps forward, putting himself in front of Myst and me like a shield.

In the next second, soldiers rush out from all sides. Tòrr squares himself against them, lowering his massive head, as I let loose an arrow.

It brings down the closest soldier, but the one behind him comes at me with a horizontal sword strike. I deflect it with a sharp kick that sends him flying backward into another soldier.

I nock a fresh arrow, take down another man.

Opposite us, Tòrr kicks a pair of swordsmen in the chest, sending them crashing into one another.

Archers positioned somewhere high release a volley of arrows. I guide Myst backward with my heels, anticipating the arrows' trajectories, and we take shelter behind Tòrr's flank just in time.

The arrows plink off his side as though hurtling against a castle wall.

I lean over to pat him. "Good boy. Good murder horse."

More soldiers close in, and Myst rears up to smack one in the jaw, sending him reeling backward. When she touches down again, I plant a kick into a soldier's chest, then deliver a sharp elbow strike to the top of his helmet.

A group of three soldiers rushes Tòrr at once, and I quickly assess their position until they line up right, then signal to Myst. She swings her rear end into the closest one so they crash into one another. The last one manages to sidestep, but Tòrr slams his head into the man's chest, knocking him on top of the pile.

Myst and I fall back into position opposite Tòrr as we face the next wave of soldiers.

"Not bad for some equines." My smug smile evaporates when a vibration travels up my legs. The wind shifts, and among the expected sweat and leather scents, there's something metallic and musty. Animal-like.

"Oh, fuck."

A goldenclaw wearing battle armor gallops through the mist with a roar that sends warm spittle flying onto my face. *Wipe my face or save my life?* Tough choice.

I steer Myst to the right as the goldenclaw swipes his giant paw at us. We dodge his strike, but in the jostling, my remaining arrows fall out of my quiver.

The bear rider taps a bullhook on the creature's rear haunch, and the bear stomps back around to face me.

I draw my hunting knife, centering my focus.

Suddenly, Tòrr rams the bear from the side. Ferra's glamour may mask his horn, but it's still *there*. As the invisible horn grates against the goldenclaw's metallic fur, sparks fly.

The bear lurches, off-balanced. The rider tumbles off his back.

"Monoceros!" a soldier shouts.

It's followed by more shouting in a language I don't speak, but their meaning is clear: Tòrr's disguise no longer fools anyone.

Roaring, the goldenclaw circles back around at Tòrr and delivers a powerful kick that sends him scuttling backward, hooves skidding over wet earth in a struggle for balance.

The goldenclaw prepares itself for another kick.

I slide off Myst's back, landing in the mud, and wave my hands over my head.

"Leave the horses alone, you gilded bastard!" I shout. "It's me you want!"

The bear lumbers around to face me. At the same time, his rider rushes me on foot with a drawn sword. I dodge the sword's downward strike, then snatch up a fallen arrow from the ground and throw it point-first at the bear.

It strikes squarely on the bear's nose—the only place its armor-like fur doesn't protect it.

The bear cries out, knocking away the arrow with its paw. As silver blood flows from the wound, the bear raises itself to its hind legs, towering over me.

More soldiers attack from the west, but I throw myself into a roll in the opposite direction and manage to grab a fallen soldier's sword as I come back up.

I swing it around, settling into a defensive stance.

Behind me, Tòrr scrambles to his feet. He moves close so that my back is against his rear end, covering one another.

The goldenclaw towers high above us, claws bared, poised to crash down.

I lift the sword in a defensive strike.

There's a terrible moment of seeing the bear hanging above me, knowing it'll be his claws through my chest, or my sword through his, when—

Everything...stops.

The bear hovers above me mid-fall.

The mist in the clearing freezes.

A tuft of goldenclaw fur hangs immobile on the wind.

The soldiers go completely still, too, with swords lifted to slash down on Tòrr. Tòrr is also frozen, his back foot lifted, ready to kick one of them into the next life.

I strain to move—even to breathe—but it's like I've turned to stone.

Movement from the corner of my eye directs me to the only people *not* frozen.

Two female soldiers in indigo cloaks step around the soldiers' motionless bodies. Their cloaks are emblazed with a star-shaped pin fastened above their godkissed birthmarks.

The first one, thickset with a long blonde braid, sweeps her hands through the mist, dispersing it in a single fluid motion until only a faint wisp lingers.

The other, a captain, raises her hands as if holding back an invisible tide. She lowers her fingers one by one, counting down from ten. She's a petite, light brown woman, and her uniform swallows her frame, but her size doesn't hinder her from wrenching the heavy sword out of my left hand.

I try to shout an objection but can't.

Moving swiftly, the other godkissed soldier unfastens the goldenclaw's heavy metal collar and bolts it around Tòrr's neck instead.

While she's trapping Tòrr, the captain strains to haul me out of the goldenclaw's trajectory. She stops to catch her breath, lips still silently counting down from ten.

She angles her sword against my neck. Her eyebrow arches in a challenge as she warns, "Don't move."

Like a wound clock, my heart suddenly lurches back to a

start. Breath rushes down my throat. Time hurtles back into motion.

I jolt forward, but the sword blade presses against my neck. Holding out my hands in surrender, I bark, "I want to see King Rachillon."

The captain presses her sword harder against my throat. "Oh, you'll see the king. It's straight to the gallows for any normal bandit, but one who travels with a monoceros? Who kills royal soldiers? Who bears King Rian's crest? You'll get a royal audience, I assure you. I'd wager that His Majesty will even do the honor of personally slitting your throat."

Nearby, the revived soldiers loop a rope around Myst's neck. Tòrr strains against the iron collar, but six heavyset soldiers hold him back with attached chains.

The moon hangs high overhead—his solarium horn is powerless until dawn.

I glance back at the captain. "You're godkissed. So is she." My eyes shift to the woman in the indigo cloak.

"And?" The captain's tone is sharp.

"I'm godkissed too," I say, narrowing my eyes. "Yet your time-stopping spell worked on me."

"It works on who I want it to work on." She removes the sword from against my neck but shoves the hilt into my solar plexus instead. "Even a monoceros."

Pain rips through my middle. As I double over, I pat the outside of my pocket to make sure I haven't lost Rian's locket with the portrait of Sabine.

"King Rachillon." I dig the heel of my palm against my aching chest. "Does he...have...a daughter?"

True surprise crosses the army captain's face. Genuinely curious, she wrinkles her brow. "What do you know of the king's daughter?"

I thrust out my wrists to be bound. "Chain me. Tie me up. String me along on the back of that goldenclaw. I won't fight. Hell, I'll even hunt rabbits for your dinner. If you take me to Sabine Darrow, then I will bow before any god, man, or woman you like."

CHAPTER 24

SABINE

S how the gods that they're not the only ones with domain over this world.

As night gives way to the first light of dawn, I stand beneath the Hall of Vale's newly repaired crystal chandelier with every eye on me.

My mind reels. My lungs seize. To be frank, I shouldn't have had so much wine.

But here I am.

"They're *gods*," I state, swaying slightly. "I can't compete with them."

Woudix's acolyte, Arden, claps her hands in delight. "Oh, Highness, try! Just because a human hasn't ever competed in fae trials doesn't mean one can't now!"

Samaur's twins pound on a table in unison. "Here, here!"

Well—this is new. Being cheered on to win. The humans at Drahallen Hall may live in the shadow of five fae gods, but they clearly enjoy seeing their masters knocked down a peg.

Still, I'm not keen to humiliate myself.

I raise my glass to the gods in surrender. "Maybe next time."

But the courtiers smell blood in the water. "Winged Lady! Winged Lady!"

"Where did they even hear that name?" I murmur aloud.

Artain rests his hand on my shoulder. "Word spreads, princess. We've all heard one version or another of the Winged Lady's attack in Duren's arena. Go ahead, give us a taste of that vicious godkissed power of yours."

I shrug out from under his hand, rolling my eyes. "I don't think so."

He scoffs, "What's the matter? Does our power intimidate you?" A wicked gleam sparks in his eyes. "Or are you not curious about the winner's prize?"

I hesitate. "What prize?"

"A sip from the Meden Cup, of course!" Samaur punches his fist in the air to the chorus of raucous applause from the crowd.

My head spins at all the noise. Frankly, I have no idea what the Meden Cup is or what vile concoction it likely contains.

Human blood? Goat piss?

Still, the thrill of a challenge has worked its way under my skin. For so many years, I wasn't allowed to have fun. To drink. To dance. To celebrate my godkiss.

"What the hell." I grin, slightly uncertain. "I'll play."

My words are met with more enthusiasm from the human courtesans, who laugh and clap in anticipation.

Artain slaps me on the back. "That's the spirit, princess!"

I cough, trying to hide how his inhuman strength nearly knocked me to my knees.

Someone—Arden, maybe? —thrusts another glass of wine in my hand, and before I second-guess myself, I down it in one long glug. That was...maybe a mistake. Wiping my lips, I scan the room tipsily, struggling to make calculations.

I rest my hands on my hips. "Open all the windows."

Paz, Arden, and the twins jump into action, unlatching the Hall of Vale's tall, arched windows. An unseasonably wintery breeze rolls in, ruffling my gown, tickling my ankles with a rush of excitement.

I roll back my shoulders, standing tall, feeling the adrenaline enter my system. This is what Rian taught me—the allure of a game, the intoxicating rush of outsmarting an opponent.

I catch snippets of conversations. Low murmurs of bets being placed. The room feels alive, and I can't help but feed off that energy.

The game is on, and I'm ready to play.

I climb onto the banquet table, knocking over a goblet, but ignore its clatter as I lift my hands toward the open windows.

Come, friends! I call. *Join our feast!*

Everyone spins toward the windows as they seem to hold a collective breath. No one here can hear my godkissed voice—not even the fae—so to them, I am merely staring at the windows.

Time stretches. A musician drops his violin, the strings squealing in protest.

Then, a storm hits.

It's a flurry of wings and feathers. First, the blackbirds come. They were closest to the castle, pecking in the kitchen garden outside. Next, a flock of tiny gold-winged finches swoop in and land on the cheese platter. One of the royal falcons, still wearing leather thongs, circles over the attendee's heads before tearing into the roast turkey. A pair of swans who usually live in the Twilight Garden fly in and fight over a crusty loaf of bread.

As more birds pour through the windows, gusts from their beating wings ripple throughout the hall, blowing over cloth napkins and leaving women to clutch their curls.

"Exceptional!" a courtesan cries.

"Look—they're still coming!" Paz's face shines in awe as he points to the windows.

More birds pour in—lapwings and jays, barred owls, a buzzard. Their wings throw shadows over the ceiling as they circle over the guest's heads, diving down now and again to pluck a treat from the banquet table.

"Not too bad for a human—" Artain begrudgingly starts, but his praise falls on uncaring ears as I sharply pivot away from the birds to face the rear wall that flanks the kitchen.

Little scavengers, I call. *Come, eat your fill!*

Gasps ripple through the crowd as the floor begins to vibrate, causing the water glasses to tremble. From the open doors, hundreds of rodents stream into the hall. Plain brown mice who live in the walls. A few timid rats from the kitchen. A family of chittering red squirrels. A pair of rabbits from the kitchen garden, followed by a beaver who waddled all the way from the river valley.

Guests exchange incredulous glances as they spin in circles to take in our company. A few attendees press their hands over their mouths, unable to contain their marvel, while others point excitedly.

"That buzzard is eating Iyre's slice of cake!" Arden exclaims with a laugh.

I stamp my heel against the table three times. ***Come, the rest of you! Join the party!***

Honeybees buzz through the windows, waltzing aimlessly until they discover the honey-glazed tarts. A cloud of iridescent dragonflies takes wing around the chandeliers. Ants creep through tiny wall cracks by the thousands, parading in fanciful lines between the partygoers.

I climb down from the bench to revel in the presence of all my woodland friends. The chamber is filled from floor to ceiling with animals that coo and chirp and chitter, and my heart feels so overjoyed that I spin in a slow circle, weaving my hands among the cartwheeling dragonflies.

A nuthatch lands on my shoulder to chirp a pretty melody. Rabbits hop between my feet, chasing berries rolling across the floor. Tiny claws delicately climb up my gown, and I gasp in delight at her familiar face.

Little friend! I exclaim.

The forest mouse perches in my palm. ***What a feast! And to think, you tried to leave.***

This place is not at all what I expected, I admit with a nuzzle of my nose to her soft fur.

The crowd gasps in awe as ladies dodge swooping owls. The Blades' self-satisfied smirks have vanished, replaced by expressions of disbelief. Iyre gapes openly, dumbfounded, at the legion of animals.

Vale slowly rises from his place at the table, clearing his throat. At the scrape of his chair, all eyes turn to him. I hold my breath, clutching the mouse in my palm, waiting.

Slowly, Vale brings his hands together. "We have our winner—Lady Sabine!"

A brief pause blankets the air like the calm before a storm...and then the crowd *erupts*.

The force of their applause deafens me, raw energy crashing around me like a tidal wave. My cheeks burn in a sudden flood of pride. Back in Astagnon, such a spectacle would have incited screams. The crowd would have tripped all over each other to escape the swarm of creatures.

But Volkany—these people—revel in what I can do.

A grin cracks my face as I nod to the lords and ladies who press forward to congratulate me.

"Humanity scores a win!" Paz exclaims, draping an arm around my shoulders.

Arden laughs as she ducks beneath a swooping blackbird. "You've done the impossible, Lady Sabine!"

"Bested the fae?" I ask.

She shakes her head, grinning. "You've found a way to make a fae party even *wilder!*"

The musicians take up a spirited tune. Laughing, Paz and Arden pull me onto the dance floor, but just as my feet begin to catch up with my head, Iyre clamps her hand around my wrist.

"Your father wishes to speak to you," she hisses low in my ear.

My good mood dims slightly as she drags me toward the head table, nudging the beaver out of our way with her boot. At the table, honeybees cover nearly every pastry, and the squirrel family has nibbled the turkey to the bone.

Iyre releases me, and I stumble, wine-drunk, before resting a hand on a chairback.

Pull it together, Sabine. "Father."

Vale folds his arms, his face unreadable behind the wild beard. "There was the matter of a prize, Daughter."

My heart begins to patter again in a tentative mixture of pride and apprehension. I dare to meet his eyes. In the fae stories I was told as a girl, "prizes" from the fae could be as much a curse as a blessing. But the spirited dance music hums through me, its jaunty chords stoking the hidden part of me that revels in this party.

"I would be honored," I croak.

His massive hand cups the narrow point of my chin. "You did well. You proved yourself a credit to me and to your mother."

His stern face breaks into a smile.

My heartbeat takes up a strange, feather-light pattern. In twenty-two years, I've never had a parent say they're proud of me. Maybe it's silly to care at my age, but standing before Vale in all his immortal splendor, I can't help but feel like a thirteen-year-old girl again, writing a letter to my father in hopes of a scrap of affection.

I swallow, fumbling with the twine around my finger.

Vale holds out his hand, and my heartbeat stumbles before I take it. He lifts our joined hands high, showing me off to the audience.

He commands in a ribald cry, "Bring the Meden Cup—if you can find it under a beaver's ass!"

Drunken laughter rips through the air until the chandeliers' crystals tremble. Servants, their grinning faces and wine-sweet breath revealing they've indulged as much as the courtiers, clear the head table.

They nudge a mallard off the gravy tureen. Gently dump a half dozen mice out of the breadbasket. All the while, dragonflies pinwheel overhead to the music.

I'm swept deeper into the chaos by Samaur on one side and Artain on the other, who wrap their arms around my back as they usher me to the table's opposite side. A dove alights from a half-finished plate, nearly crashing into my head, and I barely duck in time.

My head doesn't seem to be entirely in sync with my body. I list to the left, leaning into Samaur's shoulder to steady myself.

He laughs as he tweaks my cheek. "You hold your alcohol about as well as a suckling pig, Highness."

My tongue feels thick as I fumble for a retort. The thing is, alcohol isn't what's making my head whirl like a top. Well—not alcohol *alone*. I've never felt such a heady intoxicant as this wonderous place. Fae gods. A symphony of wings overhead. A serenade of tails at my feet.

A father whose eyes shine with pride.

It's a strange harmony that makes my chest ache for something I've never had.

Blinking, I realize servants have cleared the table in record time. It's now covered with a fresh velvet tablecloth and, on that, a single piece of black silk.

Artain lifts the simple scrap of silk. "Before she sips from Meden's prize..."

The crowd yells out the rest of the chant. "...a blindfold shall cover her eyes!"

Before I know which way is up, Woudix appears behind me, fastening the fabric around my eyes. His cold fingers brush my temple as he knots the blindfold in the back, making goosebumps lift along my skin. He's the Ender, after all. Whose knees wouldn't go weak?

I press my palms against the smooth black silk.

"Why do I need a blindfold?" I ask with a high note of worry.

Instead of an answer, I'm jostled from one god to

another as Samaur leads me back to the dance floor among the crowd's tipsy giggles.

Let's be real—I'm not *totally* blindfolded. I could ask the animals to tell me what's happening. Plus, I can peek out the bottom. Still, a part of me doesn't want to ruin the surprise. I never had a chance to play games as a child. No Blindman's Bluff with farm girls. No hopscotch with other lord's daughters.

Samaur takes both my hands in his as he shouts to the musicians, "Play 'In the Meadow of Dreamers'!"

A quick-paced tune springs to life as Samaur spins me in dizzying circles until I'm stumbling over my own feet.

"Before she sips, twelve times she'll spin..." he recites, and the audience immediately responds in a chant, "...to lose her way before the win!"

My sense of balance tilts off-kilter as Samaur catches me, holding me steady as my head spins.

"*This* is the prize?" I whisper. "Getting me dizzy enough to puke?"

He chuckles in my ear.

I peek out from the bottom of the blindfold as Samaur leads me back to the head table. The fabric is thin enough for me to make out vague outlines, and it looks like the servants have delivered a new, large platter.

Samaur guides me to my place, and then Woudix's cool fingers brush my bare shoulders.

My ears perk up at the sound of someone uncorking a bottle. The audience is doing a poor job of containing their snorts and giggles. From the blindfold's narrow bottom gap, I can peek at a suspiciously bare curve of tanned skin on the table.

Those muscles? Yeah, only one god has brawn like that.

Vale takes over the chant, reciting in his rasp, "Now comes the time for all to hush..."

The crowd laughingly answers, "...for the Meden Cup shall make one blush!"

My head feels as bubbly as champagne as my heart thumps faster, wondering what kind of fae trick I've gotten myself into.

Woudix guides me forward with one cold hand resting on the back of my neck, gently pressing my head toward the table. I hold out my hands to pat the air, making up for my lack of sight, and discover that where a plate should be, my fingers graze a taut male bicep instead.

I cheat by peeking through the blindfold gap.

Yep. As I suspected. *Fantastic.*

Artain is laid flat on the table, shirtless as usual, only this time, he's also shed his leather vest and belt. His trousers are shoved an inch beneath his navel. Someone— Iyre, judging by the flash of a long white sleeve I make out— pours a dram of whiskey into Artain's navel.

"Drink deeply from the cup, Highness," Woudix's coarse voice murmurs in my ear, and I shiver as he bends me forward.

What the hell am I doing? My lips hover a few inches above Artain's ripped abs. The blindfold hardly hides the "surprise" in store—that the "Meden Cup" means slurping a dram of whiskey out of a god's navel. It's beyond ridiculous. Childish. Perhaps the silliest thing I've heard of in my entire life.

Artain snickers, doing a poor job of playing an inanimate object.

I groan inwardly. *It's just a game.*

The crowd eggs me on as I brace my hands on the table,

feigning ignorance that the God of the Hunt is currently serving as my drinking glass.

"As a daughter of Volkany and winner of tonight's competition," I announce, feeling equally absurd and amused, "I accept my prize!"

Among the crowd's laughter, there's a ripple of commotion at the back of the hall. Raised voices tickle my ears. Guards' footsteps clomp on the floor, but the echo of their steps is muffled by all the flapping wings from my invited guests.

"To the gods!" I laugh as I make a mock cheer, then lean forward and slurp whiskey from the dip in Artain's abdomen.

The alcohol is spicy and warm, and burns pleasantly over my tongue. I straighten, grinning triumphantly, and reach to untie my blindfold—

But the room has gone strangely silent.

I pause.

Why isn't the crowd falling over themselves with laughter? Why aren't the musicians playing again? Why hasn't Artain made some asinine joke about my lips on his bodily fluids?

My fingers freeze on the blindfold's knot, suddenly uncertain that I want to see what has rendered everyone so speechless.

Mouse-talker, the forest mouse whispers urgently in my head. *Take off your blindfold. Captain Tatarin has returned...*

My stomach flips. As though moving through a sluggish dream, I tug the knot loose, and the black silk flutters away from my face.

Most of the birds have found roosts on the chandelier or

disappeared back into the night. The rest of the animals have followed the servants to the kitchen to finish off the scraps.

Guards now flank a wide aisle through the crowd, and Tati stands at their head in a mud-splattered indigo cloak, her hair mussed from her journey.

And my heart *stops*.

Because she isn't alone.

Basten stands at her side, wrists shackled in iron chains, as travel-worn and filthy as the rest of the soldiers. A vicious bruise marks his temple. He's hunched forward so that his loose, dirty hair falls in his face. He looks as though he's just fought in the arena for his life. Like he might collapse on his feet—and yet his brown eyes shine with alertness.

Until this moment, I realize, he didn't know that my father was Immortal Vale.

Or that Artain, Samaur, and Woudix were awake.

His eyes scan over Vale briefly, taking in his fey lines and pointed ears with a hunter's calm attention to detail, and then shift to Immortal Artain, splayed out on the table with a line of whiskey running down his rock-hard obliques.

The air in my lungs evaporates as I swipe the back of my hand across my lips.

A ghost—that's what I must be looking at. Someone back from the dead.

I take a shaky step forward but stop, hemmed in by the table.

Why is he chained? Is he here against his will? Did he come to save me? Strangle me? Does he remember me at all?

I inhale raggedly, the thoughts like daggers.

Oh, no, the Meden Cup! *This...can't look good.*

Here I am, dripping with obsidian jewels like the perfect

Volkish princess, teasing the God of the Hunt. I'm clearly no prisoner.

For all that is holy, I just sipped booze from a god's navel...

The blindfold falls from my slackened hand.

"Basten," I murmur breathlessly.

Basten is silent, staring ahead with dark, unreadable eyes—not at the dazzlingly bright gods, but at *me*.

CHAPTER 25
BASTEN

S abine Darrow is even more beautiful than her portrait in Rian's locket. I've seen plenty of artists embellish their subjects—adding extra curves, omitting unsightly freckles—but the real-life, in-the-flesh Sabine Darrow?

She's a *vision*. The kind that makes you forget to breathe for a second. Her black gown, studded with iron rivets and obsidian jewels, gleams in the faint dawn light like stars trapped in dark velvet. It's regal yet hard-edged, like armor. And she carries it with the grace of a queen—no, something wilder.

But it's not about the gown. It's her. The way she holds herself, chin high, like she's daring the whole room to challenge her. Her skin glows in the warm light, untouched by the dust and filth I've dragged in with me. Her hair—pure sunlit gold—brushes her shoulders in soft waves, framing a face so sharp it could cut glass. And those eyes...impossible to describe. Though, right now, they're wide with something I can't read, flickering between fear and defiance.

She's still. Frozen. Like she's caught in a moment that she doesn't understand.

Neither do I.

I both know her and don't in a way that has my insides twisting in knots.

Oh—and then there's the fae.

The *motherfucking* fae.

It's a strange world when a girl consumes my attention more than the five immortal gods who, by all accounts, should be nothing but myths. Yet here they are, lounging like kings in their palace, their fey lines glowing in the dim light, looking both amused and bored by this little banquet.

And I'm standing here, chained up like a damn criminal, trying not to let my mind shatter from the weight of it all.

I'll admit—it's a bit of a surprise. Okay, it's an earth-quaking, bone-rattling surprise. But I guess that's Sabine Darrow for you. She outshines the stars, so why not gods, too?

Hundreds of eyes bore into me, so I have to piece things together fast. Okay...the gods are real. They're awake. At least, half of them are. Plus, from the reek on their breath, they're drunker than sailors.

I can guess their identities—the tall one in a crown must be Vale—but the one I would know anywhere is Iyre.

Perched on the foot of the table, she bites into a honey-cake and takes her time licking the crumbs off her lips.

I only *wish* I could forget about that bitch.

For weeks, I've been clawing myself apart to learn every detail about Sabine. The sound of her laughter. If she snores. Which foods make her happy. I want to know everything.

Once, I *did* know everything about her.

And now?

My muscles tense like a caged beast, wrists straining until the chain between my iron shackles pulls taut with a metallic snap that echoes in the hall, making half the courtesans jump.

She took Sabine away from me. Robbed me of my memories. Left me doubting the one person in my life who's ever given a damn about me.

My gaze swings back to Sabine like gravity's pulling it there.

Her wide eyes on my shackles, she staggers forward to catch herself on the table as though about to faint and says again, "*Basten.*"

My legs nearly give out. One utterance of my name on her lips, and I'm a lost soul.

"Daughter? Do you know this man?" Vale's voice rasps like he's been sleeping underground for a thousand years.

Wait—*wait.* I blink hard.

Daughter?

I only have seconds for my mind to churn over this information before Sabine makes her unsteady way around the table, clutching onto the chair backs for support.

"Basten. I—I know how this looks." Her bottom lip trembles as she fumbles with some piece of string around her finger. "It isn't what you think. It was only a game. A stupid game..."

She comes to a short stop a few paces before reaching me.

"A game?" I repeat, confused.

She chokes back a sob as she points a shaky finger at the fae on the table. "Artain, I mean. Whiskey. The Meden Cup..."

Her words are gibberish to me, but if she thinks it shocks

me to see revelers, well, *reveling*, then she has no idea how much time I've spent in taverns.

Okay, it *is* jarring. To know her lips were on another man's body. But frankly, I don't give a fuck what she's done—she could stab me in my own navel, and I'd thank her for it.

Doesn't she get it? We're just like in the story Runa told me.

I'm Aron.

She's Aria.

Memories or not, jealousy or not, nothing can come between us.

"Do you...do you even know who I am?" Tears glimmer in the orbs of her eyes. She can't seem to decide if she wants to reach for me or not, her fingers hovering in the air between us.

I say measuredly, "I know who you are."

Her throat bobs in a hard swallow. She takes another step forward—

But like a thunderclap, Vale is there, one hand gripping her upper arm. "Sabine. Stay away from this captive."

Her eyes go round as silver coins. "Father, this is—"

"An Astagnonian war prisoner." He shoves her protectively behind him, where another fae—I'm guessing Woudix from the whole "cold as death" vibe—closes his hands around her shoulders, holding her back.

Vale wrenches my face to his and thunders, "Who are you?"

"Basten Bowborn," I mutter between smooshed lips, fighting the urge to rip my jaw out of his grasp. For Sabine, I have to play nice. "First Sword to King Rian Valvere."

Vale tightens his fingers until something cracks in my jaw. "Spying for your king?"

"No, Majesty. When I left him, it was with his blood on my fists. I'm no loyalist. King Rian does not deserve the throne. His greed will cast Astagnon into an age of darkness." Pain shoots through my jaw as I speak. "I can help you. I am the true son of Berolt Valvere. The rightful heir to the Astagnonian throne. Test my blood—it will prove my claim."

Agitated murmurs ripple through the courtiers until Vale silences them with a raised hand.

"Or better yet, ask your daughter." I point the best I can with my bound wrists. "She knows my claim is true."

Even the damn squirrels fall silent as everyone turns to Sabine.

Face pale, she stutters, "It's—it's true. The bloodtaster verified it before my own eyes. I know this man to be trustworthy beyond doubt. He and I were—to be married." She gently strokes the twine around her fourth finger. "Iyre can verify it. She took his memories."

"Iyre?" Vale asks.

Iyre takes a long time inspecting an imaginary crumb under her fingernail. "I did not see the bloodtaster with my own eyes."

The hot anger I feel for her crushes against my skull, making my fingers curl so hard into fists that I'm afraid the bones will shatter.

"You ruined my life!" Unable to control myself, I lunge toward her with a growl. I win a few feet until Captain Tatarin signals to the guards, and the iron chains pull taut. Another metallic snap echoes through the hall.

Gasps ring out from the guests.

Sabine's hand flies to her collar, her face going ghostly white, terror-stricken.

Iyre only offers the hint of a smirk.

"Enough!" Vale's thunderous voice makes the floor shake.

I bite back my hatred of Iyre, letting it simmer into hot coals in my belly as I fight to keep my breath steady.

"If I may, Majesty," Captain Tatarin says with a bow, her soft presence diffusing the tension. "I might be able to offer some evidence to support Lord Basten's claim. He was captured with a horse...and a monoceros."

Sabine's lips part in soft surprise.

Vale strokes his metallic beard before finally signaling to Captain Tatarin. "Bring the animals."

"Here?" she says, gazing up at the crystal chandeliers. "Inside?"

"*Here.*"

She leaves with a few guards, and soon, the clatter of hooves sounds in the hallway. Captain Tatarin enters, leading Myst and Tòrr by ropes in each hand.

The human guests in the hall murmur in confusion. They see two horses, not a horse and a monoceros.

But the moment the fae set eyes on Tòrr?

All five of them jump to attention as though I've dropped a powder keg in their party.

In a way, I guess I *have*.

Artain springs upright from the table, knocking over a bottle of honey wine. Iyre's eyelids flare. Even the fey lines on Vale's limbs pulse.

"By your reaction, I assume you can see beyond the beast's glamour," I say, stretching out my jaw. "I stole him from King Rian. I've traveled with him in daylight for a week

—as you can see, I'm still alive. He would have incinerated a spy."

Whispers spread through the hall, and my ears pick up on every one of them.

The horse is glamoured... It's a monoceros... Look—dawn rises outside!

Vale twists toward the early morning sun rising through the windows. "Samaur—bring night. Now."

"It's only just dawn." The God of Day brushes aside a crow to reach out the window. "We'll lose an entire day's worth of light."

"I don't fucking care! Do it now! That monoceros can burn the castle to ash!"

Samaur casts one more doubtful look at the rising sun before bringing his hands together in a clap. Orange-gold fey shoots out from his palms toward the open window. The echo of his clap makes the water glasses tremble.

The rising sun skyrockets across the sky from east to west. The shadows change. The sky brightens, then dims. The animals throughout the Hall of Vale run for cover, alarmed.

In the space of a single breath, the sun vanishes behind the western ridge.

Vale looks to the ceiling and releases a held breath. "Good."

The crowd utters words of relief amid their astonishment.

"Myst!" Sabine's joyful voice cuts through the tense chatter. She pulls out of Woudix's grasp, races across the room, and throws her arms around Myst's neck.

Myst whinnies softly, resting her muzzle on Sabine's shoulder.

Tòrr lets out a burst of steam as if to say, *Where is my hug?*

Sabine laughs, wiping away tears, and wraps her arms around him, too.

I can barely tear my eyes off her.

All this distance. I've crossed all this distance on nothing but faith, all to answer one burning question.

And the answer?

I would fall for this woman from the stars themselves.

Vale grabs my chin again, wrenching my attention away from Sabine, bushy silver eyebrows lowered as he glowers. "Which did you come for, human? My daughter or a throne?"

Another hush falls over the room as hundreds of ears await my answer. But none seem as interested as Sabine herself, whose fingers weave anxiously through Tòrr's mane, her attention darting between me and the twine loop on her finger.

Her, I want to say. *In a thousand lives, I would always come for her.*

And yet...her father currently holds my jaw in a death grip. He spent years searching for her—he won't let me walk out of here with his prized daughter.

"I don't remember your daughter," I murmur measuredly, lifting an indifferent shoulder. "Whether we were engaged or not, I cannot desire someone I don't know. I want the throne. It's my birthright. My duty. And I will see it dripping with Rian Valvere's blood as *I* sit upon it."

Sabine's face falls before she struggles to put up a mask of apathy—but I catch it.

Vale's massive fingers tighten painfully on my jaw with a bone-crushing promise. "Our brother, Immortal Meric, is not yet awakened. He alone holds the ability to discern truth. So, in his absence, we will call for a godkissed blood-taster to verify your claim. Until then, you'll remain locked and under guard."

"You can't treat him like a prisoner!" Sabine cries.

Vale snaps, and a bolt of blue energy ripples across the room in warning. Sabine clenches her jaw, though her eyes simmer with anger.

"I have the right to speak to him—you can't keep us apart," she argues.

Vale beckons Artain forward with his free hand. "Keep Lady Sabine under lock and guard, too."

"What? No! You can't do that, Father!"

His face remains stony. "I didn't go to the lengths I did to bring you here only for some human male to take you from me. You are a princess of Volkany and deserving of the privileges under that title. But make no mistake—I may be your father, but I am still your *god*."

He releases my jaw.

"As for you, Lord Basten." He circles Myst and Tòrr, assessing them. "I appreciate the gifts. Let us hope that your claim has merit. Both that you are the heir and that you did not come for my daughter. Our altars always need fresh sacrifices—and a king's blood would be especially potent."

To emphasize his power, he raises his hand to shoot a bolt of energy at Tòrr, peeling away Ferra's glamour so the monoceros stands before us in his full fae form.

Vale nods to Captain Tatarin, who rests a hand on my shoulder to lead me away. My muscles bunch, resistful, but her grip presses into me in a gentle warning.

I force my shoulders back and down.

Sabine and I share one last look before I'm dragged

away. There's an ocean of uncertainty between us. She looks pale. Shaken. She thinks I don't want her—that when Iyre took my memory of her, she also took my love.

She couldn't be more wrong.

I didn't crawl across kingdoms to walk away now. She's mine—and I'm not leaving without her.

CHAPTER 26
SABINE

I pace so long in front of my bedroom fireplace that the thick rug looks more like a game trail. All night, I've thought of nothing but Basten's face when he saw me reveling with the fae...reveling with that *ass*, Artain.

It...wasn't my finest moment.

Basten's anger at me was palpable. The metallic rattle from when he jerked his shackles still echoes between my ears. Those terrible words aimed at me: *You ruined my life.* I can only imagine the nightmare that the Valveres have spun me into, filling his missing memories with poison about the traitorous princess.

And what did I do?

Prove those vipers right at first glance.

He must *hate* me.

If only I'd been free to explain to Basten that the Meden Cup was just a game. I was pretending. The way to stay safe here is to play along, make them trust me.

I flop onto the battered rug and sink my face into my

hands. Oh, but who am I kidding? It wasn't pretend. No matter how badly I wish it were.

Ever since I arrived in Norhelm, it's been like a lantern switched on. Something about Volkany sings to me. For the first time in my life, my every move hasn't been watched. Judged. No one cares what I wear or how I style my hair. I can drink two bottles of plum wine and be cheered on for it instead of reprimanded.

Is it only about the freedom to sin? Hell, I was locked in a convent for twelve years, so I'm due a chance to blow off a little steam. But, no. If it was only debauchery I was after, I could have gotten my fill of that in Duren. The same goes for luxuries: for all his faults, Rian was beyond generous. Likewise, the riches my father lavishes on me are only baubles.

I think...it's the taste of *power* that bewitches me.

The raw potential.

Here, I'm brushing shoulders with the gods. Ancient beings who—let's face it, are far from perfect—but can bring death upon a room, trap a memory, and turn day to night.

Sighing, I slide off Basten's twine ring and hold it up to the moonlight, twirling it slowly.

Tattered. Misshapen. *Perfect.*

"I never took it off," I whisper.

Is Basten perfect? No, but he's perfect for me. *And I won't let him go.*

Slipping the ring back on my finger, I call softly, ***Are you there, friend?***

It isn't long before a pink nose pokes out from the loose chimney bricks. The forest mouse emerges and scampers onto my knee. ***You did not sleep all night. Though it is still dark, my stomach tells me it is breakfast time.***

That's Samaur's doing, I explain. *The sun won't rise all day. The darkness may help me, though—I need you to tell me how many guards are stationed in the hallway.*

The mouse trains her beady eyes on me like a disapproving governess. *What are you planning?*

Please, do this favor for me. I wrinkle my nose and hope it looks endearing. *And also pick the lock while you're at it?*

She puffs out an exasperated burst of air but climbs down my leg, tackles the tasks, and returns promptly.

Two guards at the door, she reports. *Two more at the end of the hallway.*

Thank you—now get some sleep yourself, my friend. I push to my feet determinedly and drag my desk's wooden stool to the tall armoire.

The armoire's top is adorned with detailed wooden carvings resembling vines. The maids are diligent in dusting, but they tend to overlook this spot, which is clotted with spiderwebs.

"*Tck-sssSSS-Tck,*" I sing softly aloud, cooing to the mother Barkcreeper spider who nests here with her downy egg sack.

Soon, a button-sized gray spider emerges from the shadows, wiggling her front two legs in greeting. I lower my hand for her to crawl onto my palm, then carefully descend the stool.

As a rule, spiders are hard to communicate with, but not impossible. You just have to understand how they sing. Spider songs communicate by pitch and modulation: For example, low and rounded notes mean "sleep," staccato ones mean "help," and a piercing warble means "danger."

I carry her to the door, where I lay on my belly in front of the narrow gap. I softly sing a staccato trill, and she bounces up and down to say she understands while trilling back my melody.

Then, I hold up two fingers to mean the closest guards, then two more fingers with my other hand to indicate the ones down the hall. I don't know the exact pitch to convey "venom," but I do know the note for "bite."

I quietly sing a shrill aria that repeats three times.

She bounces up and down faster, her front two legs waving excitedly in the air.

"Go, then, little friend," I whisper as I lower my hand for her to crawl under the door.

For the next few minutes, my nerves rattle. I gnaw on my thumbnail, waiting.

The desk clock keeps ticking, ticking, ticking.

Is something wrong?

Nearly ten minutes pass before the spider returns, resolutely making a bee-line onto my hand.

"*SSSsss-tck-tck-SSSsss*," she sings with such urgency that her melody stumbles over itself. "*Tck-tck-tck!*"

"I don't know what you mean. Slow down. *sssSSS sssSSS.*"

She continues to wave her front legs and sing emphatically, and I shake my head in frustration.

All I can think to do is give a high warble to clarify: *Danger?*

She immediately stills, then carefully repeats my warble backward. "*SSSsss SSSsss.*" In the language of spider songs, a backward melody means the negative of whatever the previous speaker said.

So, she means: *No danger.*

It eases my anxiety, but now my curiosity is hooked. I lift the spider back to her egg sack on top of the armoire, then tiptoe to the door and press my ear against it. Silence meets me from the other side. Not so much as a guard's sigh.

Well, spiders have never failed me before...

I crack open the door, ready to plead ignorance to the guards about how the lock possibly opened. My heart hammers hard enough to crack a rib. The first thing I see is a guard slumped against the wall, his head slack, drool sliding out of his mouth.

My hand tightens on the doorknob.

That isn't the reaction from a Barkcreeper spider bite, which leaves a victim's face bright red.

If it wasn't the spider, how did—

Movement from the other side of the hall sends my heart shooting into my throat—as I look up to find Basten.

He presses a rag reeking of chloroform to the struggling second guard's mouth and nose. Locking eyes with me, he continues to silently wrestle the second guard until that one also slumps to the floor.

The two at the end of the hall? Already knocked out.

The second guard's unconscious body sits like a boulder between Basten and me as we stare at one another, a million and one questions perched like daggers over our heads.

"I—was going to do that," I blurt out.

Without missing a beat, he deadpans, "You were going to drug a pair of two-hundred-fifty-pound guards?"

I shake my head quickly, my thoughts a jumble. "No, I mean that I had an arrangement with a spider, and..."

I take a deep breath, fingers tensing around the brass doorknob.

Start over, Sabine.

One month apart, and I've never been so nervous around him.

His gaze cuts to the twine ring, the symbol of love he gave me, but his face shows no recognition.

For the agonizing span of one heartbeat to the next, we stare at one another.

"Did you come here to put a knife in my chest?" I ask bluntly.

His eyebrows twitch. "What?"

"I don't know what the Valveres told you."

He rests one hand in the doorway, leaning over me. "They told me plenty, but I can make up my own mind about things that matter."

With him towering over me, my thighs go a little weak. In a whisper, I ask, "Do—do you remember me?"

This time, the dark pools of his eyes deepen. A long second passes. Soft, he says, "No."

No word has ever felt so heavy. My breath falters, but I try not to show the crushing weight of disappointment. I glance down at my hands, still fiddling nervously with his ring.

But there's no time for grief. Not here. Not like this.

With a deep breath, I gather the broken pieces of my nerves and thrust my hand out.

"Then I suppose it's time for introductions. Sabine Darrow. Err—well, not Darrow anymore."

I was almost Sabine Valvere.

Then Sabine Bowborn.

And now? Her Highness, Princess Sabine of Volkany?

I stammer, cheeks blazing, "I guess I don't know what I am."

He stares long and hard at my extended hand, his loose hair shadowing his expression, as my heart screams like a tea kettle gone dry.

Slowly, he lifts his eyes, his calloused hand sliding into mine. "Little violet—that's what you are."

A jagged inhale cuts across my lips. My heart freefalls into a bottomless cavern, pinwheeling with a belly-tightening yearning until I'm sure I'll never breathe again. *He remembers. He does.* If he wasn't holding my hand, the next speck of dust might topple me over.

"You...do remember?" I breathe.

Haltingly, he admits, "Like I said, I've been told a lot about you. About us."

I try to stop the crashing freefall of my heart before it slams against rock bottom. Slowly, I pull my trembling hand back.

You idiot, Sabine. Of course he doesn't remember.

"Don't believe a word the Valveres said about me being a traitor," I say in a rush. "They can't be trusted. Rian most of all. I tried to leave here. To warn you. I know you have a long history with him, but *he's* a traitor. He—he was the one who sold me out."

His eyes simmer. "I know."

"You...know?"

He reaches into his pocket and takes out Rian's Golath dime. I pull in a gasp—it's Rian's lucky token that he's never without.

Basten turns the coin from one side to the other. Serpent and Scepter. His knuckles are blanched as he holds it—the only sign of his tightly coiled anger. "When I found out, I left him with a black eye that will be hard to explain to the King's Council."

I give a grim, mirthless smile. "I'm impressed you left him alive at all. I wouldn't have."

"Believe me, I was tempted. Never been so hard to pull

my punches." He slides the coin back into his pocket, a muscle jumping in his jaw. "But if I'd left the throne vacant, Astagnon would have fallen into deeper chaos."

I pause. "Right." I hate this. The distance between us. The strange formality. I find myself having to keep from drifting closer to him, pulled like the moon to earth.

"How did you manage to travel with Tòrr and keep your head?"

This rewards me with a gruff laugh that's so familiar, so *Basten*, that it makes my heart weep. "That murder horse and I share an enemy, just like you and I do. Rian caged him. He was only too happy to flee."

He suddenly glances down the hallway, that specific head jerk that means he's heard something.

"Come into my room," I breathe. "Before you're seen."

I step back, quickly combing my fingers through my hair as I hold open the door. There's still the danger that he's here to slit my throat. Still, all things considered, a knife is the least of my fears. One cruel word from him could end my heart as surely.

He closes the door behind him, trapping us in misplaced moonlight. His eyes don't give anything away.

Whether he means to kill me or kiss me—

"I assume the fae haven't harmed you," he says slowly, "from what I witnessed."

My eyes widen. Dear gods, could I *get* more mortified?

I blurt out, "What you saw...Artain on the banquet table...the Meden Cup...I was only trying to win their trust." My throat constricts.

He prowls forward, his face unreadable, and instinct drives me to retreat a step. I croak, "Artain is an ass. There's nothing between us."

"I know," he murmurs softly.

"You—you do?" The backs of my knees bump against the bed, and with a nervous flutter of moth wings in my stomach, I realize I'm cornered. "But you were so angry."

"At Iyre, little violet. Not you."

The moths in my stomach float away. My shoulders relax, and I blink a few times, rethinking everything. When he said I ruined his life? When he rattled his chains in anger? *Iyre was standing right beside me.*

"O—oh," I breathe.

He continues to stalk forward. "As far as Artain, I know how to read lust. Widening pupils. The tang of sweat. The scent of—" His eyes fall briefly to the junction of my thighs before lifting back to my face. "Well, you didn't show any of those signs."

"Right." My voice lilts when, inside, I want to shriek with hope.

He steals another step closer, close enough that I can feel his radiated body heat. He braces his arm on the bedpost at my side, and his sleeve rides up over his forearm. He's all raw power. Dangerous. Territorial. All I can think about are the beautiful things his cruel lips have done to me.

I realize I'm trailing my fingers over my neckline, practically drooling. *Get it together, Sabine—remember, he can sense lust.*

Embarrassment tunnels into me until I'm squirming. Normally, the darkness would hide my blazing cheeks, but this man can see in the dark.

Scars on his forearm catch my eye. Squinting in the low light, I read what looks like letters.

I gasp. "My name. That's my name on your arm!"

He straightens, dropping his hand, slowly running his

fingers over the scars. A slight growl rumbles in his chest. "I couldn't remember your name. I needed it—needed it close. At least until I could get my memories back. I vowed to myself that I would find a way to wrench them from Iyre's hands."

I nod eagerly. "The day she took your memories, I saw her with a small, round, yellow bottle. She keeps it in the highest room in Aurora Tower. I haven't been able to get it— the doors and windows are warded to only let in fae, and the cabinet is locked."

A light flares in his eyes. He immediately stalks to the window, studying the spire of the Aurora Tower over the rooftops. For a few moments, I can see the gears turning in his head.

Then, he stalks back to the bed, that light in his irises blazing brighter. "I can get them."

My lips part. "You think so?"

His hand lifts as though to reassure me by cupping my cheek, but then he hesitates. His fingers fold in. "I didn't come all this way to fail. After I confront Iyre, we'll get out of here. You and me. We'll return to Old Coros and make Rian pay for what he's done."

His voice breaks with a rare note of hope.

I tug at a loose thread on my dress, looking down. "You promised me once that you'd cut out your beating heart if I asked you to. You said you'd crawl across kingdoms for me on hands and knees. You can't...possibly still feel like that? Since I'm a stranger now?"

"Sabine," he says slowly, tipping my chin up with one finger. "Cut out my heart? Little violet, I'd cut out a thousand hearts."

The space between us is so tight. So tense. My arms ache

to feel him. It's a visceral need, as necessary as water. But he's holding back—literally. An agonizing inch separates our bodies.

To kiss him, I'd simply have to tilt my chin up.

But I pace away, heat burning on my cheeks.

"It isn't that simple. My father will never agree to let me leave. And—I'm not sure I want to. I know it sounds crazy, but something about this place calls to me." I pivot sharply, facing him again. "Don't misunderstand me. I know the fae are dangerous—I'm not blind. I'd like to get my hands around Iyre's throat as much as you would. But it's complicated. Their reign isn't completely without merit. I see a glimmer of potential in them. In *some* of them. In my father, most of all."

Basten's eyes narrow a hair. I can feel the questions, the doubts.

"Besides," I blurt out, pivoting sharply again, "They have a massive army. Goldenclaws. Tòrr, now. Grand Cleric Beneveto is ready to throw the full weight of the Red Church behind them. That means thousands of churches in Astagnon will preach the fae's side—priests will even take up arms if necessary. If war breaks out, Volkany will decimate Astagnon. Millions, dead in a snap." I wet my dry lips. "But my father? He might listen to me. There's a chance we can avoid war."

He folds his arms across his chest. "I trust you, Sabine. I do. I *want* to trust you."

I stop at the bed, inches from him. My fingers close around the bedpost behind my back, locking me here, to keep my wayward body from rolling the *teensiest* bit to brush my chest against his.

I whisper, "Why did you come to Volkany? Really?"

His full lips twitch, and my stomach keels. There's such brokenness in his eyes that every fiber of my body screams at me to go to him.

A catch pulls in his throat. "I dream about you. Every night. I think about you. Every day. For weeks, I pretended I could let you go, but all the while was looking for clues. Talismans. Mementos. Anything that could trigger a memory." His voice grows gravely. "I came because I couldn't *not* come."

My fingers squeeze the bedpost harder to keep myself from falling.

"For a month," he continues, leaning over me, "The world has tried to turn me against you. The Durish people blacked out your mural. Street criers preached of the traitorous Volkish princess. I had Runa Valvere in one ear telling me that you were poison, and Rian in the other ear professing your cunning."

I breathe, "And the voice in your own head?"

He shakes his head. "What voice? There was no voice. No reason. No plan. Only my damn heart that said I had to fight a king, steal a monoceros, cross two kingdoms, and get myself captured so that I could stand here to look you in the eye and tell you that I've never believed in anything in my life—but I believe in you."

My skin aches for him, goosebumps cropping up along my bare arms as I squeeze the bedpost harder. I've never felt such a raw, frenzied need before.

Basten believes me. Despite his erased memories, he didn't doubt my heart for a second, even with the world trying to drive us apart.

Not. One. Doubt.

He's so beautiful in the dark light that it makes my heart

weep. At some point tonight, he bathed. His raven hair is now down and soft, still damp. The ghost of a beard hugs his jaw. He smells *delicious*.

My hips roll, knocking my knee against his. My face tips up so I can gaze at him through my lashes.

His lips are so damn close.

"Do I feel like a stranger to you?" I whisper.

"No, little violet." His answer is immediate.

His hand quirks, involuntarily reaching for my hair, and a tiny whimper burrows out of me. I need this. His touch. His lips. I'm so starved for him that all the air feels sucked out of the room.

My eyes sink halfway, waiting.

His hand pauses a hair away from my temple, and he's all around me, above and below and on all sides—and he finally lowers his hand.

I lean into his hold.

"Basten." My whisper is desperate, yearning. I can't stop myself from gripping his shirt in my fists, fingers coiled in the cotton fabric, silently urging him closer. "I missed you—gods, I missed you so much."

He rasps, "I want this moment with you, Sabine. You have no idea how much I want it. From now until the damn sun sets over this earth for the last time. But I need more than just this, right now, with you. I need...our *past*. I need to know more than your name, and how gods-damned perfect your lips are, and how I would raze villages to have them on me now. Like they were on *him*."

My gaze skips between his eyes, not certain what exactly I'm searching for. Jealousy? Over Artain? Yes—there's that. But the burn in his gaze goes beyond possessiveness. It goes to a place so deep I've never been there. It damn near reaches to hell and back.

My gaze drops to his lips, and my toes curl, poised to lift me up to close the distance—

He pulls me infinitesimally closer. Our bodies press together—

His head jerks toward the door. A beat passes. "Someone is coming."

I cling to him harder. "Wait. Don't go."

"It doesn't matter if I try to run—they'll catch me either way. I drugged every guard from the holding cells to your door. Wouldn't take a genius to figure out it was me. And your father? He's going to be furious."

"Wait. Let me explain to him."

He grips my upper arm, such a meager drop of the fathomless pool of touch I crave. "Whatever happens, it was worth it. Just for this moment with you. Do what you must to stay in the fae's good graces. I'll find a way for us to speak again."

He starts to pull away, and my bones scream at me to grab him, to keep him here, to wrestle him to the damn ground if I have to.

It takes the last drop of my strength to keep my hold on the bedpost.

"Basten?" I breathe.

"Little violet?"

"You will always be worth it. Worth the damn world."

CHAPTER 27

BASTEN

Five days pass while I'm locked within four extremely annoying walls.

King Rachillon's soldiers put me in the servants' wing of Drahallen Hall, on the ground level of the Stormwatch Tower wing. The room is cramped, with a bed so short my feet hang off, a piss pot and a wash basin, and a high, barred window that looks out on the kitchen garden.

But hey, it could be worse.

I showed up here claiming to have a king's blood but looking like a beggar, then pawed the king's daughter. I guess if you can't decide between putting your prisoner in the dungeon or a stateroom, this is where you choose.

They drew my blood, so now, it's just a waiting game until the bloodtaster arrives to decide my fate.

I slide open the top dresser drawer and laugh at my paltry belongings. Rian's Golath dime. A second shirt no cleaner than the one I'm wearing. The locket with Sabine's portrait.

One piece of good luck? I remember in perfect detail

every second of my interactions with Sabine since coming to Drahallen Hall.

However Iyre's magic works, only the memories from before she touched my temple are gone. Apparently, I can make *new* memories that directly involve Sabine. Which means I don't need the locket anymore. All I have to do is close my eyes and summon her perfect pout, pupils blown with desire...

Oh, gods.

There's no greater turn-on than knowing Sabine Darrow is sleeping under the same roof. Now that I've seen her again, any doubt is gone: *I know she's mine the same way I know water is wet.*

The days drag, and I get real damn tired of staring at the same water stain on the ceiling. But the time isn't a total waste. In those five days, I've overheard every scrap of gossip about what's happening within the castle walls.

And these are the key pieces:

One. Captain Tatarin departed two days ago to lead a goldenclaw team to the southern Volkish coastline to Immortal Thracia's newly discovered resting place.

Two. Vale won't launch a full-on war against Rian until all the gods are woken—which means, if Captain Tatarin succeeds in locating Thracia, he'll have four more gods to find.

Three. Unrest is growing along the border. The rulers of the neighboring kingdoms are growing worried. The Queen of Clarana has increased her troops along all borders. The Kravadan king—whose kingdom is the only one to share a border with both Volkany and Astagnon—has sent emissaries to propose a peace deal.

On the sixth day, a different set of footsteps approaches

down the hall. Unlike the guards, who reek of boot polish from two floors away, my new visitor carries the expensive scent of myrrh mixed with iron.

I bolt upright, already waiting at the door when it swings open.

King Rachillon—no, *Vale*—tosses me a bundle of cloth.

I catch it, lifting an eyebrow. "What's this?"

He rasps flatly, "Fresh clothes acceptable for royalty. Go ahead, change. The bloodtaster arrived and verified your claim, King Basten. Servants will move your belongings to a stateroom in the Aurora Tower."

His face is stiff as bark, his eyes dull. *Oh, yeah. He still hates me.*

"*King* Basten? No need for insults. Call me Lord Basten until there's a crown on my head." I toss the expensive clothes onto the bed, then grip my old shirt by the back collar and drag it over my head. I slap my dirt-lined chest. "You'll find that even under the finest clothes, I'm still a scoundrel."

"You do not appear to seek the approval of a god."

I shuck off my pants, flashing my ass before pulling on the new woolen pair. Emphatically, I say, "I don't."

He strokes his graying beard. "Nor a father's approval. Not that I would ever grant it. Sabine is not yours; do you understand? You will be granted some freedom of movement around Drahallen Hall, within limits. Go near my daughter again, however, and it won't matter that you're a king. Everyone rots the same in the dungeon."

I fasten the silver buckle and button up the brocade vest. "Marrying a future king isn't good enough for her? She'll have the richest kingdom in the known world at her feet.

Power, too—she and I will rule together as equals. What more could a father wish for his daughter?"

"Much more," he growls.

I turn away from him as I rake my sweaty hair back into a tie at my nape. Anger snaps in my chest. I could care less if I piss off the King of Fae—*Sabine* sees potential in them.

Me? I only see bullshit.

"Come." Vale begrudgingly holds open the door. "It is time we discuss what comes next."

With a low thrum of wariness, I follow him through the military offices on the Stormwatch Tower wing's lower levels, then pass through the towering central foyer. The Hall of Vale is straight ahead in the Sunflare Tower wing, but he leads me instead through the kitchen garden toward the stables.

"What exactly does come next?" I ask quietly.

He doesn't look back as he murmurs, "A deal, Lord Basten, if you are so inclined. It seems we both have something the other desires."

We pass a pair of kitchen maids, baskets of lettuce underarm, who bow to Rachillon from beneath their sunbonnets.

He signals to the stable attendants, who roll open the doors. Drahallen Hall's stable is like nothing I've seen. It's circular, for one. A high dome rises overhead. The curved outer wall houses fifty stalls, each holding a horse worth a thousand gold coins. In the center is an intricate mosaic tilework. High, round windows let in beams of light that catch the errant flecks of freshly raked straw floating in the air.

We pass a stablehand braiding a stallion's mane, then head to a round iron door that leads to a secondary, smaller, domed stable. This portion of the structure looks far older than the more modern construction of the rest of the stable.

The iron door is bolted shut by a heavy steel bar that must take ten men to slide open.

Vale places his hand on the bar, and bolts of fey blast from his palm. The lines of energy wrap around the bar, sliding it open with sheer magic alone.

"This chamber is old," Vale says, noticing how I eye the stone walls. "Older even than Drahallen Hall's foundation. The one place we can have complete privacy."

The light is low inside. The only window is an enormous circular moonroof set at the dome's apex, tightly shuttered now against even a crack of sunlight.

A single wall torch casts a glow over an opulent stall. It's the size of a small barn, with mosaic tilework in the shape of vines running along the floor. The walls are flawless white marble blocks, mortared with molten gold. A gilded tray rests on a marble column, holding golden grooming equipment: a bristled brush, hoof pick, mane comb. Not a speck of dust floats in the air here. I could eat off the mosaic floor.

"Basten?"

I turn sharply at the sound of a female voice. Sabine stands up from a stool, folding the storybook she had open in her lap and tucking it under one arm. Her eyes are wide as they dart between Vale and me. Cautious. Her plump lips part as though poised with a question.

Gods. I've fallen a thousand times. Off horses. Off rooftops. But nothing compares to the sheer weightless terror of falling in love with Sabine Darrow.

Tòrr and Myst look up from where they were happily munching honeyed oats, blinking at me in indignation for the interruption. Was Sabine...reading stories to them? Is this something she did in Duren?

A pang snaps against my ribs because where a memory should be is only a void. Blackness. And it fucking *aches*.

Tòrr lets out an irritated shriek, and Sabine taps his nose with a disapproving frown. Likewise, Myst gives his neck a nip. Chastised, he retaliates by stomping off to a marble water fountain. Myst clomps after him, chittering.

Whatever those two horses are arguing about, they sound like an old married couple.

"Tòrr is only grumpy because I was almost at the end," Sabine says.

She toys with the book, running her nail over the leather binding. How is it possible for a woman to become more beautiful in five days? I've replayed our meeting in her bedroom a thousand times, and even in my fantasies, she was a sketched-in copy of this breathtaking original.

My breath grows ragged as I take in the curve of her jewel-encrusted dress along her waist and hips to fan out beneath her ass—a style that shows little skin but leaves nothing to the imagination.

Possessiveness flares in my chest. Her hair is loose other than a tiny fishtail braid circling her crown. Her creamy skin glows with health.

But her eyes?

Their grain of fear is the only thing to mar her perfection.

King Rachillon clears his throat heavily as he steps to the center of the stall, where the torchlight reflects off the shuttered moonroof and bathes his features in liquid gold.

"Three thousand years ago," he begins, "I housed a monoceros here named Saph. She was a vicious thing.

Completely feral. Ravenous for sunlight. She burned every village in a mile-long path from the Volkish coast to Norhelm. Tens of thousands died. Artain trapped her here— right on this spot—with the immortal lasso. With Meric and Samaur's assistance, we constructed this stall around her in a single night. By the time Samaur made the sun rise again, its rays were useless to her. She was imprisoned here for one hundred years."

"What is the point of caging a monoceros," I ask, "if you do not intend to use its power?"

"In fact, I used her often." Vale turns his head toward the moonroof. "I threw my enemies through that moonroof at midnight, then left it unshuttered. If they weren't immediately stomped or impaled to death, Saph gleefully dispatched them upon the first ray of sunlight."

"Lovely," I deadpan, rubbing my beard.

"I'll do the same thing to you, Lord Basten, if you betray me. I'm sure Tòrr could be convinced to end you."

Sabine balls her hands, her gaze alternating between anger at her father and concern for me. Tightly, she says, "Don't make threats, Father. You need Basten if you want to win Astagnon. Rian won't bow to you. The King's Council won't accept any other candidate without royal blood."

"No, Lord Basten needs *me*," Vale growls. "There are other ways to win Astagnon. War will mean the deaths of millions, but so be it. Pick any man in Volkany to fuck—just not him."

Sabine's face drains of color.

Her lips pull back, ready to argue, but I lift a hand.

"Enough." I can read Vale's intentions from a mile away —this man craves war, and no bargains on our end will stop him. Only one thing can protect us now if Sabine and I want

to be together—our own army. "King Rachillon—Vale—
whatever you want to be called. I brought you a monoceros.
Your bloodtaster verified my heritage. You want to keep a
chastity belt on your daughter? Fine. I came for a throne. So,
tell me how to get it."

Vale's face is unreadable. I can't tell if I convinced him
about Sabine, but he does look intrigued by my boldness.

"We've been in contact with Kendan Valvere." He goes to
the iron door, testing to ensure it's tightly closed against
eavesdroppers. "We have a plan to overthrow King Rian.
Beneveto will travel to Old Coros to assist in the coup. His
priests enjoy diplomatic access to all of Hekkelveld Castle,
which will get our spies in. They'll capture Rian, and once he
is imprisoned, Kendan will ensure that he's tried by the
King's Council and found to be a pretender to the throne. A
bloodtaster will testify that you are the rightful heir. Rian
will spend the rest of his days in exile, and the throne will be
yours."

As Sabine hugs the storybook to her chest, she is the
portrait of calmness. But inside? Her heartbeat raps fast as
hummingbird wings.

"When will this supposed coup take place?" she asks
steadily.

"That depends on you. Both of you." Vale moves back to
the center of the stall, placing himself squarely between the
two of us. "Kendan does not know his brother's habits as
well as you do. We need to know how to manipulate King
Rian. How to isolate him from his sentinels for my spies to
attack."

The words land like a yoke on my shoulders. For as
much as I want to see Rian suffer for betraying Sabine and

wrenching out my heart in the process, there was a time—once—when I would do anything for him.

He was my rock when I was unmoored. His laughter made *me* laugh. A round of ale together, and all my worries vanished. He shared his table when I was hungry, his ear when I went on a tirade, his bed when I needed a drunken place to crash.

I stew on the memories, jaw working.

Sabine studies me, then pulls in a resolute breath and says, "Rian has an old battle wound that pains him. He admitted it to me once while he was drunk. A healer adjusts the bones in his back on the first of every month. He's sensitive about the weakness. Doesn't want his guards to know, so it's only him and the healer. He'll be flat on his stomach, face down, naked from the waist up. Without his weapons."

I briefly close my eyes. I'm grateful to her for doing what I couldn't do. For revealing his weakness. Hell, I know what has to happen—Rian's ass in exile in some prison on the far side of the Kravadan desert—but she spared me from being the one to land him there.

Silently, I tip my head in a nod to her.

Her lips flicker in a sad smile.

"Good." King Rachillon rests his hand on the round iron door. "First of the month, you say? That gives us some time. Now, Lord Basten, it is only a matter of getting you back to Old Coros before that day without having you immediately arrested as a traitor."

My eyes lock possessively to Sabine.

No—it won't be nearly that simple.

~

Like all fae castles, Drahallen Hall is set out like a star, with the Aurora Tower wing making up the southwestern point. That means the turret's pointed roof is clearly visible to any onlookers until after midnight.

Luckily, I'm no stranger to midnight escapades.

Getting to the central portion of the castle's roof is as straightforward as climbing the spiral stairs to the top, where a narrow landing leads to a trapdoor that opens into the bellringer's post.

There, below the trapdoor, I wait behind a barrel of pitch, listening for the bellringer to leave his post. It isn't long before his footsteps tromp over to the roof's edge, followed by the sound of him pissing off the side.

I carefully climb the short ladder beneath the trapdoor and push it open. Once outside, I slip behind the raised parapet wall and crouch low to stay hidden from view.

Here's where it gets tricky.

Unlike Hekkelveld Castle, whose wings are short and squat, Drahallen's reach out like five elongated points of a blade. The roofs are sharply pitched, especially at the turrets, whose points rise to a 50-degree angle.

If I tried to cross that slope, I'd only slide on my ass. The only way across is to balance along the narrow ridge cap that runs the length of the Aurora Tower wing. The wind is vicious. Bitter-cold. By the time I reach the turret, my lips are so chapped they're bleeding.

"Can't get in the window or door, huh?" I grab hold of the rough stone bricks, cold and slick with frost, and haul myself up toward the turret's base. "Then I'll go through the damn roof."

The wind whips my face as I unroll my rope, trying to throw it around the turret's iron spire. On the third try, the rope catches, and I yank it tight, using it to hoist myself up the last few feet.

Clutching the spire, I listen.

The castle is a chaotic jumble of sounds. Servants gossiping. Love-making couples moaning. Half a dozen people snoring.

I tune it all out to focus on the room directly beneath me. It's quiet. So quiet all I hear is the gentle ruffle of a lantern's flame.

Adjusting my grip on the spire, I set my hunting knife under a slate tile and pop it up. The slate tumbles off the castle's side, crashing to the river valley below.

I make the mistake of watching it fall hundreds of feet.

You idiot—eyes up.

Heart jackhammering, I pry up more tiles until I can slip feet-first through the beams.

I land in a crouch, knife at the ready.

The tower room is small. The circular shape makes it feel even tighter. There's only room for a few worktables of various heights, a wardrobe, and some wall shelves. A lantern flickers, but otherwise, there are no signs of anyone.

I'm alone. So, I don't waste any time searching the shelves.

Bottles cover every shelf, every worktable. No two shapes or colors are alike. They are all unlabeled, so the best I can do is hold them up to the light and try to guess at their contents. Before coming here, I re-read The Tale of Iyre's Memory Bottles in a borrowed copy of the Book of the Immortals, and now, the words come back to me.

· · ·

"...in a time before time, Immortal Iyre kept her prized collection in the highest tower: Thousands of memories trapped in bottles, corked with bloodroot. As Goddess of Virtue, it was her divine duty. Purify mortals' souls by stealing the memories of their most sinful experiences..."

Sinful? My memories of Sabine? More like fucking divine.

I rifle through the bottles, looking for the small, round, yellow one Sabine described before moving to a locked wall cabinet.

Finally, through the glass panels, I spot it. It's the size of an apricot. Murky yellow glass. The only one that fits the description.

"How about this for a key," I mutter under my breath. I wrap a cloth around my hand and smash it into the glass.

My heart pounds as I fish out the small bottle, which feels so slight in my hand. It's half full of a dark, sloshing liquid. My skin prickles with goosebumps, and I suppress a shiver.

Are these really my memories?

Something about the thick liquid turns my stomach, but I uncork the bottle. I've come all this way. No chance in hell I'm not taking back what's mine.

My hand shakes as I tip the bottle against my lips. After all this time.

I want to remember.

Gods, I want to remember *everything*.

A bitter, room-temperature liquid fills my mouth. I immediately gag, doubling over. My tongue revolts, ordering me to spit out the liquid until I'm retching all over Iyre's braided rug.

This is wrong.

I know that taste. I've tasted it a thousand times. On the air after each of my kills. Licked off my own busted knuckles.

Blood.

Gagging, I toss the bottle aside and, uneasy, tear through the rest of them. They each hold the same familiar smell. Blood. All of it human.

I stagger back, bumping up against the window. The wind's chill slips through the cracks to spread frost up my spine.

No.

Desperate, I grab more bottles, but they're all the same.

"Where are they?" I shout. "Where are my *fucking* memories?"

Before I can stop myself, I swing my fist into the bottles on the wall, letting out a roar.

Glass crashes, spilling blood that seeps through the floor cracks.

But I don't stop.

I smash my fists into the bottles on the worktables. I wrench the locked cabinet off the wall and slam it down over my knee. Destroying everything. Like Iyre did to me.

A shard of glass slices into my thigh, making me hiss with pain.

But I like it.

Dammit, I *need* it.

I throw open the wardrobe door, determined to ruin everything and—

A body slumps out.

Lurching forward on instinct, I catch the body and lower it to the floor. My thoughts go haywire. My senses, too.

What the fuck? A body? Who the hell is this?

He's a young Black man with shorn hair. I press my hand to the man's neck, but only out of habit. I can already hear how nonexistent his pulse is. Can smell the rot beginning in his flesh.

I drag a hand over my face. "*Fuck.*"

Looking closer, I realize I've seen him before—in the Hall of Vale, refilling Iyre's water glass. His limbs are cold but not yet stiff. He's been dead two hours at most.

His complexion is strangely pale. When I slide my fingers up his arm, I don't feel a drop of blood beneath the skin.

A deep cut on his right wrist catches my attention—the fatal wound. The callouses on his hands tell me he's right-handed, so it's unlikely he did this to himself. Besides, his left hand doesn't have the metallic scent of a blade.

Which means someone else bled him to death and shoved him in this wardrobe.

The muscles of my back shudder, reminding me how far I've pushed myself. Groaning, I get to my feet and start to lift the dead man—

A floorboard creaks outside.

Shit. Someone is coming. I grab a chair to climb back through the roof, but it's too late.

The door opens.

Iyre saunters in slowly, hands clasped like a perfectly innocent schoolgirl, looking unsurprised to find me there amid her shattered bottles.

She nudges the broken yellow bottle with her toe.

"Lord Basten. How did I know that, sooner or later, you and I would have words?"

My jaw clamps as I climb down from the chair and shove

it back under one of the work tables. "Maybe because since I set foot in this castle, I've wanted to do *this.*"

I slam my fist around her throat, shoving her against the wardrobe door. An inch from her face, I hiss, "Give me back my fucking memories, or I'll do to you whatever you did to this poor bastard."

She chokes, "I needed to renew my powers. Paz has always been more than happy to serve. His breath. His blood. Whatever I need. Of course—sometimes I get carried away with my acolytes."

My stomach roils as I squeeze my fingers. "What the hell are you talking about?"

"We gain powers from offerings. The trinkets left on our altars, for example. But the most potent offerings come from sacrifice. Human blood fills my goblets. I eat memories like sugared figs. We take everything you wretched humans can offer us, and we turn it into pure fey. I didn't bottle up your memories for some collection, human. They don't exist anymore. They became *fey.*"

She hisses the word in a strange low pitch, and the lantern throws out red-tinged sparks of crackling fey.

When I flinch away from the sparks, she suddenly latches her hands on either side of my head.

Lightning surges out of her palms against my ears.

Pain bursts through my head. I let her go, staggering down to my knees, slamming my hands on either side of my skull.

A wail rolls out of my throat. For weeks, I've imagined wringing this fae's neck until she replaced the void in my head with every memory she stole. The days with Sabine. The nights—gods, the nights.

What did I once tell Sabine about the fae?

Trust a snake and get bit, and it's your fault, not the snake's.

For once, I hate to be right.

My hand presses hard against my chest, fingers curling in like I can hold myself together.

Like I can stop my heart from breaking apart. But I can't —there's nothing to stop anymore. I'm empty.

"There were never any fucking memories," I murmur.

The words taste bitter on my tongue. I choke on them, half snarling, half gasping, as if saying them aloud might make them less true.

But nothing changes.

My knees go slack, and I slide to the floor. My vision blurs. I can't seem to focus on anything, my stare detached, everything cast in a weak shade of gray. Weakly, I kick at a broken bottle. It spins uselessly on its side, just like me.

"All this damn time..." A dry rasp catches in my throat.

I thought I could restore what was lost. My memories. My past. My time with *her*. I thought I could bring it all back.

But it's gone.

Forever.

She rubs her throat, looking down at me like I'm filth. Slowly, she bends down to whisper in my ear.

"Food, Lord Basten. That's all you mortals are to us." She pads back to the door and gracefully swings it open. "Now get out before I find myself hungry."

CHAPTER 28
SABINE

Three days and not a word exchanged with Basten. Now that he's an honored guest, he dines in the Hall of Vale—but three tables over. Each evening, I watch longingly from my window as he walks the grounds with my father, making plans. Likewise, I feel his burning gaze when I ride Myst through the Twilight Garden each morning beneath his tower.

Spying each other from afar isn't enough. We're twin shadows on the wall, so close and yet never intersecting.

And that barrier's name?

Vale. He of the fae axe that will separate Basten's head from his shoulders if we're caught together again.

I've searched for excuses to be near the guest wing, hoping for a glimpse of him, a whispered word, anything to bridge the chasm between us. But the guards' ever-watchful presence blocks every attempt.

The quiet of the evening settles around me now, the fire in my bedroom's hearth crackling as I sit with my unease. My fingers toy with his frayed twine ring, pulling at loose threads, while I imagine scenarios in which I could outwit the guards.

It's in this restless silence that I hear a rustling from the fireplace.

I glance up, half-expecting to see nothing.

But there, amidst the cooling ashes, a small shape stirs. The forest mouse, her fur dusted with soot, pokes her head out. She pauses, sniffs the air, and then fixes her bright eyes on me.

Mouse-talker, she chits excitedly. *Follow me!*

To where? I ask silently, my heart beginning to beat faster.

You shall see! We must make haste—there is a clear path to the kitchen at the moment.

The...kitchen?

She scampers to the door and swiftly picks the lock, then motions for me to open it. I peek out into the hallway, heart fluttering. It's empty.

Where are the guards? I ask warily.

One of the army captains was married today, she answers. *The soldiers were briefly called to the military offices to eat honey cakes. They will be back soon—hurry!*

She scampers along the wall so swiftly that I have to jog to keep up. We head down the narrow secondary stairs the servants use, descending until the walls take on the cool air of the basement level, then even further into a stone-lined hallway filled with storage rooms for root vegetables.

A chicken pecks at some loose straw on the floor, bobbing her head to me as I pass.

Ahead, I smell the scent of boar on the rotisserie, as well as rich roasting garlic and rosemary. The chatter of kitchen maids—broken by laughter—spills down the hallway.

Here. the mouse tugs on my skirt. She points her nose toward another storage room. ***Wait inside. I'll be back soon.***

More questions perch on my lips, but a maid might come down the hall any moment, so I duck inside and close the door.

It's pitch black—no windows, no lanterns, and I didn't think to bring a match.

But one whiff, and I don't need Basten's senses to know where I am: the castle confectionary.

My stomach growls at the aroma of freshly baked honey cakes. The bakers must have stored the extra wedding treats here. I step backward and accidentally kick over a sack—the tight space fills with a cloud of powdered sugar.

I pat the air until I find shelves, feeling in the dark around crockery pots containing the most amazing-smelling vanilla beans, nutmeg, and cinnamon. I lift the lid off a glass jar, and the rich, buttery scent of caramel sends my mouth watering.

I'm dipping in a finger for a taste when the door creaks open.

I shove the jar back on the shelf, quickly sucking my finger clean, when the forest mouse appears in the crack.

Oh. I let out an exhale. ***It's you.***

The door opens wider, and Basten's broad shoulders fill the space.

"Oh!" I cry. "It's *you*."

I pull in a breath laced with the rich sweetness of powdered sugar. I have the briefest glimpse at his handsome face—his hair raked back into a bun at his crown, his velvet-brown eyes simmering—before he closes the door to plunge us back into darkness.

"Sabine." His voice comes out of the void. "I asked the mouse to find a way to meet. We need to talk about how to get back to Astagnon." His boots scrape on the floor, stirring up more spilled sugar. "Your father will broker the deal with Kendan Valvere over the next few days. Then, he'll expect me to leave for Old Coros. I want you to come with me—if you're willing."

I blink at the deluge of information, landing on my first question. "Wait. Wait. You *asked* the mouse?"

A silence stretches, and he huffs a small laugh. When he speaks again, it's more gentle. "You'd be amazed by how friendly I've become with animals since my early days of wanting to stomp on them." A warmth bleeds into his voice —a teasing that's so damn familiar I grip the nearest shelf to keep steady.

He continues, "I learned that Tòrr can spell things out with his hoof. It made me think I might be able to communicate with other animals. I showed the mouse your portrait in a locket, and she understood."

She. It's the first time I've heard Basten refer to any of my animal friends as something other than "it," and I'm not prepared for how it makes my heart sing.

"Basten, if we're caught planning to leave together..." I don't have to finish the sentence.

His heavy boots scuff as he approaches in the dark. My breath lodges in my throat. I know that he can see every detail of the confectionary—of me—as clearly as if we were in daylight.

A shelf groans as he leans over me, bracing his arm, his body heat licking me up and down until my toes curl.

"Are you frightened?" There's a beat before he adds, "Of being discovered together? I can go."

"No!" I suck in a cloud of powdered sugar. It dulls my mind, makes me think only of hunger. Makes me wonder if the sugar in the air would make his skin taste sweet, too.

"We've been caught before," I whisper. "And we're both still standing."

His bicep tenses as it brushes against my temple. He breathes in, a hitch there that makes my heart thrum.

"You don't remember." My voice is soft, trying to hide my disappointment. "The altar at Midtane, when..." I trail off. "Never mind. You'll remember everything when we get your memories back."

He thieves another inch closer, his steps echoing. The fabric of his pants rustles as he shifts from foot to foot, and my stomach tightens, sensing something is wrong.

"About that." His voice is deep. Strangely hollow. "I confronted Iyre. I found the bottle you spoke of, but it contained only blood." He pauses. "There's nothing in that tower room but pain. Paz? Her acolyte? His cadaver is there, drained of blood. The Tale of Iyre's Memory Bottles is a lie. She doesn't keep stolen memories bottled. She consumes them just like blood." A hitch sticks in his throat. "My memories are gone. Our past—it's gone."

I feel for the shelves behind me, clinging to their sturdiness.

"Oh, Basten," I breathe, hearing the pain in his voice.

I want to go to him, but there's still this space between us. This void.

I can't help but feel that I'm to blame in part. It was me that Iyre was after when she cut a portal into Astagnon. The fact that Basten was there was only bad luck. He was collateral damage. It aches down to my bones to know that every beautiful moment we've shared is burned into my brain, and yet, to him, I'm still a stranger.

"It breaks my heart for you," I whisper, fighting the urge to reach out to him. "If there was anything in my power to—"

He cuts me off by suddenly cupping my jaw, leaning in.

A gasp cuts across my tongue. It draws in the earthy, deep aroma of honey cakes. Basten towers over me, lips an inch away, as heat floods my lower half to the point that I have to squeeze my legs.

Kiss me. Please. Do it.

I find his shirt collar and bunch the fabric in my fist, feeling the overpowering urge to hold onto him. My arms ache to hold him. I pledged every one of my days to this man. Every night in his bed.

Still—he doesn't kiss me.

Doesn't hold me like he used to.

I swallow, hard, easing my grip on his shirt. "We can find another way. A godkissed person with the ability to restore memories, maybe. Or a potion."

I feel his jaw tense against mine. "They're *gone*, Sabine."

My head falls back against a sack of pears. I swallow the saliva pooling in my mouth as I place both my hands on his chest, needing to feel the steadiness of his heartbeat. Memories flood me like flipping pages of a picture book. All our best days together. For him, now, all those pages are blank.

I whisper, "I don't want to be a stranger to you."

He shifts his stance, his knee brushing against my inner thigh. He considers his words carefully. "You aren't a stranger—you're just a dream that hasn't happened yet."

My toes go numb as all the blood rushes to the apex between my legs. It's all I can do not to clutch his shirt. If it were up to me, his shirt would be unbuttoned right now, my dress bunched around my waist.

But this is all new to him. He's grieving his lost memories that can never be recovered. He's hurt. *Give him time.*

My head bobs in a nod.

Slowly, his lips brush my temple as he whispers, "I dreamed such things about you. Filthy, sinful dreams. I've never hated the gods more than when I saw you bent over one of them, your hot lips against his skin..." He stops short as though he's spoken out of turn. Clearing his throat, he says more measuredly, "I thought it must be one of my dreams. You can't fathom how insanely jealous I was to see you like that, to realize it was real." He hesitates. "Wishing that it was *me* beneath your mouth."

My eyelids sink halfway closed, lips aching.

I can feel his breath.

He's so close.

I slowly slide my hands over his chest, near his shirt collar, where his matching birthmark resides. His skin is hot to the touch. Everything in Volkany is so cold. The wind. The floors. The fae. So, now, feeling his hot blood churning under my palm, I feel warm for the first time in weeks.

"You've been in the caramel pot, haven't you?" he suddenly tuts, and before I can think, he pops my finger in his mouth and sucks off the sticky remnants.

My whole body pulls in a gasp as heat from his mouth radiates straight to my middle, legs squeezing until it aches.

"I skipped breakfast," I blurt out.

He laughs as he releases my finger and, testingly, trails his lips over the back of my hand. His tongue darts out to lick my knuckle. "You taste like powdered sugar. It's turning me into a salivating mess. This damn place—the scents are too tempting. I wish you could smell what I can smell. Ripe pears. Cloves. *Violets*." He shifts again, his breath rasping. "Listen, Sabine, we don't have to—to rekindle how we were. If you don't feel comfortable with me—"

I twist my hands in his shirt, jerking him forward. My voice is husky as I bark, "I *want* to."

The silence stretches, our breaths strained, our muscles tense, wondering who will break the awful tension first.

Quietly, he runs his thumb over my collarbone and purrs, "Tell me—where did I touch you the first time that made you feel good?"

I silence a moan. By the gods, has there been a time he touched me that *hasn't* felt good?

My throat constricts. Memories flood me of the first time we met in my family's courtyard, when Basten lifted me, naked and spitfire-angry, onto Myst. At the time, I tried to ignore the spark. Told myself it was hatred instead of attraction.

I slide my hand over his, intertwining our fingers in the dark.

I murmur, "We were staying together at an inn. I told you I was nervous about my marriage. The wedding night. I asked you for a...bedroom lesson."

A surprised laugh rolls out of his mouth. "You, in my bed, begging for a tumble? What good deed did I do in my life to earn *that*?"

He laughs, but I can hear the pain there, too. The ache of wanting to remember.

I delicately kiss his knuckles one by one. "Well, I *was* trying to trick you. To escape."

"Sabine, if you want to escape me, it's as impossible now as it was then. Now that I have you, you're mine." He skims his thumb over my cheek and, achingly close to my lips, shifts into a deeper voice. "Did I give you a good lesson?"

My heart tumbles at the same time that the base of my belly tightens, catching me before I crash into a blubbering mess.

"You said that if I were yours, you would kiss me first here." I lift his fingers to my lips.

"And then here..." I guide his hand to my jaw.

"And then here." Our clasped hands hover over my birthmark as my voice grows husky again.

His broad hand slides around the back of my neck as he leans his weight against me, trapping me against the confectionary shelves.

"Do you think that's a lesson that needs repeating?" he asks.

My breath stalls as he leans in for a kiss.

Our lips connect. *Finally.* His warmth floods into me, and I moan all the way down to my toes. His left arm encircles my waist, folding me into his body as tight as a button. His other hand roughly cups my cheek, his fingers plunging into my hair near my temple.

The way he kisses is like a storm: a slow rumble, then a crash, then a *flood*.

My skin snaps with a delicious itch that has me nuzzling my cheek against his, my hands desperately undoing the buttons at his collar so I can breathe in the woodsmoke scent of his bare skin.

Yes. Gods, yes.

It's been so long apart. So many doubts. Fears. Longing. Suddenly, I'm like a frenzied animal as I trail my lips down his neck, tasting and licking more than kissing.

His head tips back. "Fucking *gods*."

"Powdered...sugar," I moan breathily as I lick up the rough underside of his chin. "You taste...so good."

I tug his shirt back over his shoulders, running the flat of my hand over the muscles that might as well be carved from hard oak. He spears his fingers through my hair at my nape and wrenches my head back to face his.

"Little violet." His voice is husky, hesitant, testing out the nickname. "I dreamed so often about this. Having you. Loving you. For a long time, I didn't have a damn hope in the world it would come true."

He kisses the hell out of me, his lips as feral and possessive as I remember, but there's something different. A thread he's holding back. He doesn't bite my lower lip as he knows I like; he doesn't grind his hips against mine until I'm seeing stars.

I pull back, barely able to keep up with my own breath, and ask, "What's wrong?"

He braces one arm on the confectionary shelf again, his chest rising and falling hard, his shirt falling loose on either side of his perfect abs.

"Nothing," he says, but there's a telltale hitch in his voice. "I just... I don't know what you *like*."

His words hit me like the snap of a breaking branch. How many nights have we spent exploring each other's bodies, sharing secret desires whispered in the dark? We knew each other's hearts in ways we'd never shared with anyone else.

But for him, this is our first kiss.

His bicep tenses under my touch, a raw wave of anger building in him, threatening to pull him into some black hole of frustration. I can feel him slipping—losing himself.

I grab his face between my hands, forcing him to meet

my eyes in the dark, to stay with me, to not disappear into whatever storm is brewing inside him.

"Look at me," I whisper, my voice steady even though my heart aches. *Stay with me.*

But the truth is—it hurts me, too. He's here, and yet not. It's like loving someone through dirty glass, when all I want is for him to see us clearly.

I say evenly, "I'll show you. I'll guide you this time. You and I, we couldn't keep our hands off one another. There's a reason your heart drove you here. We're fated—hearts, minds, and bodies. You showed me what physical pleasure could be." On impulse, I plunge my thumb into the open caramel jar and then tease it over his bottom lip as I whisper, "Now let me show you."

His body shudders with desire. Feverish, he takes my thumb in his mouth. He licks off the liquid caramel with the raw hunger of a feral beast.

"Show me," he says hoarsely. "Now."

The stark command does something to me. My body gives a tremor of pleasure, my pussy clenching. It's all I can do not to rake up my skirt and rub myself all over his leg. But he's still holding back—literally. An agonizing inch separates our bodies.

With my back pressed against the shelves, I roll my hips enough to brush against the bulge tenting the front of his pants.

I moan at the friction. His hand tightens on the back of my neck. "Fucking hell, little violet."

"Our first time," I pant, "You were gentle. You warned me that you wouldn't always be. That's what I want now. Don't treat me like a virgin. Definitely not like a princess. I want you to make love to me on this floor—hard."

Live coals burn in the base of my belly as I guide his hand to slide the strap off my shoulder. The front of my dress slumps down to rest above my peaked nipple, which strains through the fabric, begging for his sweet torture.

He shifts his stance, muscles flexing as he grips the shelf behind me harder, and it calls to mind a fighter in the arena, adrenaline and testosterone demanding release in the form of connecting flesh.

His cock strains at his pants—strains at me.

His hand hovers over my breast, hesitant, so slow it's killing me.

"Stop being so damn respectful," I growl, picking up his hand and roughly cupping it over my breast.

The fabric slips down another inch, my nipple springing free as it rubs against the hard calluses of his palm. I moan.

"That's what you want, little violet?" He skims his thumb over the sensitive bud, teasing. His deep voice takes on a wicked lilt that makes all the blood pour straight into my groin. "For me to bend you over one of these sacks and fuck you until you moan?"

Oh. He learns *fast.*

I'm writhing against the shelves, back arching to drive my nipple harder against his hand. My elbow connects with a clay jar, which crashes to the floor and fills the room with the heady scent of plum sauce.

"Please, Basten," I beg. "If I don't feel your mouth on me in the next three seconds, I'm going to burst like a ripe pear."

I jump as he grips the back of my neck, forcing my head up, his breath ghosting hot and heavy against my cheeks. *There*—there's the positively filthy beast I know is prowling behind his veneer of gentlemanly tact.

"It was so fucking hot to see you like that," he pants. "Cheeks flushed, lips dripping with whiskey, tongue still tasting of that fae bastard's sweat. I could have killed Artain in that moment—only because I would have traded the entire world to be in his place."

I murmur, "You can take his place now."

That does it.

He crushes his lips to mine, and I cling to him around the neck, afraid to let go. Now that he's here—real, breathing, hot against me—I can't imagine us ever being apart again.

For a dizzying number of days, I've been plunged in this topsy-turvy fae reverie where I don't know left from right, up from down. I've danced with gods. Witnessed feats that until now were reserved for fiction. Felt the crackle of pure, powerful fey.

And all I can think, as our lips meet with a relentless devotion, is how *he* is a hundred times worthier than the gods. Every drop of blood in his veins is human, and yet the raw power I feel under his skin brings me to my knees.

I vocalize a needy moan, and Basten grabs my breast almost painfully, driving me back against the shelves with one knee thrust between my legs. I drag my skirt around my hips. My thin silk panties are soaked. I straddle his thigh, holding onto his shoulders for leverage while I buck against him.

"Down on your knees," he barks, voice ragged with desire.

I fumble to the floor in the darkness, hands skimming over the flour sacks. The air is still kissed with powdered sugar, and I lick my lips, salivating.

His boot scuffs as he approaches me from behind,

sending a delicious shiver of anticipation to form a choke-hold around my heart.

Glass clinks together as he rummages through the shelves, searching for something I can only guess. There's a scrape as he drags a sack to the door, blocking it—and a wild rush of fear lands hard on me, realizing how dangerous this is.

Under my father's own roof...

Basten presses a bottle into my hand. "Go ahead, then, little violet. Play your games with me."

I uncork the bottle and sniff. Whiskey.

As my breath strains, I pat the darkness until my fingers locate his bare chest. He's leaning back against a flour sack, his legs splayed on the floor. I straddle him, and he groans as I settle myself flush with his hips.

"The Meden Cup is the prize of victors." I feel down his chest to locate his navel. The scent of ripe pears mixes with the whiskey, the caramel, the sugar...I can barely stop from drooling. "And you won me long ago, Basten Bowborn."

I slosh the whiskey over the dip in his abdomen, then set the bottle down and lean forward until my hair brushes his bare stomach. His muscles tighten, the liquid seeping down over my fingers. Trying to catch it, I seal my lips over his navel and suck.

His groan roars out of him at the same time that his stomach muscles tense like bowstrings. "That's it. Fuck. Keep going. Lick me everywhere, you filthy girl."

I run my tongue over his washboard ridge of muscles, marred by puckered, long-healed scars from countless fights.

Breathing hard, I reach for his belt's clasp.

"I want to taste you," I choke out.

His muscles shudder under my fingertips, a ripple that pulses all the way down to the bulge pressing against my hips. Sweat drips down his chest, the saltiness mixing with the earthy tang of whiskey.

His hand in my hair guides my head lower, to the cock that springs free when I finish unbuckling his belt.

In the darkness, I run one hand over its velvet shaft, marveling at the girth of it. My needy pussy throbs, soaking my panties, weakening my knees.

Tentatively, I run my tongue over the tip, swallowing down the first salty drop. His ass flexes as his groin thrusts up at me.

"Take me in your mouth," he orders hoarsely. "Suck me until you're choking on my come—and then swallow every drop."

My skin erupts in goose bumps as I line up my lips with his straining cock.

It's been a while since I did this, and I feel a flutter of doubt.

This is our *new* first time together—I want it to be perfect.

I wrap my lips around his cock, gently sucking as I bob my head up and down.

"Oh, fuck," he moans. "Oh, that's so *fucking* sweet."

I move faster, relaxing my throat to take more of him. My lips still taste like whiskey, and it's the most alluring, sinful sensation to fill my throat with his cock. His fingers tighten in my hair, guiding my head in a rhythm that matches the thrusts of his hips.

"That's it. Gods, you have no idea how beautiful you are like this. I wish you could see what I can see. Wish you could taste the air—it's a mixture of your cunt's sweet juices and ripe pears. After this, I'm going to lick you until I finally get my fill."

My swollen pussy throbs harder. My skirt is up around my backside, the cool basement air chilling my damn underclothes. My hips squirm in the air as I lean over Basten, needy and impatient, sucking him.

"Just like that," he pants, thrusting so deep into me that my eyes water. "I'm going to come now, little violet. Take it. Every drop."

I brace myself as his cock stiffens before pulsing out a hot ribbon of cum. It hits the back of my throat, making me temporarily gag, but I pull back and swallow.

Breathless, I wipe my lips.

"Good girl," he growls between breaths. "That's my good fucking girl. Now—come here."

He moves fast and confidently in the darkness. Before I know it, I feel the press of the cold stone floor at my back. He pushes my skirt up around my waist with a fevered touch, then traces his fingers worshipfully down my exposed hips until he hooks his thumbs in my panties.

Slowly—torturously—he pulls them down over my thighs.

His ragged sigh falls heavy over the darkness as he kisses my skin. "You. You. You."

I've barely pushed up to my elbows when he buries his face between my legs. The surprise of it makes my hips buck, and his hands come down to grip the curves of my hip bones, holding my lower half steady as he attacks me with his mouth.

"I want to devour you," he murmurs while his tongue does punishing things to my wet heat. "I want to lick you from the inside out like a cream-filled tart."

Dear gods.

He takes my swollen clit between his teeth, gently biting down.

"I...missed...you," I murmur between heaving breaths. "I feared I'd...I'd never see you again. I need to feel you in me. Claim me, Basten...Take me...I want to hear you moan my name so loud that you'll never forget."

My muscles are so tightly wound. Every inch of my body demands release. I'm so damn famished, so primed to be taken. I squirm on the floor, knees splayed open like a whore.

"I'll never forget you now that I have you." He grips my hips, flipping me over so that I'm draped over a flour sack, my skirt around my waist, my bare ass in the air. Like this, I can't see him, but everything is only blackness to me anyway.

Still, my bare skin tingles with anticipation.

He delivers a sharp slap to my ass that has me crying out.

"Quiet now." He positions himself over me, wrapping his big hand around my mouth. With his free hand, he lines up his impatient cock—rock hard again—with my pussy from behind. The tip nudges against my wetness with a slick sound, and I whimper into his palm, wriggling my hips insistently.

There's a clatter of crockery, and then he thrusts his big middle finger into my mouth. It's dipped in honey, the sticky-sweetness coating my throat as I suck on his finger.

At the same time, he slides into me from behind.

I'm hit with a burst of pleasure that prickles all the way down to my toes. I'm filled from both ends with him. He thrusts his honeyed finger in and out of my lips in rhythm with the pumping of his hips.

And, gods, I love this. Feeling so full. Having him nearly everywhere he can be.

"I'm going to make you come so hard," he growls in my ear as a drip of sweat from his brow falls on my bare shoulder. "That you forget there was anything before this moment. The past doesn't fucking matter, because I'm going to make you come every day from today on. Every night, too."

He rides me hard, fingers coiled almost painfully against my scalp, thrusting into me from behind with a possessiveness even more wild than ever before. He has more to lose now. He's lost me once, and he's determined not to do so again.

"Come, princess," he coaxes. "You're ready. You're nearly there. Your pussy is begging for me to break it apart...but you have to let go."

He reaches one hand to the place where our bodies connect, wetting his fingers in my juices, then tormenting my swollen clit with his deft fingers. A moan tears out of my throat, barely muffled by his palm against my lips.

Death—that's what would happen if we're caught. But for him? I'd risk Woudix's wrath and more.

I let my eyes sink closed. "Gods, Basten. Yes. That's it."

He speeds his thrusts, the friction making me feral as I slam my hips back to meet his. He slaps my ass again—so hard and unexpected—that I break apart.

Gasping, I collapse over the flour sack as waves of pure electricity snap through my body. My muscles tense and pulse before finally going slack.

I suck in deep breaths, dizzy with the aftermath of an orgasm that's still leaving my knees shaking.

Basten cleans me up with a kitchen towel from one of the shelves, then gathers me back into his arms, gently stroking my hair.

It's an echo of when we made love in the waterfall cave. My heart tightens at the memory, knowing he doesn't recall it. Still, I know that we could lose one another in a thousand lifetimes, but we would always find our way back, for another—*new*—first love.

CHAPTER 29
BASTEN

Finally, I can breathe.

Ever since that black void opened in my head and swallowed my little violet, it's felt like a cannonball has rested on my chest. It's been a struggle to put one foot in front of the other, weighted down by the knowledge that somewhere out there, a woman waits for me, and I can't even remember her face.

But tonight?

Here in the confectionery, it's a gods-damn sugar-spun dream to hold Sabine against my chest, her feather-light weight lifting weeks of punishing pressure off my bones, the lingering taste of her on my tongue every bit as sweet as the honey she sucked off my finger.

Finally—fucking *finally*—she's mine.

Her silken hair drapes over my shoulder as she traces the map of old fighting scars on my torso. Her stomach audibly grumbles like a grumpy old man, and a delicious shade of pink floods into her cheeks.

I swipe one of the honey cakes off a shelf and nudge it against her lips.

In the darkness, she squeaks before realizing what it is.

"Eat," I tease. "Or your complaining stomach will draw the kitchen maids straight to us."

She hesitantly takes a bite, her eyes rolling back as she moans at the flaky pastry. A drop of honey rests on her bottom lip, and her tongue darts out to lick it off. *Fuck.* That moan from her pretty throat has my balls tightening again already.

"So, what happens now?" Resting her head in the crook of my arm, she absently traces the cuts that spell her name on my forearm.

I blink, trying to mentally shift from honey to politics.

"Once the deal with Kendan is set, I'll have to return to Astagnon." I lock my arm around her, bending down to place a kiss on her crown. "We need to figure out how you can come with me."

I can hear her hold her breath, not saying what's on her mind.

Finally, she haltingly asks, "What if we're wrong?"

I shift, adjusting my arm around her. "Wrong about what?"

"There's so much here that we don't understand. My father, this place—there's a power here I can't ignore. I'm not sure I'm ready to turn my back on it. It might be crazy, but what if I can make a difference? Convince my father to listen to me? There's a chance I could stop a war before it even starts."

I shift again, suddenly unable to get comfortable. "We can't wait forever, Sabine. If we don't leave when we have a chance, we might be trapped here. And Rian will drive Astagnon into ruin in the meantime."

Her body tenses under my arm. "I want to see Rian punished as much as you do. But leaving Volkany instead of working directly with the fae? I don't know if that's the answer."

I rub the bridge of my nose with my free hand, trying not to let my panic show. "Every day we stay here, Rian tightens his grip on the throne. He's already scheming, and Vale—your father—will only match his warmongering tenfold. If we don't act soon, it might be too late." I pause. "I never wanted the throne. I still don't. But it's the only way to keep you safe."

Sabine slowly extricates herself from me, sitting up, hair veiling her expression. "Even though you still barely know me?"

My throat tightens with panic that she might slip away. "We have a lot to learn about each other. Or...relearn. I get it. It will be a long road ahead to get back to where we were. Hell, maybe it won't ever be the same. But I came here blindly, on a belief I couldn't shake. I trusted in you. In my dreams. In my heart. Now that I've met you, I'm more certain than ever. You and me—we just *are*."

She pulls in a gentle sigh.

I curl my fingers around hers. She softly strokes the back of my hand, then links our fingers and squeezes. "I want that, Basten. I feel that, too."

"You'll leave with me, then?" My heart wallops, waiting.

She tips up her head to look at the dark ceiling, at her father's castle looming overhead. She squeezes my hand again. "Yes."

It's all I can do not to grin like a damn schoolboy. I rattle out, "It won't be easy. I've been watching the guards. Two armed soldiers are posted in every hall. A godkissed locksmith at the main gate. If we try to run, or sneak you out, your father will know."

"What if we just walk out?" A curious hitch lifts her voice as an idea seems to strike her.

"I don't follow."

"Plume," she whispers excitedly.

I wet my lips, intrigued. "Look, if you want some feather play—"

"No, Plume is a cloudfox friend." Her eyes alight, she pulls her legs under her as she sits upright. "She told me about fae bargains. It's the only way I know to bind the fae to their word. Seal a fae deal with soil, and it's unbreakable. Do you see? We can enter into a fae bargain with my freedom as the prize."

I still lament the feather—a little. "Your father wouldn't sense a trap?"

She pauses, thinking. "So, we don't bet against my father. We'll do it all behind his back." She bites down on her thumb, excited. "We'll bet against *Artain*—he's so prideful that he can't resist a wager. He's stupid, too."

A sour taste fills my mouth at the thought of the preening idiot who had Sabine's lips all over him.

Putting him in his place? *Yeah, I'm in.*

"Hunting," I grunt. "Artain is God of the Hunt—if I can threaten his ego when it comes to his affinity, he'll accept the challenge."

She squeezes our hands together tightly. "You're the best huntsman I know, but can you best a god?"

I pause. "If I have your help, maybe."

Her eyebrows lift, surprised. "My animals, you mean.

Like how in the Everlast tournament, I called an arrowwood spider to bite your opponent." She pauses, a reluctance there. "Okay, yes. There's no other way. Tomorrow, we'll propose the wager. There's an offerings ceremony each Friday morning in the Garden of Ten Gods. It's a public event. Artain will be there. It won't seem strange for both of us to be there, too. And my father will be distracted."

I stroke the back of her hand. "Something's still holding you back."

She takes a long breath. "I don't want to see any more animals hurt. People, either. But I know that war is ugly."

"Come here, you." I pull her into my lap and stroke the hair at her temple. "If our prize is your freedom, then what will Artain wager? What does he want more than anything else?"

She buries her forehead into my chest. "I'm afraid to know."

On Friday, the Garden of Ten Gods, normally quiet, is as busy as a county fair. The walled gates are open to allow in a steady stream of Volkish commoners, whose arms are laden with offerings for the gods' altars. Woven baskets. Bolts of silk. A brace of skinned hares. At the base of each statue, the gods' altars overflow onto the ground with more bottles of wine and bread loaves than an army could eat in a month.

And this happens every *week*?

"Ah. Lord Basten. Share this drink with me?" Samaur sidles up to me with a busty redhead on one arm. His golden eyes are dulled. Pupils black like he's drunk. He smirks. "We are allies, now, are we not?"

I give a slight nod. "Lord Samaur. I'll happily share a drink, but your hands are noticeably empty."

He gives a knowing wink. "Silver chalices are one thing, but sometimes it's better to take straight from the source."

As he squeezes his acolyte's ass with one hand, he latches his lips onto her neck. A tang of blood splashes in the air, and I realize with a sickening jolt that he's biting her. I watch his throat constrict as he drinks from her vein, then pulls back with a satisfied sigh.

The wound closes up almost immediately. She looks dazed. Stunned but happy. He smacks his acolyte on her ass, dismissing her, and wipes away a drip of blood on his chin as he cackles.

As I watch her stagger back toward his altar, I think about Paz's dead body still rotting in the tower room. How long before Samaur, too, "slips" and drinks too much? Before that redhead girl is dead in another closet? And her twin?

"I'll stick to wine." My voice is hard.

Samaur cackles.

I spot Sabine near Artain's altar, her face carefully blank as she pretends to peruse a brass birdcage holding a snowy white bird. "Excuse me."

I take my time circling the other altars, pausing to help a peasant tie a donkey's lead rope to Vale's altar, then sidle up to the opposite side of Artain's altar.

The God of the Hunt himself is across the garden, flirting with a farm girl. He idly strokes an arrow, running his fingers along its sharp edge as he smiles at her.

Fixating on his altar, I feign interest in a necklace made of bobcat claws. Quietly, I murmur to Sabine, "Is it time?"

She shakes her head faintly without looking my way.

"Not yet—my father is too close." She returns to admiring the bird—a rare albino crow.

I spot Vale in the amphitheater's center, looking over the offerings as they come in. He lifts a length of fabric from a merchant, rubbing it between his fingers. I wait a few minutes for him to get pulled into a conversation by a crowd of wealthy landowners plying him with Spezian sugared figs.

"He's distracted," I whisper.

From the other end of Artain's altar, Sabine quietly unlatches the birdcage door. Her lips move silently, and the bird takes wing, hopping onto a wooden deer carving in the center of the altar.

Not a second later, Artain is beside her, having crossed the amphitheater with inhuman speed.

Though he smiles, his eyes remain cold. The arrow in his hand tap-tap-taps against the cage, a warning. He wags a scolding finger. "Lady Sabine, these are *my* offerings. Should you see something you desire, I'd happily gift it to you, but no freeing your little friends."

He begins to reach for his bow, eyes already targeting in on the albino crow, when I interject myself.

"Let me," I say casually.

I dive forward to catch the creature. It flaps its wings to evade me, but this isn't my first crow. I feign grabbing it with my left hand, knowing that means it will take off to the right. As soon as its feet lift off the carving, I snap out my hand to grab one talon.

It flaps its wings only once before I pin it to my chest. As I return it to its cage, I feel the weight of Artain's gaze on me. The arrow in his grip is stilled now.

"Piece of cake." I dust off my hands, grinning.

"Basten was known throughout Duren as the best huntsman in the seven kingdoms," Sabine chirps sweetly.

Artain's eyes nearly bug out of his head at the claim. Incredulous, he laughs as he calls to the other fae. "Samaur! Woudix! Come here, brothers. Listen to this." The two other Blades pick their way through the crowd to join us. Woudix pauses his sharpening of a dagger, sliding it back into his belt before approaching. "Lord Basten claims to be the best huntsman in the seven kingdoms."

I crook my lips in a rogue's smile. "Why, you think you're better?"

Another incredulous laugh bursts out of him, but he's leaning forward now, his eyes sparking at my gall. "I'm a god. I've been hunting for three thousand years."

"Then it would be easy for you." Sabine strokes the albino crow through the bars, gently trailing her fingers along its feathers.

"What would be easy, Highness?" he asks her.

"A test." She shrugs. "A competition."

Artain's eyes gleam with the thrill of a challenge. He flicks the arrow in his hand, spinning it in a showy arc as he turns to me. "What do you say, mortal? Shall we put it to the test?"

I lift my eyebrows, feigning surprise, and laugh good-naturedly. "Only a fool would accept a challenge from a god." I shift again, acting uncertain. "But, let's say I'm a fool...what manner of test?"

"Do you know the tale of the Night Hunt?" Artain asks, voice rising.

"You'll have to refresh my memory," I say. "I'm not much of a reader."

Artain fans out his hands theatrically, still holding the

arrow as he gestures. "Picture this. In a time before time, Immortal Solene, Goddess of Nature, wished for a rare black pearl apple. I climbed the fabled Tree of Quick to pick one for her pretty lips, with the promise of a tryst beneath the branches. As soon as she'd eaten her fill, the fickle thing transformed into a fawn and bounded away. I pursued until sunset—until night—when I set my arrow's aim upon her and made her surrender herself to our deal." His green eyes light up in wicked delight at the memory. "Trust me, the little siren wanted the chase as much as I did."

The story settles heavily in my gut.

I give a cheeky smirk. "And what, you want me to play Solene?"

Artain's face sinks into a scowl. "No, you buffoon. Lady Sabine will play the part of Immortal Solene in our little game. You and I? We will compete to capture her. Just outside the castle walls in the Vollen Forest. At sunset, the huntsman who has her captured wins. A perfect recreation of the Night Hunt."

Sabine stiffens.

A protective instinct roars up my throat. "Sabine? No— she plays no part in this. If it's a competition, then it's between you and me."

I move a step closer to her, unable to stop myself. Her eyes flicker to me, rimmed with anxiety.

"Oh, relax, human." Artain scoffs, absently tossing back his hair. He slides the arrow back into his quiver. "It's a game, not an execution. We catch Lady Sabine with our bare hands. The little mortal princess won't be so much as bruised, you have my word. In fact, we'll say that the competitors can't seriously harm each other, either, during the game."

My heart takes on an unsteady rhythm as I glance at Sabine.

"It'll be okay, Basten," she murmurs reassuringly.

"No." My voice is hard. "We hunt a deer, not Sabine."

"I've already set the rules of the game." Artain swoops down to scoop up a handful of soil, weighing it in his hand. He says slyly, "No changing it now. It's up to you to accept or decline."

My mind churns as I try to poke holes in his proposal. According to Sabine, fae bargains can't be broken. If he gives his word that she won't be harmed, then he'll be bound to that, right?

Also...it hurts like hell to admit, but I'm not sure I stand a sinner's chance of winning against the God of the Hunt without cheating. I haven't lived at Rian Valvere's side for twenty years to not learn a thing or two about cheating. If I'm to win a competition against ancient immortals, it's going to have to involve some sleight of hand. If Sabine is involved, she can help me win as she did in the Everlast.

I cross my arms over my chest. "If I win, then Sabine is free to return to Astagnon with me."

Woudix leans in and murmurs a gruff warning to Artain, "Vale won't stand for that." His hand lingers on the dagger at his belt, fingers tapping the hilt.

"Vale isn't our keeper, brother." The veins on Artain's arms bulge. There's a strange ripple under his skin where his fey lines rest as if they're about to burst through his human glamour. "Vale may be king, but the rules of the fae bargain are older than his reign. If I lose, he will have no choice but to grant Sabine her freedom." He picks a fleck of dust off his vest. "Anyway, I won't lose."

Sabine crosses her arms. "Don't I get any say in the matter of my fate?"

Artain slings his arm around her shoulder. "Come, now, princess. You don't mind playing the fawn, do you?"

"Get your hands off her." My skin bristles with a predator's ferocity as I shove his hand off her.

The fae fall silent.

Immediately, I realize my mistake and dart a look over my shoulder at Vale—who, fortunately, is still dealing with the landowners and didn't see my hands on his daughter. He's now examining a sack of gold coins, weighing it in his hand.

Sabine takes an exaggerated step away from Artain, throwing him daggers with her eyes. "I'll play as long as it's just a game. No one hurt."

"You will be perfectly safe, my lady," Artain assures me.

Woudix points out gruffly, "She's only going to use her godkiss to help him."

Artain flicks the fleck of dust off his fingers with an irritating shrug. "Two against one? So be it. It won't make a difference—in fact, it will make it all the more enjoyable. Otherwise, I'd win too easily."

"What is your wager, then?" I ask, throwing a fleeting look in Vale's direction, wanting this bargain done.

Artain continues to brush the wrinkles out of his doublet. "Oh, nothing so significant. If I win, I'll take what I always ask for and never get. Sabine, all night. When the sun sets, I'll have her until the dawn."

In one stride, I have his neck in my hand with a grip that I hope bruises his damn fae bones. "No *fucking* deal."

"Basten!" Sabine tries to pry my arm off him. I can smell her nervous sweat. Hear her quick heartbeat.

Keeping her voice low, she hisses, "It doesn't matter. He won't win. He won't get a minute with me, let alone an entire night."

I bare my teeth. "I'm not risking it."

"Well, *I* will," she says softly. Urgently. "I believe in you. Us. Together, we can outsmart him."

I stare into Artain's eyes, his smirk unwavering despite my grip around his throat. My fingers itch to squeeze harder, to snap his neck for daring to suggest such a wager.

Sabine squeezes my arm, a grounding touch pulling me back from the edge.

Slowly, I let out a breath, forcing the tension from my body. I unclench my hand, releasing him.

"Fine," I bite out. "But you lay one finger on her outside of this game, and I'll gut you where you stand."

He laughs, a low, mocking sound that grates against my skin. "As you say, Lord Basten."

Sabine crouches down to scoop up some fresh dirt with her nails. When she straightens, she pours it into my open palm.

Artain holds out his fistful of soil—he lets the grains fall through his fingers.

I do the same.

Woudix turns away sharply, striding off back to his altar with his hound trotting along to guide him, the dagger in his hand again, pointing down as he walks.

Then—locking the angry heat of my gaze to Artain's—I say, "The Night Hunt is on."

"The Night Hunt is on," he echoes vaguely, as I'm already half-forgotten in favor of the farmgirl, who is batting her long lashes at him from across the amphitheater. Distracted, he murmurs, "Await further word from me.

We'll have to bide our time until Vale is occupied. Best he doesn't hear of this wager until its conclusion."

There's a marked shift in his tone—all business, completely focused, as though he's been steering me all the while that I thought I was the one pulling strings. A chill sends the hair on the back of my neck on end.

I swap a look with Sabine, who looks equally unnerved.

Did we just get played by a fae?

As soon as I can escape the gathering, I go straight to my stateroom and throw up in the pisspot—because, now, the deal is sealed, and there is no going back.

CHAPTER 30
SABINE

"**H**is name is Rian Valvere," Matron White says dismissively as the Sisters unload me from the convent's wagon no more gently than if I were a barrel of cider. My father's courtyard gates rise in front of me, cold and unwelcoming. "The High Lord of Duren. Tomorrow, one of his men will come to collect you. Be obedient. Be virtuous. If you want my advice? Say nothing of your time in the Convent of Immortal Iyre. Neither Lord Rian nor his representative will care, and you'll only seem ungrateful to our blessed maiden, Immortal Iyre."

The wagon rolls away, the wheels grinding against the dirt, and for a moment, I swear I feel the tremor of an earthquake beneath my feet. I hope it might split the earth open and swallow them, but it doesn't.

They leave me here, in a place that should feel like home, but I'm a stranger.

I don't belong here.

I don't belong anywhere.

. . .

Every night, I watch from my tower window as the sun sets over the Vollen Mountains. In no world, in no age, could anything compare to a Volkish sunset. As dusk unfurls, phosphorescent flying insects paint the gloaming in impossible shades of greens and blues. Cloudfoxes are at their most active, scampering along the treetops. The mountains take on a purple cast, the closest ones dark indigo, and then each one beyond it a shade fainter until the last ridge is a light periwinkle so faint it melds with the sky.

I'm going to miss this.

I know I have to leave. I lost Basten once, and I won't again. Yes, things are different between us. Still an inch out of lockstep. His missing memories hang like a silk screen between us, a perpetual barrier. One that hurts every time I look at him and see him looking past me as if trying to remember something just out of reach.

One day, I have to believe we'll see each other clearly again.

The dinner bell chimes. But tonight, on my way to the Hall of Vale, something feels different. The musicians aren't playing as they usually do. Servants look pale-faced. The hair on the back of my neck prickles, and the feeling of unease only grows as I approach the open doors and am hit with a strange smell.

I barely glance at the agitated crowd filling the Hall of Vale when a voice calls, "Highness?"

Captain Tatarin strides out of the hall, herding me back into the hallway. She clasps my hand briefly. Her eyes dart, distracted. Her star-shaped pin is askew.

"Tati?" Craning my neck, I try to peer over her shoulder into the hall. "What are you doing here? I thought you led a squadron to Immortal Thracia's resting place."

"That was the plan. We made it as far as the Lunden Valley before—" Her lips stitch together to hold back her words before she admits, "Things are bad there. At first, we thought it was a plague."

My gaze swings sharply back to the Hall of Vale. Someone lets out a sharp cry.

As my nerves jangle, I head for the crowd inside.

"Highness, wait," Tati says but doesn't stop me.

The smell of singed metal grows stronger. Worried murmurs fill the air. I scan every face, looking for Basten's.

But he isn't here.

He isn't here anywhere.

My pulse kicks up as I push through the crowd until I reach what they're all looking at.

A goldenclaw lies on the smooth stones, attached to a harness pulled by two horses. She's dead. One look makes it clear. Her fur is brassy, dull. Her eyes are clouded over. The fur around her mouth is matted with dried blood.

It's Two.

A gasp slips out of me as I drop to my knees to gently touch her scarred ear. *Cold*. She's so cold. Where is my funny, warm-blooded, riddle-telling friend?

Near the head table, my father argues with his army generals. The rest of the fae sit moodily in their gilded seats, their meals untouched, as they murmur to one another in an ancient language.

Artain locks his gaze on me, his eyes flashing with unreadable intent.

Tati catches up to me, dropping to her knees as well. She touches my shoulder. "Highness, I am so sorry. I know you had a special bond with Two, and all the goldenclaws."

"What happened?" I breathe.

Tati's face pales. "The fields in Lunden Valley were dead. In every farm we came to, all the animals and villagers—it was always the same. Dead, seemingly without warning. They'd cough up blood. We didn't know what to think. There were no plaguewings. None of us took ill. It was only after we stopped to let the goldenclaws drink from the river that I put it together. Two drank first, even before our soldiers filled their flasks. She started coughing up blood immediately." Tati's eyes travel somewhere else, to some dark memory. "Poison. The entire river. It had spread into the water table. Everything west of the Lunden Valley is contaminated. Hundreds of people and livestock dead."

My spine goes ramrod straight. Any hunger I felt vanishes, replaced by a tidal wave of shock that leaves my hands trembling.

Quietly, I ask, "How?"

Before Tati answers, my father overhears and thunders, "We don't know yet how it happened, whether by intention or accident. We've taken a sample from this beast but cannot identify the poison."

"It's Thorn Apple."

I spin at Basten's voice sudden behind me, my eyes immediately scouring him for any sign of harm. He looks tired. Dark circles hang under his eyes like shadows against his pale skin. Briefly, his eyes dart between me and Artain, like his worry over our deal has left him sleepless.

That makes two of us.

"What's that, Lord Basten?" Vale rasps, drawing out his words.

"Thorn Apple." The crowd parts, and Basten moves into view. "It's similar to burdock root, but I can smell the difference. If Thorn Apple flowers are crushed and soaked in oil, then the poison won't dilute in water, and remain highly potent. It's a little-known poison. Only a few experts would know how to use it in that manner."

My father's eyes narrow. "Yet *you* know how."

Basten rolls back his shoulders. "I know how, yes. I had an incident with Thorn Apple when I was younger." His throat constricts as he swallows. "And someone else knows how, too—I told King Rian the story years ago."

I push to my feet, shoving my hair out of my face. "Rian? This was—Rian? He did this?"

Basten's eyes meet mine over the goldenclaw's body. There's so much anger there. Enough to fill the hall twice over. But his pain? A hundred times as much. A pain that makes me want to reach out to him. To close the gap.

But I can't—not here. In front of my father.

"Considering the border wall, that would mean King Rian must have poisoned the river on the Astagnonian side before it enters Volkany," Tati explains.

"He wouldn't." My voice falters. "To do so, he'd have to poison a portion of Astagnon, too. Kill his own people."

The crowd erupts with speculative murmurs.

"Are his forces on the move?" one of the generals asks Tati.

"Not as of yet. Not from what we've seen." She clears her throat. "King Rian has to know his forces are not strong enough to face our army. If I had to guess, I'd say this was a stunt to prove his power to the kingdoms of Kravada and Clarana in hopes of garnering their support."

"Generals," my father says sharply. "Meet me in the council chamber. We need to retaliate, and it needs to be swift. Dramatic. Send a message right back. The rulers of Kravada and Clarana will think twice about siding with King

Rian when they hear how many bodies fall in our wake." He lowers his heavy gaze to Basten. "Lord Basten, ready yourself to depart when I give the word. The faster the Astagnonian people bow to us, the fewer lives we'll lose. Where's Beneveto? Someone drag him out of the opium den and tell him to get on a horse to Old Coros *now*."

Bile rises up my throat, and I press a hand against the base of my ribs, my other hand squeezing into such a tight fist that my fingernails cut into my palm.

I will kill Rian myself...

I force my hands slack before my skin breaks from the pressure of my anger.

My father and the generals spare no time, only consulting for a few minutes with Tati before striding out of the hall.

"Oh, where's the damn fiddler?" Iyre asks, frowning out at the crowd. "Can't we get some music? More wine? And you—you, guards. Drag that dead beast out of here before it stinks up the whole castle."

I narrow my eyes at her, but before I can say anything, I feel a hand on the small of my back.

"Come, Highness." Artain deftly guides me through the crowd to where Basten stands. Then, he leans in between Basten and me, a wicked curl to his lips. "Looks like we have our chance to play, mortals. Vale will be in meetings all night and tomorrow with his generals. Tomorrow, meet at dawn, before the Seventh Hour bell. At the southern gate— it leads to the Vallen Forest. I'll give the rest of the game guidelines then."

I glance at Basten, my heart thundering, but his eyes are fixed on Artain while his jaw clamps tightly.

"We'll be there," Basten says hollowly, the words falling like stones.

Artain's smile never fades. "Excellent. I do so look forward to a good hunt. In any case, there's no turning back now. The deal has been struck. It must be seen through. In a way, I suppose you could say that the game has already begun."

A chill creeps up my spine. I can feel the threat laced in his words, the edge of danger.

Basten and I share one more look—and in the reflection of my sunken eyes in his, I know that neither of us will sleep a moment tonight, too.

CHAPTER 31
BASTEN

awn breaks with all the subtlety of a sledgehammer.

Blazing rays cut across the horizon to torch my eyes. I swear that Samaur, that smug God of Day, cranked up the sun just to irritate me.

I tighten the straps on my leather breastplate one final time before descending the central staircase two steps at a time, headed for the southern gate that lies between the Aurora and Hailstrom Tower wings.

My breath grates. I flex my hands, anxious. Gods know I've spent hours agonizing over this bargain's terms, trying to sniff out any fae trickery. Decades with Rian have sharpened my sense for deceit like a bloodhound's nose, but I'm not dealing with second-rate cheats here.

For my own sanity, I run through the terms again.

From dawn to dusk, the game is in play.

Competitors may bruise but not break, bleed but not perish.

To the winner goes the prize.

See, when I lay it out like that, it all sounds safe. I can't fathom how Sabine could be harmed when the rules explicitly forbid it.

So then, why do my bowels feel like they're about to blow?

When I shoulder open one of the southern gate's heavy double doors, blood-orange sunlight burns against my face.

Before me stretches the seemingly endless expanse of Vollen Forest. Twisted pines reaching for the clouds. A bleak ridge in the distance high above the Ramvik River. A whispering wind.

I stride toward a small treehouse pavilion constructed six feet high in the crook of a sprawling oak's branches, where the gods are already lounging in their human glamours.

"Lord Basten. Good of you to join us. I was afraid you wouldn't show, and it's no fun to win on a forfeit," Artain drawls from where he's draped over the pavilion's steps, basking in a band of golden sunlight with a Wicked Weed pipe in hand.

Iyre sits one step below him, drumming her nails on a green glass bottle half filled with a dark liquid.

Woudix and Samaur are in the pavilion, with Hawk, speaking quietly as they study the forest horizon.

Artain saunters down the stairs, sidestepping Iyre, to size me up with that damn smug smile. "You *are* still playing, yes?"

Do I have a choice?

"I wouldn't dream of ruining your diversion," I utter. "You're certain that Vale isn't aware of our bargain?"

Artain folds his arms over his half-bared chest, tossing a perfect lock of hair coquettishly off his forehead. "Vale is with the generals, drafting a plan to charbroil a few thousand villagers to make a nice straight path to the throne for *you.*"

I shouldn't let this pretty bastard get under my skin— but damn, how I'd love to sink my fist into that smirk.

I cut to the chase. "Where's Sabine?"

The words have barely left my lips when the delicate scent of violets wafts into the morning air, chasing away the gods' purulent scents of iron and myrrh. I hear her soft footsteps long before she reaches the southern gate, but I'm still not prepared when she steps out into the dawn light.

When priests speak of angels, they speak of her.

She wears tall boots and wool military trousers that still have Captain Tatarin's hemlock scent on them. The captain is a few sizes smaller than Sabine, so the pants squeeze Sabine's ass in a way that reveals every curve—like a gods-damn map to paradise.

Her face is free of makeup. Bare. Natural. I struggle to swallow. Like this, she reminds me so much of my dreams of her—of us—sleeping together under stars instead of crystal chandeliers.

"Lady Sabine." Artain offers a wolfish smile. "The key player in our game. Without you, Lord Basten and I would be left with nothing to compare as huntsmen but our shafts." He shoots me another smirk. "I speak of arrows, of course."

This fucking asshole.

Equally unamused, Sabine crosses her arms tightly over her chest. She looks as calm as if she's spent years putting up with fae rogueries, but I can hear how shallow her breaths fall. How much she's fighting to hide her nerves.

She tucks back a strand of hair, eyes briefly landing on

me with a waver of uncertainty. "We're here, Lord Artain, so give us the rest of the game guidelines."

Artain points to the bellringer's post, visible on the castle's rooftop. "When the bellringer signals Seventh Hour, the hunt will begin. You, my little fawn, may scamper about anywhere within the boundaries of Vollen Forest. One hour head start. At Eighth Hour's chime, Lord Basten and I will set out from the farthest points of Aurora Tower and Hailstrom Tower. The huntsman who captures your pretty little tail and brings you back to this pavilion at dusk wins."

Sabine nods, adjusting the band of her trousers.

I shift my weight from foot to foot, chewing a damn hole on the inside of my cheek.

Sweat pours down the back of my shirt. My skin prickles with every breeze. I can't shake the uncanny feeling that's been plaguing me since making this damn bargain: *Something is wrong here.*

My brain might not see it, but my senses do.

"And if neither of you catches me by dusk?" She casually tosses back her hair, but she's sweating as much as I am. On her palms. The back of her neck. Places only I can detect.

"In that unlikely event, the game is forfeit." Artain shrugs. "A draw." He laughs mockingly as though he knows that a draw will never happen.

She shoots back with as much derision: "And, what then? We toss a coin to determine the winner?"

"Certainly, if that's what you like." He winks.

I interject impatiently, "We're losing daylight. Everywhere within the forest is fair game?" Out of the corner of my eye, I pick out the tallest trees for easy branches to climb, where I can get a high vantage point to look for Sabine.

"That's right, Lord Basten. That high ridgeline to the

southwest, the Ramvik River to the east, the Norhelm road to the northeast. Those are the boundaries."

I wipe the nervous sweat off my brow, pretending to rake back my hair. Okay, this? I can deal with this. You could give me all the land from the port of Thrassos to the Kravadan border, and Sabine and I would still find each other.

"You'd better hope Vale doesn't find out about this," Woudix intones from the pavilion, taking a long toke from the pipe before passing it to Samaur.

"It bears no consequence," Artain snaps defensively. He rests his hands on his hips, his open leather vest revealing a line of sweat running down his muscles. "When he does learn of it, he'll be pleased that I found a way to keep his daughter safely in Volkany."

His nostrils flare. He shades his eyes to look up at the sun. "When will Seventh Hour strike, Samaur?"

"Ten more minutes," the God of Day answers, lifting the pipe to his lips.

I pull in a deep breath. Trying to get a head start by picking up on scents. Though I'll admit, it's hard to focus on game trails with Sabine so achingly close.

Her hand rests just three inches from my own as she scans the forest for her own strategy. It takes all my self-discipline not to brush the back of my hand against hers. The faintest scent of powdered sugar clings to her hair, and it's so intoxicating that I can't be blamed for forgetting all about the forest.

I feel confident. Artain has millennia of hunting experience, sure. Oh, and magic. But Sabine *wants* me to find her. It's two against one.

Really, I almost feel bad for the guy.

Artain picks up his bow. "Time to take our places."

I pick up my own bow, slinging it and my quiver over my shoulder. Then, gently, I touch Sabine's chin and, for a brief second, everything else falls away. "I found you once, little violet. I'll find you again."

She leans her head into my palm. "We'll find each other across any distance."

Artain chuckles darkly. "So serious, aren't you both? Please. It's a *game*."

I feel an itch somewhere in the center of my back that I can't scratch. My instincts whisper that this isn't a game, no matter how they dress it up with rules and wagers. If there's one thing I've learned, it's that nothing in this world is ever as straightforward as it appears, especially when the fae are involved.

But what choice do we have?

As if reading my mind, Artain spins back around with a finger raised.

"Oh! I almost forgot." A wicked curl tugs at his lips. "There's *one* more thing to mention."

CHAPTER 32

SABINE

That pretty fae *bastard*.

The Night Hunt is on the verge of starting. Any second now, the rooftop bellringer will signal Seventh Hour, when I'm supposed to run into Vallen Forest and hide. Already, I feel the pull of animals in the woods calling to me, standing by to help me. Sensing my need.

But now? A shiver runs up my limbs. I exchange a nervous look with Basten as I hug my arms close.

"You can't change the rules now, Artain," I spit.

"There's no change." Artain plucks a tiny green inchworm off his tunic. "The deal we struck is binding. It's really more of a...footnote."

My stomach tightens. I don't have time for this. I only have an hour to get a head start from Artain. Once that bell rings, I need to *run*.

"What kind of fae bullshit is this?" Basten demands, the cords in his neck straining.

Artain holds the inchworm up to the light, watching it crawl down his finger. "If Lord Basten wins, you'll be free to leave Drahallen Hall with him, Lady Sabine. As per our terms. However, at that point, our game will be over. Including its binding rules. There will be nothing to stop me from putting an arrow in his skull *then*." He puffs on the inchworm to send it flying into the air. "How's this for a footnote? If Lord Basten wins, I kill him right after."

My cheeks blaze red. "That isn't fair!"

Artain smooths a wrinkle out of his tunic. "It *is* fair. It adheres to our deal."

Anger floods me as I fight the urge to grab his bowstring and wind it around his neck. As much as I want to see his pretty eyes bulge out, I have to be smart. Quick thinking, too. Because that bell is going to ring at any moment. And Artain won't wait around twiddling his thumbs for me to argue with him.

"You gods-damned lying bastard." Basten draws his hunting knife in one smooth move. "If we can kill each other outside of the game, then I'll do the honors now, before it even starts."

He lunges for Artain, but Artain has his bow at the ready. *He was waiting for this.* Basten's blade catches Artain's bow in the center, deep enough to stick in the wood. Artain gives a cold smile as he draws his own hunting knife with his free hand.

"You're welcome to try," Artain hisses.

"Basten, don't!" I yell. "You can't win hand-to-hand combat against a god!"

But Basten ignores me, circling Artain in a fighting stance.

Gods, he's going to get himself killed.

"Wait!" I lurch forward to grab Artain's sleeve, holding his arm back, and say in a rush, "End the game now. Or wait for the bell and end it then. You've won, Artain. That's what you want, isn't it? I'll spend a night with you!"

"Sabine, *no*." Basten wrenches his knife out of Artain's bow with an angry grunt.

"It's that or your life!" I tug harder on Artain's shirt, twisting the cotton in my fingers to jerk him around to face me. "It's an easy choice. One night and it's over."

Artain looks down at my hand on his bicep with a calculated smile that makes me feel like I've walked into a trap.

"An easy choice? Hmm, perhaps not *that* easy. You see, princess, when we set the terms, I didn't say one night. I said that when the sun sets, I'll have you for the entire night." He toys with the edge of his blade. "And the sun sets *every* night."

I rip my hand away like he's on fire, retreating with fear building in each step. "No—no, that's a lie. You always joke about spending *one* night with me. One."

He uses the knife blade to clean a spec of dirt from under one fingernail. "That's your fault for assuming that's what I meant when I set my wager." He shrugs impishly. "*Every night* with Lady Sabine. Vale might not like it at first, but he'll come around. Who could be a better prospect for his precious daughter than a god?"

My throat closes up, choking me, but Basten interrupts before I can spit pure fury at Artain.

"You planned this all along, didn't you?" His muscles twitch, but he marshals his temper and slams his knife into a tree trunk instead of Artain's skull. In a tightly coiled voice, he says, "No weapons. No powers. No game. Just you and me—we decide this here and now with our fists."

"No." I plant my palms on Basten's broad chest, shoving him back from Artain. But he might as well be an anvil. He barely budges. His eyes glow like hot coals, his skin burns beneath my hands. I shout, "He'll kill you!"

The tendons on his neck bulge out as he bares his teeth. "I'd sooner die right now than see you bound to be *his* slave every night."

I shove my heels into the ground to brace myself as Basten pushes against me, trying to get to Artain. "Hey. Hey, look at me! This is what he wants—to pit us against each other. So he can win the game!"

"It isn't a fucking game anymore, Sabine! It's your life! It's every night!"

In the distance, the bellringer signals Seventh Hour.

Oh, no.

No, not yet...

My stomach drops.

The bell's echo reverberates from my toes to the tips of my fingers, pressed against Basten's chest, leaving me feeling as hollow as that damn brass bell itself.

In a flash, the breath vanishes from my lungs. I try to heave, but my ribs crush inward like I've been slammed by the bell clacker, unable to get air.

My eyes lock with Basten's. In all the time I've known him, I've never seen bald-faced panic burn in his pupils. But now, they're blown big as pennies.

The bell hasn't even stopped ringing when he murmurs hoarsely, "Sabine."

A ragged cry tears from my throat. "Basten—I'm sorry."

Throwing all my weight forward, I dig the heel of my palms into his left lower ribcage where he was hurt in the Everlast. He clocks my movement a fraction too slow to stop me.

Groaning, he doubles over to clutch his side.

I trip backward in a blind rush, hands snagging in doghobble bushes, as a phantom pain pinches in my own ribcage.

"I'm sorry," I choke. "I can't let him kill you."

Basten tosses his head up, hair already sweat-soaked as it streaks his forehead. "Sabine, don't run!"

But I have to.

Can't he see? If I stay, then he dies.

His shouts are barely afterthoughts as I turn and tear through the doghobble like the frightened fawn that I'm supposed to play.

At the edge of my periphery, I see Artain pluck one of the doghobble leaves I brushed by, crushing it in his hands and burying his face in his cupped palms to memorize my scent.

Screw Artain. Screw all of them. I fell right into the beautiful trap they laid out for me, baited not with honey wine and gowns but with the promise of freedom.

Of a family. Of a home.

They made me feel like I *belonged*.

But I can't think about that right now. It's not just Artain I'm running from. I have exactly one hour to put some distance between me and Basten, too. I don't have a sliver of doubt that he'll get himself killed to keep me out of Artain's possession, if he can.

I know what he thinks of himself: A sinner. A street rat. Only good for his fists. But what *I* see is the heart of a king beneath the bruises, someone who would travel to the ends of the earth to keep me safe even if it means tipping himself head-first into the underrealm.

Once I'm far enough into the woods that I can no longer see the castle spires above the trees, I stop at a pine tree, catching myself against the rough bark, taking a second to find my breath.

Overhead, a crow caws.

Pressing my forehead against the bark, I murmur aloud, "Basten will do everything he can to catch me. I need to run. To hide. To confuse his senses."

My mind stirs with a flicker of possibility. Slowly, I lift my head and squint at the crow. They're always bringing me little tokens—acorns, shiny bits of metal, pretty rocks.

Friend, can you bring me something specific?

It tilts its head. *What object, bird-talker?*

I lick my lips, thinking of what could be close by. *A quartz stone. And anything metal—iron or steel.*

It caws again and flies away.

As I wait, every second stretches like a taut bowstring, and my panic fills the silence. My breath rasps. My pulse hammers. I want to crumple. To curl in the dirt like autumn leaves. To shatter into dust.

But I *can't*—the only way to keep Basten alive is to keep moving.

My head jerks up just in time to see the crow circling back. It drops two objects at my feet: A hunk of raw quartz and a rusty steel belt buckle that it must have scavenged from a soldier.

Moving fast, I arrange a handful of pine needles over twigs. My hands are shaking, but after a few strikes of the quartz on the metal buckle, I manage to get a spark.

Blast—it goes out.

Hunching over, I concentrate and get another spark. I breathe oxygen onto the spark until it catches and starts smoking. I stand up, fanning away the smoke, coughing as it spreads.

That will confuse him.

The crow flits its wings. *Go left, bird-talker. To the river. The water will hide your sound.*

I start moving again, veering toward the left. Soon, the ground slopes sharply downhill toward the Ramvik River valley. I can't spot the river through the trees, but I can make out its shushing roar.

Will it be loud enough to mask me from Basten's ears?

I start down the slope at a run, but after about twenty feet, my boots slip on damp leaves. I lose my balance, slamming onto my left hip, skidding downhill a few feet until I can grab ahold of a root. "*Dammit!*"

Damp, loamy earth stains the backside of my trousers, leaving my lower half clammy and cold. I push to a careful stand and brush the soil off my hands, frowning down at the skid marks my boots left behind. If Basten comes within a quarter mile of this slope, he'll spot my tracks in a blink.

Still, the only way to the river is down.

So, I grab hold of twisting rhododendron branches for balance as I descend, trying to hop from rock to rock so I don't leave prints. It's painfully slow going, and I'm not even sure it's effective. My boots leave damp prints on the rocks, just as they did the dirt. I might as well be painting a bright red blaze that says: SHE WENT THIS WAY.

I crouch down to unlace my boots, then knot the laces together and sling them around my neck so I can walk on dry sock feet.

It isn't long before the rocky outcropping ends at a cliff. I dare a peek at the Ramvik River, fifteen feet below, its whitewater cascades sluicing down a canyon.

If it were the slow-moving Innis River back in Astagnon, I might risk jumping in. I could let the current carry me downstream, where hopefully Basten wouldn't think to follow.

But the Ramvik River is a beast. Filled with rocky water-falls, I wouldn't make it twenty feet before falling over a cascade and crashing onto jagged rocks.

So, I skirt the cliff's edge, balancing as best I can as I follow the river upstream. More tangled rhododendrons block my path and require contortion to squeeze between their branches. Roots snag at my socks. Rough bark scrapes my arms. I finally reach the loud, rushing river's bank, and follow it upstream.

Now that I have some degree of cover, I rack my brain for a way out of this. Artain screwed Basten and me both. Here we thought we were so clever to trick a fae into a bargain, but we should have known all along that *we* were the ones being played.

Take stock of your options, Sabine.

If Basten catches me, I might as well drive an arrow into his skull myself. I don't doubt for a second that Artain will make good on his threat, no matter how much I beg other-wise. Basten has a king's blood, but he's still human. Artain wouldn't think twice about stamping out his mortal life.

Which leaves letting Artain catch me. It would be easy enough to accomplish. Vallen Forest is filled with creatures who would gladly lead me to Artain's location once Eighth Hour tolls.

I could simply fall to my knees and surrender.

Basten would live.

But what would happen to me?

A chill settles into my bones as I picture my future as Artain's nightly plaything. Not just one night, but *every* night. Until now, he's behaved for my father's benefit. It's as if I've been living in a grand performance, unaware that the spotlight has only shown on what the fae wanted me to see: the smiling acolytes offering their blood, the hedonistic parties, a doting father.

I never thought to pull back the curtain to see the shadows lurking backstage—until Basten arrived.

And if Artain wins?

I close my hand over my neck, rubbing my thorn-scratched skin as if Artain's pointed incisors were already closing in on my jugular.

I duck beneath a branch, my feet pounding the earth as I try to put as much space as possible between me and Artain. Initially, I'd dismissed him as a harmless fop, but I see now how wrong I was.

My stomach lurches as I swallow down bile, fighting against the terrible images that fill my mind. How many nights can I fend him off? Ten? Twenty? A hundred? He'll have me on my back eventually, taking what he wants.

No—I *won't* let that happen.

As the ground turns muddier, I stop to tug my boots back on as I try to think my way out of this. Would my father even let Artain carry out either threat? I'm his daughter; he wouldn't want me reduced to a god's toy. And letting Artain kill Basten would be political suicide, when the fae need him to deliver Astagnon.

On the other hand, I'm thinking of my father as rational. Fair. *Human.* When in reality, his fae mind is probably as devious as Artain's.

Twisting Basten's ring, I take stock of my surroundings. I'm about two miles from the castle's southern gate. Maybe less, since it's slow going to move through the underbrush.

That's not nearly enough distance for—

A distant, faint bell clangs through the trees, halting my thoughts.

My stomach drops.

"Oh, *hell*."

How has it already been an hour? Immediately, my pulse flares, stoking my dwindled energy until I'm back to running through the woods. Now that Basten and Artain are on the hunt, I have to keep my wits about me more than ever.

Friends. I project my thoughts through the trees. *I need your help. Is anyone there?*

For a moment, there is only silence, but then, a red-breasted robin swoops down. He flies alongside me from branch to branch, cocking his head in interest. *I am here.*

Thorns lash at my arms, shredding my shirtsleeves, but I push through them. *I need you to gather robins and have them track two huntsmen coming this way. One is fae. The other human. Can you do that?*

Hold tight! The robin flits off into the canopy.

Leaves crunch to my left, and I snap my head around to see a doe gliding alongside me, her graceful strides like a whisper through the underbrush.

Why do you run, human? she asks curiously.

I'm being hunted. I pause to climb over a fallen trunk before continuing. *Is there somewhere I can hide? Somewhere difficult to track?*

As the doe lopes beside me, her soft brown nose twitches. *Den near the still-water pond. We deer hide there from hunters.*

She stops and points her nose to the right, back toward the way I've come. My chest heaves as I pause, turning to look back through the trees. There's a gap where a widow-maker must have fallen, and it gives an unobstructed view of the top spires of Drahallen Hall.

The hair lifts on the back of my spine. The last direction I want to go is backward, but what choice do I have?

I nod, breathless. *Take me there.*

Hiding is a risky strategy. It means voluntarily trapping myself. Easy prey. But the other choice is continuing to run and that's...not ideal either. I'm already out of breath. My muscles ache. Not to mention that running means spreading more tracks across the forest.

The doe darts down a game trail I hadn't noticed.

I follow her at a run, thankful for a clear path after miles of brambles. My ears pick up on the roar of flowing water again, but when I glimpse a waterway ahead, it isn't the raging Ramvik. It's a medium-sized tributary stream about ten feet wide.

The doe follows the game trail along the riverbank for about a quarter mile before my feet sink into soft mud. When I lift my foot, water immediately fills the depression.

Just ahead! the doe says encouragingly.

We follow the tributary to its source: a large, marshy pond surrounded by river birches, with a beaver's den damming one end. I can hear their squeaky voices coming from inside, sounding like burbling water. A grey heron languidly strides through the water, and a fish jumps on the other side. Dragonflies buzz around the reeds.

I pause, struck.

It's a beautiful scene. Peaceful. For a second, my heart latches onto this brief window of calm.

Then, the robin lands on a branch beside me, hopping in agitation, and my bubble of calm pops.

Did you find them? I ask, stomach knotting.

He fans his wings, a signal of warning. *The human huntsman is at the high river cliff.*

I swallow a dry lump in my throat. Basten has already tracked me to the cliff? How is he moving so fast? I can only hope I didn't leave enough tracks for him to follow, but I know his skill.

And the fae huntsman? I tighten my hands into fists.

Harder to track. The robin hops to another branch. *He moves fox-fast. He—*

A second robin lands on the neighboring tree, frantically fanning his wings. *The fae is headed this way!*

I suck in a gasp. "That's impossible. Not even the fae can move that fast."

But a second deer bounds out from the copse of river birches, her white tail flashing in warning as she runs. *A huntsman! A fae huntsman comes!*

The first doe nudges me sharply in my side. Urging me to follow the other deer. For a second, I'm frozen, eyes scouring every shadow to see if they'll take on Artain's form. But then my senses snap back into place, and I run.

Pumping my arms, I catch up to the deer. A third has joined, running alongside me. They scamper over a small hillock and then vanish, seemingly straight into the ground.

I come to a skidding stop, pinwheeling my arms, afraid I'm about to tumble through a fae door.

But it's only an eroded space beneath massive tree roots. A herd of six deer huddle within, so tightly packed that I can't tell which limbs belong to which bodies.

The deer are quiet as clouds, perfectly camouflaged by the dirt walls. I could walk two feet away and not see them.

Quick. The young doe wiggles her ears at me. *Hunker down with us!*

I have to wriggle head-first through the narrow space between the exposed roots. It's a tangle of knobby knees and clattering antlers as I scramble to the back of the den. The deer move in front of me, their warm bodies hiding me from sight. I can feel their quick heartbeats flutter beneath soft fur.

A robin lands at the edge of the den. *Not a sound, now! He approaches!*

I clamp a hand over my mouth to muffle my breathing. Artain doesn't have Basten's godkissed hearing, but he's still God of the Hunt. He's spent thousands of years honing his senses to track his quarry.

A young doe gently presses her head against my arm, and only then do I realize I'm shaking.

"Sabine!" Artain's voice tears like thunder through the woods.

Oh no. *Oh, gods, no.*

My muscles clench as I try to hunch further into the den, wishing I could disappear into the dirt. Ninth Hour hasn't even struck—and he's already found me?

How did I *ever* think I could make it until sunset?

"I know you're here!" he calls. "You leave a trail as wide as a goldenclaw, princess. Here's some advice for next time: get yourself a pair of boots with a tread that doesn't catch every dirt clod in the forest. You might as well have drawn me a map."

My toes curl in my boots. This can't be happening. He can't win this easily. I refuse to spend every night of my life at his beck and call, satisfying whatever lurid fae needs he can dream up.

A twig snaps loudly close by—that can't be an accident. Not with him. He *wants* me to know he's closing in.

I brace my hands over my head, huddling closer with the deer. My mind races. A part of me wants to just end it. This terrible torture. This awful anticipation. At least that way, I know Basten will live.

But for how long? a voice warns in my head. *You know he'll get himself killed trying to free you from being Artain's plaything.*

"Where are you, princess?" Artain's voice cuts with a sing-song lilt. "Do I need to stab my knife through every fern until you squeal?"

The game's terms state that he can't harm me, only catch me. Still, that's little reassurance now, when a much darker fate awaits.

"Ah...what's this? A strand of your hair caught on a branch? By this hill marked with deer prints?"

Fear jolts through me as his voice blasts mere inches outside the den. I press my palm harder against my lips, but I can't hide my rickety breath.

There's a terrible moment of silence, and then a scuff as his boots come to stand at the den's opening.

I'm trapped. Cornered.

So afraid that I might piss these damn trousers.

He stoops, smiling like a jackal as he peeks between the roots. "Hello, princess."

In that instant, something changes. *I* change.

Awakened by fear, it's like a different self takes me over. Some deep energy explodes through my skin.

Suddenly, I'm outside of my body, fracturing into six different pieces. Those pieces slam into each of the huddled deer, and before I can blink, the deer herd burst out of the den. A hoof smacks into my thigh, sending pain shooting through the muscle. The young doe knocks my other leg over as she bounds out of the den. The big buck's antlers crack against my temple, but I barely feel anything.

Because I'm not in my body anymore. I'm in *theirs.*

I puppet the deer herd on pure instinct and adrenaline, barely cognizant of my actions. My fingers twitch as I force the deer's bodies to knock Artain to the ground.

The first two deer out of the den side-swipe him, making him lose his balance. A third gives him a sharp kick with her hind legs, sending him stumbling to the left.

But the damn bastard is still standing.

Baring my teeth, I dig my fingers in the air with a forceful shove. The big buck lashes forward with the same forceful movement, head lowered. He crashes his massive rack into Artain, who tries to escape the strike but doesn't make it in time.

An antler spears his left shoulder.

My breath catches. *I can hurt him—how?*

The terms said they couldn't hurt me or each other...but no one said *I* couldn't.

I jerk my hand back. The buck mimics my act, pulling out his antler.

Could I even...*kill* him?

With a grimace, I brace to shove my hand forward again to direct the buck to stab Artain in the heart this time, but before I can—

Artain moves inhumanly fast, swinging around his bow. He draws and nocks an arrow, pulling back the string to aim at the buck.

Reality slams back into me—my lungs, my heart—as I'm thrown out of the buck's body and returned to my own.

I scramble to regain control over the deer, weaving my fingers to direct their movements.

Go! I scream in my head. *Run!*

But the deer are sluggish from the aftereffects of my possession. Their feet wobble. The buck shakes himself, lilting to the right. He charges Artain, but Artain easily tucks into a roll to evade him.

When he rises, it's with his bow drawn again. He fires at the youngest doe, bringing her down with an arrow straight to the heart.

"No!" I scream.

Artain nocks again—two arrows this time. He aims and fires both simultaneously to take down two more does as they flee through the doghobble.

I flail forward, clawing my way out of the den.

Artain whips around to nock another arrow. Before I can reach him, he fires on the mother doe, who crashes into a river birch. Her little fawn bounds after her, bleating, and Artain trains his sights on it as he nocks yet another arrow—

I look away as there's a sickening squelch.

My heart aches, but it's too late. *I did this to them. I'm a monster. I got all of them except the buck killed...*

No.

No—if anyone here is a monster, it's the man with the arrows.

With a battle cry, I burst out of the den and throw myself on Artain as he aims a sixth arrow at the buck.

I wrestle the arrow from his bow, throwing my hip into his side as I snap the arrow over my knee.

The buck takes off into the woods—the last of his herd.

Gasping, I launch myself onto Artain's bow, trying to pry it out of his hands. His initial surprise gives way to a slow cackle.

"Little princess, you want a tussle, is that it?"

My vision bleeds into red as I slam my knee up toward his groin, but he blocks me with a downward swing, gracefully catching hold of my thigh in the process. His fingers dig into my ass as he drags my body flush against him.

"We're going to have a *lot* of tussles, starting tonight, then every night after," he says breathily. I struggle, but he swipes my foot out from under me, slamming my back down against the riverbank.

Climbing on top of me to pin down my limbs, he forcefully smooths the tangled hair off my face. "We can start early, if you like." He laughs. "After all, we have a long time until sunset."

I should be disgusted, but I'm still too brutalized by the raw pain of losing the deer herd to feel much of anything at all. Their still-warm carcasses bleed out around me, their blood running in rivulets around the depression where Artain has me pinned.

He grabs my head and twists it toward the closest deer carcass.

"See what happens?" he murmurs in my ear. "When you use your power against me?"

"Their blood is on your hands," I spit, cheek smushed to the mud. "And I'll make damn sure you don't get a chance to harm another breathing thing in this forest—including me."

Before Artain can offer a retort, I bring my knee up between his legs.

This time, I catch him unaware. His eyes bulge as a moan peals out from his lips. In the split second that his guard is down, I dig my heel into the ground and use the force to cantilever my hips upward, throwing him off me.

I press myself to my hands and knees at the pond's edge.

"Sabine. You will soon regret resisting me!" As he swipes an arm for me, I gulp in a breath and fall backward.

I plunge into the water—

—where everything is dark—

—and cold—

—and deadly—

—until a small, squeaky voice with a hint of burbling water calls, **This way!**

CHAPTER 33

BASTEN

As Ninth Hour rings from the distant castle, I crouch by a game trail, studying the trampled grass. There's no mud here to capture a footprint, but it's clear enough that something heavier than deer passed this way. The grass's bend suggests a person weighing around one hundred twenty pounds with a running stride of forty inches.

I lower my nose to the grass to breathe in.

There.

Sabine's violet blossom scent slams into me like a shot of adrenaline. It's heady. Intoxicating. But then, I grimace and spit into the dirt. Her normal scent is tainted by the bitter bite of her fear. Thinking of her, fearful and alone, makes my stomach revolt.

"If that fae bastard has touched you..." I mutter between clenched molars. I grip a fallen branch, squeezing so hard it snaps. I close my eyes, imagining it's Artain's trigger finger.

You're a fool to fall for his tricks, I berate myself for the hundredth time. Growling, my muscles bristle as I think of his pretty-boy smirk. The urge to strike something is overpowering, and I settle on giving myself a good smack in the jaw.

Pain shoots through my head, but I only growl again.

It doesn't hurt *enough*.

I need my physical pain to match my inside pain. It's my fault that we're trapped in this twisted game. I thought I could outsmart a fae. Still, that wasn't even my greatest mistake. If I could do everything over again, I'd have taken that first look at Immortal Vale in his fae regalia, thrown Sabine over my shoulder, and gotten the hell out of Drahallen Hall on Day One.

Now, I've put her in danger. And if the only way to spare her from the fae's bottomless well of depravity is to win, then I'll fucking win.

Even if it means putting myself in the grave.

I open my eyes and stalk forward after Sabine's trail.

It's a tricky thing, tracking her. I don't mean that it's *difficult*. On the contrary, it wouldn't be easier to follow a guide rope. Her scent is splashed on every tree she brushed by. If that wasn't enough, it's more than clear by the animals' reactions that she's passed this way. Robins cluster in the branches overhead, watching me like her guardians.

When I say "tricky," it's because I don't want to catch her too fast.

The way I figure, this game won't end until sunset. So, if I catch her now, I have to hold onto her for seven more hours until dusk. Which is an eternity when you're trying to cage a spitting wildcat. I might not remember our past together, but all it takes is one look to know she's a woman who puts up a fight.

And her screams?

Might as well be a blazing signal fire to draw Artain straight to us.

So, it's best to let her run—on a leash, of course. Her scent tells me that she's about ten minutes ahead of me. Which is perfect. That's enough space so that her spies don't fly off to sound the alarm, but I can snatch her quickly if needed.

The game trail splits, and I sniff the air. Sabine turned left toward the tributary stream, following a female deer. A bird was with her—probably one of those robins, judging by the faint scent of mealworms, their preferred snack. The other forest smells are expected: rotting mushrooms, fox scat, pine resin.

I don't detect a glimmer of Artain's wild mint scent.

I take the left trail along the riverbank. I should be relieved that there's no sign of my competition. It means Artain hasn't found Sabine's trail yet, which makes sense— he lacks my heightened senses. But the bastard is nearly godkissed fast. And smart.

That's why I keep glancing over my shoulder, scanning the shadows. If he's so quick, why hasn't he swept through the forest by now?

Yeah, I don't like this.

As I round a bend, a sound ahead brings my feet to an abrupt halt.

A human sound. A woman's. A *yelp*.

My heart smashes against my ribs as my body screams at me to run toward the sound. To move. But I force myself still.

Is it a trick?

I cock my head, straining my ears. The gods-damned stream's burbling cuts my hearing range in half. Normally, I could pick up on a squirrel's chit from half a mile away, but now, I strain even to hear a leaf fall nearby.

Then, I hear it again, clear this time.

That's Sabine's cry. No mistake. It's a quarter mile ahead, and I can hit that distance in a minute and a half.

I tear through the forest, ignoring the ache in my muscles. For Sabine, I'd run until I collapsed, bruised and spent in the dirt. I'm not sure which churns harder, my heart or my mind. I have to get to her. The world will burn before I let that fae bastard place his filthy hands anywhere near her.

As soon as I round the stream bend, I pick up on their scents:

Artain's wild mint aroma meanders through the air like oil on water, oozing confidence. Whereas Sabine's violet scent cuts straight to my nose with the sharp tang of fear. It coats my tongue, driving me into an even faster run.

I crash out of the woods at a clearing at a pond's edge. As I skid to a stop, I throw out my senses to take stock of the situation.

Artain is on his knees at the water's edge.

The water laps against the bank—recently disturbed.

Five dead deer lay bleeding out into the trampled grass, gold-tipped arrows shot with godly precision into their hearts. The tang of their blood hangs in the air, but beneath it is the salty scent of Sabine's tears.

Artain clocks me immediately.

He jumps to his feet with inhuman speed, tossing a pebble casually in the air and catching it. "Well, well. Lord Basten. Perhaps not a bad huntsman after all—though you're too late."

In a flash, I have my bow drawn, the arrow aimed square at his chest.

"Where is she?" I demand. "I can smell her all over you."

There's a new edge of cruelty in his eyes, though I suspect it was always lurking beneath his smiling facade. He strokes his chin, eyeing my arrow with unsettling calm. "The terms state we can't kill one another."

"Fuck the rules—I'm dead anyway, right?"

He tosses the pebble again. "Go ahead, then. What part of "immortal" don't you understand? Let that arrow loose and see how much it slows me down."

Anger burns through my forearm as I strain to hold the bow drawn. Every instinct screams to let my arrow fly. Maybe it won't kill the bastard, but hey, at least for a minute, it would wipe off that smirk.

"I'll ask again," I challenge. "Where. Is. Sabine?"

Artain flings the pebble into the stream, where it skips twice before plunging underwater. When I narrow in my vision on the sinking pebble, I can make out water plants still disturbed beneath the surface, as though something large swam recently through them. The trail leads toward a beaver's dam on the opposite shore.

"The beavers," I realize. "They helped her."

"Doesn't matter." He combs his fingers through his hair to tame it back into place. "She'll be soaking wet now. Even easier to track. I'll have her back under me in five minutes to finish what we started."

My arrow point trembles as rage blurs my vision. "You. Don't. *Touch*. Her."

"Oh, I'll do much more than that when she's mine every night." He draws his hunting knife in one smooth flick of his wrist. "I just have to put you in the grave first."

We begin to circle one another. Sunlight winks off his blade. My arrow is drawn but aimed downward.

He moves first, feigning a stab forward, but at the last minute, kicks a rock with exceptional aim at my head.

I bat it away, ducking. *He's testing my reflexes.*

When I straighten, I use the momentum to swing the end of my bow at his midsection. He dodges, then tackles me from the side, slamming me down to the streambank. We grapple in the mud, boots spilling and sliding. I try to wrestle the blade out of his hand.

"Mortal weapons can't kill me," he reminds me. "And if you maim me and break the terms, then I win."

"Guess I'll have to be clever, then. Think like a fae."

I wedge my leg between us, boot against his chest, and throw him off me. While he scrambles to his feet, I draw my own knife and slash against his leg.

"Bleeding is allowed," I growl. "I could just drain you. Tire you out."

I rush him, slashing again, this time at his arm. He evades me with an upper block, cuts his blade across my shoulder, then slams the hilt into my solar plexus.

I double over, gasping for air, then come up shoving my shoulder into his midsection and throw him back into the pond.

He lands with a splash. I stomp in after him, sheathing my knife, then grabbing his vest lapels to shove him under the water.

He burbles, struggling for air.

My arms burn, but I throw all my weight into holding him underwater. His flailing leg manages to hook around my ankle, and he knocks me down with him.

We both splash in the water, struggling to go after his knife. He tries to pin me under the surface, but I twist away, crawling back onto the shore.

I grab my bow, breathing hard as I get to my feet.

He emerges from the water, hands empty. His eyes dart to his bow lying in the grass at the base of a rocky slope.

"Go ahead," I grunt. "See if you can make it."

His eyes flash, calculating. In a burst of speed, he lunges for his bow. Immediately, I nock an arrow in my own—but don't aim for him.

Instead, I swing my arrow toward a thin root halfway up the slope that holds back a mass of dirt and rocks.

I let my arrow fly as Artain grabs his bow.

The root snaps in half—without its support, a landslide begins.

Artain can't get out of the way fast enough. Dirt rains down the slope. Rocks follow. Some the size of my fist. A few as large as a wooden chest.

I jump back, bracing my hands on my knees, as I scan the slope.

When the dust finally settles, Artain is buried up to his neck in loose rocks.

Limping forward, I spit in the dirt. "Try to get out of *that*."

Where dirt doesn't cover his face, cuts and bruises do. As he strains against the rocks, he spits, "Your victory is also your death sentence, don't you get it?"

"You don't begin to understand what I'd do for Sabine." Gripping my upper arm, I secure my bow behind my back, double-check I have my sheathed knife, then splash into the shallow water toward the beaver dam.

I pause, sniffing.

There's smoke in the air.

It's faint but undeniable. Blowing in from the west,

about a quarter mile away, where the forest buts up against the jagged Vallen Mountains.

Smoke means fire, and a wildfire always comes with the acrid scent of lightning. But I don't smell lightning now—only a tang of iron and minerals. Which means this wildfire is human-made.

"Sabine," I murmur. "What did you do?"

I break into a run, clenching my molars against the pain that shoots through my shoulder with every jostle. If my little violet started a fire on purpose, then I need to reach her before the smoke dulls my senses.

On the one hand, I'm impressed. Few tactics could slow down both me and Artain, but smoke is one of them. It masks scent and taste. Not to mention, reduces my seeing distance by half. Hell, the fire's roar muffles sounds, too.

On the other hand? I'm fucked if I don't catch her before Artain gets himself free.

I crash thigh-deep through the water, and once I'm within a few feet of the dam, the bright scent of blood hits me like a drug. It's fresh. It's *hers*.

I channel my anger into following her trail. Now that I know she's bleeding, it's child's play. From the scent, I can tell she spent a few minutes hiding inside the den with the beaver family before swimming out to the far shore, where she crawled onto a sandy patch.

I scoop a handful of sand to bring to my nose. *Violets.* But the worst kind—stained with blood.

The grass is bent where she crawled through, and my feet break into a run, following her scent as surely as if she'd painted arrows on the rocks. There's a break in the trees ahead where the sun winks through.

It's past Tenth Hour, judging by the sun's location.

Smoke blows thicker. Coming from the north, now. *The fire is spreading.*

Sabine's tracks fade once I hit a rocky outcropping, but her scent remains strong. I pause to drop into a crouch to touch a blood drop. She can't be that badly hurt, or else I'd be following a river of blood. That's some small comfort.

As I study her blood, another drop falls beside it—this time, it's mine. With a grimace, I clap my hand over my blood-stained shoulder.

Sabine's scent cuts toward a game trail marked with deer sign, and I hustle in that direction, moving cautiously now. Her scent is strong here, beneath the smoke.

She's close.

My eyes dart to the nearby trees, searching for her winged spies. She doesn't have my hearing, so she won't hear my approach, but her minions will.

Coughing from the smoke, I push through a cluster of huckleberry bushes and see a cave ahead. I came across this cave before when I was setting traps throughout the forest, so I know that it doesn't have a rear egress.

Her scent pours out of it—she's in there.

I spare a moment to lift my head to the sky, shoulders sagging in a rare moment of relief. As clever as she is, hiding in a cave isn't the smartest move. Maybe she's desperate. Blinded by grief from the deer herd whose scent still clings to her.

"Sabine!" I step out of the bushes. "It's over."

I can hear her soft, shallow breaths echoing inside the cave.

About two hundred feet to the north, flames lick at the underbrush. I wipe away a bead of sweat.

"Come out, sweetheart!" I drop my tone into a gentle

beckoning. "You did well. Starting the fire. Hiding in the beaver den. But there was no world where I was going to let that bastard take you. This is how it was always going to end."

I listen to the quiet rustle of her clothes. Glance at the encroaching fire—one hundred fifty feet off now, moving in fast.

But she still doesn't come out.

Tightening my jaw, I say, "Now isn't the time for fighting one another. I'm going to win this damn game whether you like it or not. You're going to walk out of this kingdom free as one of your birds, even if it means a knife in my heart."

Still...nothing.

Growling to myself, I shift my approach. Fine. If my little violet wants to play hide and seek, I'll play.

"I'm coming in," I call in a hard tone.

I'm two strides toward the cave when a flurry of activity erupts from the darkness.

Hundreds of bats shoot out like arrows, flapping their wings in my face as their hard little bodies slam against me, knocking me around like a straw dummy before dispersing up into the smokey trees.

Fuck!

My pulse scrambles to regain its rhythm as I hunch over, raking my fingers through my hair in case any of the little devils got tangled in it.

As my breath heaves, I toss my head up—

To see a monster crashing toward me.

I have a split second to process a thirty-point buck thundering out of the cave with his massive antlers lowered at my torso. Sabine rides on his back like a goddess straight out of a legend, gripping the base of his antlers, her hair whipping behind her as her eyes fix on me like dagger points.

Fuck me.

So, she's *not* ready to surrender, I take it.

I stand my ground, quickly calculating my chances. The buck is forty feet away—it'll be on me in three seconds. My hand instinctively grabs for my bow. I can have an arrow in the animal's heart in two.

I nock the arrow and pull back the string, closing one eye for aim.

But as my vision hones in, I can't seem to fire. Beneath the reek of smoke, the air still smells faintly of Sabine's tears. Her grief over the deer herd is real.

"Just do it," I growl to myself.

I steady my aim again, though my fingers shake. *Dammit.* I'm a huntsman. I've killed hundreds of deer and never thought twice. But there's something different now that I've found Sabine. It doesn't matter if I've forgotten our past. Somehow, her pain is my pain. What she cares about, I care about. I never would guess in a million years that Wolf Bowborn would hesitate to take an animal's life, but this is what she's done to me.

She's given me a fucking heart.

"Dammit!" I hurl my bow to the ground as the buck closes the distance between us. One second left. A half a second.

I throw myself to the side as its antlers barrel forward. One point catches me in the right side, and pain explodes across my ribs. I grit my teeth as I come up from the roll, tossing the sweaty hair out of my eyes.

Think fast, Basten.

I don't want to kill the buck, but I can't let Sabine

escape. Right now, they're retreating fast. The smoke will hide them completely in another second.

Adrenaline sets my muscles on edge as I scan the immediate forest, calculating where I laid my traps. I pick up a rock and pitch it to the right of the fleeing buck.

The animal spooks to the left—right into the tripwire I secured before between two birches.

There's a crash as the buck slams to the ground with Sabine still on his back. A cloud of dust kicks up as Sabine falls off sideways, tumbling into a pile of leaves. I hear the air shoot out of her lungs.

She groans, temporarily stunned.

The buck scrambles to his feet, stumbling only briefly before regaining his footing, and then bounds off into the encroaching smoke.

I race to Sabine's side and drop to my knees. "Little violet!"

I roll her onto her back as she coughs, her eyes unfocused, blinking hard at the sunlight through the clouds of smoke. A cut on her temple oozes blood. I quickly feel along her limbs for any broken bones, relieved that she's only twisted an ankle.

I cup the back of her head to gently lift her up. "Easy. Don't move too fast."

She coughs again as her eyes begin to focus.

Glancing at the spreading wildfire—one hundred feet off—I brush the wet hair off her forehead as I murmur, "It's almost over. Soon, you won't have to fight anymore. We're together now. All we have to do is keep moving until sunset. I left Artain incapacitated, but that bastard will figure a way out to free himself sooner or later."

She latches onto my forearm, where the scars that form

her name peek out from my torn sleeve. "Basten. The buck—"

"I didn't shoot him."

She lets out a relieved sob. Slowly, she tries to push to her elbows but winces from a bruised rib.

I won't lie, we aren't in the best position here.

We're both soaked, dripping pond water, which will leave an obvious trail. Both bleeding, too. Wildfire is rapidly approaching. She can't run on that twisted ankle.

And the sun? Shit, it isn't even Eleventh Hour. Dusk is eight hours away.

You need to get her the hell out of here, idiot! a voice announces in the back of my head.

But I can't take my eyes off her.

Tonight, I'll die for her, happily putting the noose around my own neck, but before that light disappears forever?

Cupping her jaw, I capture her mouth with my own.

Warmth floods into me, laced with the taste of violets. My chest seizes up with so much damn love that it feels like I might float away.

She pulls back and gently wipes the blood from my jaw. "Basten."

My heart starts pattering like rain on a tin roof. When this perfect woman says my name, I'm fucking lost.

She tilts her chin up for another kiss, and I'm only too happy to oblige. She lifts herself onto one elbow, sliding her hand around to the back of my neck, where her fingers weave in the hair at my nape.

Brushing my rough lips against her velvet-soft ones, all I can think is that this one kiss is worth giving up my life for. Its aching softness leaves me breathless in a new way. A way that has me exploring every curve of her mouth, searing this kiss into memory so that when I die in a few hours, I'll be remembering everything about this moment.

She lives in more than memories.

Breath shallow, I pull back to rest my forehead against hers.

"It might be madness, but I love you, Sabine." I lock my hand around her arm, afraid to let go. "Screw the past. The future, too. We have right now together, this moment, and it's all I want."

She clutches my good shoulder, biting her bottom lip as though pained. "I love you so much, Basten. Now and forever."

She vocalizes a soft moan as my teeth scorch across her bottom lip. She twists her hand in my torn shirt, instinctively grabbing on.

This is what my life has led to.

The chance to keep her light shining forever.

The heat from the wildfire toasts my left side. Though it kills me, I break the kiss and slowly ease my arm around her waist. With her twisted ankle, it will be slow going with me carrying her over my shoulder, so we can't risk staying here any longer.

"Come on, little violet," I coax as I help her sit up. "I'll carry you back to the southern gate—"

She interrupts me by slapping away my arm. Her eyes are clear now, powerfully fierce.

"What?" she stammers. "No."

"No? Darling, there's only one way this game ends, and it's when I carry you to the finish line over my shoulder to claim my win."

She shoves herself up to a sitting position, her wet shirt

clinging to her chest. "So Artain can slit your throat? Basten, I'm not going to let that happen."

My eyebrows slide upward. I thought she understood that this kiss was our last.

The determination on her face is so damn adorable that I find myself laughing at the idea that she thinks this can end any other way.

But as soon as I chuckle, her face goes dark.

She pushes to her feet, not looking at me, glancing at the wildfire closing in. She tests out her ankle, winces, and takes a single hobble.

And that's when I realize she's serious.

I shoot to my feet next to her. "Like hell, you aren't."

She rakes her damp hair off her face so she can glare at me. "I'm not letting you sacrifice yourself for me."

I laugh again, though I don't mean to be cruel. Simply realistic. "Darling, you don't have a choice."

Her jaw flexes. Her lips twist angrily. Gods, I love seeing that defiance sparking in her eyes, but what does she think she's going to do to stop me?

I urge her toward me with my hand. "Come on, Sabine."

She retreats a step, glancing over her shoulder as though she's primed to run. "You don't get to do this. To be a martyr after we went through hell to be together again. You might not remember our past, but I do. I remember every beautiful day. Every night when you held me. Every morning when you made me coffee and hid your grumpiness until you'd had some yourself. The midnights. The dawns. I remember every second—and if you think those end today with your death, you're wrong."

In the distance, I faintly hear the far-off bellringer signal Eleventh Hour.

I pinch the bridge of my nose, steadying my temper.

"I might not remember our past," I start, "but I remember plenty else. I remember pummeling other boys so hard that their skulls cracked. I still hear Onno's dying whimpers at night. Don't you get it? Sabine, I've killed innocent men. Tortured women whose only crime was hearing gossip about the wrong person. When I say my life meant *nothing* before you—"

My throat closes up.

After a breath, I continue more measuredly, "My life was less than worthless. I was a blight on everyone I crossed paths with—until I met you. I'd pay any price to remember our past, but it isn't going to happen. The memories are gone. And I don't care, understand? Because I finally have a chance to do one worthwhile thing in my life. And then all of my mistakes will be worth it. This is my chance to make up for everything. Because I can save *you*."

She watches me carefully, warily. I take another step forward, reaching for her, but she hobbles two steps back and ducks under a branch, putting it between the two of us like a shield.

She shakes her head hard, eyes flashing. "Don't talk like you don't have a reason to live."

My temper is boiling over now. I could never be angry with her, but I'm starting to panic at the idea that she will keep fighting me.

"Only one of us is leaving this kingdom, and it has to be you." I tear open the leather pocket on my breastplate to hold up Rian's Golath dime. "You have to ride to Hekkelveld Castle and show Rian Valvere what happens to those who betray you."

I thrust out the coin, but she refuses to take it.

She keeps that damn branch between us as she shouts, *"You're* the rightful king of Astagnon. The people need you on that throne. We know now what kind of twisted games the fae can play. Do you think my father is any different from Artain? We just haven't seen his true colors yet. If anyone can protect Astagnon from them, it's you."

I pinch the bridge of my nose, glancing up at the high sun. "Gods dammit. I'm sorry, little violet, but we don't have time for this."

I lurch forward and grab her arm, dragging her out from behind the branch. She winces as she puts weight on her twisted ankle. Guilt stabs between my ribs.

But this is what I have to do.

When I pull her against me, she struggles like a wildcat. "Let me go!"

"Sabine, get it in your head that *you're* going free, not me."

"I won't let you do this!" She manages to wrench one hand free and grab my bow from the ground. She smashes the pointed end into my bleeding shoulder. Pain jackknifes through my upper half, making my muscles slacken.

She slips free from my grasp, staggering back against the tree trunk with the bow clutched in hand. "Stay back, Basten. I'm warning you."

Pressing one hand to my shoulder, I growl, "I didn't liberate you from Rian only for you to land in another lunatic's hands! Artain will have you on your knees for him each night until they're bloodied. You're a gods-damn princess. A queen. I'll die before I see you bow to *anyone.*"

A sob bubbles up her throat as she clutches my bow across her like a shield. "Please, Basten. Just walk away."

I see red, and I slam my fist into a towering elm to dull

my raging fear. My knuckles burst, blood drizzling out. But the pain feels good. Grounding. Motivating.

Taking a deep breath, I shake my head. "Not happening, little violet."

I hesitate for a heartbeat before stalking forward. Gods, if only there were another way.

But this is all I get. One heartbeat. One fantasy. One last kiss.

Then, I start toward her again.

"I said you aren't *dying!*" She hurles my bow at me, and in the split-second that I'm distracted by swatting it away, I don't hear hoofbeats until it's too late.

She twitches her fingers in the air.

The thirty-point buck tears out of the bushes at too close a distance for me to run. I can barely stuff Rian's Golath dime back in my pocket before the animal smashes its rack into my chest.

The wind heaves out of me as I'm thrown against the tree trunk.

Fucking *hell*.

Grimacing, my vision refocuses—I look down to see at least a half dozen antler points stabbing into me.

I can feel a broken rib. A sharp pain in one of my kidneys. Still, it's clear this was a warning strike. The antlers only pierce a half-inch deep. The buck could have done a lot more damage if Sabine had wanted it to.

I pant as I grip the base of the buck's antlers with both hands, then strain to wrench them out of me, screaming from the effort.

"Basten, stop!" Sabine cries.

Her eyes are wide. Incredulous. She underestimates the lengths I'll go to get her free.

Groaning, I push all my weight against the buck until I can fully free myself from its antlers. Blood immediately pours from more stab wounds than I can count, and for a second, my knees soften before I can straighten again.

Tears pour down Sabine's cheeks. "Stop!"

"Not...going...to...stop," I mutter.

Grimacing, she twitches her fingers, and the buck tries to drive forward again. It's a battle of wills as we wrestle together.

"Then I'm sorry for this. I really am." She thrusts her hands forward in the air in the same position as the buck's antlers. "Again!" she screams.

The buck digs his hooves in the dirt and thrusts forward harder, throwing his three hundred pounds of muscle behind the effort.

I try to hold him back. Straining. Grimacing. But I can't. His antlers stab into me again, right through my ribs, dangerously close to my organs this time.

A cry rips from my throat as pain swallows me.

Digging deep, I grab the beast's antlers with renewed determination and prepare to fight him for another step toward Sabine.

"Basten, please!" Tears stream down her cheeks. "Don't make me hurt you again!"

"I'm not—going to stop, little violet." I wheeze. "You said I promised I'd—I'd tear out my beating heart if you asked it of me. I meant it. I mean it now."

"But I'm not asking!" she shouts.

"Doesn't—matter. My heart...is yours. It was always yours."

Tears stream down her face.

I'm losing a lot of blood. My vision is blurring. Until

now, I've heard the crackling of the encroaching wildfire clearly, but it's at the point where I struggle to hear my own rasping breath.

I muster my last ounce of strength and lurch forward toward Sabine.

Her sobs sound dim, too far away, as she says one more time, brokenly, "*Again.*"

The buck thrusts forward one last time.

I reach out a blood-soaked hand toward Sabine—but then it falls.

I slump forward over the buck's antlers, pinning me to the tree, as the world goes black.

CHAPTER 34
SABINE

ods, no!

As I rush to Basten's side, I pray to everything between the grass and the sky that he survives. The Ender can take anything on this green earth except for him.

Enough! I say to the buck. ***Step back!***

I press against the buck's shoulder to guide him from where his antlers pin Basten to the tree. There's a sickening sound as the points slide out of Basten's torso. Fresh blood bubbles out of a dozen puncture wounds to paint his shirt crimson.

Unconscious, Basten slumps forward over the buck's rack.

Lower him down gently to the grass, I say to the buck, heart pounding.

The buck lowers this head, and I collapse next to Basten, hands hovering over his wounds, afraid to touch his chest. Afraid I'll make it worse.

"Why didn't you stop?" I sob, clenching the grass. "I didn't want to do this to you!"

Gods help me—he's lost so much blood already. My fingers tremble an inch above his blood-soaked clothes. A creeping panic begins to close up around my throat.

You did this. You killed him. Just like the deer.

I squeeze my eyes closed as panic sets in, turning away to dig my fingers into the grass. I need the grounding force. The cool wash of dirt. Slowly, my breaths begin to steady, the earth beneath my nails anchoring me back to myself.

Only then do I dare open my eyes.

I ask the buck, ***Can you carry us both?***

He nuzzles Basten's arm to test his weight before answering, ***Yes. But not far.***

I shove to my feet, reaching down to clutch Basten around his underarms as I strain to lift him. ***As far as you can, then. Back to the castle. Fast!***

Basten weighs twice my weight, and it's an arduous task for the buck and me to roll him onto the buck's haunches. The only choice I have is to position Basten stomach-down over the buck's back so that his legs fall on one side and his arms on the other. Which means putting pressure right on his puncture wounds.

If he were conscious, gods, he'd be cursing black and blue. I'm half surprised he doesn't snap to only so he can growl in pain.

But he remains dangerously pale.

I look up to gauge the sun. I'm not as good at reading time that way as Basten, but it's clear that it's hours before dusk. Which is a long time for Artain to find us. For Basten to bleed out.

I swing one exhausted leg over the buck's back, sitting high near his shoulders in front of Basten's body. Gripping the base of the buck's antlers, I nudge his ribs with my heels.

Go.

He takes off at a run as my fire spreads into the clearing behind us.

With every jostle, I wince in fear for Basten. His blood pours down the buck's rear legs until, when I glance behind us, blood-stained hoofprints mark the mud. The smoke and wildfire will help hide us, but still, that blood trail might as well shout our location to Artain.

Don't worry about that now.

The buck knows the way to Drahallen Hall better than me, so I concentrate on holding on. Trees fly by us as I blink away tears. The wind tosses my loose hair. Robins swoop from branch to branch, following my path.

Bird-talker, they whisper. **Bird-talker. Bird-talker.**

As if speaking my name is some kind of a prayer. Like I'm a god to them instead of a desperate girl with thorns in her hair.

The smell of smoke fades behind us, and for a disoriented few minutes, the air is replaced with the smell of pine. Then, I get a whiff of the unmistakable, strong fae scent of myrrh that can only mean a fae is close.

My heart tumbles into a freefall.

To the southern gate, hurry! I tell the buck.

He stumbles, exhausted, as he finally emerges from the trees by the covered pavilion.

It's empty. No sign of Woudix or Artain or Iyre.

At the sound of hoofbeats, however, Hawk bursts out of the Woodland Garden, snarling. Woudix strides up behind her, his head swinging toward our sound as he splays his hands, readying his deadly power.

"Hold," he commands Hawk. "Who's there? It isn't sunset for eight more hours."

Samaur runs out of the gate behind him, staring in incredulity. Iyre stumbles after him, fingers tangled in her long red braid, quickly finishing it with shaking hands.

"What are you doing here?" she demands as she ties off the braid. "Where is Artain?"

Exhaustion eats at my bones as I slide off the buck and signal for him to lower himself.

Iyre paces in a tight circle around us, her cheeks blazing red, toe-tapping anxiously, but I couldn't care less about supplying her answers.

Carefully, I roll Basten's body off the buck's back and feel for a pulse.

Come on. Please, Basten. Please still be with me.

There! It's faint, but the tiny flutter fills me with hope. Urgently, I rip the sleeve off my shirt and tie it as a bandage around the deepest wound in Basten's chest.

"I asked where Artain is, human!" Iyre shouts, tugging her braid in frustration.

"In the woods!" My voice bursts out of me like a flock of crows. I can't swallow back my burning anger as I spit, "Where the hell do you think? He's out there. *Losing* this damn game of yours!"

Samaur shoves past Iyre, clutching his scabbard strap hard, blinking his golden eyes fast. "Wait. Wait, the human huntsman won? That's impossible."

The high note of disbelief in his voice sounds like a rooster at dawn.

Unlike the other two, Woudix remains calm. He slowly crouches, touching the ground as though sensing something. "No—he's dying. He hasn't won anything."

"Dying? How? Artain wasn't allowed to kill him," Samaur sputters.

"Artain did not do this." Woudix stands and slowly tilts his head in my direction.

"Ha!" Iyre smirks so hard that her left eye twitches. She can't seem to stand still as she paces around us. "*You* killed your lover, princess? Now *that* is a twist!" She cackles. "So, Artain wins by default."

"No," I say steadily. "The game isn't over."

I curl my blood-soaked fingers inward, marshaling my anger, squeezing so hard that Basten's blood drips onto the grass.

Go, I say to the buck. ***With my thanks.***

As he hobbles back into the woods, I can sense his exhaustion. His pain. The last thing I want is for another innocent animal to get further caught up in this twisted game of gods.

Iyre cries, "Of course, it's over! There's only one competitor left!"

I run my bloodstained hands down my wrinkled grown. "Neither competitor caught me. I came back here on my own. Even if one of them had, the Night Hunt doesn't end until dusk. A lot could happen before then."

"Lord Basten will die long before dusk," Woudix murmurs. "He barely has a few minutes' life in him."

My pulse kicks up, threatening to trample me under its pressure, but I force myself to pull in a breath.

"I know." I spin to face Samaur. "Which is why *you're* going to make dusk come early."

The God of Day jerks back as though I've slapped him, his hand falling from his scabbard strap in disbelief. After blinking a few times in surprise, he slowly settles into a full-bellied chuckle.

"Oh. Sure. Right." He slaps Woudix on the shoulder. "We're taking orders from a human now, did you know that?"

"I'm serious." I close the space between us and grab his scabbard strap. An inch away from his face, I hiss, "I know you can do it. You did it when Basten brought Tòrr to the castle in daylight hours. Do it again now, or I'll reduce Drahallen Hall to rubble. And everyone in it. Including those pretty twins you like to bloodsuck on."

Out of the corner of my eye, I see Iyre's smirk fall, while Woudix rests a hand on the knife at his side.

Samaur's eyes widen. He flicks an uncertain look to Iyre, who slowly shakes her head.

He forces another laugh. "And how will you do that, little human? Hmm? This castle has stood for three thousand years. You couldn't bring it down even if you commanded every animal in this kingdom to try."

"I don't need every animal," I say. "I only need one."

The ground begins to rumble under my feet. It starts softly at first. If I wasn't waiting for it, I might not feel anything at all. A chill breaks across my skin as I widen my stance. Steadying myself. With Samaur's scabbard strap still clutched in my fist, I stare at a fixed point on the high stone wall that separates the castle's Woodland Garden from Vallen Forest.

Samaur frowns as he senses my attention shift. "The gate! Iyre, shut the gate!"

Her red hair flashes in the sunlight as she lurches toward

it, but before her hand grazes the iron latch, an explosion rings out.

A shockwave tears through the castle, sending a fiery burst scorching up toward the sky.

Iyre stumbles backward, off-balance.

I duck, sheltering my head behind Samaur's broad shoulders.

"What the fuck?" Samaur yells.

Another explosion crashes inside the castle, this one closer. The ground rattles underfoot. Startled screams ring out from inside the towers.

In an instant, Samaur drops his human glamour. Fey lines burst across his skin as he latches his hands on my wrists. "What the hell did you—"

A third explosion slams through the southern gate. Wood and stones are thrown upward. A wall of heat blasts through the air. Sparks rain down like fiery embers. More screams ring out from inside the castle.

Iyre, closest to the gate, is flung fifteen feet backward, her spine crashing against a stump as wooden beams crash around her.

Broken bits of stone rain down as I clutch my arms over my head.

Samaur squeezes my upper arms so hard I cry out in pain. His sunlit eyes are wild with adrenaline. "What the *hell* did you do?"

Woudix holds out his hands, bruise-black fey crackling at his fingertips with the promise of death itself, ready to strike—but to defend Samaur or me, I'm not sure.

My chest heaves as I wrestle against Samaur's hold. "I didn't do anything—*he* did."

As the dust settles, Tòrr strides through the breach in the southern gate.

His black mane and tail ripple over his powerful muscles, and his coat is caked in stone dust. His monoceros horn—fully exposed to the sunlight—stabs toward the sky like an abalone sword.

Heart racing, I strain on tiptoe to peer through the decimated gate to make out two more equal-sized holes in the walls that flank both the Hailstrom Tower and Sunflare Tower.

As soon as I catch my breath, I point out to Tòrr wryly, *You know, you could have done that with a single explosion.*

Don't question greatness, little fae, Tòrr retorts as he lifts his chin high so his mane whips in the wind.

I don't have time to reign in his ego, because the moment he lifts his horn to the sky, Samaur drops my wrists and holds out his hands toward the monoceros instead, golden-orange fey bolts sparking at his fingertips.

"Don't try to stop him," I choke out. "You might be the God of Day, but *he's* the one who wields the sun's power."

To my right, Hawk growls low in her throat, and I whirl toward her and her master.

"The same goes for you, Ender," I tell Woudix. "Before you can spread your fey two feet, Tòrr will reduce you to ashes. I doubt even the God of Death is impervious to a solarium hit—but I'm willing to test that."

Rubble shifts to my left, and Iyre extricates herself from the pile of broken wood. Dust covers her from her hair to the hem of her white gown, and her exposed skin is covered in deep, bleeding gashes. Yet, almost immediately, her wounds begin to heal.

She narrows her eyes at me and croaks, "The monoceros stall is unbreachable. You couldn't have gotten him free."

I blink at her, with Tòrr standing behind me as my only answer.

She scoffs, rubbing a scrape on her throat. "How? It takes ten men to slide open the drawbar. No animal is that strong except the monoceros itself. Or a—" The arrogant lift of her upper lip slowly lowers. Hoarsely, she mutters, "Or a goldenclaw."

I rest a hand on Tòrr's withers. "All goldenclaws want is someone to listen to their riddles. They'll do anything for a patient friend."

Iyre tips her head downward like a predator, glaring at me through her eyelashes as a line of silver blood rolls down her forearm. "I told Vale this charade of his wouldn't work—keeping you in the dark. We should have told you the truth from the start. Like the other times. And if you'd resisted again? Bend you to our will."

Her words prickle my mind. Keeping me in the dark? What does she mean, about them being fae?

Basten moans, stealing my attention. I fall to my knees by his side.

"Basten? Basten!" I stroke a tender hand down his blood-soaked temple. "Hey, you're going to be okay—I'm going to get you help."

As fear weaves between my ribs, I throw a glance over my shoulder at Vallen Forest. A robin flits from one branch to another.

I ask in a rush, ***Where is the fae huntsman?***

He has your trail, the robin replies. ***He approaches fast.***

Swallowing, I glance at the high sun, and then thread my fingers through Basten's blood-soaked hair. "Samaur, do it. Now. Bring dusk early. And I'll save your twins before Tòrr launches another blast."

Samaur rests his boot on a broken hunk of stone, leaning forward with golden eyes sparking. In this instant, he's never looked less human. "Go ahead. Plenty more fawning little humans where those two came from. Twins aren't *that* rare."

Coldness settles deep in my belly. "You'd throw away your acolytes so easily?"

One look at their frigid faces—Samaur, Iyre, even Woudix—and the answer is an obvious *yes*.

"I'll have Thracia soon, anyway," he scoffs. "Then, I'll need acolytes less for companionship and just for blood— and they don't have to be pretty to give me their veins."

Feeling sick, I scold myself with an inner lashing that I thought the fae could be anything but cruel.

I whip back to Basten, whispering, "Hold on. Don't you dare die."

I shove to my feet and rest a hand on Tòrr's muzzle. He presses his nose into my palm, reassuring me that we're in this together.

Then, I face Samaur.

"What about something you hold more precious than your acolytes' lives, then? My father toured me around the fae artifact room. The one that's housed in Cloudveil Tower. So many objects that would be devastating to lose—but maybe none as much to you, in particular, as Thracia's Midnight Vase."

Samaur immediately strides toward me like he's going to wring my neck. "You scheming whore, you wouldn't dare. That's her most prized possession."

"Try me. Try *him*." I tweak Tòrr's nose, and he tosses his

head in confirmation. "You might not care about your acolytes, but you're fated to love Thracia. The God of Day and the Goddess of Night. You said it yourself—you win her over each Return with the midnight vase. Without it, do you think you can still earn her favor? Is it worth the risk?"

Samaur's fey lines burn brighter as his rage rises to the surface. He glances at the sun, and Iyre strides up to deliver a sharp smack to his cheek.

"Don't you dare consider it! Not over some bauble."

"A bauble? That bauble wins me Thracia every Return," he snarls. "We know her location. She's almost at my fingertips. I've waited a thousand years to be with her again."

The tension between them is thick enough to cut, and I curl my toes as I look over my shoulder at the castle. Dammit, we don't have time for this. Every second they argue is a second that Basten might slip away. The fear of losing him lodges so thick in my throat that I can barely swallow around it.

A robin swoops down in front of me, flapping hard in warning.

The fae huntsman is—

Before it can finish, a gold-tipped arrow slams into the bird's breast with enough force that feathers burst out. The robin tumbles onto a piece of rubble, its neck hanging at an impossible angle.

A scream pierces the air—my own.

As my fingers tighten in the base of Tòrr's mane, I spin like a whip, ready to lash out.

At the edge of the woods, Artain holds another arrow at the ready. "Hello, princess. This time, I'll shoot straight through your damn lover's head and roast his brain on a spit."

And it's Too. Fucking. Much.

Anger floods me like a raging river, drowning me in a torrent of fury. Bile rises up my throat, choking me with bitter rage until every nerve ignites. My vision blurs as I feel a scream clawing up from the depths of my chest, ready to rip free and end this—once and for all.

CHAPTER 35
BASTEN

My thoughts scatter like leaves in the wind. I can't tell what's real and what's a dream anymore. But if I'm dreaming, then hell, *let it be this one.*

Let me dream of her.

Her smile. Her power. That fire in her eyes when she looks at me like I'm more than a street boy with bloodied knuckles. Maybe I can't remember our past, but I can *feel* it. It's as alive in my bones as my marrow, giving me strength. I guess one fae tale was true, huh, Sabine? We're Aron and Aria all over again. The Fate-Spun Lovers. Destined to find one another.

But it's more than that, isn't it? It's about choice—choosing you each time, in every lifetime, cost be damned.

I don't care if I never recover a single memory of us. I'll make new ones. Even if it's only this. Here. Now. One final memory. Hearing the rumble of your voice nearby, as quiet as a stream but just as capable of reshaping the world.

And if my last *first* memory is of saving you?

Then I'll die happy.

Because I feel the blood leaving. Emptying like an over-turned glass. And I don't care. I want you to have all of it, all of me, because it will all be worth it to know that I found you, I looked in your eyes, and I saw every answer to every question a man could ask.

Sabine, I'm not afraid to die.

Not if it's for you.

CHAPTER 36
SABINE

rtain points the arrow at the one target he knows will break my soul—Basten.

The fire burning in the pit of my stomach catches and spreads until I feel like I'm wildfire itself, ready to rip through the world and leave nothing but ash in my wake. The times I've felt this angry before were the ones when I slipped into the minds of animals to force them to do my bidding.

And now? I'm not working with birds and mice. Not even tigers.

I have a *monoceros*—and he could burn down the world.

My vision sharpens as I slide my hand along Tòrr's neck, feeling his strong pulse as my own changes its rhythm to match.

I'll do it.

I'll burn *everything*.

Tòrr stomps, releasing a burst of steam from his nostrils. This time, when I reach into his mind, he doesn't resist like the other animals did. Instead, I'm greeted by a flicker of red-hot glee—he's just as bloodthirsty as I am.

"Tòrr." I speak the name that holds so much power.

We're going to push each other to lose control. I can feel it. I'm ready. He's ready. Ready to end it...

"Stop!" Samaur's golden eyes sizzle as he extends his hands wide, muscles so tensed the veins in his arms pop out.

My heart skyrockets to my throat, and for a second, my rage falters. Will he...will he do it?

One clap. That's all it takes.

"Stop," he seethes, "And I'll give you what you want."

"Like hell, you will!" Artain lowers his arrow an inch but keeps the bow drawn, ready to fire. "If you turn day to dusk, I lose the game."

"So? I'm not losing Thracia for your stupid game!" Samaur yells. "You want to toy with mortals, fine. Risk your own damn neck—not ours."

He jerks his head toward Woudix and Iyre, who are both still braced to aim their fey against Tòrr if he tries to use his solarium horn.

"This is all about your fucking ego, anyway," Samaur spits at Artain. "About sticking it to Vale by tricking his daughter into being your plaything. In a fae bargain that he can't do a thing to break. It's *him* you want to play against, isn't it? Not this human. Not her. You're only using them to get to Vale."

A muscle bulges in the side of Artain's jaw. "Vale will thank me when I win, and Sabine is bound to Volkany. To me."

"Oh, get over yourself!" Samaur yells.

His palms connect. Like a crash of thunder, the clap reverberates with a ground-shaking burst of orange-gold fey.

I drop low, clinging protectively to Basten's arm. The sky immediately darkens. Purple shadows stretch across the mountains. The temperature drops. Birdsong stops. A confused rabbit darts out of the bushes and into its den. The sun streaks across the sky like a shooting star to sink below the horizon.

In the west, the last shard of the sun's orb vanishes behind the mountains.

"Dusk," I whisper in disbelief.

It's real. It happened.

More confused shouts come from the castle's direction. First, there were the explosions. Now, dusk has come hours early. Courtiers and servants alike must think the world is ending.

A soldier runs up to the shattered gate, taking in the scene with wide eyes, and I call, "Fetch a godkissed healer. Lord Basten needs help!"

None of the fae attempt to stop the soldier as he unsteadily runs back into the castle. They're all focused on me, not the man bleeding out at their feet.

"It's over now." I push to a stand, wiping Basten's blood onto my shirt as I stare at Artain, daring him to challenge me. "It's dusk. The game is over."

"It's not fucking over," he snaps.

"*You* set the terms." I speak measuredly because one wrong word with these tricky assholes, and they'll twist it. "The game ends at dusk. Natural dusk or not, it's still dusk. You didn't catch me. Neither did Basten. I evaded both of you until the end. We have an unbreakable bargain."

Artain lets his bowstring slacken, though he keeps the handle clutched with white knuckles. He takes the arrow in his other hand, squeezing the shaft so hard I can't believe it doesn't shatter.

"She has you there, brother," Woudix states quietly.

"*Fine.*" Artain's pretty features are twisted now, ugly. "So, it's a draw. That's what all this was for? A fucking draw? That's what you and your fae monster want?"

He jabs the arrow in Tòrr's direction, and the monoceros responds by lowering his horn like a battering ram. Now, post-dusk, he can't harness his horn's solarium, but I'd bet a hundred coins that no fae could survive a monoceros horn through the heart.

Artain wants to rattle me, but he can't. Keeping my shoulders squared, I press on. "We agreed to a coin toss if the game ended in a draw."

Artain's eyes nearly pop out of his head as he huffs incredulous little laughs, antsy feet pacing over the rubble. "A coin toss...? What? But...you were jesting. You weren't *serious!*"

"Maybe, but I'm serious now."

And oh, am I. Basten's life is bleeding out of him into the grass, and I've never been more deadly serious in my life.

Artain falls silent at the tone in my voice, blinking hard at me as though it's the first time he's paused to look beneath the pretty gowns and seen *me.*

Whatever he sees makes him swallow a knot of fear. "Fine. Whatever. So Lord Basten and I will toss a coin to determine the winner—you're only prolonging the same game. It's pointless. Not to mention, I don't know how the hell you're going to get an unconscious man to toss anything."

I rake my sweaty hair off my face. "That wasn't our bargain. I didn't say anything about you and Basten. I said *we* would flip a coin."

His pouty lips purse as he sputters little breaths, waving his hands in the air. I can tell he's about to ask what difference it makes, when the realization crashes over him.

His face pales. The fey lines running down his abs flicker in intensity like a sputtering flame about to go out. Hoarse, he says, "You devious little thing."

I pat my trousers and shirt pockets, pretending to feel for a coin. "Your bow can't help you now. It doesn't matter if you're the best huntsman in the kingdom. There's no skill to a coin toss. It's up to chance now. Fate." When my pockets turn up empty, I drop down to dig in Basten's pocket. "Here—I'll even let you toss it."

I pull out Rian's Golath dime and throw it to Artain as though it's any other coin.

Like I haven't played this exact game before.

He steps forward to catch the coin with a mixture of indignation and anger. A dangerous combination in a fae. Especially one as prideful as Artain, who, until a few minutes ago, thought I'd be on my knees for him tonight.

Gods, it feels good to prove him wrong.

"This is ridiculous!" Artain raises his closed fist around the coin. "We haven't even set terms—"

"Yes. We have. Same terms. You win, I spend my nights with you. I win, and I have my freedom. I can walk out of here whenever I want—and you don't *touch* Basten."

I can see the indecision turning cartwheels in Artain's eyes. This is outside of his wheelhouse. Immortal Popelin is the God of Chance, the patron god of gamblers, sinners, and competitors. If Popelin were to weigh Rian's Golath dime in his hand, he'd instantly realize that it's a weighted coin.

But wherever Popelin slumbers underground, he can't help his fae brother now. And for the first time since I set foot in this kingdom, I see fear in Artain's eyes.

"No," he sputters, casting his hair back in his signature hair-toss, though it feels even sillier now. "No. You twisted my words." His attention latches onto Iyre. "Iyre! Iyre, you heard the terms. Use that perfect fucking memory of yours to remind this *human* of what was said."

Iyre's lips pull in frustration as she hunts for something to say. It's clear in the flare of her nostrils that she can't contradict me. Finally, she spits, "Just toss the damn coin. You're a fucking *god*. You'll win."

Artain whirls on Woudix next. "Do something. Bring death to her lover unless she takes the loss—he's practically dead anyway!"

Woudix strokes Hawk's head at his side, his face emotionless. "It was your game, not mine. *You* play."

Artain garbles a curse before turning to Samaur. "Clap your damn hands and bring back dawn!"

Samaur rolls his eyes. "I can't go *backward* in time."

"Fuck!" Artain punches the air, pacing, until a light shines in his eyes. "Captain Tatarin! She can take us back to this morning! Can't she? I don't know how the hell her godkiss works...someone get Captain Tatarin here right fucking now to—"

"No."

A deep, unmistakable rasp travels over the rubble from the direction of the busted gate.

The sound raises the hair on my neck like I've walked through a graveyard.

Judging by Artain's even paler face, he feels the same.

My father, in full fae regalia from his Battle Helm Crown to the fey lines radiating from his cheekbones, steps over a splintered piece of wood with terrifying calmness as he looks over the wreckage of the southern gate.

"Vale." Artain recovers fast, giving another hair toss. "B —Brother. I'm glad you're here. You can settle this disagreement."

"Disagreement?" Vale hisses the word like a snake.

Artain blanches. "Well—"

Vale cuts him off as he rests a hand over his anatomical heart brooch. "First, I feel the earth shake. Holes are blown in my castle walls. Then night comes half a day early. The screams are so loud throughout the towers that I had to leave the council chamber, where we're planning a *war*."

Artain looks on the verge of dirtying his pants.

Truth be told, I don't feel much more confident. I shift from foot to foot. There's no way of knowing what my father will do. On the one hand, Artain went behind his back to trick us into this game. Vale would be well within his right to bring down one of his axes on Artain's perfect head.

But Vale is *fae*. No matter the lengths he went to find me, he'll always be fae. Fickle. Deceitful. Deadly.

Which has me throwing glances between Tòrr and Basten, trying to calculate my chances of saving us all.

"Now, I have to clean up more of your messes, Artain?" Vale's voice is dangerously low as he makes his way around a minefield of fallen stones. I snap my attention back to him, breathing through my fear, afraid to hope. He continues, "Every thousand years, you find new ways to fuck up, don't you?"

"It was only a g—game," Artain sputters.

Vale continues, "A game? You know as well as I do how deadly the consequences of fae games can be. I heard Sabine recount the terms just now. This was the stupidest gamble you could have made, and now she's called your bluff." His arm flies out to grab Artain's pretty chin. He pulls the sputtering god dangerously close to his face. "Toss the coin."

Artain's jaw hangs open as he searches for words. Between smooshed cheeks, he babbles, "If she wins, she could leave."

"You should have thought of that instead of assuming you couldn't fail. *Idiot.*" He shoves Artain away by the jaw with enough force that the God of the Hunt trips backward over a fallen joist, barely catching his balance. "You bound yourself to a fae bargain. Now, you have no choice but to play this to the end. Toss. The. Coin."

Artain massages his jaw, testing out the joint, as his sculpted chest rises and falls hard. No fae likes to be put in his place—but he knows better than to argue with Immortal Vale.

With an angry sneer, he holds out his fist with the coin. He shoots at me, "Call it."

"Serpent."

My voice is barely audible. Basten's face is paler than I've ever seen it. He has to have lost nearly two liters of blood. The makeshift bandage is soaked through. His chest barely moves when he breathes—at any moment, it might not rise again.

"Scepter." Artain spits bitterly, tosses the coin, catches it, and slams it on the back of his opposite hand.

There's a terrible moment when I'm afraid I got it wrong. That I didn't remember which side always lands face-up. Or that Artain somehow knows the coin is fraudulent, is toying with me.

No creature—fae, human, animal—breathes as Artain lifts his hand.

I cry out as the coin toss is revealed in my favor, relief flooding me like sunlight melting through ice. I didn't realize I was holding my body as tensely as a bowstring until my muscles finally uncoil. The blood rushing to my ears quiets. I press my hands against my sides, feeling the cool, still-damp fabric to ground myself.

"I won," I murmur.

Artain turns away, letting out a sharp curse.

Woudix's face flickers with the faintest streak of satisfaction, though I doubt he feels joy for my win—I can't imagine he cares about me. He doesn't care about *anything*. Except, that is, the cruel delight of seeing another fae bested.

Iyre and Samaur are silent, still as their statues in the Garden of Ten Gods. If they had the power, I think they'd like to disappear into the background, outside of Vale's reach with his axes.

They might as well be granted their wish because Vale doesn't glance at them.

He only stares at me.

"It's decided, then." His voice feels strangely distant. Oddly, impossibly calm. "Sabine wins her freedom."

Something itches up and down my skin, warning me that this is too easy. My father spent twenty-two years trying to find me. He sent a goddess and half an army to bring me back.

Is he really going to let me go?

He signals to a group of soldiers inspecting the southern

gate's damage. Matter-of-factly, he says, "Send a stretcher to take Lord Basten to the infirmary. Fetch the stablemaster to return Tòrr to the monoceros stall—and tell him to do a better job locking up the goldenclaws next time."

The soldiers bow before rushing back toward the castle, picking their way over the rubble in the twilight darkness.

"Woudix. Samaur. Iyre." Vale snaps. "Lock this idiot in the dungeon until I decide his punishment."

Artain gapes, resting a hand on his hip as he tries to protest, but his fellow Blades and Iyre shove him around with enough glee that he finally holds up his hands in surrender. He follows them toward the castle, throwing a possessive glare back at me.

In the distance, two soldiers jog toward us across the Woodland Garden with a stretcher, but they're still half a minute away.

For a moment, I'm alone with Vale.

My father's strange calmness makes the hair lift along my arms like a ghost whispered across it. I fold my arms across my chest, rubbing away the goosebumps, and lift my chin to face his ethereal beauty.

"You'd let me go?" I ask. "Just like that?"

He slowly runs a hand down his tangled beard. "You were bound in a fae bargain. You won your freedom. Naturally, after the lengths I've gone, I want you to stay here. But what I feel bears no consequence. I cannot force you."

I shift my weight from one foot to the other, locking my knees to keep myself upright. My entire body is heavy with exhaustion. I feel wrung out from worrying about Basten. My father's words should fill me with relief, so why do I still feel uneasy?

This could be another fae trick.

Or...is that only paranoia talking? I can't find any faults in Vale's logic. I *did* outsmart Artain. I followed all the fae rules. Even the King of Fae himself is standing here telling me that I'm free.

Gods, I don't know. I'm too damn spent to keep standing. Too tired to think straight. All I want is to know that Basten is safe and then to collapse into days of sleep that would fold around me like a cocoon.

"Good," I murmur. "Okay."

My voice rings hollow—because I'm empty. Depleted. I sway on my feet by the time the soldiers arrive with the stretcher, and it's all I can do to murmur soft reassurances in Basten's unconscious ear as they cart him off to the Aurora Tower.

And then, it's done.

It's over.

My father watches with an inscrutable look that makes it impossible to know his true thoughts. My legs finally give out. When was the last time I had water? Food? I'm bleeding from dozens of scratches, a rash of bruises blooming along my arms and legs.

I stumble forward—

—and catch myself on Tòrr's horn, which he lowered to me like a helping hand.

Take me away from this damn castle, I tell him.

No one argues against a monoceros, not even King of Fae.

Tòrr uses his muzzle to lift me onto his back, and he carries me to the stable, to Myst's stall, where I collapse in the soft, clean hay.

Outside, Tòrr stands watch by her stall door.

Myst sinks down to curl up beside me, nuzzling her velvety nose against all of my sores.

As I drift off—*I'm free, Basten is alive*—I feel little paws climbing over my shirt. The stable's mice form a warm blanket on top of me. A snake comes to lick the blood from my arm.

And the spiders?

The spiders sing me to sleep.

CHAPTER 37
BASTEN

F*uck.*

Everything hurts.

The pain tearing through my chest makes me feel like my bones are being slowly ground into dust. Every breath is a curse—but also a reminder that I'm alive.

Because of Sabine.

She saved me. Of course she did. The stubborn, beautiful thing. The only person who could outsmart a god while damn butterflies flit around her head like a living crown. Or were the butterflies only in my dreams? Eh. Awake. Asleep. Doesn't matter—I can't get her out of my head. And maybe that's the point. She's always been there, hasn't she? Buried somewhere even Iyre couldn't reach her.

Pushing me.

Daring me.

Urging me to dream beyond what a street boy fighting in the ring could imagine.

Lying here, half-dead, it hits me—what exactly have I been trying to escape? A chance to change things? To help abandoned kids like me? All these years, I've been hiding out in the woods, or in Rian's shadow, afraid to take a good look at myself in the mirror.

And see the king I am.

Sabine saw it. Something worth saving. Hell, something worth taking me to death's door and back again.

So maybe it's time to step out of the shadows.

And wear the damn crown.

But by the gods, I'm not doing it without her at my side.

CHAPTER 38
SABINE

Days and nights settle back into their age-old dance around the earth as Basten heals. Each day, I visit him in his curtained-off infirmary room in the Aurora Tower, making sure to open the window wide so he can feel the southern breeze to remind him of home. He cycles in and out of consciousness, slowly improving from weak moans to curses strong enough to make even the most hardened nurse blush.

What can I say? I fell in love with a man with the mouth of a bandit.

My father calls in godkissed builders from the royal army, who use their powers to efficiently clean up the rubble and install scaffolding to repair the castle's broken southern gate. It feels impossible, but only a week after the Night Hunt, life falls back into a routine in Drahallen Hall. After five days in the dungeon without wine, women, or Wicked Weed, Artain is set free by my father. If you ask me, he got off easy. It's a thought I share with anyone who will listen—pointed ears or round.

It was only a game, everyone laughs off.

But it wasn't. It wasn't a game at all. A game is a fantasy. A pantomime of real life. The fact that the fae court believes our lives are as expendable as wooden chess pieces tells me all I need to know about this place.

About them.

Right now, we have an alliance, but it feels shaky as autumn leaves. I tell myself that it can last—that peace is possible—but something tells me that sooner or later, our fragile deal might fall.

If that happens? I might have to put a permanent end to their games.

Once and for all.

Lately, old memories have been stirring back to life in my mind. About Matron White. About the Sisters. I was just a girl then—naive, hopeful. Blind to how bad things were. Now, those memories take on a different color. I see things I didn't notice as a girl. I see the violence of the world around me—the storms that raged, the branches that fell—as if nature was answering my silent cries for help.

And then there's Rian.

I considered him a brother, he said to Tati. *Now, I won't stop until he's muzzled. Chained. Broken as a hunting dog that bit its master and will never see sunlight again.*

When Basten and I leave this place, I won't just walk away. I'll carry vengeance with me. I'll destroy everyone who's wronged me, break every hand that's fallen on me in violence.

One by one.

I'll ruin them all.

Because I'm not that naive girl anymore—my eyes are wide open.

CHAPTER 39
BASTEN

"Look at you, sitting up and everything!"

An absolute vision stands in the open partition of my infirmary room, holding two steaming bowls of venison stew.

Sabine has never looked more beautiful than in a simple, soft sage gown, backlit from the hallway's window so that her golden hair glows, with an adorable streak of ash on her chin. Only this time, she isn't just a vision at the edge of my sight. She's more than a dream. My heart clenches like that moth that's finally captured its flame and lived to tell the tale—but if I'm being honest?

It's the mouth-watering stew that makes me *really* groan.

My stomach growls so loudly that one of the nurses passing through the hallway flinches in surprise before continuing down the hall.

Sabine looks down and giggles.

"Get in here, you," I order.

She perches her pretty ass on the side of my bed and sets

one bowl on the side table, blowing on the other as she stirs it with a wooden spoon. My mouth fills with saliva, and I'm unsure which I'm hungrier for—Sabine or my supper.

"Slow sips. It's hot." She spoons a bite in my mouth, and I moan as the savory flavors of rosemary and meat burst across my tongue.

Every damn one of my muscles aches, but still, I'm perfectly capable of lifting a spoon myself. I keep my mouth shut, though, because if she wants to play nurse to me? *Yes, please.*

Once I've finished and licked the bowl, she fusses with the sheet over my bare torso. Her thumb skims the dozen new puncture-wound scars across my chest.

Her brow sinks low in concern. "How are you feeling?"

"Not dead."

She rolls her eyes softly, gently slapping my shoulder. "Tell me truly."

Her lips are pursed in worry, and that adorable streak of soot still marks her chin. I know that she feels guilty. She *did* have a thirty-point buck pin me to a tree, after all. And even though Vale's healer was godkissed, it still fucking *hurt.* But I force a smile as I sit up straighter, hiding how my muscles bristle against the pain.

"I'm fine, Sabine. Fit as a damn ox. Stop worrying." I tweak her chin to wipe away the soot, then hold up my thumb in question.

"Oh." Embarrassed, she wipes at her chin. "I was helping Tati roast potatoes for the goldenclaws."

"Goldenclaws like vegetables?"

She blows the hair out of her eyes with a grin. "Goldenclaws and their salads...who knew?"

She smooths her palm over my chest, still playing the

nursemaid, and something awakens in my veins. Something decidedly not *medical*. Now that my stomach is full, a different kind of hunger is stirring.

I place my hand over hers to guide it lower on my torso, down to my navel, where the sheet sits low on my hips.

The most delicious rose color blooms across her cheeks. She glances over her shoulder at the hallway, where nurses pass every few minutes on their rounds.

"Basten, not *here*."

"Close the curtain," I bark.

"You're recovering! You nearly died!"

I growl into her ear, "Exactly. I nearly died. And do you know what I thought of at that moment?" My breath hitches. "I thought... I don't care about the memories Iyre stole. I don't grieve a lost past. Not anymore."

The words come out low as if I'm hearing them myself for the first time. The part of me that fought so long to hold onto what's gone now falls quiet.

She waits, eyes big.

"Because now?" I continue haltingly, chest tightening, "I went to hell and back, and all I could think about was a future with you."

A gasp cuts across her tongue. "Can we have a future... without a past?"

The question hangs between us, and for a moment, I let it. My heart still aches from what was lost, but it's softer now, less of a gaping wound and more of just another battle scar.

A realization begins to sink in.

"Someone told me once that you live in more than memories." I pause. "That's the woman I want—the one here, now. That's the only you I want."

She finds my shirt collar and bunches the fabric in her fist. Her lips tremble as she whispers, "Do you mean that?"

I wrap my hands around hers. "Little violet, I've found my faith in the unknown. I find it whenever I look at your face."

That ache around my heart fades as I see my love for her reflected in her eyes.

I continue softly, "You're no stranger to me—you are my heart's other half. The Aria to my Aron. If you'll have me, then I want nothing more than for you to tell me stories every night about how it was when we first met. The first time we spoke. If I was a damn gruff asshole. What I said when I first saw you use your godkiss." I lower my voice, a smile tugging at the corners of my mouth. "Our first kiss. The first time we..."

My voice halts as I tuck a strand of hair behind her ear. My hand lingers, my rough thumb caressing down her cheek. "I want you to tell me everything, read to me like you do those damn horses, and then? Then, I want to make new memories. I want to kiss you again and again for the first time. I want all our firsts—again."

She places both her hands on my chest as if needing to feel the steadiness of my heartbeat to reassure her that this is real.

"That's all I want, too. A new start. With you."

I grin rakishly, raising my knee, nudging her closer. "We can start right now, princess. Making new memories. Let me show you how much I've recovered."

I know that having sex with Sabine in a tiny, stiff hospital bed will hurt like hell, but fuck it. I can't get her scent out of my nose. For days now, I've been lying here with nothing to do but imagine her warm little mouth on every part of my body that doesn't ache.

Hell, even the ones that do.

To my delight, she doesn't protest. *My little wildcat wants me, too.* She stands up and closes the curtain, hiding us from the nurses' incessant glances, and then comes back and lays a finger across my lips.

"We'll have to be quiet," she whispers. "You can hear a feather land through those curtains."

My response is to take her finger in my mouth, suck on it, then gently bite down on her knuckle.

Her eyelids flare as I hear the telltale rush of her blood thrumming through her veins.

I shove the sheet even lower to reveal the very convenient fact that I'm naked. My erection tents the sheet, straining against the thin fabric. Keeping my voice low, I order, "Pick up that pretty skirt of yours and sit on my cock."

I crave her so badly that my bones ache. My skin tightens, tugging at the already sore scars, but the pain just further awakens my senses.

Sabine glances at the curtain again, but I grab her jaw to keep her attention on me. I lean forward—even though my body screams at me in protest—to make her forget about anything other than this kiss.

My lips claim hers with a scorching burn, and she presses hers back at me. Her hand comes up to thread through the back of my hair, nails raking against my scalp in a way that pulls a moan from deep in my throat.

She tastes like rosemary stew and violets and everything good in this world.

And I can't fucking get enough.

I push forward to settle my mouth harder over hers,

tasting and sampling, before biting down on her bottom lip. A sigh slides out from her lips as she skims her hands over my chest, careful to avoid the fresh scars. Her hips rock on the side of the bed, antsy.

Gods, I fucking love seeing her so eager.

"Straddle me," I order. "Now."

I shove the sheet back over my erect cock and grip her hips to guide her to take its place. She swings a leg over me carefully, fussing as she tries not to rock the bed too much as she climbs on.

Impatient, I growl, "You aren't going to break me. Now sit on me like you mean it."

I grind my hips upward to rub my erection against her silk panties. Her pupils dilate as she chokes on a long, throaty moan. Her hands press against my chest like she needs to hold on. Her fingers dig hard into my skin.

Fuck—now *that* hurts.

At my wince, she immediately pulls back with wide eyes. "Basten?"

"Don't you dare stop." I grip her by the throat to pull her back into a kiss.

Our lips graze together, first slowly, then more feverish. I coax her lips apart with my tongue and then slide it inside to lick the roof of her mouth.

Her thighs instinctively tighten over my hips, and I groan.

"I—" she pants. "I don't want to hurt you."

"Hurt me. Please. Hurt me."

Her hips slowly rock against my straining cock, her body already primed for me to take her even if her worries hold her back. Breathy, she moans, "Don't be stupid because you're horny. We have to be careful."

I drag her skirt up over her ass and give the left cheek a solid slap. She yelps in surprise, her eyes wide as saucers, then claps a hand over her mouth as she glances toward the curtain.

"Slap me back," I order, offering up my cheek.

Our hips are already rocking together, finding a steady rhythm despite the slip of fabric still forming a barrier between us. I can feel her growing wetter. It does dangerous things to me to know that she's already gushing in anticipation.

She huffs, frustrated. Glances at the curtain.

Then slaps my left cheek *hard*.

The sharp sting spreads throughout my face in a way that has me choking on desire. Twisted, I know. Believe me. But that's where my head is.

"Gods, Sabine. Can you feel what you do to me?" I grind my hips up against hers.

Her breath goes shallow, causing her breasts to tighten and lift. I slide my palms up her sides to run my thumbs along the underside of them. The tops tease me from her neckline until I can't resist. I shove one dress sleeve down over her shoulder and free her right breast, then claim it between my teeth.

Her hips buck against mine as she lets out a moan.

"That's it. Moan. Scream my name. I don't care if every damn nurse in the castle hears."

Her hands lock around the back of my neck as I tease her nipple with my tongue. Her back arches, begging me to take the sensitive bud deeper. I suck and roll it until it's tight as a button.

I push her back by the waist to watch the beautiful flush roll across her skin.

"Sit on my face," I growl. "I want to taste you."

She hesitates, thumb lightly brushing against one of my scars.

I tear her hand off me, running my lips lightly over her sensitive palm as I threaten quietly, "Sit on my face, little violet, or I'll have you on your back screaming so loudly the nurses will think you're dying."

Her eyelashes lower. "You're a beast."

Half my lips pull back in a wicked smile. I settle back against the pillow as she climbs over my torso, lifting her skirt to drape over my upper half. She holds herself up with her knees against my ears, clinging to the headboard.

Her pulse tells me she's nervous but excited—and gods, that drives me wild.

I push her panties to the side. Then, I breathe in deeply, the sweet scent of her arousal like a wine I could drink forever. She's so wet that I can tell from her shallow breath that she's embarrassed, but my little wildcat has nothing to be embarrassed about. Her slickness only pushes me faster toward my need.

"I could taste you all night." I finally give in to my throbbing need and lick along her center.

She bucks her hips as the headboard groans under her tight grip. "Gods, Basten. Don't stop!"

"That's it, little violet. Come on my face."

Her trembling muscles finally give in as her climax crests, erupting from her throat as a cry she can barely muffle against her sleeve in time. I keep sucking at her clit relentlessly to milk every last twitch and throb out of her.

Spent, her thighs slacken. Panting, she gathers her skirt and sinks backward off of me to the side of the bed.

Her eyes are unfocused. Lips glistening and swollen. So damn beautiful that I never want that look to leave her face.

"Here," I coax, pushing to my own knees to guide her to lay flat on the bed. "Be a good girl. Lay back."

Every move makes pain ricochet throughout my body, but I clench my molars and ignore it. I take my cock in my left hand, stroking gently, so full of need that if I don't get inside her in the next ten seconds, I might combust.

I press a hand to her shoulders to ease her down.

Still dazed from her climax, she gapes. "No—you'll *really* hurt yourself, Basten. You said you wouldn't!"

"I lied, darling. Now, get on your back. I want to watch your face this time when you come."

Before she can pout at me again, I silence her protests with a kiss. She gives in, surrendering to her own desire, warring with my lips as she sinks back on the small mattress. I wedge my knee between her thighs, one hand going to stroke the soaked fabric of her panties.

"Are you ready for me?" I break the kiss to ask.

Her hips wiggle, her breath so shallow that she can't speak.

I hike up her dress and take my time sliding her satin panties down her legs. Then, I take a moment to stare at her perfect pussy, glistening and ready for me to worship it.

While I watch, I rub my tip along her folds, reveling in the way my touch makes her breathe so shallow that her tits bounce. I've dreamed about this so many times. Taking her. Making her mine. It's almost enough to make me believe Immortal Alessantha rearranged the world for us to be together.

But that fae bitch isn't even awake. How do I know?

Because no fae would ever let us be this happy if they had the power to stop it.

No—we have to make our own magic.

"This is how I want it," I murmur, tenderly sweeping the hair off her face. "I always want it this simple. Just you and me."

"You and me," she echoes, her soft eyes swallowing me whole.

I take her slowly this time. I'll be honest, I'm not sure my ravaged body gives me much choice. Our first time having sex in the confectionary was wild. Desperate. Sugar-coated.

Or rather, the first time for *me*. *She's* experienced us having sex countless times. I want her to tell me about every sizzling, hair-pulling, sweat-soaked romp. But this time, there are no fireworks. No explosions. Just a steady burn that has me worshipping her with every slow thrust.

When we come, it's together.

Eyes locked.

Both our palms pressed against one another's mouth to keep us quiet. Our bodies tremble then melt together, limbs fitting perfectly together as I gather her in my arms.

She lays against my chest, gently tracing the circular scars from the buck's antlers.

"Do you think you can stand? Ride a horse?" She keeps her voice a barely-there whisper, even though we're no longer trying to muffle the sounds of our sex. Her pulse picks up as she glances anxiously at the curtain.

"When you're ready to leave, I'll be ready, too. Name the day." I keep my voice low, too, though it itches at me that we both instinctively whisper.

We shouldn't have to. Vale gave us permission to leave

together. So why does the air still hold a chill like something is wrong?

"You think your father will try to stop you?" I ask haltingly, hesitant to voice my thoughts.

She twirls her hair around one finger pensively. "He can't. If anything can be trusted in this kingdom, it's a binding deal. He even said so himself. I know that he wants me to stay here, but he can't force me to."

I nod.

It kills me to see her nervous about what should be a good thing. So I try to stoke some confidence in the both of us as I cup her cheek and give a smile. "Hey. You and me? We beat the gods. We can sure as hell beat Rian Valvere."

She smiles back at me, though it doesn't quite reach her eyes. "Now *that* I'm looking forward to."

The jesting slowly bleeds off her face, and a strange distance settles into her eyes. Coldly, she murmurs, "I'm looking forward to punishing everyone who wronged me."

The hair on the back of my neck lifts at the strange tone in her voice. But if anyone's earned some good, solid revenge, it's her. And I'll happily be the sword and knife and arrow at her side, if she wants me to be.

She snaps back into the present, a renewed light in her eyes as she squeezes my hand. "Tomorrow."

I nod. "Tomorrow, then, little violet."

We lay in bed, holding one another until the sun sets outside. I can't help but feel that we're juggling the same silent hopes and fears. I've seen what can happen between one day and the next. The world can turn on its axis.

We may think we're free now—but the gods may have one last trick up their sleeves.

CHAPTER 40
SABINE

Freedom is a strange thing.

When I was in the convent, I used to climb the tallest yew tree to look over the stone walls at the distant mountains. The wind would blow through my hair, whooshing against my cheeks, calling to me with the promise of freedom. From those branches, I would watch the townspeople go about their day. The old shepherd herding his flock to the stream. Boys and girls dragging their feet to church. The butcher making his deliveries.

At any moment, any of them could have left.

They could have dropped their shepherd's crooks and never come back.

Even gone to Salensa to see the ocean.

But no one ever did, even though I know the wind whispered to them, too. Their bodies weren't locked behind stone walls, but their minds were. It's simply human nature. We stay where we were born. We follow our parents' footsteps. We do as the gods tell us.

But now, as I stand in my bedroom high in the Stormwatch Tower with the wind blowing through the open window, I whisper back to it:

I'll go where I want this time.

"Are you ready?"

I turn toward Basten in the doorway. He has a knapsack slung over one shoulder, his bow and quivers around the other. He wears black travel clothes, but they're much finer than the cotton ones he used to wear. These have black embroidery at the cuffs and collars and are tailored to fit his broad shoulders to perfection.

His hair is loose. Freshly washed. He's actually *shaved*. To see him like this, I can't help but think I'm looking at a true king.

I rest my arm on the windowsill so the forest mouse can scamper up my sleeve and settle under my collar. I've sewn loops for it to hold onto—it will be a long journey, after all.

Then, I take one last look at my bedroom.

The twisting, living vines no longer look strange to me. To be honest, I can't imagine ever living in a place without nature bursting through the walls. Drahallen Hall is a place of contradictions: broken but beautiful, ancient but novel, haunting yet serene.

I place my hand in Basten's. "Ready."

We take our time descending the central stairs as I wonder when—if—I'll ever see the intricate carvings again. My maids wait in a line at the bottom of the stairs to bow to me in turn. The last one drapes a fur stole over my shoulders.

"Autumn can bring a brutal frost to these woods, Majesty. Best you stay warm."

Plume floats up to nip at the stole, tail wagging. I pat the soft tufts of hair on her head with a smile. *Don't worry, little troublemaker. I'm taking you with me. A cloudfox sidekick can be immensely helpful in Old Coros.*

She yips, floating in a pinwheel.

We head to the stable, where Myst is already saddled along with a chestnut horse named Ranger for Basten, their saddlebags stuffed to the brim with hard cheeses and rolls that the kitchen insisted on packing for our journey.

"Soon, pretty girl." I rest my head on Myst's forehead as she stamps her restless hooves. "Just a few more goodbyes."

It takes ten soldiers to slide open the bolt on Tòrr's palatial stall door. Guards armed with broadswords flank me on each side, but I roll my eyes and wave them away as I step into the cool darkness.

A single, round glass lantern hangs from a high hook like the moon—just as Tòrr likes it.

He snorts a burst of steam. *You're late. Thought you were not coming.*

And miss your complaining? Never. I smile a little sadly as I tweak his bottom lip.

I'm going to miss the big lug, but at least I know he's well cared for here. Since he arrived, he's filled out to the size of a tank, his glossy black fur taking on a new, healthy sheen. Rian never understood how to properly take care of a monoceros, but here, at the seat of the fae court, he's treated as a prince.

This isn't goodbye forever. I press my forehead against his. *We have an alliance with my father. Once Basten is on the Astagnonian throne, I'll convince my father that we need you with us.*

A nervous flutter kicks up in my stomach. For all my promises to Tòrr, if I've learned one thing here, it's how fickle the fae are. Yes, we have an alliance...but for how long?

Tòrr blows a gentler snort that ruffles my hair. **The least you could do is leave Myst with me.**

I run my fingers through his long mane. **You'll have to woo a new girlfriend.**

After a kiss on his nose, then a tour through the golden-claw stable to play one final round of riddles—and a catch in my throat at Two's empty stall—Basten and I head back inside Drahallen Hall to speak to my father.

The Hall of Vale looks strange in the light of day, with all the curtains wide open, the tables pushed back. I've never seen it so bright. Empty like this, it feels almost reverent.

Our footsteps echo as we approach the head table where my father sits with Iyre, Samaur, Woudix, and a wan-looking Artain.

My feet drift to a stop.

For the first time, I realize that there are ten seats along the length of the head table. With a jolt, I think: *It was never meant as a dining table. It's an altar for the full court.*

Now, with only five of the ten places filled, it looks like a harmless enough scene, but it makes my stomach turn to think of how powerful the court will be if—when—all ten seats are taken.

I bow to my father, then squeeze Basten's hand for him to do the same. Which he does—lukewarmly.

"We're packed," I say as I rise, my voice echoing tinnily in the large space. "If we leave now, Basten says we'll reach the border by Wednesday at nightfall."

All five fae wear their human glamour, yet there's something so otherworldly about my father, even in that form, that my stomach tightens.

Painfully slowly, he pushes back his chair. The legs groan against the stone floor. In slow, measured steps, he walks around the table to stand before us.

Time ticks impossibly slowly as he stares.

I squeeze Basten's hand so hard that I'm sure both our knuckles blanch.

"I wish you'd reconsider taking Captain Tatarin and her soldiers," my father finally rasps. "For safety."

My shoulders ease, and only then do I realize how tightly I was bracing them. I glance at Basten with a quick smile. "We can travel faster and more unnoticed if it's just us."

Basten nods but doesn't match my smile. I can feel his pulse thrumming in his fingers with such impatience that I know he won't smile again until we're miles from these walls.

"I suppose the time has come, then." To my surprise, my father extends his arms.

For a...hug?

I hate that my first instinct is doubt, but could anyone blame me?

I start to step forward, and Basten bristles, clenching his hand to hold me back.

"It's okay, Basten," I whisper.

His lips purse like he's chewing something distasteful. He makes a show of resting his hand on the quiver strap across his chest. This time, when I tug my hand out of his, he reluctantly lets me go.

My footsteps echo hollowly as I cross the stone floor to my father, where after a pause, I wrap my arms around his broad chest. Truth be told, I meant for the hug to be perfunctory. When it comes to paternal hugs, I'm woefully lacking. Charlin Darrow used to pull my small limbs off his neck and curse me whenever I tried.

So, when Vale sincerely surrounds me with his thick arms, his beard tickling my cheek, I swallow down a lump of emotion. I didn't know it could feel like this. Paternal. Protective. Vale isn't human, so rationally, I know better than to believe that we'll ever have a functional father-daughter relationship.

But this?

This makes me want to cry for all the years I went without it. For what *could be*.

"This wasn't supposed to happen this way." He speaks softly. "You forced my hand."

Peeking around Vale's shoulder, my gaze lands heavily on Artain. He looks like he's lost a good twenty pounds in the last week. His skin has a sickly pallor from the dungeon's low light. Perhaps a few new wrinkles around his sneer. I don't feel anything for him but resentment—*he* was the one who forced the Night Hunt, not me.

"I wish things had happened differently, too," I confess, chewing on my bottom lip. "But I'm grateful to have you as my father. The next time we meet, I'd like to start afresh. No lies this time. As soon as we arrive safely in Old Coros, I'll send a messenger crow to let you know. Basten and I will win over the Astagnonian people for you—and then, when you come, we'll be a family."

"Yes." My father's hands fall away, though the ghost of them holds on a little longer.

I take a step back, adjusting my cloak around my shoulders. I add, "In the meantime, take care of that grumpy fae horse. I wish there was someone who could play riddles with the goldenclaws—"

When I look up from smoothing my cloak's folds, there's a knife in Vale's hand.

And my heart stops.

I know that knife. It's the Serpent Knife from the fae artifact room. The one used in the Sacrifice of the Golden Child. To turn the fae into gods.

Time suddenly seems to move strangely. Too fast. Too slow. I feel like I'm hovering above myself, watching the blood drain out of my face.

"Sabine!" Basten screams my name as his footsteps sprint across the floor.

Time slows.

Vale grabs my wrist with godly speed. I should tug away. I should at least *try*. But I can't break free of the crushing realization of what's about to happen.

I was right, I think dimly. When my father first showed me this knife, I felt a jolt of unease, of foreboding.

"The Tale of the Golden Child," I murmur quietly, almost in a trance. "You brought me here to...to sacrifice me. Didn't you? This whole time, this was the plan. To bleed me out on your altar."

"Human sacrifice *is* required." Vale's rasping voice is sickeningly matter-of-fact. Remorseless. Utterly cold as ice.

My blood roars between my ears with enough force that it feels like my skull is on the verge of splitting open. I try to jerk my arm away, but he holds on tight.

He tilts his head. "A deathless death."

"Sabine!" Basten yells again, sprinting, this time so close that his fingers almost brush my sleeve.

But he isn't fast enough.

Not this time.

A second before he can pull me away, my father stabs the Serpent Knife into my heart.

It's a violent, brutal move. My ribs crunch as the blade stabs all the way to the hilt, pain bursting across my chest in searing waves.

Vale lets go of the knife and takes a step back.

I stare at him in disbelief.

My hands paw uselessly at the knife hilt at my chest. I stagger backward a step. My knees buckle from the pain, and I fall—

—fall—

—into Basten's arms as he drops to one knee to sweep me up in his arms. Catching me, as he always catches me.

"Sabine!" He slowly lowers me to the floor and shakes me. "Sabine! No—for all that is holy, *no!*"

His eyes are so wide with horror that I can see the whites all around. A drip of sweat lands on my face—or maybe it's his tears. His lips tremble as his head rocks back and forth, back and forth.

"B—Basten..." I stammer.

"No!" He hugs me, his lips caressing my temple, his fingers knitting in my hair. "Sabine, don't leave me. Not again. It nearly killed me the first time. I won't survive it again. You hear me?" He pulls back, his eyes dark with fear. "I love you. I loved you when I didn't even know you. And now that you're here, real and warm in my arms, I can't let you go. Not now, not ever. Please, Sabine. I don't know how to be without you, and I don't want to learn. Don't leave me."

My vision goes hazy as darkness creeps over me.

"*Basten,*" I whisper.

I feel it again—my soul slipping free. Hovering above my physical body while it watches Basten sob against my cheek. He holds me so tightly his knuckles blanch. He begs in a shallow breath for me not to go.

The same moon, I try to tell him. *We'll always see the same moon.*

But the darkness swallows me whole before I can.

CHAPTER 41
BASTEN

They killed my little violet.

It can't be real. This beautiful girl in my arms whose pulse is painfully absent. Whose lungs don't rise and fall. Whose half-open eyes don't blink.

A roar builds inside my skull.

This can't fucking be *real*.

A visceral pain slams into my chest. My jaw locks. My muscles clench so tightly that I fear they might snap, but I don't care. I want the pain. I need it. The pain drowns out the bottomless pit of fear that yawns at the edge of my vision. There are few things in my life that have scared me.

Losing Sabine?

This fucking blows them all away.

My skin burns hot as the churning rage inside me comes to a boil, ready to erupt and scorch the earth around me until Drahallen Hall is nothing but a pile of steaming rubble. The fae were worried about Tòrr bringing this place to the ground? Wait until *I* unleash everything I'm capable of. I might be human, but I have nothing to lose.

432

And the only thing now I want to gain?

Payback.

Someone is going to die for this. For killing my little violet. Payback won't bring her back, I know, but it will damn sure answer the rage shredding up my heart.

Damn the fae.

Damn this fucking castle.

Damn every last thing in this wrecked world except for the heartbreakingly quiet girl in my arms.

An anguished cry tears from between my teeth as I howl up at the ceiling.

When my pain finally has no other place to go, I slowly lower Sabine to the floor, taking care to set her pale body down gently, and wipe a bead of splattered blood off her cheek.

"I swear to you, little violet," I vow, lips shaking. "They will pay for what they've done to you."

I stroke her cheek one final time—and leave my last drop of tenderness in that touch. When I push to my feet to face the fae court, it's without a shred of mercy in my soul. My body is nothing but a weapon now.

"You never fucking deserved her!" I shout.

I charge at Vale. King of Fae. I have nothing but my two fists, so I'll make them be enough. With adrenaline and heartbreak simultaneously pushing me forward, I feel like I could rip the heads off these glowing bastards.

Vale opens his hands palm-down to release bursts of blue fey toward the floor. It's just a warning, which is his mistake. He should have struck me dead when he had the chance.

"Fucking *fae*." As I get within a few feet of him, one of his eyes twitches a second before he aims his fey at me. That twitch is enough of a tell that I have time to duck, sliding on my knees past his left side. With a flick of my wrist, I unlatch one of his battle axes from the holster on his back. When I come up to my feet behind him, it's with his own axe swinging.

My senses pick up the sounds of the other fae scrambling to their feet with astounding speed. The air crackles with the smell of a coming storm as they ignite their fey— but they aren't fast enough to stop me.

"This is for Sabine!" I bring the axe down toward the junction of his neck and shoulder. My lungs scream out all my rage, my pain, my heartbreak as I bring the axe down.

Five inches away.

Three.

One.

And something happens. Something is—wrong.

My arms are locked. My legs, too.

Fuck.

I throw all my strength into trying to move, but I can't so much as blink. I'm a damn living statue. I'm the only one— the fae are still rushing in my direction.

"Stop, Lord Basten!" Captain Tatarin comes into my view, her hands extended like she's holding back a tide, her face awash with desperation. She begins to lower her fingers to count down the seconds until her spell ends.

Eight more seconds. *Seven.*

"This isn't the way!" she says in a rush. "You don't understand what you're doing!" She throws a desperate look at Vale. "Highness, let me talk to him. You need him, remember? He'll deliver Astagnon to you."

Six seconds.

My lungs burn from wanting to breathe but not being

able to. While I'm struggling, Vale calmly steps out of my axe's trajectory.

Slowly, he nods.

Five.

From behind the table, the four other gods approach, their eyes sparking in cold amusement at my misfortune.

As Iyre, Artain, Woudix, and Samaur surround me, Captain Tatarin continues breathlessly, "Lord Basten, hear me out. Human sacrifice *is* the key to awakening the fae, as Sabine figured out. The fae thrive on our blood and breath and prayers, but to awaken them requires the taking of a full human life."

Four seconds.

I gather my strength, ready to unleash it the moment I'm free.

Captain Tatarin's eyes flick briefly to Vale, whose fey bolts surge from his palms like blue lightning, ready to strike me dead. She continues, "But all the fae tales that speak of them slumbering in underground tombs? The scribes got it wrong. There were never tombs. The fae slumber for thousands of years, yes, but not in dirt."

Three seconds.

Frankly, I could care less what Captain Tatarin has to say to defend the fae. She's guilty by association. A human who willingly works with demons deserves the same fate as them. The second her spell breaks, she'd better get the hell out of my way, or it'll be her blood on my hands, too.

Two.

My peripheral vision is nearly 300 degrees, which means I can see all the fae except Woudix, who stands directly behind me.

Captain Tatarin's hands begin to shake as she lowers

another finger, saying quickly, "You've heard the rumors that King Rachillon's godkiss is waking the fae? It's true. King Rachillon—Lord Vale—has the ability, but to do so, he must—"

One.

Adrenaline sparks from the soles of my feet to the tips of my ears, ready to unleash hell on these bastards until the floor is polished with their silver blood.

Almost. Fucking. Time.

She says in a rush, "—he must kill the human to awaken the fae inside—"

Now.

I don't give a fuck about her explanations. There's nothing she could say that would spare every one of them from dying as violently as possible for what they did to Sabine. I can taste the crackle of danger in the air. It shoots electricity across my tongue, burns down my throat.

The second Captain Tatarin lowers her final finger, and her spell breaks, I detonate.

My muscles discharge all the coiled rage they've been holding under my skin as my axe slams down to the empty space where Vale had been standing. Seamlessly, I continue the axe's circle to bring it around, using the momentum to build power, and give a battle cry as I aim it at Vale's torso.

"Lord Basten, don't!" Captain Tatarin shrieks.

Vale's fey ignites faster than my senses can pick up. It shoots straight to the axe, whose copper blade conducts the electric current, transferring it to my arms until even my molars buzz. My vision dims. Pain explodes throughout my body.

Artain lunges for the axe. Even weakened, he has nearly

twice my strength and easily wrenches it from my numb hands.

Still, I recover fast and, while his hands are occupied, swing my fist straight into his sculpted jaw. Such a strike would send a human male to his ass, but Artain's chin barely snaps back.

Woudix grabs me from behind, locking my arms behind my back.

With a growl, I strain against his frigid hold.

"You want to rain death upon me?" I shout. "Fine. Do it. I have nothing to live for. You bastards took the only thing I care about. But not fucking *yet*."

I slam my head back into Woudix's face, which surprises him enough to slacken his grip. I drop to a crouch and deliver a donkey kick to his midsection. It off-balances him —but he rightens his stance in record speed.

From the corner of my eye, I see Captain Tatarin lift her hands again to freeze time once more, but Iyre clamps the captain's hands behind her back.

"No need for that again, Captain," Iyre purrs.

Eyes wide, Tatarin struggles against the fae's hold.

Samaur and Vale come at me from either side, sparking orange-gold fey bolts to my left and blue ones to my right. Caught in the middle, I'm about to be a fucking barbeque. The only reason Vale's fey didn't burn me to a crisp before was because it struck the axe, not me.

This time, there's no mistaking their aim.

I widen my stance, braced like an animal, pain racking my ribs. If this is the end for me, so be it. I'll join Sabine in the underrealm or whatever world comes after this mortal life. Because there is no life without her.

I'm coming, little violet, I just have to unleash hell first...

Woudix comes up from behind to grab me again in a headlock. I slam a kick back toward his knee, but he dodges the strike, bringing his knee up into my kidneys. I wince from the blow as I throw every ounce of strength I have at trying to get free. But the male is fucking strong as marble.

Artain snatches the Serpent Knife from the floor and holds it against my neck.

I go still.

The God of Death pins me from behind. The God of the Hunt has a knife at my throat. The Goddess of Virtue is holding back the only person who can help me. And the God of Day and King of Fae are ready to electrocute me from either side.

A frustrated growl tears at my throat.

"Brother?" Samaur asks Vale, his eyes sparking with anticipation for the permission to end me.

Vale lets out a tightly coiled exhale as his eyes sear into me. I'm supposed to be the key to Astagnon for them. Without me on the throne, they'll have to wage war. But for all I know, Vale is weighing how much war will cost him over the satisfaction of ending me.

"Kill him," Vale rasps.

My stomach plummets. *I'm sorry, Sabine. I couldn't avenge you. I tried...*

Samaur gives a cruel purse of his lips, but before he can strike me dead, the room goes dark.

It's as though someone drew the curtains all at once.

There's a split-second pause where the fae look towards the windows, as confused as I am. The bright daylight has suddenly gone dark. Black storm clouds now snuff out the sun, roiling with a vicious wind as thunder cracks above the roof.

The Hall of Vale shakes from the thunder as rain begins to pelt the outer walls.

Samaur lowers his hands a half-inch as he braces against the next earth-shattering peel of thunder.

This time, when the ground shakes, it doesn't stop. A tremor runs throughout the floor until cracks open between the polished inlaid stone tiles. The cracks widen, angling the tiles in a cattywampus disarray. The shaking intensifies until the chandelier's crystals clink together. Vale's axe on the floor clatters and dances.

"An earthquake," Iyre murmurs in a hollow voice that almost sounds like fear.

More thunder cracks outside, this time with lightning that briefly illuminates the outlines of dozens of birds flapping at the glass windows.

No—wait. *Hundreds* of birds. Their wings beat at the glass until it rattles in its panes, threatening to burst open.

Crows. Doves. Robins. Eagles. More species than I can even begin to count, pecking and clawing at the glass.

The closest window suddenly bursts open under the pressure, and the flock pours through like a river breaching its banks.

"Hold him! Don't let him go!" Vale orders, jabbing his finger at my chest.

Woudix's headlock tightens around the back of my neck, but I can feel his unsteady pulse in his veins. Whoever is causing this storm, it isn't one of them.

One of the floor cracks widens into a jagged line down the Hall of Vale. The two halves tip precariously as a chasm opens. A surge of water spouts upward, defying gravity, bringing with it fallen branches and river rocks.

Holy fuck, it's the damn Ramvik River.

A trout flops out onto Artain's boot, who jumps back with a cry.

More thunder crashes overhead as the birds break through another window, pouring in to swarm in foreboding circles overhead. A dove swoops down to claw at Vale's face, and without flinching, he shoots out a bolt of fey.

The dove falls dead to the ground.

Without warning, a twisting tree root erupts from the chasm in the floor. It's thick as a python, zigzagging across the broken stones to wind itself around Vale's ankle. Another root shoots out to circle Artain by the waist, hauling him away from the Serpent Knife.

The hall's doors crash open as loud as thunder itself, and a goldenclaw lopes in, its teeth bared.

Samaur aims a bolt of fey at the bear, but it turns its neck so the blast merely skims off its metallic fur. The creature backs him up against the table with a roar that hurles bear spittle all over his pretty face.

Dazed, I fight to keep a steady stance, grateful for years of military training that have my muscles snapping into a familiar fighting pose.

The storm pelts rain against the blackened windows.

The birds dive down to peck at anything that moves.

The tree roots spread over the floor as the earthquake chasm widens.

And then?

Sabine Darrow's dead eyes snap open.

END OF BOOK THREE

∼

Ready for more? Sabine, Basten, and Rian are headed toward a collision of love and hate in book four, *Cold Stars Midnight Glow*. Order it now!

P.S. Join my mailing list to get a steamy deleted scene of Basten dreaming about Sabine in *Steel Heart Iron Claws*.

A Note from Evie

To my dark-hearted readers, thank you for continuing in the Godkissed Bride adventure! I can't wait to bring you *Cold Stars Midnight Glow.*

If you loved this series, will do you me a favor? Five-star reviews can make or break a book—other readers **really depend on your feedback** when deciding what to read!

Rate White Horse Black Nights
Rate Silver Wings Golden Games
Rate Steel Heart Iron Claws

I am so lucky this book found all of you and has a special place on your shelves.

xo, Evie

Made in United States
Troutdale, OR
11/03/2024

24418774R00272